TIME AND DESTINY

Time Trilogy - Book One

Colleen Reimer

COPYRIGHT PAGE

Dedication

I dedicate this novel to all those who are searching for direction in
their lives.
Sometimes the revealing of our destiny can come in unorthodox
ways.
Far be it from God to stick to conventional methods although he is
allowed to work in whatever way he chooses.
Out-of-the-box methods are not beyond his litany of choices.
Be prepared!
After all, he is God.

Acknowledgment

I wrote the first draft of this novel many years ago, 2002 to be exact, and recently decided to dust it off and get it going again. After some intense slashing and reworking of the book I was ready to let people take a look and offer suggestions.

There are a few friends and family I would like to thank for bringing Time and Destiny to the printed page. Linda Rayner did one of the first proof-readings for me and made some corrections. My daughter, Felisha, proofread it and made some amendments. My son, Jeremy, also read through and gave his approval. My friend Jenn Kononoff also read the manuscript and marked some revisions.

I want to thank my editor, Julene Schroeder, for the awesome work she has done, not only in editing my manuscript but also as a "Beta Reader" because she also gave suggestions on which parts/chapters were unnecessary information. Her assistance helped to condense the book, kept the story line moving and make for a better reading experience for my readers.

My husband and our four children have been a huge support for me. Jerrie, my husband, has been my greatest advocate, allowing me to explore my creative side. He is such a blessing to me!

I also thank God for the gift of writing. Without him this book would not exist.

My readers also deserve a huge thank you for following my work and reading what I write.

CHAPTER 1

2008

Tessa March hugged one side of the sidewalk, the sun filtering through the new leaf cover overhead, creating dappled shadows around her feet. This particular street of her hometown in Chelsey, Minnesota was always pretty this time of year. Her friend, Richelle, walked beside her, her designer high heels clicking rhythmically against the concrete. Luke, Tessa's other close friend, skirted the opposite side of the walkway, his sneakers giving off a soft plodding sound, emphasizing the stark difference between her two comrades. This was rare, the three of them together. Not since high school had they all been together like this. Tessa had missed it more than she realized.

Luke arrived this afternoon in his "green thing," his car, which had clearly seen better days. After meeting Tessa at the college, they waited for Richelle, who took the bus to meet them there. The decision was made to go on to the restaurant by foot and relive some old memories. They used to do this often during their grade twelve year – walk places together – but the usual thing had been their joint trek home from school.

As they walked, they passed through a subdivision with opulent mansions lining both sides of the street, ornate stone fences surrounding each fine manicured lawn and large gates keeping intruders out. The mature trees in this neighborhood were what Tessa liked the most when she walked here. This wealthy neighborhood was a very well-kept area of Chelsey and these grand homes were like candy for the eyes.

They approached one mansion that stuck out like a sore thumb. It was baffling as to why one of these huge properties had been neglected to this degree. No one had occupied it for as long as Tessa could remember.

Luke said, "Hey, girls, look at that old thing. It sure hasn't improved any in the last while. It looks more ramshackle than ever."

"And scarier too," quipped Richelle.

An involuntary shiver ran up Tessa's spine. She'd heard rumors that the house was haunted, something she highly doubted. Luke had at times suggested exploring it and admitted he had gone into it once with one of his buddies. Touring the untended and rickety house had never been a temptation for her. Richelle had always balked at the idea. It wasn't the feminine thing to do and it seemed dangerous. It was dirty, dusty and falling apart, with boards liable to break at any step. Not that Tessa knew any of this, but just looking at it from the outside gave her imagination free reign.

"It looks creepy. The floors are probably rotten and it's likely full of spiders and cobwebs," stated Richelle emphatically.

Tessa nodded. "I agree. I wouldn't set foot in that place for anything."

"It's not that bad, you two. It's actually quite an interesting house. When Darren and I went through it years ago we found some neat stuff. I even swiped a few things I found. Maybe the three of us can check it out after our meal."

"Well, it'll be over my dead body!"

"If you insist, Richelle, but I'd rather have you go willingly."

"Are you threatening me?"

"Just trying to give you some incentive," Luke chuckled.

Richelle punched his arm.

He looked annoyed as he rubbed the spot.

A smug smile teased Richelle's lips.

Luke stopped, turned and stared at the dilapidated mansion. Tessa felt obligated to wait for him. Richelle took a few steps, stopped, turned and looked back.

"What are we waiting for?" she asked.

"I'm not sure," admitted Tessa.

"I really want to explore this place again."

"You're not serious, are you?" asked Richelle.

"Yeah, actually I am."

Tessa stared at him for a moment. "Not today though, right?"

Luke turned toward them and said, "Why not? We can do it after lunch."

Tessa felt her knees weaken. She looked at Richelle, who was shaking her head.

Richelle said, "Absolutely not! I am not going in there."

Tessa felt a moment of relief.

"Yes, you are," Luke said. "I've been gone for a full year of university and the first people I'm with are you two. Joining me on an adventure is the least you could do for me."

Tessa couldn't formulate any sensible argument even though fear was riding her back and making her hands sweat.

For once Richelle stood speechless, her mouth open in quiet objection.

"Okay," Luke said, walking toward them, "that's settled."

"Hold on," Richelle said, moving to step beside him and taking up the center. "I haven't promised anything."

"I know but I'm not going in there alone."

Tessa said, "Do we have to do this today? I've had a rough week, cramming for exams, not much sleep."

"We're doing it today, so stop making excuses," Luke said.

"I'm not! I'm not doing it," Richelle declared.

Luke looked at her. "So you're opting to be tackled and manhandled into it?

Richelle gave him a glare. "You wouldn't!"

Luke's laugh lightened the mood and he changed the subject. Tessa hoped he'd also changed his mind about the old house.

A moment of silence ruled as she tried to decipher how their walk had turned into this ridiculous dare. Richelle was also unusually quiet.

Richelle broke the silence. "I don't know how you two talked me into walking this whole way."

Tessa glanced over at her. "We could have taken Luke's car."

"That green frog? Never!"

"My car's perfectly fine," insisted Luke, the pretense of insult on his face.

Richelle released a sound of disgust through tight lips. "If you call persistent lurching fine, then yes! Your 'green thing' could have bounced us down the road all right, but would have messed up my hair."

Luke put a hand to his chest and said, "Now that would have been a catastrophe! We couldn't have Miss Barbie with

3

disorganized hair. What would people think?"

Richelle gave him an irritated glance. Luke's favorite nickname for Richelle was "Miss Barbie Doll" and she thoroughly lived up to the reputation, nails perfectly manicured and painted, hair consistently, professionally coifed, makeup done to the nines and her wardrobe looking runway-ready at all times. She was a vision of beauty, always had been. Even now, with her new shoulder length bob, bleached blonde hair and short mini skirt, cars slowed as men looked back for a second glimpse.

The exchange between her friends made Tessa smile. Those two could really get under each other's skin. Hopefully they'd behave today. After high school, they'd all gone their own way but now, with her college training complete, her last exam just written, Tessa was thrilled to be here, surrounded by her old friends. Luke had just finished his second year of Engineering at the University of Minnesota and Richelle worked at a prestigious hair salon in town.

"Just remember your promise," said Richelle.

"Which promise was that?" Luke said with a grin.

She punched his arm again. "If I get blisters on my feet, you're carrying me all the way back."

"I didn't promise that!"

She punched him harder this time. "Don't you dare go back on your word!"

Luke chuckled and rubbed his arm again.

"You should have brought sneakers along," Tessa suggested, pointing to her feet.

Richelle sighed. "Yes, I probably should have worn something more sensible."

Luke couldn't resist, "I can't imagine it. That would be like Mr. Frog getting a paint job and acting like a limo. It just wouldn't fit."

"When you put it that way…" Richelle let the sentence hang. "I can be practical, you know. After work I love just lounging around in my sweats and a big shirt."

"No way! You're way too prim and proper for that," said Luke.

Tessa ignored their bantering and pointed left. "We can cut across here. It'll save us some time."

"Great," Richelle said.

The three turned at the intersection and walked in silence for a while.

This part of Chelsey, Minnesota, an older residential section, held stately mature trees that overshadowed the street with long branches, creating a tunnel of greenery around them. The dappled shadows sifting through the leafy cover made unique patterns on their faces as they headed down the sidewalk. The clicking cadence of Richelle's high heels on the sidewalk added a calming touch.

They turned onto Main and Tessa could see the restaurant up ahead. "Okay, you two, there it is."

It had a neon sign in front, which read, "The Eating Place."

"Oh, that's very original. Couldn't they have come up with a more dignified name?" asked Richelle

Luke said, "Stop complaining. As long as they have good food, I'm up for it."

Richelle said, "It's funny; I don't think I've ever been to this restaurant. I can't even remember seeing it before."

Tessa could attest to that. "You're right about that! I've been working here for a long time and you haven't dropped in even once to see me."

Richelle looked dumbfounded. "I haven't, have I?"

"No." Annoyance flashed through Tessa at the reminder. How often had she visited Richelle at the salon for a trim? Not once had Richelle returned her gesture.

"Gee, I'm sorry, Tessa. From now on I promise I'll swing by once in a while."

Tessa gave her a skeptical look.

"I will! I promise!"

"Okay. I'll hold you to it." Tessa pointed to the place. "It used to be a large donut and coffee shop before the present owners renovated it. It's been 'The Eating Place' for two years now. They've done a great job in transforming it. It's nothing fancy but the décor is quite pretty."

Once inside, they were immediately greeted by the cozy feel of the place. The colors were warm and inviting in muted shades. Dark green tables were surrounded by wooden chairs upholstered in a striped fabric. A few booths lined the walls. Windows, with bright floral valances, ran along the outside walls. Brightly-colored paintings hung on the walls, small spotlights highlighting each one.

Partitions throughout the restaurant gave optimum privacy to all its patrons. From the wide beams up above, plants trailed down, giving the place a greenhouse effect. The colors would have been overwhelming in their most basic shades but with the toned-down hues they gave the entire room a calming quality.

The hostess seated the three at a booth in the corner. After ordering and enjoying a delicious meal, they spent a few hours catching up. Tessa found herself thoroughly enjoying this special time with her friends. Since she and Richelle both worked in the same city, they saw each other from time to time. It was Luke's presence they had missed.

Tessa turned to him. "What will you do this summer? You found a job, right?"

"I got a job with a local engineering firm. I don't know if I'll be able to do any real hands-on engineering but it'll be a learning experience. Being bossed around like an errand boy would not impress me. I want to get both hands into engineering and not waste my time being the gopher or getting coffee for the boss. Hopefully this will be a stepping-stone to something greater."

"You didn't want to work in construction again this summer?"

"No. Being a laborer, I did a lot of grunt work. Doing the work wasn't a problem, I could handle it; but I didn't want to do that again. I want to use my training this summer, get some experience in engineering. I'm pumped about it."

Tessa said, "That's great. I'm sure you'll do more than run errands, though. You're good at whatever you do. They'll see that and promote you quickly, I'm sure."

"Thanks for the vote of confidence. I'm positively hoping for that." He turned his attention to Richelle and asked, "So how's your work going at the salon?"

Diverting attention was something he was good at. He never allowed conversation to dwell on himself for long.

Richelle's eyes lit up. "I love it! My costumers are great. I've developed a real relationship with a lot of them. I don't enjoy hearing about all their problems, though. It seems like that's all I hear some days and it gets a bit depressing. It's like beauticians are part psychologists, therapists or something. Some people have no one else to talk to so they dump on us. It's not always like that, though. Most days I like my job. Hairdressing is creative and keeps changing – a new head to work on or a new person to get to know. I have a lot of regular customers who have been very faithful to me. And if I do have a bad day, I give Tess a call. She's seems to know just what to say. She's a great friend. Did you know that, Luke?"

"Yes, who wouldn't love Tessa?" They both turned to look at her.

"You two are going to make me gag!" She knew her friends meant what they said but all the accolades made her feel uncomfortable.

Richelle turned to Luke and asked, "How has university been this past year? Are you passing your courses or is it a totally lost cause?"

"No!" He shook his head. "It's not a lost cause. I know I was kind of careless in high school but I've shaped up a lot since then. I have to admit, girls, that my marks have been fairly decent. I prefer the parties and the football games over the studying, to tell you the truth, but I have applied myself this year." He grinned boyishly.

"So you haven't found yourself a girlfriend in Minneapolis?" Tessa had wanted to ask Luke this all afternoon and she'd finally found her chance.

"No, nothing permanent anyway. I've dated girls here and there but I'm not ready for anything serious. How about you, Tessa, are you seeing anyone?" Luke looked pleased to turn things around quickly.

Tessa smiled and said, "Well, actually yes I am. His name is Cody Fields. We've been dating for about two months. He's a nice guy but we're not really that serious. We're quite different from each other so I'm not sure if it's going to work out. He's very religious and talks about God all the time."

"But you're religious," stated Luke.

"I'm a Christian, yes, but I can't quite relate to Cody's zeal. He's a little over the top. I don't see things quite the same way he does. A note in his defense," she held up a finger, "he's very considerate and kind."

Luke said, "The very reason you're dating him."

"Yeah, but I'm still not sure. There's something about him I

7

just don't get. Anyway, I won't break up with him, at least not yet. We'll see what happens."

"Wow, I was hoping you'd still be unattached and available this summer."

"Why is that?" Tessa gave him a grin.

"Well, I'm still as free as a bird and was hoping we could hang out. I know Richelle is taken, right?"

"Yes, Luke, I'm still taken and glad of it."

"Humph… No accounting for tastes." He turned up his nose in aversion.

"Hey watch it! Charlie is a much better man than you and that's even on his worst days."

Luke gave her a harsh stare. "Did I ask for your opinion on Charlie's character, or on mine for that matter?"

"You absolutely did when you came down on him!" Richelle looked wounded.

"I can't help it that you chose someone like him. He's easy to pick apart."

"He's a wonderful guy!" Richelle protested loudly.

Tessa decided to interrupt their little feud. "Luke, we can still get together this summer. I'm sure Cody wouldn't mind if I spend some time with you. I've told him quite a lot about you and he actually wants to meet you."

"Now isn't that a breath of fresh air, compared to some people we know?"

Richelle stared daggers at him. "And what's that supposed to mean?"

"Hey, was I speaking to you? You sure are touchy where Charlie is concerned, aren't you?" The sparkle in his eyes betrayed his enjoyment.

Tessa wondered if it was time to referee again. Richelle and Luke usually got along okay, if constant barbs and haranguing were considered amiable traits. They were at each other all the time, Luke with his smart quips and Richelle with her quick comebacks. It was entertaining listening to their constant bantering back and forth and Tessa was a good audience. She definitely picked friends with a gift of the gab. After listening to a few more derogatory comments fly back and forth between the two, Tessa finally said, "Okay you two, behave yourselves."

Luke turned his attention to Tessa. "So what's the plan? You're not keeping your job here at The Eating Place, are you?"

"Actually I am keeping it for now."

Luke looked at her quizzically. "I thought you told me that you got a job at a law firm, in their accounting department. Did that fall through?"

"No, but it starts in the fall. I'll keep my job at The Eating Place till then. I'm actually starting full time at the restaurant tomorrow."

"And I bet you can walk here from home, can't you?" asked Richelle.

"Yeah. Or I can take the bus if it's too cold. It's been perfect. It's saved me buying a car. I always take the bus if the weather's bad or if I'm late."

Luke said, "Sounds great. I have another two years at the U of M before I'm done. I won't be working full time for a while."

Richelle said, "But you do have your own car, that lovely 'green thing.'" She gave him a condescending smile.

Luke, with arms crossed on the table, leaned toward Richelle and said, "It gets me from point A to point B."

"And that's about all it does. It's barely still holding together."

Luke looked irritated again. "And where's your car? How come you took the bus to the college?"

With a sheepish look, Richelle said, "It's in the shop right now."

"And you're mocking my car?"

Richelle responded with a shrug. "At least my car isn't an old relic."

"No, but it is a lemon!" retorted Luke.

Having had about her fill of their verbal jousting, Tessa said, "You know we should probably pay and get going. We've been here for four hours; can you believe it?"

"Are you serious?" Richelle grabbed her cell and glanced at the time.

"Not that I'm tired of your company or anything. I just finished my last exam and I suddenly feel exhausted. I've had too many late nights of studying this week."

"Yeah, I need to get going too. I'm meeting Darren later tonight." Luke and Darren had been friends in high school and they'd both gone off to different universities. "I called him earlier and this was the only night that suited him until next week sometime."

"You know what? I'm going to pay the bill," stated Richelle. She looked contemplative for a moment. "Or maybe I should only pay for Tessa since Luke's being so obnoxious about Charlie and all." She glowered at him again, then continued. "I've been the only one with a steady income so I think it's only fair that I pay."

"Oh, Barbie Doll, that's so kind of you!" Luke stood, leaned over, took her face in his hands and kissed her on the mouth. He pulled back, with a sudden look of alarm. "Oh no, maybe I shouldn't have done that! What's Charlie going to say when he finds out? He's so jealous; I think I'll have to leave town – and I just got here!"

Richelle looked sheepish. "Yeah, I know. Charlie is very over-protective of me. It is kind of tiresome but he's also very sweet. I won't tell him, Luke, so never fear."

Richelle paid the bill and as the three of them walked toward the door she turned to Luke. "Are you going to hold up your offer of carrying me back to the college parking lot?"

"You didn't think I was serious, did you?"

"A promise is a promise. I'm not that heavy and it'll be a good workout for you."

They left the restaurant and stood on the sidewalk.

Luke looked at Richelle and said, "Okay, come here and I'll hoist you up."

He bent down, Richelle jumped up on his back and he grabbed her legs. Her arms draped around his neck and her legs hugged his middle as he slowly straightened to a standing position. It looked odd with her short mini skirt revealing too much leg, too much of everything. Tessa shook her head at the sight.

He carried her a few yards and laughed loudly. "Now what would Charlie say if he saw us like this. He'd have an absolute fit."

"Okay, let me down! That's far enough!" Richelle glanced around anxiously as he set her back on her feet.

"You're a little nervous, aren't you? I'd say Charlie has a real hold on you, girl." He smiled devilishly.

"I don't want to upset him, or I'd let you carry me the whole way back." She yanked her short mini skirt down, correcting its distortion.

Tessa chuckled and said, "You two would definitely draw attention doing that."

"Since when have Richelle and I been afraid of a little attention? It's only now with Charlie in the picture that she's turned chicken on me."

Richelle only shook her head.

As they walked, Luke and Richelle returned to their bantering. Tessa felt a keen sense of belonging, being with them.

Tessa suggested they stay on Main Street this time but after Luke gave her a knowing look, he insisted retracing their steps back. As they approached the row of mansions, Luke pointed out the deserted one with the chipped paint, broken windows and crooked shutters.

"Are you girls ready to check it out?"

"No," Richelle replied immediately.

"It'll be fun."

"Luke, you know how I feel about that place," Tessa said; yet an odd feeling of adventure tugged at her. She concluded it must be the result of the stress of college having been done and being with her best friends. She felt safe. It was a surprising realization.

Richelle sighed loudly. "Well, Tessa, it couldn't hurt, at least not too much, and since Luke just won't shut up about it, let's just do it and get it over with." She gave Luke a patronizing stare and appeared pleased at her ability to retaliate for the Charlie thing at the restaurant.

"Gee, thanks," Luke said, looking miffed. "And I thought you said it would be over your dead body before you'd step foot in that place." His look of offence gave way to an air of excitement.

"Well, I did say that. If I fall through the floor and hurt myself, you'll be held completely responsible. And you better promise to protect me from any creepy, crawly things." Richelle looked suddenly unsure and gave Tessa an anxious glance.

Tessa couldn't believe it. "You mean we're actually going to do this?"

Richelle shrugged.

Apprehension gripped Tessa at the thought of going in there. The tremendous satisfaction on Luke's face encouraged her to be brave.

"Are we ready?" Luke looked at the two girls in full expectation of their agreement.

Tessa eyed Richelle. She looked as nervous as Tessa felt, both unsure of the wisdom of their tentative decision.

"Okay, here we go." He hurried ahead and opened the expansive but rickety gate, causing it to groan loudly in resistance. It hung lopsided from its rusted hinges as he held it for the girls.

Tessa and Richelle stopped at the entrance to the yard and looked at each other dubiously.

"Are you sure about this?" asked Tessa

"No!"

"Come on girls; I'm here to protect you. It'll be another adventure to add to our memory bank. I promise, you won't be sorry."

"Should we trust him?" asked Tessa.

"Probably not. Luke is definitely not to be trusted." Richelle gave a small, nervous grin.

"That's enough, Richelle! Get in here, you two, or I'll drag you in!" Luke stepped forward as if to grab hold of them.

The girls raised their hands in surrender then slowly walked through the gate. It was unkempt, last year's brown overgrown grass and weeds dominating the yard. There were some big, majestic trees on the property that were beginning to bloom, now that spring had sprung. A paved pathway filled with deep cracks led up to the house, spring grass peeking through in places. The pathway divided in front of the house and went off to each side of a large landing at the front. The landing extended almost the whole length of the house with steps going up to it on two sides and a railing surrounding it. Large windows graced the front of the house, the glass now shattered and lying in pieces on the landing and most likely also on the floor inside the house.

There were three entrances, the main entrance in the center with large double doors and two smaller doors on the sides of the landing, all three located beneath the roof jutting out over the landing area. It was a large, two-story building with once-ornate moldings running along the roofline. Some of the molding had broken away and some pieces hung precariously and swayed in the wind. Large symmetric columns held up the roof section over the landing, which was reminiscent of the obviously beautiful home it once was. It was unthinkable that it had been left abandoned like this.

Tessa had often wondered whatever became of the owners and why they would have deserted this home. Looking at it now, in such ruin, yet surrounded by other mansions which were pampered and in full regalia, made her heart sink.

The three of them entered the yard and slowly sauntered down the pathway, studying the house as they went. Tessa looked up at the large limbs jutting out from the tree above them, its branches full of new growth. Suddenly she noticed a few snowflakes descending from above, one landing on her nose, but before she could respond, Richelle let out an ear-piercing scream. Turning her gaze ahead, Tessa froze in fear at the sight before them.

"What in the world is going on?" Luke shouted louder than his usual volume.

"This is bizarre. How can it be snowing? It's the first week of May. And look...." Richelle's voice was quavering. "The ground and everything is covered with snow."

It was true. Somehow they'd stepped into a winter wonderland. Tessa shivered as she said, "How could that happen so fast? This is too weird!"

The three friends stood perfectly still for a moment, shocked at the instantaneous transformation all around them.

Tessa's skin crawled and she shivered with the sudden onslaught of cold. Snow was falling heavily, a steady stream that was piling up by the minute. The heavy snowfall made the house nearly indiscernible, the screen of white blotting out much of the view.

Richelle said, "It's freezing."

"Let's get out of here now!" Tessa said as she turned to go.

Luke pointed to the house and said, "Wait! Look there. It's hard to see with all this snow coming down, but isn't someone standing over there on the landing?"

Tessa turned back and joined Richelle to stare in the direction he pointed. She squinted and concentrated with difficulty, fear tap dancing against her ribs. After her eyes adjusted, she slowly began to make out the silhouette of a man. He stood perfectly still, watching them. The suspense in the air thickened and her fright escalated. The urge to turn and run was overwhelming. Rumors of the house being haunted hit her with force. Anxiety played a rhythm up and down her spine. This was downright crazy!

Luke and Richelle didn't move a muscle and Tessa felt she should not leave her friends, at least not now.

CHAPTER 2

Richelle turned suddenly and said, "I'm leaving."

Tessa turned to join her. "Me too."

"The snow started just as we passed this big tree," stated Richelle. "It should switch back to normal on the other side."

That's what Tessa was counting on. But looking back the way they'd come, snow blanketed the entire landscape. Even the road was coated with a layer of white. Old-fashioned cars crawled along at a snail's pace. As the realization hit, Tessa stopped to stare.

Luke's voice beside her made her turn to him. "Look at those vehicles. They're ancient. Have we gone back in time?"

The idea was preposterous. Tessa was sure that they'd switch back to normal any minute. Both she and Luke started for the gate.

Richelle, walking ahead of them past the tree and heading for the street, stopped and turned around. "Don't say that, Luke! Let's just get out of here." Fear filled her eyes.

"Hold on, girls," Luke said.

Tessa stopped beside him. With her hand on the gate, Richelle turned to look back.

"We're already on this side of the tree. We switched over to winter on the opposite side, closer to the house. Shouldn't we be back to spring by now?"

"Luke, we have to get out of here!" Tessa felt desperate to escape.

"Okay," he finally agreed. "Maybe when we're out by the sidewalk, things will switch back."

The gate was open and Richelle stood on the opposite side waiting for them, holding her bare arms, her legs shivering. Luke and Tessa stepped through the gate and stood with her for a moment.

"Nothing has changed," Luke stated the obvious.

"But why?" Richelle sounded frantic. "Why is this

happening?"

"I don't know." Concern began to fill Luke's face, his spirit of adventure starting to vanish.

Tessa said, "Maybe we should backtrack the way we came. Perhaps then things will shift back."

Richelle turned on the spot and started walking. It was clear she was willing to try anything to get back to the familiar. Her high heels slipped on the icy walk and, after wobbling back and forth precariously, she finally found her footing again. "Luke, come here!" she demanded.

He hurried to her and extended his arm to steady her.

Tessa stepped in beside them, walking gingerly to avoid slipping. Her worn sneakers had little traction and she had no desire to wipe out and end up on her bottom. The cold was seeping through her thin sweater and her capris did little to warm her legs. A quaking had taken hold of her middle which she didn't think the cold had anything to do with. The bizarre situation they were in brought on a wave of anxiety.

After walking past two more properties, the snow persistently falling and the landscape remaining in a blanket of white, Luke finally stopped and said, "This isn't working. There were two cars on the street earlier but since then there's been no action at all. The only person we've seen was back at the old place. I say we head back there and see what this is all about."

"I don't want to go back," Richelle insisted through chattering teeth.

Luke looked exasperated. "We can't keep walking in this weather. Did you see those cars?"

"Yes," Richelle said cautiously.

"They were ancient. I don't think we're in Kansas anymore, Dorothy."

That thought had occurred to Tessa but having Luke say it made her fear escalate.

"Where do you think we are?" asked Richelle tentatively.

Luke said, "It's more like 'when.' We're still in Chelsey, Minnesota but at an earlier time."

Tessa didn't have a clue how to respond to that and Richelle's only reaction was a confused and terrified gaze.

"Let's head back to the house and see who that man is and

what he wants. Maybe this has something to do with him."

Tessa couldn't keep her fear under wraps any longer. "What if it's a ghost? What if all the rumors are true about the house being haunted?"

"That's ridiculous!" Luke said. "There are no ghosts. Unless you girls want to keep walking and freeze to death, I suggest we turn around and go back."

Richelle shivered violently. "I'm terrified!"

Luke stepped closer to her and wrapped his arm around her shoulders. "We'll be okay. We just have to stick together."

Tessa took up her position on Luke's other side and lifted his arm. "Warm me up too."

He positioned his arm around her and they retraced their steps back to the rundown mansion. Tessa felt a smidge safer with Luke's arm draping her shoulder. Her inner quaking didn't abate much but at least she wasn't facing this alone.

They made the short trek back to the crooked gate, walked through to the yard and passed the massive tree along the trail to the house. As they neared the landing, Tessa couldn't help but be reminded of something she'd experienced before and she wasn't eager to dive into another unknown.

The closer they got to the house, the clearer the man's form on the landing became. Tessa could now make out that he wore a long, black trench coat and a black fedora sat tilted on his head. Standing as still as a statue, his eyes stayed riveted on them. His silent, immobile pose creeped her out.

Why is he just standing there watching us? What's his problem?

They slowly made their way to the left side steps of the landing. The man stood in front of the door on the left side of the landing, waiting for them. When they reached the bottom of the stairway, he broke the silence.

"Why don't you come inside? It's freezing out here." He turned, opened the door and disappeared within.

Tessa said, "I don't like this!"

Through quivering lips, Richelle said, "Well, I'm going to take him up on the offer. This mini skirt isn't exactly made for winter and my toes are freezing in these high heels." She was shaking and shivering. Being so frightened and outside in these conditions was clearly taking a toll on her.

"You didn't dress too smart today, did you, Barbie?" Even with the tension of the moment, Luke still took the time to tease her. Richelle pierced him with a deadly glare.

Luke turned back to the steps and said, "Come on, girls; let's go in." He took his arms from their shoulders and took their hands in his.

Tessa felt like a little girl needing encouragement. Fearful thoughts plagued her as she took the first step to the landing. Brushing her dread aside, she allowed Luke to lead her to the top.

Directing them across the landing, Luke stopped to stare at the front window. Tessa's eyes were glued to what she saw. Warm light flowed out from intact panes of glass.

Luke shook his head and said, "This is crazy. This used to be a dangerous place to walk with all the broken glass around, but now everything looks in perfect condition!"

"Are you sure we should go in there? This is giving me the heebie-jeebies!" Richelle backed away from the door.

"She's right, Luke." Tessa quickly agreed. The tension in the air felt thick enough to cut with a knife. "We don't know what's in there." With panic clutching her throat, it was hard to breathe.

Staring at her, Luke asked, "Well then what do you suggest? Run back to the snow-covered street?"

Tessa shrugged uneasily. No ideas came to her that made any sense.

"The only choice we have is to deal with what we've got. We need to go in there and find out why this is happening." Luke looked suddenly charged with energy. "I'm curious too. Just think of the stories we can tell after this. No one will believe us but it'll make a great tale."

Richelle said, "Come to think of it, this would make a great story to tell to my clients, you know. Maybe it would give me a break from their soap operas. It'll be my way of cheering them up. They won't believe me either but it could make for some great conversation." Nervousness always made her chatty.

Tessa knew that objecting would make little difference. Her bones were aching with the cold and going inside was the only reasonable solution.

"Okay let's go for it!" Luke started for the side door and

opened it for the girls. Richelle walked through cautiously and Tessa tagged behind slowly, apprehension clouding her reason.

Luke followed them inside and closed the door. Immediately warm air flowed over them. Their shivering gradually subsided. The mystery man in the fedora and trench coat had disappeared. They looked at each other but with a reassuring wink from Luke, they started toward the front lobby of the house.

As they came around the corner, they entered a massive foyer which faced the main, center doors of the house. The foyer was bigger than any room in Tessa's house. The grand entrance area boasted a central, large round table holding a huge floral arrangement, whose aroma drifted toward them. On either side of the foyer, two chairs and a small table were positioned as small sitting areas. Impressive houseplants were placed about the entrance. Substantial, beautiful paintings by iconic artists hung on the walls. The wealth displayed caused the threesome to stare in awe.

From the open-style ceiling hung a massive crystal chandelier with enough lights to light an entire home. It sparkled and shone and made the entryway bright and cheerful. Two curved stairways wound up on either side of the foyer, ending on a landing overlooking the grand entrance.

The floor was a highly polished, light beige marble. Tessa could see her reflection when she glanced down. An expansive area rug lay beneath the round table in deep, rich colors of green, burgundy, and gold with a cream background.

With such beautiful decorating and positioning, everything about this room spoke wealth. There was not a sign of disregard or abandonment anywhere; nothing was broken, no dust showed and everything was in place. Either the lady of the house was a remarkable housekeeper or they had very good help.

The three of them stood in wonder, trying to take it all in.

Tessa looked at her friends. "Hey, you two, your mouths are hanging open." She allowed a small smile as her inner quaking began to subside. The grandeur and beauty of the home had taken the edge off her guard and her defenses had started to crumble.

Richelle gazed dumbstruck. "Well, look at this. Isn't this just amazing? I've never been in such a gorgeous house in my entire life. I hardly know what to say!"

"Now that's a first," said Luke with a grin.

Richelle reached over and punched his arm.

"Really? Again? You need to stop hitting me!"

"Then stop saying stupid stuff!" Richelle retorted.

Rubbing his arm, Luke ignored her, took a step into the room and said, "I just don't get it. How could this have happened?" He turned back to stare quizzically at the two girls. "We were walking across the yard to an abandoned house one minute and suddenly, here we are in this gorgeous mansion with everything in place and not one thing broken! Explain, please!"

Tessa just shook her head. How could one explain this? This was beyond comprehension and her skin began to crawl again with the absurdity of it all.

Richelle shrugged her shoulders and said, "I have no clue. This is the weirdest thing I've ever experienced! What do you think is going on, Luke?"

"I haven't the slightest." He looked around the foyer somewhat nervously. "I'd love to investigate though. You know, seeing that we're here and everything. Why waste the moment, right?"

"I'm just wondering where the man in the trench coat disappeared to," Tessa said.

"Yeah, where and why did he go?" asked Richelle.

"He invited us in so I assume we're supposed to be here."

The sound of agitated voices began to trickle down the stairs from the second story and all three turned in that direction. It was clear the voices were heading their way. Tessa felt relief that she and her friends were standing behind the table, nearly hidden by the large floral arrangement. Through the veil of blooms and greenery, she soon noticed an older man appear on the top landing by the left stairway. Their unobtrusive spot behind the flowers hid them well and they stayed, waiting to see what would happen. The man, his hair winter white, descended briskly, talking. A young woman descended behind him.

"I told you, Mary, the party has been planned and we're not changing it. How, at this point, could we possibly un-invite all the guests? It's totally out of the question."

"Dad, I'm just saying that school has been very stressful for me and I was hoping when you said a 'small get-together' that that's what it was going to be. I wasn't expecting to have over one hundred people invited. It's just too much for me right now."

Mary's father reached the main floor and went to a doorway between the two stairways and opened it. He turned and said, "I don't know what's wrong with you. You've been too reclusive lately and it'll be good for you to see your friends and family. I have to agree that the schooling was difficult; after all, you did finish a four-year course in two and a half years. That's very impressive, even to me. I thought you'd be thrilled to celebrate after such an accomplishment. I don't know what you're so upset about."

Mary's father walked into the room, leaving the door ajar. Tessa could see a large wooden desk in the middle of the room with bookshelves lining the back wall. Mary entered the room and stood before her father while he sat down at his desk. He looked at her with a mixture of exasperation and disappointment. Mary's back faced the door and the three watching could see her hands clenched tightly behind her, fidgeting and shaking slightly. Her dark brown hair trailed down her back in a braid, nearly reaching her waist.

Tessa whispered, "Do you see how nervous she looks? Why would she be so afraid around her father?"

The other two only shrugged and kept watching.

"I was just hoping for a quiet evening with a few close friends, that's all. You should know how much energy it took for me to finish this course so quickly. You placed huge expectations on me and somehow I managed to succeed. But I must admit the last few months have been very difficult. I just don't know if I can handle so many people around, at least not right now."

Her father looked stern as he glanced up from his paper work. He held up his hands and said, "That's enough, Mary! I don't want to hear another word. It's been settled and we're not changing it. The party is fully planned for tomorrow night. Your mother has worked feverishly with the cooking staff to ensure a magnificent evening for all. The menu's been determined and all the arrangements have been made. It's sure to be a relaxing and enjoyable evening. It would be nice if you'd show some appreciation for all the work poured out for your benefit."

"I'm sorry, Father." She spoke dejectedly. "I don't mean to complain. It's very kind of you to do this for me. All I'm saying is that I would have appreciated being asked what I would have liked, that's all." She turned and walked out of the room. Her father watched her retreating back with a look of confusion and shook his head.

As she approached the three hidden behind the flowers, they could see her face clearly for the first time. She was a very pretty girl, but dark circles drooped beneath her brown eyes and her face looked deeply distraught. It seemed to Tessa that Mary was in need of an extended vacation.

Mary looked to be the same age as the three of them. According to her clothing choices, they were definitely from a different time period. The pretty dress hugging her thin frame had a light yellow background, covered in a rose and dark yellow floral print. It was modest with a delicate lace collar at the base of her neck, a narrow waist with a skirt which flared out below it, ending about mid-calf. Light-yellow, two-inch heels graced her feet. They had a strap across the top, which buckled at the side.

She turned to close the office door behind her and when she faced into the room, they noticed her lip quivered. Stopping, she raised her hands and covered her face.

"She's an emotional mess," Luke whispered beside Tessa.

"You can say that again," Tessa agreed. The sight of Mary in such distress tugged at her heart strings.

"She obviously hasn't tried cosmetology. She hasn't seen any stress!" Richelle decreed quietly.

Just then a well-dressed lady came from one of the hallways and stopped short at the sight of Mary, concern flooding her eyes.

"Mary, what's wrong?" She rushed over and embraced her.

Mary quickly pulled her hands down. "Mother! Oh, I'll be fine."

"Tell me what's wrong."

After a deep breath, Mary said, "It's the party. I wasn't expecting you two to go to such lengths. I was hoping for a small gathering. There'll be so many people. I'm not sure I'll be able to cope." Her lip quivered again.

"Come with me, Mary. Let's go into the sitting room and have a cup of tea together. I know it's been difficult for you lately but now that university is over you can relax. I'd love to sit with you and talk like we used to. Come." Mary's mother took her by the hand and led her to a room off the right side of the foyer. The door to the room stayed open as the two disappeared within.

Luke said quietly, "Have you noticed that they haven't seen us yet? Isn't that a little strange? I mean it's not like we're hiding or anything."

Tessa whispered, "Maybe this big flower arrangement is bigger than we thought. Perhaps it's totally blocking us."

Richelle began moving to the door where mother and daughter had gone. "It feels a little strange listening in on their conversation. I feel like a peeping Tom."

"Oh yeah, it looks like being a peeping Tom has really got you bothered, Richelle," Luke declared, also moving closer to the sitting room.

"Alright, I'm coming too." Tessa followed right behind. They all stood to the side of the open doorway and listened.

There must have been another door leading into the room because they heard it open and close and Mary's mother speak to someone. "Esther, would you please bring us some hot tea and some of those cheese biscuits we had for lunch?"

"Yes, Mrs. Hardington, I'll bring them right out."

Now Tessa knew the mother's name, at least her last name. She could hear Esther walk back across the room. Peeking around the corner, she saw her leave through a side door. She was wearing a servant's outfit, a modest dark dress with a white apron overtop, tied at the back. Mary and her mother were sitting kitty corner to each other on the couches located in the room. A huge fireplace on the far wall had a fire glowing in the cavity. It looked warm and inviting. Three beautiful burgundy couches in a "U" shape faced the fireplace, a rich oriental rug tucked between them. Mary sat on the couch facing the fire and her mother sat on a side couch gazing at her daughter.

Tessa did a quick overview of the scene then pulled back out of sight. As she did, she bumped into Luke and Richelle who had also moved up with her to take in the scene.

"Move back and give me some room," Tessa whispered. "Don't you know we could get thrown in jail for sneaking into someone's home like this?"

Luke and Richelle put on stricken faces as they looked at each other then grinned. They truly were enjoying their "peeping Tom" experience. Luke said, "We were invited in."

"By a vanishing ghost!" declared Richelle.

"Don't say that!" demanded Tessa. "I'm nervous enough."

Mrs. Hardington's voice drew their attention. "Now, dear, why don't you tell me what your plans are, now that you're done your schooling?"

"My plans, Mother?" Mary's voice squeaked. "Have I ever been able to make any plans of my own? What you really want to know is what Father's plans are for me. Isn't that right?"

"Let's not get into that, okay? Your father loves you and wants only the best for you. I know he can be a bit demanding at times but it comes from his deep affection for you. He wants the best for both of us."

"What if Father's plans don't seem the best to me? I mean, managing a bank is something I've never desired. That's been Father's dream."

"You know, Mary, maybe it's because he doesn't have a son. He's always put his dreams for a son onto you. Ever since he opened the bank many years ago he's dreamed of passing the baton to you. And you must know by now that you're worth more than ten sons to us. You're a treasure to both of us. You know that, don't you?"

"Yes Mother, you've told me often. I don't doubt your or Father's love for me. But I do feel that he's pushing me into something I'm not capable of. I'm not a banker or a manager of a bank. I don't think I'll ever fit into that role."

"But you've trained for it, dear." Confusion laced her voice.

"Yes, I've been trained but it's not what I want. I don't understand why Father can't see that."

"Your Father believes nursing is a pointless career, financially unviable."

"But that's my dream!" Mary's voice shook with her declaration.

"I know, dear."

"I want to help people; I've told Father that repeatedly. He refuses to listen."

Her mother remained silent.

Mary continued, "I only wish I had some peace about my future. All I feel is dread and it gives me so much anxiety."

"You really feel only dread?"

Silence followed.

"Why?" asked her mother.

"I don't know. It's an awful feeling! I truly wish I was excited about working at the bank and learning all Father can teach me."

"Well...," Mrs. Hardington hesitated a moment. "I have a feeling that once you start and feel comfortable there, things will all fall into place. Your father is so excited about having you work with him. You should hear him brag to our friends about you. It's almost embarrassing. It's apparent he's very proud of you, dear."

The three friends could hear a door open again and the clattering of a tray. The serving lady, Esther, was returning with the hot tea and cheese biscuits. That sure sounded good to Tessa right then. They had finished their lunch hours ago and her stomach was talking to her.

"Thank you, Esther. You may set the tray down right here. We'll help ourselves," Mary's mother said.

They could hear the sound of the tray and Esther leaving the room, followed by the clinking of china teacups and the tinkle of spoons stirring their tea.

Mary spoke first. "Why do you think it's so important to Father that I learn banking? There are so few girls that even work. It's almost unheard of. None of the girls that I grew up with have ever gone to university, or even had the desire to do so."

"I don't know, dear."

"When Father suggested that I take further schooling I wasn't opposed to it. I had always wanted to do something else with my life. Getting married and having children right away never appealed to me." A moment of silence, then she continued. "All my friends ever wanted in life was to get married and have babies. I couldn't relate. When Dad suggested taking accounting and bank management, I told him flat out, 'No.' I suggested a nursing career but he wouldn't hear of it. He had already made up his mind what he wanted me to do."

"Mary, don't start again. We can't change your father. He is who he is."

"It just seems so unfair of him! He has never even considered what I wanted. It's always been what he wants for me. I can't help but feel angry, Mother! There's nothing I can do to change my situation and I feel trapped."

Mary's mother said, "I can see that would create some anger in you. Perhaps you could try to look at it as an opportunity and it might help change your perspective. If you continually concentrate on the negative aspects, then of course you'll feel angry. You must remember that your father has provided you with a great education, an amazing opportunity. Very few girls are ever given that chance."

"I know all this and understand it. I'm just really concerned with how I feel. I've never felt this way before. My emotions are all mixed up, like a ball of yarn all tangled and knotted and I have no idea how to undo it."

Tessa peeked into the room again.

Confusion clouded Mrs. Hardington's face. "What do you mean? I don't quite understand."

Mary spoke in a whisper, as though afraid her father might hear. "There's been tremendous pressure on me for such a long time. I feel nervous and uptight continually, my emotions are jittery and there's this heaviness that weighs so tightly on my chest that it's hard to breathe. I'm afraid something is about to snap. I don't know what will happen when it does. It frightens me, Mother!"

Mary appeared almost frantic for a moment. Mrs. Hardington's concern was apparent and was also evident in her tone of voice when she spoke. Tessa pulled back out of view.

"What do you mean, dear, that something will snap?"

"I don't know. All I know is that I'm not who I used to be. I once loved socializing with my friends. Crowds never intimidated me and I loved parties. Now I'd much rather be a hermit. To be with a mass of people frightens me. I feel so edgy all the time and tears come too easily lately. I'm sorry, Mother; I wasn't going to unload on you. Please forgive me. I'll truly try to enjoy the party tomorrow night. I know how much work you went to in order to get the party ready." Mary's voice broke and they could hear her cry softly.

There was the sound of Mrs. Hardington rising and moving toward her daughter. "Dear Mary, I'm glad you told me this. I never realized how difficult it was for you. I knew you were having a hard time but I never imagined it was taking such a toll.

I'm sorry we went to so much trouble with the party. We could have kept it simple. I wish you had told me your wishes earlier and I could have steered your father into a smaller gathering."

"It'll be all right. It's all planned and I don't want to disrupt things for you." She sniffled. "I just hope I can keep my emotions under control. The last thing I want is to embarrass the two of you."

"We'd never be embarrassed of you! We love you and are proud of you. Dear, your hands are shaking." They could hear the rattling of a cup and saucer. "Listen, why don't you go up to your room and have a quiet evening to yourself. I'll send one of the servants to your room with some dinner later on. I'll explain to your father why you're not at the table and I'm sure he'll understand. Tomorrow I want you to have an undemanding, quiet day and do whatever you'd like. I'll take care of the preparations for the evening. Come on, Mary, I'll walk you upstairs if you'd like."

"Thanks, but I'll be fine on my own. I will take an early evening though and spend some time in my room. Thanks for listening to me, Mother. I love you!"

Tessa peeked around the doorway again to see them rise and give each other a hug. "They're coming this way, you two. Let's get behind that floral arrangement quickly!" They speedily moved into position just as Mary and her mother exited the sitting room. Mary headed upstairs and her mother went into the office and closed the door.

"Well, should we listen in on another conversation, or what?" Luke asked.

Richelle said, "I don't know if we'd be able to hear them with the door shut. I think maybe we've heard enough?"

Tessa was thinking the same thing and nodded. Listening to Mary whine and complain had been tiresome.

Richelle said, "I wonder whatever happened to that guy in the trench coat. Do you think he was Mary's father?"

"I don't know. I think the guy in the black trench coat was a lot taller and he didn't have white hair."

Luke said, "Wow, Tessa, you really took note! Wasn't he wearing a hat outside? How could you tell what his hair color was?"

"I don't know exactly. I must have seen dark strands sticking out from under his hat. I just wonder where he's disappeared to."

"It is odd." With hands on his hips, Luke scanned the foyer carefully for any sign of the trench-coated man. "He invited us in here and vanished. That's super weird! Maybe we should take off. I think I've seen and heard enough anyway."

"Does all this girly emotional stuff scare you?" Richelle grinned wickedly.

"No, but I don't want to hear any more of it either. It sounds like this Mary's father runs the show around here. If I were her, I'd tell him where to stick his ideas and move out on my own."

Richelle shook her head. "Well, they do live in a totally different time period. Their ancient clothes are a dead giveaway. Things were different back then. Girls couldn't just move out on their own that easily without a job to support themselves. It sounds to me like she really was trapped into doing what her father wanted. I'm glad we live in the twenty-first century. I sure wouldn't want my parents telling me how to live my life!"

Richelle had moved out after high school and enjoyed her freedom. The tenuous relationship she had with her mother, the grating on each other's nerves, had encouraged her independence. Getting along at a distance seemed to work much better for the two of them.

Luke said, "I wonder if we'd be able to come back tomorrow and check out the shindig. I'm just imagining all the food they'll have." His eyes lit up at the thought. "If we actually have gone back into the past, I wonder if it could happen again."

Tessa couldn't believe the suggestion. "What if we're seeing ghosts, ghosts from the past? What if this place is just a mass of haunted hallucinations? Do you really want to hang out here?"

"I don't think they're ghosts, Tessa," Luke said, concern in his eyes.

"Then what is this?"

"I suspect we've stepped back in time."

Richelle made a musing sound. "That's kind of a cool thought. I wonder if that's what's happened."

Tessa said, "Even if the clock has turned backwards, who knows if this will ever happen again. Maybe this is just a one-time freak occurrence."

Richelle said, "That's true. And even if we came back tomorrow and switched to the past, I feel uneasy being here, listening and snooping around. It just doesn't seem right."

Luke responded, "Oh don't worry about it, sweetheart. I'm sure it's okay. That guy wouldn't have invited us in if it weren't."

"But," Richelle said, "we don't even know where this guy is so how do we know if he's legit or not. Maybe he's an intruder himself. He's probably sneaking around the house and swiping stuff while we're occupied listening to these people's conversations. He could be a thief! We should call the police and let them handle this."

Luke stared at her in a dumbfounded way. "You're getting carried away, Barbie Doll! Breathe deep and relax. Don't get so worked up."

She crossed her arms and gave him an angry stare.

"Remember, this house is actually abandoned. No one lives here anymore so the police wouldn't find a thing and you'd end up looking like a fool. I'm sure the trench-coat guy is around here somewhere. We just have to find him." He started toward the left side of the house, where they had entered, to search for him. "Maybe he's waiting for us in this room over here."

Just then Tessa saw something move up on the landing. Glancing up, she saw the man they had just been discussing. "Luke, up there," she whispered.

Luke turned to look. The man was still wearing the black trench coat and fedora. They watched as he started down the left side and walked deliberately, carefully down the stairway. The three moved over to the side of the round table in the foyer and waited for him to approach.

Tessa squirmed as he headed straight for them, a stern gaze in his eyes. He stopped before them and turned to look directly at her.

She cleared her throat nervously and said, "So you're still here. Why did you invite us in? Do you live here?"

"I invited you in because you needed to see and hear some things. There's a party being held tomorrow night and you need to come back and attend. You are personally invited to come and join us." With that he turned and walked down the hall.

The three friends stood in shocked silence and watched him disappear down the dark corridor.

"That was strange. He didn't really answer my questions. He just invited us back for tomorrow. What a peculiar man." Tessa's mind was spinning from the surreal conversation.

Luke gave a grunt. "Wow, we're invited to come back for the party. I wonder if he has the authority around this place to be inviting total strangers?"

"It would be interesting to come back and see," said Richelle.

Tessa couldn't believe Richelle's nerve. "I don't know. This is way out of my comfort zone. Doesn't it make you two worried? I mean, whoever heard of being hurtled into another time zone? We see it portrayed in movies but this is us, you guys! I feel really uneasy about this whole thing."

"We should at least consider the offer," Luke said.

"Please, let's just go before those two come out of the office." Tessa headed toward the side entrance but when she realized the others were still standing close to the stairway, she stopped, turned and looked at her friends in bewilderment. "What?"

Luke looked perturbed. "I think I'd like to come back tomorrow. Would you join me?"

She raised both hands, palms up. "I don't know."

With a tentative look, Richelle said, "If Tessa chickens out, I'm pretty sure you can count me in but I need some time to evaluate all this first."

"Tessa?" Luke asked.

"I said I promise to think about it. That's the best answer I can give you right now."

He continued to stare at her.

It was clear Luke was planning to come. Tessa could see the excitement building in his eyes. The whole thing was way too bizarre for her liking. She couldn't wait to get out of this place and back to normal. Hopefully they would switch over into their world. The thought of not being able to go back caused her heart to race. Plus, there were no assurances that everything would turn out all right at the party. With a house full of people, there would be no place to hide. What would they wear so they wouldn't stick out like intruders? The fear of something going wrong seemed too much of a risk at the moment.

Luke's eyes stayed locked on hers. She shrugged her shoulders to signal her uncertainty then turned and headed for the door once more, anxious to get out. The other two followed her slowly. They headed outside, into the yard, the snow crunching under their feet as they headed toward the large oak tree.

Being outside in the cold air was a relief. Tessa could see Richelle starting to shiver again. Her own light sweater didn't help ward off the cold either and yet the feeling of liberation outweighed the discomfort she'd felt inside.

"I wonder when we'll snap back to the present. Do you remember at what point we switched time zones?" Luke was walking slowly, taking note. "Weren't we just past that big oak tree when it started to snow?"

"What if we don't switch back over?" asked Richelle apprehensively.

Tessa had the same dread.

"That wouldn't be good," admitted Luke.

They walked side by side toward the tree and, as they did, they could see across the street where the snow blanketed everything. It was starting to darken outside and the windows in the mansions across the street were ablaze with lights. Old-fashioned cars drove slowly down the snow-covered road. One car swerved as it tried to increase its speed on the icy surface and quickly slowed to a snail's pace once again.

Tessa stopped to take in the unreal situation and Luke and Richelle joined her to stare at the sight. As the car faded from view down the street, Tessa stood transfixed in her spot. If she wasn't so spooked, the sight would have been amazing. Not only had the house transformed but everything around it had too. Luke and Richelle continued on and she scooted up to join them as they walked beneath the snow-laden branches of the big oak.

Richelle said, "I hope the time changes soon. My toes are starting to freeze up on me again."

Tessa was starting to feel the effects of the cold breeze as well. They were all dressed for a warm spring day, not for cold temperatures in the middle of winter.

As the three of them walked under the tree, it suddenly turned bright outside like someone had flicked a switch in a darkened room. The sun was shimmering brilliantly in the western sky as it was starting to descend toward the horizon. It was late afternoon and they still had a few hours of daylight left. They could hear birds chirping in the tree above them and see new buds on the branches. The snow was gone and the ground beneath them was now a mixture of last year's brown, overgrown grass, some fresh green sprigs, and weeds. The air had turned instantly warm and a slight breeze made everything smell fresh and new.

They turned around to look at the mansion they'd just come from. It looked as forsaken as ever, a shell again of its former beauty. They stood for a while in silence, gazing at the empty husk of a home. It looked sad now, considering the grandeur and magnificence it had once enjoyed. Tessa couldn't help feeling an emotional letdown at the drastic contrast.

Luke finally broke the silence. "I wonder what caused us to go back in time."

No one answered.

"Maybe there's a magnetic field around this house that transported us back. It could be what drove these people away. Maybe they were constantly being shifted into different time zones every time they walked through this magnetic field. That could be why they left everything and never came back. Perhaps that's why no one's ever lived here again."

"It could be. It sounds kind of far-fetched to me, but anything sounds believable after what we just saw." Richelle rubbed her arms, trying to warm up.

Tessa was in no mood to discuss the possibilities of what transported them in time. Her only interest was in getting away from there. "I have to go and get some things done before tomorrow. I start work early." She headed to the gate with her two friends following. "I've had enough excitement for one day."

"I believe the excitement is only beginning – that is, if we all come back tomorrow night," said Luke.

"Maybe," Richelle said tentatively.

Richelle's veiled answer irritated Tessa. They'd always been united in their aversion to going anywhere close to the abandoned house. Richelle's tentative "maybe" bothered her. Walking back to the college, Luke and Richelle discussed the bizarre experience and their hesitancy began to give way to anticipation. Tessa didn't say a word as she noticed their excitement increasing. All she felt was a rising dread.

When they reached the college and before they all went their separate ways, Luke turned and said, "Hey, Tessa, I've been thinking about something all the way back from that house. Did you notice that the guy in the trench coat hardly paid any attention to Richelle or me? When he spoke he looked straight at you the whole time. I wonder what that's about?"

Richelle nodded and said, "Yeah, I detected that too. Do you think this is about you, Tessa?"

Yes, she'd certainly taken note of that detail too. "I don't know what it means but it doesn't make me feel any better about going tomorrow night, that's for sure."

"Hey, don't worry about it," said Luke. "I'm sure he meant it for all of us. He did invite all of us back for tomorrow. Have a good walk home, Tessa, and we'll see you tomorrow after work." He turned back to Richelle and said, "Let's get going, Barbie."

Richelle had asked him for a ride home, surprisingly, since she always mocked his car. After the two jumped into the "Green Thing" and sped off, a puff of dark smoke ejecting in their wake, Tessa started her walk toward home, wishing she felt even a tiny bit of peace.

The more she deliberated over the afternoon's events, the more uncomfortable she grew. Time travel didn't just happen. It reminded her of an experience a few years back – something she'd kept secret and well hidden. Now the past was flooding into her present and she hated it.

What was the point of going back to see what happened to people who lived so long ago? What relevance did this experience have to her life now? The only purpose it served was to increase her stress level. She didn't see any good in that. And listening to Mary complain and cry was even less incentive.

CHAPTER 3

The morning dragged after the breakfast rush and Tessa's mind wandered to the events of the previous day. The absurdity of the whole thing plagued her as she tried to focus on her customers. It was nearly impossible.

One customer, a very stern-looking woman in a stiff suit, asked for the third time to have her coffee cup refilled. Tessa chided herself for being so distracted. A number of customers had complained over exactly the same thing throughout the morning. She really needed to concentrate if she expected any tips at all. Another table of three business types complained about having to wait fifteen minutes just to have their order taken. She apologized profusely and yet they still glared at her. She couldn't really blame them; her mind was not cooperating and couldn't be persuaded to concentrate on the present.

Martha, the manager on duty, had made mention of Tessa's sidetracked attention and the complaints that filtered through the place. It was rare for Martha to be pleased about anything so Tessa didn't take her irritation too seriously. Although the woman's agitation caused her some guilt, she couldn't seem to change the direction of her focus. Now, as the morning slowed, it was easier to keep up and apply a little more effort. Martha eventually stopped monitoring her efforts and with it came some semblance of peace.

Tessa was thankful for the quiet evening she'd had the night before. After walking over to the pharmacy to pick up a few things, she headed home, made herself a sandwich for dinner and started on her laundry. The house was empty and quiet and she had been glad of it. She had been in no mood to discuss her day. Her parents had gone out for dinner with some friends and arrived back at the house quite late. Mac, her sixteen-year-old brother, had a basketball game and had been home late as well. Joe, her fourteen-year-old brother, had baseball practice and his friend's parents had brought him home around nine-thirty. The solitude of the evening had been a balm to her frazzled mind.

However, the attempt to get some sleep had only resulted in fitful tossing and turning. It seemed like hours passed in the futile attempt to get some shut-eye. The consequences of her sleepless night were glaringly evident now.

She looked at the clock over the kitchen door and noticed it was only ten thirty. The morning was ticking by far too slowly. With weariness dragging her down, it felt more like three in the afternoon. After shaking aside her exhaustion, she rubbed her eyes and breathed a heavy sigh.

"Tessa, did you hear what I said?"

She looked up from the tray she had set down on the counter at Martha who was gawking at her.

"What's wrong with you?"

"I'm sorry. I didn't get a lot of sleep last night and I'm a little out of it today."

"I've noticed," she said accusingly. "How are tips so far?"

"Not the greatest." Tessa reached for two tumblers, filled them halfway with ice and placed them under the fountain drink machine and pressed the correct buttons.

"I'm not surprised. You're making far too many mistakes for someone who's so experienced. Lack of sleep? That's the only thing bothering you?"

"Yeah." She had no desire to get into anything with Martha, who would never understand anyway. She chuckled. If Martha had any idea what was on her mind, she'd have an absolute fit.

Martha glared at her. "What are you laughing about?"

Had she actually laughed out loud? Tessa smiled sheepishly and said, "Sorry, I was thinking about something."

Martha turned, holding a full tray of drinks in one hand, the lines creasing on her forehead giving away her annoyance. "Get over whatever is affecting your work and concentrate. I will not tolerate having customers aggravated by your lack of effort. If you can't put in an honest day's work then maybe you should find someone to take over your shift. This is no laughing matter."

"I can handle it. I'll be fine."

The bell over the door jingled and a couple entered. Martha

pointed to them as Patrice, the hostess, seated them by the window. "Look, why don't you go wait on them and see if you can manage it without blundering this time."

Tessa released a frustrated sigh when the woman finally walked off. Considering the circumstances, she thought she had managed fairly well all morning. If Martha only knew what she was dealing with, she'd give her some space. But, good old Martha saw only what she wanted to see. If there were any mistakes made by any of the waitresses, Martha was sure to point them out liberally.

Just before lunch, Tabitha, another waitress, entered through the front doors. She'd worked at The Eating Place a few months now. Tessa and Tabitha had hit it off right from the start, one of the bright spots of being employed there. Tessa had given her some tips on waitressing when she'd first begun. She was a natural from the start – friendly, outgoing – and could strike up a conversation with any stranger. Tabitha's natural extroversion complemented Tessa's quieter nature.

Tabitha waved as she headed to the back to hang up her sweater. She returned, attempting to tie the apron at her back. Stopping in front of Tessa, she turned around and held the strings out. "Can you help me with this?"

"Sure." Plates of food were waiting on the serving counter, ready to go, but first she helped Tabitha.

All the servers had to supply their own clothes but there were guidelines set out for them to follow. The requirement was light beige pants and a white shirt. The restaurant provided small, white aprons, with pockets in the front to carry pens and note pads for order taking.

After tying the apron, Tessa turned back to the plates and set them on her tray.

Tabitha said, "Thanks," and hurried off to a table in her section.

The lunch hour grew progressively more hectic and Tessa was surprised that her ability to concentrate was improving. Less irritation and disappointment were being voiced over her service. Perhaps the trauma of the day before was beginning to wear off. She sure hoped so. Maybe all she had needed was some time for the strangeness of the experience to fade.

To Tessa's disappointment, a few minutes into the lunch hour and things began to disintegrate. Exhaustion from lack of sleep really began to take its toll. Endless duties, a crowded restaurant and not enough help all joined to stress her already taxed emotions. The mistakes started in earnest and when she felt she couldn't listen to another disgruntled customer, she noticed a familiar face at the entrance. Tessa stopped and watched the hostess, Patrice, seat him at a table for two. He looked her way and waved.

When she had a minute, she went over to his table.

"Hi, Cody! I didn't know you were coming in today."

"Hey! I decided to drop in. I haven't seen you in a while."

"It's been less than a week." She wasn't sure she was pleased he was here. Her feelings were still unsure where he was concerned. At times she was thrilled being with him and at other times she felt anxious and uncertain.

"It's been too long for me. I didn't want to bother you while you were doing your exams. I knew you were having a busy week."

"Why don't you come sit in my section so we can chat? This is a busy time for me so I can't sit down right now but we could slip in a few words while I'm rushing around. I have a lunch break around two or whenever it slows down, if you want to wait around that long."

"I'm on lunch break myself and don't have much time. I'll come over and sit in your section, though." Cody grabbed his briefcase and followed Tessa to a table she pointed out.

"How's work going now that you're done your classes?" Cody asked after he was settled.

"Don't ask! This isn't my best day!"

"Why's that?" Cody folded his arms on the table and looked at her in deep interest.

"I can't concentrate today. I'm making tons of mistakes. I guess going from exams and school to working a full day is a big switch."

"I'm sure you'll settle in eventually."

"Yeah."

"Excuse me!" someone shouted from a few tables down.

Tessa turned to Cody and said, "I'll be back."

She went to see what was needed. After refilling their drinks, checking on another table and bringing out food to a third, she headed back to Cody.

"So, how's the life insurance business going?"

"Great. I had a few appointments this morning and I have a few this afternoon too. It's been extremely busy lately. I'll have to go to the office after my appointments and finish up some paper work. You know, Tessa, maybe we should go out for dinner tonight, celebrate that you're done exams. I know you've been excited about getting done. How about it, are you up for it?"

"Well, you know Luke's back from university, right? Luke, Richelle and I were together yesterday for a while and we had kind of planned getting together again tonight."

"Could we slip in dinner before that?"

"Well…I could probably fit it in before I meet up with them. Is that okay with you? I don't want you to feel like I'm trying to squeeze you in." But that's exactly what she was doing and she knew it. She was actually relieved she wouldn't have the whole evening with Cody. With her unsettled feelings toward him, an hour or two at dinner was plenty.

"That'll work with me. Maybe we could plan a date on the weekend again."

She shrugged. "Maybe."

"Till what time do you work today?"

"I get off at four-thirty. Why don't you pick me up five-thirty at my house? That should give me enough time to get home and change."

"Great!" He gave her his order and then pulled some paperwork out of his briefcase.

As she worked, she thought about her relationship with Cody Fields. He was a good friend and he treated her with a lot of respect, almost too much respect. They hadn't even held hands yet to this point or kissed. A part of her felt relieved. Some of the other guys she'd dated in the past had been interested only in one thing and nothing serious had ever ensued. She enjoyed the fact that they could simply be friends for a while and she wondered at times whether they were going to be any more than that. He was likable enough but it was hard to tell what he wanted out of the relationship. Her roller coaster feelings didn't help either.

Cody shared her beliefs; he was a Christian and wasn't shy

about sharing his faith. He had a tremendous excitement about spiritual things and a great love for God. It was intriguing. She had never felt that way. She loved God but without his intensity.

They'd met through a mutual friend, Marcia, at a Christian music concert. He immediately took an interest in her and asked her out within the week. Tessa found him comfortable to be with, like being with one of her brothers. To be with him felt safe somehow. The only thing that made her uncomfortable was when he talked deeply about spiritual things. It made her squirm and she wasn't sure why. However, the comfort level they shared on most points kept her from tossing him.

Cody attended a small church of about seventy people. They called themselves "Church on the Move." They didn't have enough money for their own building so they rented a store in a strip mall and renovated it to suit their small congregation. Cody was the youth leader and enjoyed sharing his love for God with them. His enthusiasm seemed to be contagious. Tessa had attended a few of the meetings and although she didn't participate in the discussions, they intrigued her.

On the other hand, Tessa attended a large church a few blocks from her house, which was a known landmark in the city. It had been built at the turn of the twentieth century, had been there for as long as anyone could remember and had a robust membership of around eight hundred. New people seldom joined, so she knew most of the parishioners. She felt comfortable at Chelsey's Community Church, having attended there since she was a child.

Church on the Move was a bit of a stretch for her. She went with Cody once in a while for his sake but still preferred her own.

Cody ate his lunch quickly, and since Tessa was much too busy to talk, said good-bye and left. After her lunch break, she struggled to focus on work. There were still some stragglers finding their way in, but her mind continually wandered to the old mansion and she dreaded the coming evening. If only she hadn't agreed to accompany Luke and Richelle. Hopefully they'd forget all about it.

The last hour was a dichotomy with the restaurant nearly empty. It dragged and yet flew by at the same time. Plenty of opportunity arose to visit with Tabitha but Martha's time was also freed up to harp on any mistakes. She kept giving commands to the two girls, keeping them occupied. There was always something to clean and Martha was more than pleased to keep them both busy.

Tessa was computing the bill for her last table when she noticed Luke walk in. She headed to the table where two women sat. Their empty plates of dessert sat to the side and they were still sipping on cups of coffee. After placing the bill on the table, one of the women immediately pulled out a twenty and handed it to her. She headed to the till to get the change.

Luke waved at her from the door

She waved back, returned the change to the table and walked to the entrance where Luke waited.

"Hi, Luke."

"Hi there, pretty! How was your day?" It felt good to have him drop in like this. She didn't realize how much she'd missed his cheery greetings this past year until this moment.

"It went fairly well, considering the circumstances."

"What circumstances?" He looked puzzled.

"Well, I couldn't get that old mansion off my mind all day."

"Just what I wanted to hear! I can't wait to head over there."

"Well…actually I've been dreading going back. I don't know if I want to go and besides, Cody stopped by and wants to take me out for dinner."

Disappointment clouded his usually cheery look. "What? You can't back out on us now! Remember, you promised us last night that you'd go." He looked upset. "Richelle won't be too happy about it either. She's getting off early just so we can go."

"Oh, you two!" A feeling of resignation and despair swept over her. "I suppose we could still go but it would have to be after dinner sometime. Cody wants to take me out to celebrate me finishing up at college. As long as you don't mind waiting for me, I could still go." A light bulb moment hit her. "Or you two could go on without me if you'd like." She crossed two fingers behind her back.

"No, no, no! You're not getting off the hook that easily."

Disillusioned resignation set in fully. Luke was much too stubborn to give in.

"I'll let Richelle know we'll be meeting a bit later than we'd planned. Why don't we meet at that coffee shop on the corner before that row of mansions start? What's it called again?"

Tessa thought for a second and then said, "Michael's Mocha Shop."

"Oh yeah, that's it. We'll meet there, let's say eight o'clock." He looked at her for confirmation.

"Okay, that should work. I'll see you later then." Luke gave her a kiss on the cheek and walked out. As Tessa picked up her tip from the last table, she could hear him starting up his green car and, from the rattle of it, that beast hadn't improved much over the past year. It had always been noisy but it was sounding worse than ever. He wasn't one to tune up his vehicle too often but, by the racket it was making, it sounded like he really should.

So, she was going to the old house. In a way it was exciting but all the unknowns sent chills down her spine. She hung up her apron in the back staff room, scooted out the front door in relief and started on her walk home.

At five-thirty sharp, Cody arrived and drove them to the best steak and lobster place he knew of. Tessa didn't like eating heavy meals so she decided on one of the chicken breast entrées on the menu. Cody feasted on a twelve-ounce steak. The way he devoured his meat made her smile.

Distraction overtook her enjoyment of the meal and she aimlessly picked at her food. After the meal they caught up on what they'd been doing and she realized again how easy he was to talk to. Of course she purposely left out the mansion fiasco. There was no point in going there. There was no reason to spoil a nice, relaxing evening. She suddenly wished she could spend the whole evening with him. His excitement about life was contagious and right now she could use a good dose.

"So how do you feel about staying on at The Eating Place for the summer? I know you weren't too thrilled about it at first."

"I think it'll be okay. I know the ropes and most of the girls are easy to work with. My only concern is Martha. She's always picking at my mistakes and rarely smiles. I don't know if she's even capable of it."

Cody grinned.

"It was hard keeping everything straight today. I had a lot on my mind and I'm hoping tomorrow will be easier."

"I'm sure it will be. Working full time can be hard to adjust to, especially being on your feet all day. I know you'll do great. Who wouldn't love to have you as a waitress at their table?" He smiled sweetly at her.

Tessa didn't know what to say. She felt uncomfortable and looked away. His words did please her, though.

"I was thinking. Maybe the two of us could go to the youth worship time in the park on Saturday night. A bunch of different youth groups are getting together. Would you be interested? I'm taking the youth group from our church and I'd love to have you join us." He gazed at her expectantly.

Going with a whole group of people wasn't her idea of an intimate occasion. She'd much rather have time with him alone. Would they ever get more serious or would their moments together continue to consist of short meetings and surrounded by people? Was he even interested in more? She tried not to look too disappointed. "I guess that would be okay."

"I'll pick you up around seven. Most of the youth can drive or their parents will take them. We'll swing by the church to see if anyone needs a ride and then we'll go on to the park. I'm looking forward to it." He looked thrilled that she'd agreed.

It warmed her insides. At times his feelings showed he was interested in more than friendship. Sometimes he did something romantic like this nice dinner but mostly they hung out with his youth group or some kind of church function. It caused some frustration on her part. It was really difficult to get to know him when they spent so little alone time together.

She asked him to drop her off at Michael's Mocha Shop after dinner. Luke's car was already parked by the curb in front of the shop. Cody stopped, let her out and she stood on the sidewalk and waved as he drove off.

Michael's Mocha Shop had been there for a number of years and had gained quite a bit of popularity among the youth. It maintained a steady flow of business and boasted many unique coffees, a solid selection of teas, frosted drinks and pastries. This was one of her favorite coffee places.

The exterior of the place was a dark brown stucco with bold gold-lettering spelling out the name above the door. As she stepped inside, the rich, dark colors of the interior greeted her. The tables and chairs of the booths were stained a dark brown and upholstered in a rich rust, gold, brown and off-white, striped fabric. There were gold light fixtures on the walls by each booth with tulip sconces extended out from each fixture. The effect of all the richness of the décor made the shop feel homey. Inviting framed pictures of various coffees, teas and desserts hung on the walls.

As Tessa walked in, she could see Richelle and Luke at a table toward the back. They both looked up as she walked toward them. He stood when she got there, a gentleman at heart.

"Luke, sit down! It's only me! You don't have to get up for me unless you were planning to use the men's room."

"No, I don't need the men's room. I'm just so glad you showed up. I had to give you a standing ovation." With that he started to clap, then reached over, grabbed her and gave her a big kiss on the lips.

It left her completely flustered.

"I'm sure glad you're here, darling. It wouldn't be the same without you."

Tessa recovered and shoved him. "Oh stop it, Luke. I told you I'd be here." She sat down and turned toward Richelle. "How long have you two waited?"

"Too long, Tessa. I think there's something going on between you and Cody. I believe it's more serious than what you've been letting on. You're always so quiet about him. Why is that?" Richelle gave her an inquisitive stare.

"Don't start on me. I almost didn't come you know. Cody and I are friends and that's all for right now. We're not serious."

"Yeah, yeah, we've heard that before. What about Duncan? You always said that wasn't serious either but he wouldn't stay away from your house. We couldn't get close to you while you were dating that guy. How long did that last? Wasn't it like a few weeks?" Luke sure could bring up some bad memories.

Tessa cringed at the recollection. "It was two months."

"Okay, two months. That got serious fast and you kept saying, 'We're only friends.' It didn't look like 'only friends' to us. He was all over you all the time."

"He was a creep. After two weeks I knew I wanted him gone but he just wouldn't take no for an answer. It took me six weeks to finally shake him. I wanted friendship and he wanted something more. Conflict of interest is what brought the end to that relationship."

Richelle said, "I was so glad you finally gave him the boot. It was like I lost my best friend. I couldn't get close to you because Duncan was always hanging around. He was like a leech! Eleventh grade brings back some bad memories when it comes to Dun."

"Richelle…" said Luke.

Tessa knew by the smirk on his face where this was going. She wished he'd take it easy after just arriving in town. He was about to ridicule her choice in men. Richelle could get so defensive, especially concerning Charlie.

"What about your leech? Charlie won't leave you much room either. He has to know what you're doing every second, doesn't he?"

Anger flashed from her eyes. "He's not a leech! Luke, he's not that bad!"

He raised his hands in surrender but it was clear her response brought him great enjoyment.

"He's very jealous but as long as he knows who I'm with and where I'm going he gives me some space. Hey, when you love someone, you accept a lot about that person even though he isn't perfect. That's how I feel about Charlie. He's sensitive and sweet and he'll do anything for me. What else could I ask for?"

Luke looked pleased to answer. "Some room to breathe for one. I couldn't handle that kind of relationship. I'd feel claustrophobic with someone like that taking up my space. I enjoy my freedom too much and couldn't handle being tied down to one person. But you can't just get up and go, Richelle; you have to pass everything by Charlie. I'm not ready for that." He raised his eyebrows. "I don't think I'd ever be ready for that."

"Just wait, when that certain girl walks across your path, you'll be smitten and everything will change. Suddenly you'll be infatuated and you'll do anything to be with her. Falling in love will change you." Richelle wore this "I-know-what-I'm-talking-about look."

He shook his head. "Maybe women don't mind giving up control. Men on the other hand don't want their woman ruling their lives. It's oppressive. Don't you find Charlie oppressive?"

Richelle looked hurt and angry. "Stop it, would you? You keep downing the man I love and it's ticking me off! You have never been in love so you're no expert on the matter. Like I said before,

Charlie's a great guy. I wouldn't be with him if I found him oppressive. He's fun to be with and he treats me like a queen. That's all I have to say about it and I wish we would change the subject."

"Hey, you two, have you had anything to drink yet?" Tessa knew it was time to calm the storm again. She felt in no mood to play referee right now but she was even less in the mood to listen to a fight.

"Hey, Richelle, I'm sorry if I hurt your feelings about Charlie. I'm sure he's an absolute sweetheart in every sense of the word. I guess I just don't see him the way you do, that's all."

"Well, then I'd appreciate it if you'd just shut up about it. I don't want to hear any more of your comments about my boyfriend!"

It was time to step in. Tessa said, "All right, how about some cups of decaf coffee all around? I'll go get some at the counter and I'll even get some pastries too. Maybe that'll quiet you down for a while. What kind would you like?" They could be so childish.

"Make my coffee with caffeine please and no pastry for me." Richelle's voice was laced with irritation. Her eyes betrayed her anger as she flashed them back to Luke.

"I'll have a coffee and one of those twisted pastry things," said Luke with a smirk. He obviously found the conversation very amusing.

When Tessa arrived back with the coffee, the mood at the table had changed. Richelle was actually smiling and Luke was laughing. "What happened here while I was gone?"

"You see, Tessa, we don't always need you to rescue us from our arguments. We actually can act like big kids and make up." Luke said with a huge grin on his face.

"We didn't make up at all. Luke's still in the doghouse! He just told me this corny joke and it made me smile, that's all. I'm still mad at him!"

"Oh, but you can't stay mad long. Look at this face." He pointed at his boyish good looks. "It's too innocent-looking and adorable to stay angry at."

"Get real, Luke. If it's so adorable, then where's the woman on your arm? I don't see anyone drooling over your face."

"Okay, Luke and Richelle, stop it or else I'm leaving. I had a hard day of work, hurried home to change, went out for dinner with Cody and then rushed over here to hear this? If you two keep this up, I'm out of here. I'm not going to spend my evening listening to you argue and fight. You both do need a referee and I'm not up to it tonight so either stop it or goodbye."

Luke stuck out his hand to Richelle and said, "Truce?" He was always quick to let things slide.

Richelle, on the other hand, wasn't. She sat there; arms crossed, and stared at him with a scowl on her face. "You don't deserve to be forgiven."

"Did I ask to be forgiven? I don't remember that part." His hand still stuck out.

"You are such a jerk!"

Tessa got up with her coffee cup in hand. "Okay you two have a great night. I'm going home for some peace of mind."

"No wait, Tessa." Luke jumped up to stop her. "Okay, Richelle, I apologize. Would you please accept my apology? I won't say bad things about your Charlie again. He's sweet and wonderful and all that. Now can we kiss and make up?"

"You had better keep your promise, Luke. I'm not amused at all! If you'll wipe that smirk off your face, then maybe I'll accept your apology."

He looked as serious as he could, got down on one knee and said, "I am truly sorry for the pain I have caused you this evening, my dear Barbie. I promise you it will not happen again. Is that good enough?"

Richelle rolled her eyes. "All right, Luke. I'll forgive you. Now get up. You're making a fool of yourself."

He slowly stood.

"Just remember, you're still on thin ice."

"I'll behave, I promise," he said as he sat down.

They all took a few minutes to drink their coffees and Luke finished off his pastry. It sure looked good but Tessa was still too full from dinner to have anything but a drink. It was nice to have things quiet at the table for a change and she reveled in the peace for a few minutes. Richelle didn't seem to be much in the mood for any small talk at the moment and it was nice that Luke was stuffing his face; it kept him quiet for a while.

When he finished, he looked up and said, "Are you still up for a party?"

"That depends if you can behave yourself," Richelle stated. "I should have brought Lacy's dog leash along. Maybe that would keep you in line." Lacy was a shiatsu, a gift from Charlie on their one-year dating anniversary.

Luke sang out lustily, "Don't be cruel to a heart that's true."

People looked over at the spontaneous entertainment. He seemed oblivious to the attention he was drawing.

"I'll behave myself, I promise."

"All right, let's get going then." Tessa didn't want to get home too late. Her feet were aching from standing all day; she wasn't used to being on them that much. "Can we all ride in your car, Luke? My feet are so sore!"

"Sure that's what it's here for. Let's go, gals."

They drove up to the old mansion and stopped right in front of it. They all stayed where they were for a moment, staring out at the debilitated thing.

Richelle said, "It must be getting close to nine already. Look how dark it's getting and how spooky those windows look. I never did like the dark. It gives me the creeps."

"I hear you, girl," said Tessa. It did look ghostly with the elongated shadows across the front yard, throwing most of the front into darkness.

"It's not that dark yet, girls. Come on, let's go." Luke opened his door, exited and waited for them on the sidewalk.

Luke draped an arm over Richelle's shoulder and the other over Tessa's as they joined him on the sidewalk facing the mansion. "I'm here to protect you so you'll be fine."

"That's what I'm concerned about. You're not much help tonight." Richelle moved Luke's arm off of her shoulder and moved a step away from him.

"Touchy, touchy!" He shook his head and looked at her with disappointment.

"Hey, buddy, you did it to yourself."

Tessa shook her head in despair at their constant friction. She turned her attention to the house before them and noticed that it looked particularly dark and foreboding this night. The moon gave off a filtered light through the thin cloud cover, making the shadows in the yard move ominously.

Luke undid the lock and the gate, which opened with a screeching resistance. "Okay, here we go." He grabbed both of the girls' hands and led them through the gate.

Goose bumps formed as Tessa walked toward the tree and she knew it wasn't from being cold; it was a warm spring evening but the anticipation of what lay ahead sent shivers up her spine. She wished she were anywhere but here at the moment.

CHAPTER 4

The anticipation and tension was thick enough to cut with a knife as the three approached the big oak tree. Luke let go of their hands and led cautiously, the girls nervously taking up the rear. He was steps ahead when he finally turned around, excitement glowing from his eyes. Grabbing them by their hands once more, he started pulling them along.

"Okay, show some enthusiasm here because we're about to switch over into whatever year it is."

Richelle said, "That's easy for you to say. I'm shaking like a leaf and you're asking me to show enthusiasm?"

Tessa threw Richelle a glance of mutual trepidation. Her skin crawled in panic and she felt completely unprepared for whatever was about to happen. The intensity of the moment crowded around her, making it difficult to breathe. She pulled at her sweater, buttoned up to her throat, for more air. Luke's hand wrapped around hers gave a small token of security.

They walked a few steps past the big oak and then it happened. Just like that, again everything suddenly changed. Snow blanketed the ground around them, the path beneath their feet the only cleared area. The walk had obviously been shoveled clean this very day because mounds of snow were piled on each side. The lights from the house splayed across the snow-covered yard, casting a yellow glow everywhere it touched. All three stood deathly still and studied the changed landscape.

The house was alive with activity as bright lights shone from almost every window. Music, emanating from inside, radiated through the glass partition. Tessa looked back and noticed that Luke's car was nowhere in sight. What she did see was a row of old-fashioned vehicles parked on the road beside the curb. She wouldn't have known the year or make of the cars. Not that she cared.

49

Boy, my mind is going! This is crazy! How can we have slipped back in time? It just doesn't make sense. This should not be happening! I'm so stressed! Why did I ever agree to come?

Luke interrupted her thoughts "We are definitely in a different time period. I sure wonder what year we're in."

Richelle said, "Look back there. Do you see all the cars parked on the street? There must be a lot of people here for the party tonight!"

That bit of information only helped to increase Tessa's fears. She glanced at Richelle and noticed for the first time that her friend had dressed quite warmly with sensible sneakers and a sweater that she was presently draping over her shoulders.

"I see you came prepared this time."

Richelle responded, "Well, I sure didn't want to freeze today. Better safe than sorry. I see you're dressed warmer too."

"I hate being cold!" admitted Tessa. Richelle grinned and it helped loosen her fear a notch. Tessa turned to Luke. "How come you didn't dress for the weather?"

He wore khaki pants, a t-shirt but no jacket.

"Hey, we won't be outside that long. I'm expecting to be enjoying a party, not a snow fight!" He stooped down as if to pick up some snow. The girls both yelled at him and, with a smirk of enjoyment, he reluctantly abandoned his idea and kept walking.

As they approached the house they could see decorative lights hung from the roof of the outside veranda. Lanterns were arranged along the railing and placed on each step of the stairway leading to the veranda. The terrace had been cleared of all snow and large flower arrangements stood at various places.

Hmm...I wonder how the flowers can survive the cold?

Tessa noticed all the lights combined gave a rosy glow to the snow-covered yard. Gone was the dark, dreary look, replaced by a home fully-lit and party-ready.

As they drew nearer, they could see people walking around in the house, eating, laughing and talking. The three friends walked very slowly, trying to take it all in before they got too close.

Gingerly, they ascended the left-side stairway to the veranda. Tessa didn't have the nerve to go right into a house full of people she didn't know so she wandered around the terrace and gazed at the extensive decorations. She stopped in front of one of the large floral arrangements and could tell at this close range that the flowers were artificial. They were arranged in large ceramic containers, set upon finely-sculptured marble bases.

She turned to see if her friends were still with her. Luke and Richelle stood toward the center of the terrace and gazed into the windows, watching the activity within. Walking toward them, she felt edgy being so clearly visible to the guests inside. With all these lights scattered in profusion just outside the windows, guests inside would easily be able to see them.

"Guys, I think we should stay as unobtrusive as possible. Standing here in full view of the guests isn't too smart." Tessa moved away from the window and scanned the veranda. "I wonder where the guy in the trench coat is?"

Luke moved toward her. "I don't know. He's the one who invited us so I'd think he'd let us in."

"Well, I'm not going to stay out here and freeze, that's for sure." Richelle started toward the center doors where all the action was taking place inside.

"Richelle, I think we'd better use the side door instead. We wouldn't want to make a scene right from the start," said Tessa.

Richelle considered this and slowly turned back to join them.

"What if he doesn't show?" asked Luke.

They suddenly all noticed movement by the door and turned in that direction simultaneously.

The trench-coated man stood at the side entrance, so still that he looked like a molded statue, studying them with a serious, no-nonsense expression. Questions bombarded Tessa at the sight of him.

Where did he come from? I sure didn't notice anyone approaching or any door opening. How could he possibly have appeared so quickly without us noticing him? This is too weird!

Luke was the first to approach the man and the girls followed. "Hi there, sir. My name is Luke Trent, and your name?" He held out his hand to shake the man's hand but was completely ignored. Instead, the man turned toward Tessa and said, "I'm glad you came. Follow me." With that he turned, opened the door and led the way into the house.

The three friends looked at each other and Luke whispered, "That was downright rude. He didn't even look at me and totally ignored my hand! Did you see that? What a jerk! I should give him a piece of my mind."

Richelle whispered, "Now you know what it feels like to have the shoe on the other foot for a change. You can give but you can't take, is that it, Luke?"

"Come on, you two; he's holding the door for us." Tessa was the first one through with Luke and Richelle following.

Tessa turned to see Luke give the man a harsh look as he walked past him but the man didn't seem to be affected at all by Luke's ire. She glanced over and tried to spot the action in the foyer but it was around the corner, hidden from view. The home was full of noise, though, evidence of a crowd in attendance. She turned back to her friends and noticed that the man who had escorted them inside was gone. Luke was searching around frantically. He opened the door and looked out onto the veranda.

"What are you doing, Luke? Looking for your heart?" asked Richelle with a smile, her arms crossed.

"No!" he said in exasperation. "That jerk in the trench coat opened the door for us and then vanished into thin air. I was just wondering where he could have disappeared to so quickly. Did you two see where he went?"

Tessa said, "No. He was here a minute ago. Where could he have gone to so fast?" His sudden appearances and departures were unnerving. The fear that had started to abate was coming back with a vengeance.

Richelle looked nervous. "He keeps inviting us back here like he's our tour guide or something so you'd think he'd at least stay with us to show us around. He's really freaking me out." She shuddered.

Luke said, "Who is this guy? I mean, he told us to come in and then treats us like that. I can't believe his nerve. I wish I'd had the chance to give him a piece of my mind."

"I don't think anyone needs a piece of your mind."

"Did I ask for your opinion, Richelle?" He glared at her and shook his head before turning toward the foyer. "Come on, you two, let's go join the party."

Tessa glanced around once more for any sign of the man, but it seemed he really had disappeared into thin air. Maybe he'd show up again during the party or when they were ready to leave.

52

She followed her friends around the corner and as soon as they entered the main lobby area, they were bombarded by the sights and sounds of an era long ago. A crowd of people was congregated in the lobby. The large table and floral arrangement had been moved to the side, creating a natural dance floor in the large entrance. A live brass band was set up in front of the office door between the two stairways leading to the second floor. The tune being played was unfamiliar, yet reminded them of years gone by.

The three of them stayed close to the wall and tried to look inconspicuous. It was completely impossible with their modern clothing, which contrasted so strikingly with what they saw the partiers wearing. But surprisingly, no one had noticed them yet. Tessa was thankful for that, but the fear of what would happen once they did, made her hands sweat.

Well, we're here so whatever happens, happens! Huh!
Courage. That's a strange sensation. Where did that come from, I wonder?

Tessa rubbed her sweaty palms on her thighs and scanned the room nervously. She estimated that there were over one hundred people in the big entrance room, but even with that many, it didn't even seem over-crowded. The men wore suits and ties and some were even in tails. The predominant choice in the ladies' party wear was floor-length gowns and the wide range of colors flowed together like a beautiful, moving painting. The extravagantly-made gowns in rich colors, of silk, taffeta, organza and many other fine fabrics were breathtaking. It was mesmerizing to watch their skirts swish as they flowed and moved to the dance.

The people in this room were obviously wealthy. Only the finest materials graced their frames and only the purest gems and stones sparkled from necks and hands. It was quite an astounding sight, one Tessa had only seen in movies.

It was beautiful to watch these couples hold each other in close embrace and sway to the music. The contrast of the men's dark suits with the colorful, elegant gowns of the women was spectacular. Tessa had to admit that the music was graceful and peaceful but it certainly was different than anything they were used to. It didn't have much punch to it and she hadn't recognized any of the music so far. Even so, she found her head moving to the streaming sound.

"You're enjoying this, are you?" asked Richelle.

"It's kind of peaceful," whispered Tessa.

"Yeah, it'll put me to sleep soon," mocked Luke.

Tessa ignored him and watched the room. A refreshment table was located on the far side against the wall. It was full of all sorts of delicacies. A large punch bowl stood on one table surrounded by cups. Beside it stood coffee and tea urns with all the fixings. The kitchen staff ran back and forth, replacing plates of food, cleaning up spills and checking on people to see if they had everything they needed. Other staff members took dirty plates and cups away and brought freshly-washed ones in their place. It was a hub of activity, with some busy serving and others enjoying.

The entrance area was elaborately decorated, featuring much attention to detail and beauty. Wonderfully-arranged floral arrangements filled with roses, carnations, daisies, irises and day lilies, were placed all around the room. Each large vase was filled with varying colors that made the room look vibrant. Tessa could smell the fragrance of the blooms wafting through the entrance.

Now, how is it possible I'm smelling flowers? This isn't even real! This house is empty, rotten and ready to be condemned! I don't get this!

Candles were lit at various locations around the room. Some were placed all over the refreshment tables; long candlesticks, three to four feet in height, stood against the wall at different places. The effect of the floral arrangements and the iridescent light combination gave the room an intimate feel. There were also thin tapers attached to holders on the railing of the stairways going up to the top floor landing. On the second level, large lanterns were positioned close to the banister, the candlelight giving off a soft glow.

Tessa wondered how they could have managed to secure the candles on the railing. The light from the large chandelier that hung from the open ceiling had been turned down low and, with all the other soft glow of lighting throughout the room, it gave the whole entrance a serene effect.

The three of them stood mesmerized for a long time taking it all in. People were laughing, dancing, eating and enjoying the generosity of the Hardingtons. Everyone appeared to be having a great time.

"Isn't it weird that we haven't been noticed yet?" asked Richelle.

"Yeah, I was thinking the same thing," said Tessa. Not that she wanted to be noticed. The mere fact that they were here again, in another time dimension, was enough.

Luke said, "All I can think of is all the food! I'm nervous as all get out and yet all I want to do is eat."

Richelle looked over at him. "You are a hopeless case!"

He gave her a crooked smirk and said, "So, what do you think? Should I try to nab some food?"

Tessa felt nervous just thinking about it. "I don't think that would be the best idea." It was hard to decide how to act. If they'd really traveled back through time, perhaps interfering with the party wasn't such a good idea.

Richelle said, "I think we should just watch for a while. See what happens."

Luke complied for a while but when a servant came close by, carrying a tray of appetizers, Luke pushed off the wall, said, "I'm starving," and walked a few steps toward him.

Fear and curiosity vied for dominance as Tessa kept her eyes glued on the exchange. As Luke approached the servant, she had a feeling this wouldn't turn out very well. The young servant walked right toward Luke, his head turned away as though he didn't see him there.

Luke stopped and said, "Excuse me. Could I have one of those, please?"

The man didn't break his stride, Luke backed up a step but the fellow walked right into him, through him and kept on going!

Luke yelled, "AAHHHH!"

Pinpricks of fear scurried up Tessa's spine as she watched Luke's terrified response.

His eyes were filled with shock as he turned to face the girls, his face an ashen white. He looked sickly as he walked back to join them. With a shaky sigh, he slumped back against the wall as if all his energy had suddenly escaped and breathed deeply.

Tessa touched his arm and asked, "Are you okay, Luke? That was freaky!" Her stomach turned sickeningly. One glance at Richelle told her she was shaken as well.

Richelle said fearfully, "That was too weird! It's like we're back in time but we're really not here."

Luke said, "Yeah, the people are here, we can see them but we can't interact with them. They can't see us. It's as though we're ghosts."

Tessa said, "And did you notice? No one in the room reacted when you screamed. They simply kept on dancing, talking and laughing!"

Richelle said, "Well, that does simplify things for us."

"How?" asked Luke, still shaken.

"It means that we can go wherever we want and no one will know the difference. Since they can't see us, no one will question our presence here. It definitely relieves the pressure I was feeling." Richelle let out a sigh of relief, although nervousness still played around her eyes.

Tessa didn't blame her. Luke's experience had put all of them on edge. "Richelle has a point, Luke. Our clothes won't make us stand out and no one will ask us how we got in. We'll just have to be careful to stay out of the way so people don't walk through us. We'll be able to go anywhere we want without being noticed." The thought brought tremendous relief. Her breathing eased and tension slowly left her shoulders.

"Well, I'm still recovering from the shock of having someone walk right through me. That was too bizarre! Besides which, I'm still hungry!" He stood quietly for a while, a highly unusual occurrence. "Well, the first thing I'm going to do is get into that office and find out what year it is. There must be a calendar in there somewhere."

Richelle said, "How are you going to do that? The band is standing right in front of the office door. You'll have to sneak back behind them somehow without walking into or through anything. It'll be tricky." She actually looked concerned for him.

"I'll manage, Barbie Doll." He headed for the office but this time took extra precaution, dodging his way through. He slipped behind the band, hugging the wall and disappeared into the room. A few minutes later he reappeared and skirted his way back to them.

"You two are too scared to move, aren't you? You're still in the same spot I left you."

Tessa shrugged and gave a small grin.

Richelle said, "Whatever. So, what did you find?"

"The calendar on the wall read 1946 and it was open to the month of January."

"Then no wonder they're dressed so anciently." Richelle lifted her nose in disdain. "I wouldn't be caught dead wearing gowns like that."

Tessa said, "That's a year after World War II ended. Wow!"

"Yeah, you're right," said Luke.

Richelle nodded. "That's interesting. My grandfather was a soldier in that war."

Tessa looked at her, "Really?"

"Uh-huh."

Tessa said, "Well, what should we do? We can't eat any of the food or have anything to drink. All we can do is watch."

"I wonder where Mary is. I haven't seen her at all. Have you?" Richelle scanned the room.

Luke said, "No, I haven't seen her either. I saw some people our age walk into the sitting room earlier. Maybe she's in there with her friends. Let's head over and take a look." He started to the other side, past the refreshment tables to the doorway into the sitting room. The girls followed him, being careful not to bump into anyone. It was a little nerve-wracking as they dodged the dancing couples. They entered the sitting room, stood next to the door and surveyed the scene.

There were quite a few young people in the room, some sitting on the couches and some standing around a large grand piano located to the right of the room in the corner by the window. On the far wall, a fire burned warmly in the fireplace, heating the room and giving it a cozy feel.

Tessa noticed Mary standing by the piano, listening to a young man play. The music sounded familiar. She had heard it before on one of her parents' old records they still played from time to time. It was Eddy Duchin's "Let's Fall in Love." The young man kept looking at a pretty girl dressed in a dark purple gown and gave her a smile now and then. When he finished, he rose and gave the purple-gowned girl a kiss.

Mary immediately looked away, turned and walked over to the couches. "Is there room for me here, Hilda?"

Mary seemed uncomfortable with the piano situation and

Tessa wondered why.

Hilda scooted over and patted the seat beside her. "Of course."

"Thank you." Mary sat down and released a heavy sigh.

Hilda turned to Mary and asked, "Why don't you play a piece for us?"

"I'm very out of practice and I'm not much in the mood for playing right now."

"Oh, nonsense," Hilda whispered quietly so no one else could hear. "Just because Henry played a love song for Rosy doesn't mean you shouldn't play."

The three snoops were close enough to pick it up.

"Come on, I'd love to hear you play. It's been such a long time. Please would you do it for me?"

"I'll be awful. I must decline." Mary looked irritated by the pressure.

"Alright, don't worry about it; you don't have to play if you don't want to." Hilda looked disappointed but stopped pressuring her and the two talked quietly.

It was obvious that they were friends. Tessa turned her attention to assess the people in the room. From what she could tell, there was definitely some pairing going on. Some couples talked quietly in private closeness. Many were obviously still free and available as girls and guys congregated together in groups, talking and laughing.

Tessa noticed Luke saunter toward the piano, stand for a time and look at the grand musical instrument, a beautiful piece of furniture. He raised his hand and ran it through part of the piano. Turning, he shrugged and smiled in amusement, then walked back to join them.

"What was that about?"

"Well, I touched the back of the couch that Mary and her friend are sitting on and it's actually here. My hand didn't go through it. I know that there were couches here when I explored this house before. There is some furniture in the room that obviously still exists in our time so I can touch it and my hand doesn't penetrate it. But I don't remember seeing that piano when I came before. It seems to me that if something is here in the present, in our time and space, we can touch it and feel it, like the walls and any furniture. But we can't feel anything that has been taken out. I just wanted to check out my theory, that's all."

"So you're saying that if we sat down on these couches they would hold us?"

"Yes, Barbie, they would hold us, but I suggest that you wait till they're vacant."

"Don't worry, I'll wait!"

Tessa noticed the servant, Esther, come into the room with a tray of clear glasses filled with a fruity looking drink. She offered some all around and most people took one. Mary lifted her glass to her lips and her hand began to shake terribly. She quickly lifted her other hand to steady her cup.

"Mary, what's wrong? Why is your hand shaking like that? Are you okay?" Hilda stared with wide eyes.

"I'm fine. I'm just a little exhausted and frazzled from the hectic pace I've had. I need some time to rest, that's all. I'll be fine." Mary smiled weakly in reassurance and yet her eyes betrayed her uncertainty. She got up and said, "I'll be right back. If my parents ask about me, tell them I'll be returning shortly."

Hilda stared at her in concern but only nodded.

Tessa looked over at Richelle and said, "I'm going to see what she's up to. Do you want to join me?"

"Sure, I don't want to miss anything. How about you, Luke?"

"She's probably going to use the ladies' room. I think I'll pass on that. I'll stay and see what happens here. Have fun in the bathroom." He waved to them as they left the room.

The two girls followed Mary as she dodged some guests and headed down the hallway past the right stairway and what looked like the kitchen on the right. There were servants steadily coming and going from the room. Richelle and Tessa were careful to avoid the activity as they followed her down the hall, which ended in a set of double glass doors.

As they entered, Tessa could see that this room extended from the house and had windows on three outside walls. It was a magnificent room with a beautiful view of the back yard, although at the moment, the enclosure was mostly covered in snow. Big trees were situated all over the large yard and there were cleared walkways which led to a large gazebo in the center. It was lighted and enclosed by windows and appeared usable even in the winter months. Its octagonal shape was surrounded by snow-covered shrubs. A birdfeeder stood just outside the windows and there were a few birds there now, feeding and flying about in the soft light emanating from it.

Tessa and Richelle stood near the back wall beside the door and watched silently.

Mary went to look out one of the windows, stood there silently for a while and breathed deeply, releasing a slow pent-up sigh. Her shoulders started to shake and she began to cry softly. "If only I were a bird...I'd fly away...so I could be all alone." Her voice choked as the tears continued to flow. "I'd never come back. Oh, God...I can't handle my father's expectations anymore. He hems my life in on all sides...and I have no room to breathe...or be myself. I feel like I'm breaking down...and I don't know how to stop it."

Her soft sobs filled the room. After a few moments she straightened her shoulders some and looked around, her depression obvious. Tears glistened on her cheeks. She headed for one of the end tables, picked up a lace napkin, dried her face and sat down on the love seat.

Tessa hoped she wasn't in for another blubbering session. Although she felt some sympathy for the girl, she didn't understand Mary's trauma. It still seemed so surreal being here and watching someone in the 1940s. She didn't see the sense or reason in any of it. So why was she starting to feel something for someone she didn't even know?

Tessa studied the room further. Everything was decorated in white and antique white, giving the room a soft, feminine feel. The chairs were stained a dark cherry and were covered in a fabric of antique white lace. There were four chairs and two love seats and all were decorated identically. Two end tables had the same dark stain as the chairs. Large plants in ceramic pots, white with gold trim, surrounded all the chairs.

Tessa sensed something on the wall directly behind her and turned to look. In line with her head was a large framed oil painting. It was a garden picture that added to the softness and tranquility of the room. That's probably why Mary had come here, looking for some peace of mind. She turned back to study Mary as she sat on the love seat, deep in thought.

The girl was dressed in a deep maroon gown, which had a

scooped neckline, the bodice tapering down to a slim waist. Her sleeves extended to her wrists then widened out in a ruffle that covered most of her hand. The gown was floor length and flared out flatteringly at the bottom. A large diamond pendant hung just above her bodice neckline, held in place by a gold chain. Her hair was up, secured by a gold and diamond clip. She looked beautiful, graceful and more like a model – a troubled model – than a future bank executive.

Tessa and Richelle heard a noise at the door and turned to see Henry walk into the room. He was the one who had played the song for Rosy. Mary jumped up at the intrusion.

"Henry, what are you doing here?"

"I could ask you the same thing. This isn't where the party is."

"I just needed some peace of mind and time to think. Are my parents asking for me?"

"No, your *daddy* isn't asking for you!" He stared at her accusingly.

She averted her eyes and fidgeted with her lace napkin. Henry slowly walked up to her, took her hands in his and, as he did, she looked up at him in surprise.

"What are you doing? What about Rosy?"

"Mary, why do you let your father control your life like he does? You know that it's not what you really want."

"What else can I do? I don't want to disappoint him. I'm his only child and I feel obligated to please him."

"I know you still love me. I can see it in your eyes."

"Henry, please don't!" She pulled her hands away, sat back down and turned to look outside.

He sat down beside her and said, "Well, I'm still desperately in love with you."

Mary turned to him in disbelief.

Henry continued, "I don't know what to do. Your father hates me and has forbidden our relationship. I suppose he wants someone more educated for his daughter. It's not like my family is poor; I think we've done very well in business. I was surprised that my parents and I were even invited to this party. Maybe it was something your father wanted to flaunt in my face – his beautiful, educated daughter, ready to manage his bank, someone who will never be a part of my life. What are we supposed to do with our love, Mary? Should we ignore it and pretend we love someone else?"

Her eyes swam with sorrow. "Well, I haven't fallen in love with anyone else." She raised her hands in frustration and let them drop in her lap. "This is pointless! It's not accomplishing anything. My father has forbidden our relationship, so what are we to do?"

"We could elope." He looked at her with hope.

"I couldn't do that to my parents. It would break their hearts. I know my father is a demanding person but he does adore me. I just feel so trapped right now. I'm hoping that in a few years he'll give me more space. I need to prove to him that I'm a capable adult, that I can make wise choices. I don't expect you to wait for me." She averted her eyes. "If you're falling in love with Rosy then you need to do what you need to do. Right now I can't go against my father's wishes. I'm sorry, Henry."

He looked away. "I don't understand why you're doing this. You need to live your life and stop living it for your father. I wish I could make you change your mind." He sighed heavily. "I have a feeling that I'd be wasting my time. If that's the decision you've made then there's nothing else I can say. I can't promise I'll wait for you. A few years is a long time."

Falling silent, he waited for her response but she didn't reply.

Henry stood. "I'm going back to the party. Are you coming?" he asked as he started toward the door.

"I'll be there soon." She gave him a tortured look. "I wish with all my heart that things were different. I never wanted to hurt you. To be truthful, I don't know how I'll go through life without you. If I could change the situation without hurting my parents, I would."

"I know." Sorrow emanated from his eyes as he looked at her. "Somehow we'll survive." With that, Henry left the room.

Mary put a hand over her mouth and slumped back into the love seat, fighting her emotions so that she wouldn't cry. They could hear someone coming down the hall and Mary straightened up as a servant stepped into the room.

"Mary, your father is asking for you. He's been searching for you and wants to make an announcement in front of all the guests."

"All right, Clayton, tell him I'll be right there." Clayton nodded and left the room.

With great effort, Mary slowly got up, straightened her gown, stood for a while to gather her thoughts, released a ragged breath then left the room.

Tessa and Richelle looked at each other.

Richelle spoke first. "I can't believe that she's so gutless! Why doesn't she just stand up to her father and tell him where to stick it! That's why I left home when I did. I couldn't handle my parents ruling my life. She's so wimpy!"

"Well, I don't understand her decisions and emotions either but she is living in a different time period and things were done differently back then. Maybe she doesn't have any choice. What would she do on her own? She's under tremendous pressure from her father. It seems so unfair. My parents have never pressured me like that. They've always supported me and my dreams and they've never tried to control my life."

"She still seems like a wimp to me! She has no backbone at all!"

Tessa said, "I wonder what kind of announcement her father's going to make."

"I suppose we should go see what'll happen."

"Maybe Mary will snap out of it and give her dad a piece of her mind."

Richelle started toward the door. "I would love to see that. Telling her dad off in front of all those rich guests of his would be a hoot! That's what I'd do. I'd show him that he couldn't rule my life!"

They entered the foyer and carefully inched their way around the guests. They positioned themselves close to the wall and out of the way. Tessa scanned the room for Luke but he was nowhere to be seen and she wondered where he'd gone off to.

All eyes were turned toward the band, where Mr. Hardington stood with Mary, facing their guests. He cleared his throat and began.

"Thank you all for coming. This is a night of great celebration. My Mary," he turned to acknowledge her presence beside him, "has shown her capability in managing money and has excelled in all areas of study. She has made her mother and me very proud. She was rewarded with high honors in all her subjects, something that is vital for someone who will be entrusted with people's money. Mary is honest and hard working, has shown her talents over and over in the last few years and I'm thrilled that I am going to start training her in business and banking affairs. I know that a woman in a man's world is an uncommon happening. I also recognize, however, when a woman has the ability to make it in the workforce."

He turned to smile at his daughter. Mary looked distressed by the speech, her face a chalky white and her hands fidgeting horribly within the folds in her skirt.

Mr. Hardington continued. "Mary has always been a bright girl and a studious learner and I want her to start work with me as soon as possible. She has had a very busy schedule the past two and a half years and I'm sure she would like to rest but I feel that getting right to work will be the best medicine for her. Immediate practice will only cement what she has gleaned so far and will keep her learning intact. If she agrees, I would like her to begin work with me on Monday. That said, her mother and I would like to present her with a gift." He turned to look at his wife who walked toward the two of them with a wrapped box in her hands.

"I would also like to say a few words, if I may." Mrs. Hardington turned to face her husband, who nodded his agreement. Standing beside him, she turned to face the guests. "Our Mary is a very special girl. She's been the sunshine of our home, our only child. We always knew that she was special. Even though banking and money management were not her first choice, she has done remarkably well. I believe she will excel in whatever direction she goes."

Mrs. Hardington turned to face Mary before she continued. "We love you, Mary, and this gift is a little something from us to congratulate you for your accomplishment." She held up the wrapped box and everyone clapped and cheered.

Mrs. Hardington held the box in her hands. Mary lifted the lid off and peeked inside. She reached in and pulled out an intricately-crafted wooden desk set which held a gold pen in its holder and her name engraved on the front. It read, "Vice General Manager," and then her name, "Mary Hardington." Next she pulled out a beautiful frame, displaying her diploma.

Mrs. Hardington said, "It's for your office wall, dear."

Mary stood speechless, appearing flustered and anxious.

Turning to her parents, she finally said, "Father, Mother, thank you for the beautiful gifts. They will be put to good use. And thank you for all your kind words. I hope I won't disappoint you. I will always try my best to make our bank competitive and appealing. Father, I also look forward to the pleasure of working with you."

Turning to the assembled guests, she said, "Thank you all for coming to congratulate me. Your presence means a great deal to me. I appreciate your kindness and well wishes. Thank you." As she finished, she backed up a few steps, exhaustion in her eyes, as though it had taken everything for her to stand there and say those few words. Her face appeared more ashen than ever.

Her father said, "The night is still young and there's plenty of food left. The dance floor is still open. Everyone enjoy!" Mr. Hardington turned toward Mary and whispered something to her. She nodded and the two of them walked onto the dance floor. The band started up, playing "The Way You Look Tonight" by Fred Astaire and he led her in a waltz to cheers and clapping.

Tessa and Richelle watched father and daughter dance around the room. After the dance was done, Mary's father handed her off to a handsome young man who had been watching them intently. The hand-off was done close enough that Tessa and Richelle could hear their conversation.

The young gentleman held out his hand respectfully. "Dear Mary. Would you care to dance with me?"

"Hi, Richard. How have you been?" Her stance looked stiff and she didn't appear overly thrilled to take his hand.

"I've been well. I'm keeping busy with work and finishing up my last courses at the university. It's been very busy for me. I guess that's something that you can relate to. How exciting for you to be able to work with your father and as Vice General Manager at that. It's very impressive! I'm sure you're excited."

"Well, not as excited as I should be, I suppose. It's been like a whirlwind the last few months. I feel I haven't had a chance to catch my breath." She looked distracted and struggled to keep eye contact.

Henry watched the two from across the room. Their eyes met and locked for a moment. Mary tore her eyes away.

"We'll have to make more effort to get together now that you're done your studies. I'll be done in a month and then I'll be able to focus on work and developing more of a social life." He smiled with anticipation, his eyes riveted on her.

Mary didn't reply to his statement but held out a hand and said, "Should we dance?" They swirled away to the music and the two girls couldn't hear any more of their conversation.

"I don't think Mary is too impressed with Mr. Educated. I think her father is more intrigued with him than she is," Richelle said. "Her father's trying to dictate her love life too? This is so pathetic!"

"It's frustrating to watch. I do wonder, though. This Richard guy is handsome and seems to have a lot going for him. I wonder why Mary doesn't like him."

"Maybe he's too full of himself. Some people that have it all seem to know it and flaunt it. It tends to be repulsive."

Richard was tall, handsome, with dark, short-cropped hair and carried himself with a lot of confidence. The dark suit and the dark tie he wore over a crisp white shirt only accentuated his good looks. With Mary's deep maroon gown swirling around him and her beautiful features, they made a stunning couple. Mr. Hardington must have thought so too because he watched them with keen interest from his position beside the band.

Tessa had a hard time taking her eyes off the pair gliding around the room. The handsome couple seemed well matched in height and looks. Many eyes in the room were glued to the dancing duo, Henry's especially.

Her thoughts turned to Luke again. "I wonder where Luke has snuck off to? I wonder if he heard Mr. Hardington's speech?"

"I was wondering about him too," admitted Richelle.

They both searched the room but there was no sign of him in the foyer.

Richelle grabbed Tessa's arm tightly and pointed to a young woman standing beside one of the tables holding a floral arrangement. "Who is that? I know her from somewhere."

Tessa studied the woman and shook her head.

"Doesn't she look familiar to you, Tessa?"

"We're in the year 1946. She probably isn't even living anymore. No, I don't recognize her at all."

"I know this might sound crazy but I know her. I absolutely know I've seen her somewhere."

"That's ridiculous, Richelle. It's not possible!"

"I know it sounds strange. And I don't know how it's possible to see someone that I recognize. It's sending chills up my spine!" Richelle held tightly to Tessa's arm.

Her grasp was beginning to pinch. Tessa peeled Richelle's hand off to relieve the pressure.

Richelle glanced at her apologetically. "Sorry about that."

They both studied the young woman Richelle had pointed out. She was close to their age and monitored Mary and Richard as they twirled around the foyer. There was no sign of pleasure on her face over the situation. It must have been her mother beside her because she gave this young woman a poke with her elbow and motioned for her to go interrupt the dancing couple. The young woman followed her mother's advice and started onto the dance floor. Tapping Mary on her shoulder, the young woman said, "I'd like a turn, if you don't mind."

"Now, Nancy, that was a bit rude, don't you think?" Richard gave the girl a look of exasperation.

"It's all right, Richard. I'm feeling a bit tired. Why don't the two of you go ahead?" Mary looked relieved as she turned and walked away.

Richard's eyes followed Mary while she exited the dance floor and he reluctantly turned back to dance with Nancy.

With a look of exhaustion, Mary leaned against the wall and watched the dancing couples. Henry and Rosy waltzed by and when Mary noticed them, she turned and walked back into the sitting room.

Tessa saw movement on the stairway and peered up to see Luke descending. She nudged Richelle and pointed in his direction. "I wonder what he's been up to."

"He sure is making himself at home, isn't he?"

After maneuvering his way through the crowd, he stopped beside them and said, "Well, I did some exploring. It's quite an impressive house, I have to say!"

"What are you doing sneaking around? Aren't you embarrassed at snooping around in someone else's home?"

"Barbie Doll, don't sweat it. They're not really here anyway so it won't make any difference. I'm curious how the rich and famous live. The bedrooms are amazing. The furniture is solid wood which looks like it's been imported from somewhere. The bedding was amazing too but I'm not into describing that. You'll have to go look for yourselves."

"How many rooms are there upstairs?" Tessa asked.

"I didn't count, but there are a lot. There are also some sitting rooms. The largest one has a fireplace. There's even a big balcony off the sitting room at the back of the house. It really is an impressive home!"

"I wonder if all the servants live here too. I wonder where they sleep." Richelle looked at Luke for an answer.

"There's a door on the left side hallway on the first level which leads down to the basement. I didn't go down but from what I could see it was completely furnished and decorated. That's probably where the servants' bedrooms are. I did notice something unusual upstairs though."

"What?"

"One of the doors was closed and strange noises were coming from the room. I didn't have the nerve to check it out."

"Wow! What in the world?" Richelle looked spooked.

Luke said, "Maybe next time I'll have the guts to investigate."

The lines creasing Richelle's forehead indicated her reticence.

Tessa said, "Leave me out of that one. I don't care to know what's in that room." Even to think of venturing back here again was stressful enough to last her a good while.

Richelle pointed toward the door where the butler was retrieving winter coats from a side room and handing them to some guests. "Some people are leaving."

"It must be getting late. I feel like we've been here for hours." Tessa's long shift at the restaurant and the tense evening had taken its toll and she could feel exhaustion overtaking her.

Wandering around, the three friends watched and waited as the house slowly emptied. It became easier to avoid people. The guests gradually said their thanks and congratulations and left. The three made their way into the sitting room and saw, to their relief, that the couches were empty. They sat down carefully, making sure that the couches actually existed and would hold them up. It was a relief finally to take a load off their feet. On the far side of the room, the logs still burned in the fireplace and made it feel warm. They discussed the evening, all they had seen and heard.

Luke said, "You should have seen Rosy after you left to follow Mary. She stuck by Henry and followed him around like a puppy dog. It was pathetic. For some reason he didn't seem that taken with her. He sings her a love song, kisses her and then acts like he doesn't even like her. After his song he hardly paid her any attention, basically ignored her. When Mary left, his eyes followed her and it didn't take long till he excused himself and left the room too. I guess he needed a break from his admirer."

Tessa and Richelle filled him in on what had happened in the back sunroom.

"Well, that explains a lot," said Luke.

"What do you mean?" Richelle's curiosity came quickly and predictably.

"I guess you could say I did more snooping than I had originally intended." He looked somewhat embarrassed. "It must have been Mary's room because there was a diary lying on her nightstand."

"You didn't?" Richelle looked shocked. "Don't you know how sacred a girl's diary is? That is unforgivable!"

"Well, I tried to pick it up but my hand went right through it. So I started searching the room. I rummaged through Mary's closet with no success. It took a while but I finally figured out a way to manipulate the diary without it actually being in the present time. I surmised that if I could find an item that was present in both time worlds, I could take that item and use it to turn the pages."

"Wow! Impressive."

"The question is: did it work?" asked Richelle.

Luke's grin was answer enough. "It did. At first I fished around the closet for a clothes hanger but there was nothing tangible for me to hang on to. It took me a while to figure out what to do next. That's when it hit me. When I came to check out this house with Darren years ago I remember seeing some junk lying around on the floor close to the closet. I got on my hands and knees and felt around."

"And…" asked Richelle when Luke stopped talking.

"And…I found what I thought I'd find. I hit the jackpot. With a clothes hanger in hand I was ready to do some snooping."

"Do you mean to tell me that you actually read it? You read a girl's diary without her permission?" Richelle looked incredulous.

"Look, she's probably an old lady by now or maybe even dead so what does it matter?"

"That's no excuse, Luke, and you know it. You had better never try that with me."

"Just tell me where you leave yours and I'll be sure never to touch it."

"Oh yeah, like I'd tell you where I leave my diary! You sure won't have the chance." Richelle sneered. "So what did you find out?"

"I thought I just committed a big no-no and now you want to know what I read? Aren't you contradicting yourself a bit?" He grinned crookedly, his head cocked sideways.

"Well, it's too late now. You've already read it, so spill the beans."

"I thought diaries were personal and confidential. It would be wrong of me to tell you."

Richelle looked completely flustered. "Stop it, Luke, and just tell us."

He turned toward Tessa. "Do you think it would be right for me to tell her?"

"Would you please stop goofing around and tell us." She'd had enough of his stalling and felt just as curious as Richelle.

"You two girls amaze me! You're totally as willing to pounce on Mary's diary as I was. I never thought I'd see the day that girls would betray…"

"Luke!" Richelle and Tessa yelled together then looked at each other, shaking their heads in exasperation.

"Okay, okay, I'll tell you." He chuckled and then began, "I looked back over the past few months. Mary wrote about Richard and how she feels about him. It's seems that her father has been trying to get those two together for some time. She wrote that Richard seems too taken with himself ever to care for anyone else or to be good husband material."

"She doesn't sound that impressed with him."

"Yeah, she wrote that her heart belongs to someone else and she admits in the diary that she'll never fall in love with anyone else. Her father disdains the man she loves, who happens to be Henry, the guy at the piano. He looks at Henry as a common man and not good enough for his daughter."

"That's awful!" stated Richelle.

"Her dad's not very nice, that's for sure. Mary wrote that she knows Henry's good enough for her but that she doesn't feel deserving of his love. Henry apparently served in the war and was awarded a medal of some sort. The way she wrote about it, it's clear she's pretty proud of him but she feels inadequate in many ways and believes that she will never make anyone a good wife. It sounds to me like she has a major self-image problem."

Richelle nodded.

Tessa felt sudden sympathy for the girl and anger at her father's manipulating ways. "Well, I don't blame her, knowing that she has a father who continually tries to rule her life. It's so oppressive. How could she ever develop any kind of self-confidence when she's never allowed to decide anything for herself?"

"Well I'd say it's her own fault. Why doesn't she stick up for herself and tell her father off?" Richelle crossed her arms and looked disgusted.

Tessa considered this for a moment and then said, "I don't know; it's hard to understand it all. Mary obviously feels very pressured."

Richelle retorted, "I'm sorry, but I just can't relate to Mary's lack of backbone!"

"Are you two done? Did you want to hear the rest of what I found out?"

"Yes, go on. What other ridiculous things did she write down?"

"Well, Richelle, since you're so concerned for her, I'll tell you."

"Thanks."

"She wrote about her grandmother, Eunice."

"Oh, don't you love these names, Tessa? They are so ancient."

"Would you be quiet and let me talk?"

"Like what, you're the only one that has something to say?" asked Richelle.

Tessa rolled her eyes. They were starting back at their bickering again and she was not in the mood for it.

"I'm the only one with something worthwhile to say." Luke said with a smirk.

"I think I'll just go up there, find that diary and read it for myself if you want to be so difficult."

"Be my guest!"

"Okay, you two, stop this. Luke, what did the diary say about Mary's grandmother?" Tessa had completely enough of the childish squabbling and was tired of waiting for it to blow over.

Luke was about to get into the details when they heard an ear-splitting scream that vibrated through the house and ricocheted right through their skin. It had an echo effect that bounced back and forth then slowly faded.

Tessa shuddered at the sound.

Luke jumped up from his seat and ran into the foyer. Tessa and Richelle followed him. They could hear the sound of pounding feet and people yelling, trying to sort out where the screaming was coming from. All the guests were gone; the foyer was empty. Tessa noticed the tables of food had been cleared and everything was cleaned up. The servants came running from the kitchen into the entrance area to see what was going on and the room soon filled with pandemonium.

The screaming, which seemed to have come from the second floor, began again. This time it continued uninterrupted, making the hair on their necks stand on end. There was shouting, agitated voices and scurrying of feet but it was hard to make sense of any of it.

"Well, you two lovely ladies, should we go and check it out?" Luke's eyes betrayed anxiety.

One glance at him and Tessa knew he wasn't as confident as his words sounded. She wasn't sure she wanted to know what was happening either. The evening had suddenly turned into chaos. Leaving right now seemed the sensible thing to do.

CHAPTER 5

"I want to leave," Tessa managed to squeak out.

Richelle said, "I'm not leaving at the most suspenseful part! We'll never know what happens if we take off now. I'm going to find out what's going on." She started toward the stairs but looked back to see if the other two would follow.

Luke took hold of Tessa's arm and led her to the flight of steps. Reluctantly she allowed him to drag her along. Richelle ascended ahead of them but her movements were edgy. Tessa found her feet tripping on the edge of the first rise; they weren't cooperating at all.

Frantic voices were heard from the top floor along with the spine-chilling, ear-splitting screams. An indiscernible, faint banging noise mixed with the cacophony of sound and Tessa also detected some muffled, intermittent shrieks.

They had nearly reached the second floor when Mr. Hardington came running out to the top balcony. All three of them froze on the stairway. He shouted for one of the servants to come. Within seconds they heard footsteps running down in the foyer and a servant appeared at the bottom of the stairway.

Mr. Hardington said, "Call the doctor at once and insist he come to the house!"

The servant hurried off to fulfill the order and Mr. Hardington turned and disappeared down a hall.

The three friends slowly ascended to the second floor landing and headed in the direction Mr. Hardington had gone. Tessa realized to her relief that the banging had stopped. It was one less mystery bombarding her senses.

Down the hall Tessa noticed a closed door on the left.

Luke pointed to it as they walked past. "This is the room that I told you girls about, the door that's closed where I heard strange noises coming from." Someone started knocking from the inside

73

and all three of them jumped in unison.

"That's where all the banging was coming from?" Richelle asked.

"I guess so," Luke said with a shrug.

"I wonder who's in there?" Tessa's voice cracked.

"Do you think that whoever's in there will come jumping out at us?" asked Richelle nervously.

Tessa could feel the tension building around her. Fear of the unknown was unbearable.

Luke said, "I have no idea. I guess that's the chance we're taking."

"Maybe it's locked," said Richelle.

"Hopefully it is," Tessa agreed.

"Here's for hoping," Luke said. "Let's go find out who's screaming." He led the way down the hall.

The shrieking led them to their destination. Wails of distress no longer echoed around them, the howls came at them in full force. It was like standing before a bull horn.

They stood before the open door and Luke turned to the two girls and said with some volume, "This is Mary's room."

They cautiously stepped in, not knowing what to expect. Tessa cringed at what she was seeing and hearing.

"This is where I saw the diary on the dresser," Luke interjected with raised voice.

Mary sat cross-legged on her bed holding a piece of clothing with a vicious grip, her mouth opened in a continual scream, her eyes shut and her head shaking back and forth wildly. The noise in the room was enough to rouse the dead.

Mrs. Hardington stood beside Mary's bed, a frantic look on her face. Mary's father stood by the window, his arms crossed and his face in a state of shock as he gazed dumbstruck at his daughter. When Mrs. Hardington spoke, her voice came out softly and calmly, belying her frazzled exterior.

"Mary, please tell me what's wrong. Please, just calm down and tell me. I'll do whatever I can to help you. You need to stop this carrying on, dear. Please calm down and talk to me." Tears flowed down her cheeks. "Please, please, Mary, stop screaming and tell me what's wrong." She attempted taking Mary's face in her hands but with Mary's violent shaking, it dislodged Mrs.

Hardington's grip.

Mary's father stepped forward then to help, his former sheen of control and confidence gone.

Tessa wondered if he had tried to calm Mary earlier with no success.

Mr. Hardington said angrily, "Mary, I told you to stop this right now! This is outrageous! Stop it, do you hear me?" He grabbed her by the shoulders and shook her hard. Oblivious to her father, she continued screaming and shaking. It only seemed to antagonize him further. With his brow deeply furrowed, he lifted his arm, brought it down and, with open hand, slapped her hard across the face. Letting out a wounded yelp, Mary fell back against her bed then slowly sat back up again, holding one hand to her face. She never let go of the piece of clothing as her head resumed shaking and her screams became more intense.

Mrs. Hardington moved forward immediately, gently pushed her husband out of the way and said, "Dear, please don't do that to Mary again." She stroked her daughter's back, trying to comfort her as best she could.

"I'm trying to snap her out of this!" Mr. Hardington declared in defense. "I don't know what else to do." He paced, one hand rubbing his forehead in consternation. "I'm going down to see if the doctor's here yet. Stay with Mary and try to calm her down." With that he turned and walked out of the room.

The three friends looked at each other. Tessa's eyes had been glued on Mary since she walked into the room but now she allowed her gaze to survey the room.

It was beautiful. No expense had been spared by the Hardingtons on their only daughter. Mary sat on a large canopy bed with elegant posts, each approximately six inches thick, tapering to about three inches on top. Over the top was draped a beautiful yellow Battenberg lace topper, with a tasteful ruffle cascading from the sides. The bedspread was of the same yellow fabric, quilted in a butterfly pattern with Battenberg lace on the edges where the bedspread hung down. A large bay window overlooked the side of the house with a floral valance and side panels that draped down to touch the floor. The window seat tucked inside the bay was piled with pillows in the same yellow, white, light green and lilac shades as the cushions arranged on the bed.

There were numerous pieces of fine furniture in the room but one thing in particular caught Tessa's attention. Mary's room had a large closet in the corner but beside the closet against the wall was a makeshift clothesline. Beautifully tailored outfits hung on it neatly, facing the room. They were in a variety of colors and each one had a big red bow on it.

They're gifts from her parents! New outfits for her new career.

There was one outfit missing from the neat display. The empty hanger still hung in place with the discarded bow on the floor. Tessa glanced back at Mary.

That's what she's holding onto so tightly.

"Guys, look at those outfits hanging by the wall." Tessa pointed to them.

Richelle said, "Huh! New clothes for a new job."

"She doesn't seem that thrilled with the new digs," said Luke.

Richelle giggled.

Tessa stared at her and said, "This isn't funny! How can you joke about something like this?"

Richelle shrugged her shoulders. "I find it completely bizarre. This is too way out for me. Mary's got major psychological problems. They need to admit her to a nut house! And I am so done with listening to this screaming. I am absolutely ready to go."

"Do you realize how insensitive you sound?" asked Tessa.

"So what? There was a girl who lived here in 1946 who had some mental problems. I don't really care to know any more. I've been working all day at the beauty shop and my feet are killing me. Her screams are deafening! I just want to go home and relax for a while. I can't handle any more of this. You two can do whatever you want. I'm out of here!" With that she left the room.

Tessa couldn't bear the screaming either but she did feel slight compassion for Mary. With what she'd found out that day, her heart had softened toward the young woman.

Luke said, "Well I guess that's that. I can't blame Richelle, you know. This high-pitched drama is getting on my nerves too. I have to agree with her this once. I'm ready to leave."

It was funny. Tessa knew she couldn't handle much more of the ear-splitting noise either. It was getting late, plus she'd been on her feet all day too. Tomorrow would be another busy day at the restaurant. Saturdays were always demanding. But for some reason she couldn't tear herself away, at least not yet. There was a strong pull urging her to stay. It was unexplainable but she knew she had to stay.

"Why don't you go ahead? Give Richelle a ride. I'll take the bus home in a while. I just have to find out what happens."

"Okay, beautiful, take care of yourself." He gave her a peck on the cheek and walked out of the room.

Mr. Hardington entered just after Luke exited. Tessa wondered if Luke nearly collided with the man.

It wouldn't have been a collision. Luke would have passed right through him. Maybe I should follow Luke and get out of here.

Mr. Hardington's voice stopped her.

"Doctor Maxwell is on the way. I called to double check on him and his wife said he left a few minutes ago and should be here shortly. Has Mary said anything intelligible yet?"

"No, dear, she won't stop this screaming and shaking. It's so unnerving! What's happening to our dear Mary, William? I just don't understand." She placed both hands on her cheeks and gave her daughter a troubled look.

A twinge of guilt swept over William's face. "Mary tried to tell me the night before the party that she didn't want that many people around. I didn't listen to her."

Mrs. Hardington sighed sadly. "She also told me last night that she felt overwhelmed with her life. There's been too much pressure on her. She admitted that she was afraid something was going to snap inside. I wonder if this is what she meant."

William looked incredulous. "She actually said that to you? She felt like she was about to snap? Elizabeth, why didn't you let me know?" He looked unnerved over the information.

Elizabeth choked back more tears. "I should have taken her more seriously. In hindsight I realize I should have told you."

"I'm not sure what we could have done to help her." He rubbed his chin. "I always thought Mary was stronger, able to handle responsibility."

Mrs. Hardington sat down on the edge of Mary's bed and rubbed her daughter's back. "Do you suppose she's taking the same path as your mother?"

"No, Elizabeth!" His sudden explosive outburst shook the

room. "We are not going to entertain such thoughts! Mary's a strong, intelligent girl. She's nothing like my mother. Maybe she just needs more time to recuperate than I had initially thought. Perhaps we pushed her too hard."

"But your mother had a hard time dealing with life too."

"That's enough, Elizabeth! I will not discuss my mother now." With that said, the doorbell rang and William left the room.

Tessa could hear a faint commotion downstairs. The front door opened and closed and she could hear William call the doctor upstairs. One set of feet hurried up the steps followed by William's desperate voice explaining things as they headed down the hall. The two were in deep conversation over Mary's condition as they walked into the room.

"So when did all this start?" asked Dr. Maxwell.

"She started screaming around 11:30 this evening. Elizabeth and I had just retired to our bedroom after the party we threw for Mary. It was then that we heard terrible sounds coming from her room. We can't fathom what could be causing her to act this way."

"This is most unusual." The doctor went over to the bed to observe her.

Her volume had lessened somewhat but she still shook her head frantically and screeched intermittently. Her eyes looked glazed and not focused on anything in particular.

"I don't know if I've ever seen something quite like this before. I've seen cases similar to this but not this bad."

Elizabeth asked, "What are you saying, doctor? Is there anything you can do for her?"

"I'll need to check her vital signs but it might be difficult with her flailing around like this. Could you two help hold her down while I check her?"

Mary's parents tried but Mary became even more hysterical and her shaking worsened. William exited the room and called for the servants to come and help. Two men appeared shortly, still wearing their uniforms.

After instructing the two men what to do, they positioned themselves around Mary but looked unwilling to manhandle her. At first they half-heartedly grasped her arms but as her flailing grew stronger, they took a firmer hold and forced her down onto the bed. The doctor quickly got into position. He checked her hcartbeat, pulse and also the pupils of her eyes. Straightening up and still holding his stethoscope in his hands, he looked as confused as before.

William asked, "Well, what's the diagnosis? What's wrong with her?"

Doctor Maxwell turned toward him and said, "I can't tell that there's anything out of the ordinary with her physical condition. Everything seems fine. I can sedate her for the night but I'm not sure anything else can be done for her right now. I brought some sedatives along and I can give that to her if you'd like. If she's still acting up tomorrow and there's no change, then I'd suggest bringing her to the hospital."

"But why is she doing this?" asked Elizabeth.

"Just from observing her, I would deduct that she is completely drained emotionally. I would surmise it's due to excessive stress. Has she experienced too much undue pressure lately?" He gazed quizzically at Mrs. Hardington.

Elizabeth looked reluctant to admit it. "Yes."

Doctor Maxwell turned to William. "And, would you agree?"

He shrugged his shoulders in irritation. "I don't know. How would you rate undue pressure? What is bearable for one could be too much for another. Isn't this true?"

"Yes. Everyone has a different tolerance level for the encumbrances of life."

William looked unwilling to admit anything.

Doctor Maxwell continued, "Mary has deep, dark areas beneath her eyes, suggesting that she's carried a tremendous burden and that she hasn't had enough sleep. Has she had a difficult time in any way the last while?"

Mr. and Mrs. Hardington looked at each other. Elizabeth said, "Yes, she's struggled lately. She finished a four-year university course in two and a half years and I do believe it took a real toll on her. She admitted feeling exhausted."

William appeared defensive. "I don't believe it was too much for her. She never complained at all till the other night."

Elizabeth said, "I feel so bad about this. I should have listened to her." She burst into tears and reached for Mary's hand.

Mary had settled a fair bit. James and Tom had released their hold as soon as the doctor was done his routine check on her and they now stood back waiting for further instructions. Mary remained on her back but still flailed back and forth somewhat. The screams had turned more into hoarse screeches, which had lessened in volume considerably.

"Men you'll need to hold her again while I give her the sedative so don't go anywhere." Doctor Maxwell reached for his bag and extracted some medication and a needle. As he prepared the injection, the men returned back into position.

Elizabeth moved from the bed and left the room. Tessa supposed the needle situation was too much for her to handle.

It took a few minutes for the medication to take effect. Soon Mary grew limp and her shaking subsided. The intermittent screeches turned into whimpers as her body relaxed. Elizabeth returned and, after covering Mary with a blanket, sat on her daughter's bed, took her hand in hers and stroked her damp hair back from her face. Rivulets of sweat streaked across Mary's forehead and seeped down to her ears and hair. Elizabeth cried softly as she watched her daughter settle and calm.

James and Tom left the room to return to their tasks and William went with the doctor. Tessa followed them, staying close to hear their conversation.

"Tell me the truth, Doctor. I want to hear the complete truth. What do you think we're dealing with here and how can it be treated? I want Mary back one hundred percent as soon as possible."

"I don't know what assurances I can give you. This kind of thing is hard to diagnose. If what I believe is true, I highly suspect it's of an emotional nature. It deals with the psychological part of a person. It's not that easy to treat. It can take a great deal of time, depending on the severity of the emotional stress."

"What are you saying? Can't you give me any time frame as to when she'll be better?"

"I'm sorry, Mr. Hardington, there's nothing else I can tell you. If Mary's still uncontrollable tomorrow, bring her into the hospital and we'll give her something. If this continues for some time you might consider putting her into an institution that is accustomed to dealing with this type of issue."

"What do you mean 'this type of issue'? Mary's not crazy and we would never put her into an institution! She's a strong and very bright girl!"

"I'm not saying that Mary's crazy but she is dealing with something serious right now that she's not able to cope with on her own. There are places that can help people who are dealing with emotional instability which can get them back on track."

William looked extremely agitated. "I appreciate your expertise but I believe you're very wrong about her. She's not going in that direction. I'll see to that."

"I truly hope I'm wrong," said the doctor with complete sincerity.

When they arrived at the foot of the stairs, a servant appeared, carrying the doctor's coat and hat.

William said, "My servant will see you out. Thanks for coming out at this hour." He then turned and, without another word, walked briskly to his office.

Tessa stood at the bottom of the steps and watched Doctor Maxwell leave. She wasn't sure what to do. William's voice drifted from the office. She headed that way, where the door stood slightly ajar. Inside she could see the phone to his ear.

"Yes, yes I think I would appreciate that and my wife would too. All right then, we'll see you soon. Bye!" He set the phone down and dropped his face into his hands. He sat that way for some time. Minutes passed before he lowered his hands, stared at his desk and shook his head. "How could she do this to us? I just don't understand. After all my plans and all her hard work. Why would she do this? Why, why, why?"

Tessa wasn't sure what to do next. Should she leave? One thing she did know and that was she needed to get off her feet. Heading to the sitting room, she tentatively sat down on one of the couches. In the fireplace, only soft embers glowed and yet the room still felt toasty warm. She gratefully allowed her body to relax, leaned her head back and closed her eyes.

I wonder who Mr. Hardington called this time of night. I wish I had heard more of the conversation.

A sound to her right brought her to attention. She opened her eyes and noticed the man in the trench coat standing by the bay window and staring at her. Tessa sat upright, surprised that she'd completely forgotten about him for the evening. It spooked her that he intruded without notice.

"How long have you been there? Were you watching me this whole time?"

"I only just arrived."

"Where were you during the party? I never saw you after you invited us in."

"I'm glad you came tonight. It was right for you to be here. You need to come back again. You'll know when the time is right."

"Who are you and why is this happening?" She had so many questions and he seemed expert at avoiding them. He had quite the nerve to keep telling her what to do.

"My name is not important."

"Why won't you tell me your name? What's the big secret?"

"I'm not permitted to tell you my name." The man walked around the couch and sat on the next couch over from Tessa.

"Why?"

He smiled calmly before speaking. "I'm an angel sent by God to deliver a message."

Tessa felt dumbfounded. "Why would God send an angel to me?"

"I don't know. He knows something neither one of us does. I'm instructed what to show you. I'll be obedient and reveal to you what He tells me. The rest will be up to you. The success of the message will depend on your response."

"I don't know what that means."

"You'll have to ask God. As you seek Him, He'll show you what you need to do. I have to go now." The angel stood. "Just remember – you need to come back. You'll know when the time is right." He then headed for the door.

Tessa sat glued to the couch in shock. As the angel was about to leave the room, Tessa quickly found her tongue.

"Wait! Please wait! How will I know when I need to come back here? What will be the sign?"

The angel didn't stop or respond.

Getting to her feet, she raced to the foyer. It was empty. There was no sign of the trench-coated angel. Even after a careful search, she came up empty.

She sat down on the first step of the stairway, leaned her elbows on her knees and rested her chin on her hands. Sighing heavily, she felt more tired and confused than ever. Why would God send her an angel and what in the world was he trying to tell her? Why would he bother with such an elaborate plan? Why not just say it in a Sunday morning service through the pastor? Wouldn't that be a whole lot easier? Was she really worth all this trouble?

The doorbell rang and Tessa watched as a servant rushed to open the door. An older gentleman stepped inside, wrapped in a heavy winter coat and galoshes. He discarded his coat and boots and handed them to the servant. The office door squeaked open and William appeared in the doorway.

"Welcome," said William. "Come join me in my office."

The older gentleman tucked a book under his arm, reached for his briefcase and walked toward the office. Once inside, William closed the door to within a crack.

Tessa rose from the stairs, walked toward the room and peeked through the sliver of space that was open.

William spoke first. "I'm so glad you were willing to come out at this hour of the night, Pastor Reed. I didn't know what else to do. As I told you on the phone, Mary is not herself. Her behavior has been extremely disturbing this evening. She screams and shakes wildly for no reason. I just don't know what to make of it."

Pastor Reed's voice was low and calm. It was soothing enough to put Tessa to sleep if her curiosity wasn't so mobilized.

"What did the doctor tell you? You did have a doctor assess her, didn't you?"

"Yes, yes. The doctor said it's emotional in nature and that it will take some time for the adverse effects to diminish. Mary's been under a lot of stress and I suppose it's taken a toll on her. I thought perhaps you could give some words of wisdom in this situation."

"I'm very glad you called. I'm always willing to come and make house calls to my parishioners in need." His gravelly voice gave a sense of strength and stability. "Why don't you explain fully what happened here tonight."

"I don't know what got into Mary. My wife and I had this wonderful party for her this evening and she seemed to really enjoy herself. Her new position at the bank is starting on Monday and the opportunity I'm giving her is the dream of a lifetime. I am so excited to be able to start working with my daughter, you know, teach her all I know about banking. I thought she was looking forward to it as much as I. I have to admit, she seemed a little apprehensive but I never, not in a million years, thought she'd respond like this. I don't know what to think, how to sort it all out and I was hoping you could shed some light on the situation."

"Hmm...," said the pastor, thoughtfully. "Well, you have to remember what has taken place in your family in the past."

"The past has nothing to do with what's happening to Mary!"

"You do have to admit that there are similarities."

"My mother is nearly seventy and Mary is a bright, young woman. You should see Mary's university marks. She was honored as top of her class. There's a big difference between the two!"

"All right, let's leave your mother out of this for now. I do agree that Mary is a bright girl."

William sighed heavily, then continued. "So what do you think is happening to her and what advice can you give as far as what we can do to help her?"

"Considering that she's smart and quite capable, I don't see any reason for her condition to remain. Given time she should snap out of this and resume her normal activities. According to you, William, this shouldn't be happening."

"That's correct. This should not be happening. I've done everything in my power to ensure she's a success."

"And yet, here we are. Why do you think that is?"

"That's why you're sitting across from me. I invited you over to give me some answers. We attend church faithfully and give generously. Why would God do this to our Mary?"

"Perhaps it's not really Mary's issue. Maybe it's her only choice."

"I don't understand."

"She's responding the only way her body can respond right now. I don't know what has taken place between you, Elizabeth and Mary but whatever has taken place, Mary is reacting accordingly."

Silence filled the space for a moment. Anger laced William's voice when he spoke. "So you're saying that it's our fault? Elizabeth's and mine?"

"I don't know. Only you know what's gone on here. There's a reason…"

"I have done nothing wrong!" shouted William. "And I don't appreciate you coming in here accusing me of wrongdoing!"

"I am only asking to try to find answers. I'm saying that for some reason Mary is responding quite intensely to the plans you've laid out for her. Why would that be?"

"I don't know." Williams voice sounded strained and on edge.

"You are quite strong in your opinions," commented the pastor gently.

"It takes strength to run a big ship," William said with pride. "Mary needed to learn that. Without strength she never would have made it in the banking industry."

"But if you tried to strong-arm Mary into fulfilling your plans, it might just be backfiring on you. Have you in any way tried to control Mary's future or manipulated her choices?"

"Stop!" William's voice sounded drained and angry. "I invited you here to help and all you do is accuse and demand answers from me? What is this?"

"I'm sorry. I am not trying to bring further agitation. I'm throwing out questions to help you process what could have gone wrong."

"Nothing has gone wrong! Mary is the one with the problem and I need help fixing her." By the look in his eyes, hopelessness was threatening to overtake him.

"I don't know how to fix her, William. I'm only a man. God is the only one who can help now."

"And how will he do it?" His anger and frustration returned.

"We can pray and ask God to help her."

"Like he helped my mother? Is that how he'll do it?"

"There is hope, William. He promises to meet our needs and he loves Mary more than you ever could."

"In my experience, God's love is undependable and sporadic. I've found that the only thing I can put my trust in is getting things done on my own."

"So your faith is firmly planted in yourself?"

Tessa heard the scrape of a chair on the hardwood.

William said, "I think you should leave. In hindsight, this wasn't the best idea. I'm tired and I've heard enough."

Through the crack Tessa could see William's red and angry face.

Pastor Reed stood as well and answered, "You do believe we have an enemy and that he wages war against us, don't you?"

"I don't know about all that." William let out a short, cynical laugh.

"I'm trying to encourage you, William. God is an ever present help in trouble. You're in a heap of trouble and if you'll put your trust in God, he will not fail you."

"You think Mary's condition is because of how I've treated my mother. Is that correct? This is all my fault. I've brought this on myself. That's what you're trying to tell me?"

"Your relationship with your mother is between you and God. I can't respond to that. I know that she lives with you and that you provide a roof over her head and food to eat. That says something."

"That's right. I do take care of her. That's more than can be said for others and their parents."

"That's true. But there are rumors out there. Only you know how you're treating her. Remember, you won't stand before me and give account of your ways. Your judge is Almighty God. He knows all things."

William's face was beet red. He headed for his office door, opened it wide and waved for Pastor Reed to exit. He tugged at his shirt collar and loosened the top button.

They entered the foyer, William yelling for the servant to bring the pastor's coat and boots. The servant came scurrying from down the hall, retrieved the things and handed them to Pastor Reed.

William said, "We have attended your church for twenty some years, supported your building projects and when we need some help, this is what you give us? You come in here with accusations and questions. Have I ever asked for your help before? No, I haven't! This will be the last time. I want you to leave my house now!"

"I'm sorry you took my words as rebuke. I wanted to help you, William."

"You're not much of a man of God if this is how you treat those whom you are supposed to be a shepherd over." William took a step forward in warning.

The reverend's strong voice took on a subdued tone. "I'm

sorry you feel that way. I will be praying for you and your family."

"We don't need your prayers."

With that William opened the door and the pastor stepped outside. Rev. Reed looked relieved for the fresh air. William slammed the door and turned around. His face still blazed bright red and his chest heaved in anger.

"What was all that about, dear?" Elizabeth stood at the top of the steps wringing her hands, her eyes registering concern.

"That's the last time we ever step foot in a church again! I'm done with religion! It's a complete waste of our money. It's never done us any good and I don't ever want to see that man again." William stomped off to his office and slammed the door.

Elizabeth stood still for a minute looking utterly weary and sad. The events of the evening seemed to have aged her a few years. Tessa watched as the woman slowly turned and walked off.

Shock kept her feet planted in the foyer for a while. There was so much that she had witnessed here tonight. She didn't know what to make of it. Her emotions were raw and traumatized by it all. Tears threatened under the strain of her frayed emotions

That's it! I'm calling it a night!

Tessa walked out of the house, the chill of the winter night wrapping around her. She hardly noticed, her mind full and overloaded. As she passed the big oak tree she switched back into the present. Darkness had fallen.

She walked down to the bus stop and boarded the next available one heading to her neighborhood. The bus was virtually empty. It was a welcome treat. Taking a seat in the centre of the bus, she stared out at the shadowed buildings speeding by, her mind a whir of thoughts.

My summer is starting out terribly bizarre! What was that angel talking about anyway? It seems so unreal! I don't get all this. If only I could make it all go away! I want my normal life back! And how am I ever going to function at work tomorrow?

Releasing an agonized sigh, more thoughts bombarded her.

I suppose normal isn't possible now. If going back in time was just some fluke thing, I could run away. But since I know it was an angel in the trench coat, sent by God, how can I abandon this? I'd be running from God, wouldn't I? Either I ignore what I've seen

and heard and live with the consequences or I try to embrace what God is trying to show me.

The decision facing her seemed monumental and terrifying. Both options had merit, but also consequences that she wasn't sure she was willing to live with.

As the bus came to a stop in her neighborhood, her mind was a mass of tumbleweed blown by a strong wind. She wasn't sure she'd ever sort this out.

CHAPTER 6

The next day proved more difficult than Tessa had anticipated. She felt more exhausted, mentally and physically, than she could remember. That was saying a lot, considering her recent wrapping up of assignments and cramming for exams.

Sleep had evaded her until three in the morning and her alarm blared bright and chipper at six-thirty. Her shift at The Eating Place began at eight.

The cool morning air during her walk to work didn't help to slap her awake as she had hoped. Her feet dragged along unwillingly.

When she arrived at the restaurant, she learned that Martha wasn't working. That bit of news was the first positive thing of the day. Tabitha was already there and gave her a cheerful hello. Tessa tied her apron around her middle and made sure she had a pad of paper and pen for the orders.

After a deep, steadying breath, Tessa headed toward the section she was assigned. Patrice had just seated two groups in her section, a family of four and a couple.

Things became more hectic as the day progressed. Saturdays were always busy, especially breakfast. Her lack of sleep and her mind on the Hardingtons caused her to make plenty of mistakes and she kept forgetting what her customers had asked for. There were numerous comments dished her way, complaints and angry words that only helped to discourage her. Low tips were the sign of improvement needed. She had plenty of signs today.

Tessa found herself checking the clock on the back wall above the kitchen frequently as the day dragged on. Her shift ended at three but it seemed like an eternity. The mansion and the happenings back there were uppermost on her mind. She struggled to keep orders straight and her concentration in check.

After her last table paid up and she handed them the receipt, she headed to the staff room quickly. Getting out of this place was her main objective at the moment. She untied her apron, hung it on a hook and grabbed her purse and sweater. As she was slipping into her sweater, Les Jones entered the room. She cringed involuntarily. If Les, the owner, followed her in here, then her performance really was less than commendable. She faced him nervously, concerned with what he'd say.

He stopped by his desk, leaned one hand on it and said, "Is everything all right, Tessa? You seemed quite preoccupied today. I was just wondering what's up?"

"I'm sorry, Les..." Tessa started to explain.

"You don't have to apologize. I just want to know what's going on."

"Something happened last night that upset me a great deal and I had a hard time getting it off my mind. I promise I'll try to keep it from affecting my work from now on. The way I was serving the customers today was not in line with your expectations and I apologize for that."

"Well I'm not considering laying you off or firing you, if that's what you're thinking. I just want to be sure that you're okay. I have stuff on my mind some days too. I get that. It's important to learn to keep personal situations and work separate. We owe it to our customers."

"I'll work on that, sir."

"Sir? My name's Les. Call me Les."

He had told her this numerous times. She kept slipping on that one. He was in his early thirties, had started the restaurant with his father's backing and was doing amazingly well. She had great respect for him and the "sir" kept slipping out.

"Okay, Les. I'll be sure to take it easy this weekend. I'll be fresh and ready to do my best on Monday."

"Actually you can have Monday off. I have enough help but I'll see you on Tuesday at 8:00 a.m." He gave her a reassuring smile.

"Thanks. I'll be here Tuesday then." Two days in a row should provide enough time to get the mansion off her mind.

"You're welcome." Les turned to leave.

"Have a great weekend!" said Tessa and followed him out.

"You too."

As she stepped outside, a few raindrops hit her face. She was surprised how warm it was despite the cloud cover. It had been overcast all day but the downpour had held off and she hoped the sky wouldn't drop its load as she walked home. She didn't mind a few drops but she hadn't planned on a soaking. A warm breeze gently blew on her face as she began her walk, which had a calming effect after a hectic and difficult day. Taking a deep breath of the fresh, moist air, she willed her mind to focus on anything but what had brought her so much turmoil today.

Tessa realized she'd be walking past the old mansion on her way home. She was in no mood to bring back those disturbing memories but she didn't have the energy to walk the few extra blocks to avoid it so she walked as briskly as her energy could manage.

As the mansion came into view, her mind wandered back to all that had taken place there. She longed to know what it was all about and why an angel had been sent to her. Why would God send her an angel? It still didn't make any sense.

She'd never developed much of a prayer routine but she had prayed last night while struggling to get to sleep. Reading a few verses and saying a short prayer before shut-eye had always seemed to suffice before. She freely admitted she wasn't a deeply spiritual person. So, why would God send the angel? Why was he going to all this trouble for her?

She had questioned him last night about the mansion experience. Not that she had expected an audible voice or anything. There wasn't a lot of faith inside her for any kind of answer. Confusion still dominated her emotions. She had no further insight into the reason for it all and longed for some clarity.

Better yet, she wished the whole thing would go away. The satisfaction with the direction of her life a mere two days ago was gone. Her future accounting job had given her great anticipation. Getting to know Cody was another bright expectation. Now those things faded in the shadow of this angel business. The whole mansion debacle was really messing up her neatly planned life and it irritated her to no end.

The idea that God was trying to tell her something was completely unfamiliar to her, even though it was somewhat fascinating. But honestly, she was in no frame of mind to have her life redirected. Had she ever asked for this? Why was God doing this to her? It made her angry just thinking about it. The further she walked, the more upset she became. By the time she arrived home she was all worked up. Her plan to crash and catch up on sleep for the first hour flew away. She was way too agitated to rest; anger had replaced her weariness.

The place she called home was in an established neighborhood of the city of Chelsey, with large trees that towered over the houses. It was a pretty house with beige siding, white shutters that hugged the windows and a front porch enclosed by a white railing. A well-used swing hung on the left side of the porch. It was a little tattered-looking but still in good condition. A good coat of paint was all it needed.

Her parents were meticulous in their care of the house and she couldn't help but feel pride in it. It wasn't so much the house as the feeling of home. Peace ruled here. Her parents loved each other and they kept the family close.

Inside, the house was elegant but homey, a cute bungalow with three bedrooms on the main floor. Their lower level was fully finished and that's where her two brothers had their bedrooms. They liked to hang out in the large family room down there, play video games, watch movies or work out with their weights. The rustic fireplace gave the space an inviting feel.

Tessa's bedroom was on the main level with a bathroom separating her room from her parents' room. The extra bedroom upstairs had been converted into an office. It wasn't a large house by any means but it was practical.

She'd always been close to her parents, with a special bond with her father. Their characters were somewhat similar; he was very gentle, easy to talk to and always supportive of her. They could discuss nearly any subject and he never ceased to be a fountain of wisdom. He was very knowledgeable on almost all topics, a good sounding board while she was in school, and she'd learned a great deal from him.

Her mother was also supportive but in a quiet sort of way. They could have good conversations at times but that didn't happen as often. Her mother worked full time and, though busy, showed her love through acts of service. Thinking about them brought a smile, even with the mood she was in.

After changing into track pants and a t-shirt, Tessa walked to the kitchen, poured herself a tall glass of iced tea and headed out to the roof-covered porch. She let her body slump down onto the porch swing. It felt wonderful to get off her feet finally, sit down and relax. After finishing her iced tea, she swung herself sideways and put her feet up on one end. This spot would be ideal if only her thoughts would stop racing in circles.

She closed her eyes and wished that she could bring some peace to her troubled mind. The light drizzle that fell during her walk now turned into a steady stream of rain. She felt her damp hair with one hand. It would dry eventually. The raindrops pattered and splashed on the walkway leading to the house and clattered on the porch roof. If her mind would stop its spinning, this noise could put her to sleep in no time. Forcing her shoulders to relax, she longed for the tension of the day to dissipate.

Closing her eyes wasn't helping. She felt as alert and agitated as before. A noise on the porch caught her attention and her eyes snapped open. Sitting upright, she glared at the unwelcome intruder.

She blurted out, "Why are you here and what do you want?"

The man in the trench coat, the angel, was standing on the porch steps looking at her. He stood there for a few minutes in silence. The peace in his eyes was mesmerizing. He finally moved and came a few steps closer.

"I've been sent to encourage you. You've been afraid and upset about all that you've seen. Don't be afraid of what God has for you. Let God's peace lead you and you'll know what is right. Remember that you will never feel fulfilled until you accomplish God's plan for your life. It is a good plan."

As the angel spoke she could feel peace washing over her mind, her emotions and her entire being becoming calm. It was like being caught in the eye of a storm. Where her thoughts had been spinning out of control, there was suddenly great rest. The drastic change shocked her but she gladly welcomed it.

"Thank you! I feel it! I needed that so desperately."

"Thank God. It was his peace that I brought. I'm only the messenger. I'll be going now."

"Wait! You forgot to tell me about the sign. How will I know when it's time to go back to the mansion? Could you please tell me?"

Although he didn't crack a smile, his eyes were laughing. "I'm not allowed to tell you. You have to trust God to show you." With that he turned, headed down the steps and across the front yard to the sidewalk. He turned right and passed a row of pine trees until he was hidden from view.

She watched until she could no longer see him. Awe and amazement flooded her. Her life had become a series of unpredictable events. She had always known that angels existed, but she had never thought she'd ever see one or that they would play any vital role in her life. Surely they had more important things to do than to waste their time with the likes of her. To have one appear to her was revelatory.

Tessa closed her eyes and soaked in the peace that still flooded her. What a difference the angel's presence had brought. She thought over his words about him bringing God's peace to her, not his own. His words about her fulfilling God's plan confused her. She had always thought she was pursuing the area of her interest, the gift she'd been given.

Have I ever asked God what his plan is for me? I can't remember ever doing that.

For some reason all her careful planning and preparing for the future seemed insignificant. After all her schooling why would she now doubt the direction she had chosen? She and her father had discussed her course numerous times and they had always come to the same conclusion. Accounting was what she was good at, a natural aptitude. So why did she doubt now? Although peace was still pervasive, the questions still begged answers.

Leaning her head against the swing, she pondered that her life seemed to be getting more complicated by the day. Things had shifted so dramatically and it was taking a toll on her. To adjust to the supernatural appearing around her had created a new nervousness to which she was unaccustomed. She always thought she had a good grasp on reality, God and all that, but that perception was slipping through her fingers rather quickly. What she had been so sure of now seemed vague and blurred. It was a very unsettling realization.

If only I could understand all this.

Maybe trying to understand it all was the problem. Perhaps she was agonizing over it too much. After all, the angel said she needed to trust God. Maybe it was time to set some of her rationale aside and go by faith. She struggled with that concept. Organization and planning were her strong points. It was difficult to let those go.

Mac, her brother, was home. He rushed up the walk to the house, rain pelting down on him.

The difficult questions would have to wait for now. Peace still hovered around her, for which she was very grateful. She prayed that it would stay because it sure was hard maintaining it on her own.

Mac bounded up the steps deep in thought. He stood with one hand on the doorknob and shook his head wildly. Water flew in all directions. His head was soaked and his clothes dripped from the downpour.

Tessa said, "Hi there, bro."

He swung around in surprise. "Oh, hi there! I didn't even notice you. What are you up to?" He walked over to the swing and sat down beside her.

"I'm taking a load off after work. It was crazy busy today. I needed some time off my feet." The way Mac was staring at her made her squirm. "What's wrong? Do I have something on my face?"

"No," Mac said with a grin. "You look different somehow and I feel this incredible calm around you."

"Peace?"

"Maybe, I don't know. It feels good."

Mac wasn't one for many words. It shocked Tessa that he could actually feel the peace that still surrounded her.

"I've been feeling the same thing for the past little while. It's amazing that you sensed it as soon as you got close!"

They sat quietly for a moment before Tessa asked, "What have you been up to today?"

"I was at Jon's for a while. We watched a movie." He stood and said, "I should get going. I've got basketball practice in an hour and we have a game tonight. Are you coming to see me play?"

"I can't. Sorry. I'm getting together with Cody tonight. There's this youth worship thing at the park. I wish I had known about your game. Will you have any more before the end of the season?"

"There'll be two more as long as we win tonight. Our team's doing awesome. We've hardly lost any games." His eyes lit up at the admission. "Why don't you come and watch me play more often?"

Guilt played a drum roll beneath her ribs. "I've been pretty busy lately with exams and all." She glanced at the dark grey clouds hovering overhead. "If this rain keeps up, Cody's youth thing might get cancelled. If it does, I'll see if I can talk him into going to your game."

"That'd be great. Anyway, I've got to run." With that he stood and headed inside.

Just then her parents' car pulled into the driveway. It stopped and her mother exited. After getting her umbrella out and opening it, she popped the trunk, pulled out her packages and headed to the porch. She stopped when she saw Tessa.

"Hi, Tess," she said, shaking water off her umbrella and closing it.

"Hi, Mom. What were you doing?"

"Shopping, as usual. It's your father's birthday tomorrow and I bought a few things to celebrate."

Tessa brought her hand to her mouth then lowered it again to admit her oversight. "I totally forgot about his birthday! I need to get him a gift."

"Why don't we say that the gift I bought is from both of us; that way you don't have to go out again? You must be tired after work. I know that Joe and Mac bought your father a gift together so they're prepared."

"Well, I guess that would be okay. What did you get him?"

"Why don't I show you?"

Her mother separated a bag from the others and pulled out a box. After opening the top flap, she lifted out an ornament of a golfer. His arms were extended over his head, a club in his hands, ready to hit the ball sitting on the green before him. It was a well-made ornament, not gaudy-looking like most and contained a great amount of detail with rich-looking colors.

Her father would love it. He was an avid golfer and had often admired these tacky ornaments in store windows. Her mother had found a gem. Where he'd put it she wasn't sure but she was confident he'd appreciate it. He didn't really need a thing. This would be a perfect gift for him; he could set it on his desk at work and daydream.

"It's great, Mom. He'll love it! Let me know how much it cost and I'll chip in. Where is he anyway?"

"You can't guess?" She waved the ornament around.

"Golfing in this rain?"

"Rain or shine." She chuckled. "It's his Saturday ritual. This morning he asked me to go with him but the sky looked unpredictable and I had too many things to do. He went with Mark Hunter from down the street."

"He's the guy with the motorcycles, right?"

"Yes, he loves his motorcycles and golfing. I'm glad your father and Mark have become good golfing buddies. It gives me a break. I enjoy it but every Saturday is just too often for me."

Tessa smiled. Her mom loved nothing better than to putter around the house

"Well, I need to get dinner started. Will you be here?"

"No, Cody is taking me to dinner."

"You should bring that boy over here sometime so we could meet him. I'm so curious about him."

Tessa smiled. "I'll do that eventually, I promise."

"Okay, dear, I'll hold you to that." Her mother reached for her packages with one hand, opened the door and went inside.

CHAPTER 7

It rained steadily all evening and the youth event in the park was cancelled so Tessa and Cody went to see Mac's basketball game together. Mac scored quite a few points for his team and Tessa could tell he was excited she was there to watch. He kept glancing in her direction throughout the game. Mac's team ended up winning and after the game he headed over to where they were sitting. He couldn't stop talking about all the awesome plays and moves his team made. Mac had plans to celebrate with his friends so, after congratulating him, Tessa and Cody headed to a restaurant close by.

They settled into a booth and both ordered hot chocolate. It was still cool and damp outside and the hot drink seemed like a good choice. They discussed Mac's game while they waited for their order. It grew quiet between them for a few moments.

Tessa leaned forward and rested her arms on the table. "You know we've been friends now for a few months and sometimes it feels like I hardly know you."

He gave a small smile. "Why's that?"

"You don't share much about yourself. I'm curious about what you're really like." She immediately felt awkward with her admission. Cody's intentions in this relationship were still vague and perhaps she was being too forward.

He remained quiet, looked down and studied his hands. Slowly he raised his eyes, looked at her and said, "I hesitate to open up because the times that I have, it has tended to scare people off."

"Why?"

"Maybe I'm too intense for most people. I'm very passionate about my faith and the things that are important to me."

Tessa only nodded. She couldn't disagree.

"I suppose I don't want to risk frightening you off." He looked at her and smiled but his eyes spoke caution.

"Well, I wish you'd take the risk. We'll never know if we're compatible if we don't get to know each other." She did it again. She could kick herself for appearing so eager to advance their relationship. What if he wasn't interested?

"I guess that's true."

The waiter brought their hot chocolate. It was steaming hot and smelled terrific. Tessa held hers to her lips, blew to cool it and took a small sip. It tasted heavenly and warmed her insides.

After a sip from his cup, Cody set it down and said, "What would you like to know?"

"You could start with your family. You've never told me anything about your family."

Cody nodded and looked nervous. "Well..., all right. I come from a small family; I have one sister and a mother. My father left us when I was nine and it was the most difficult thing I think I've ever gone through. He just up and left and I never saw him again. My mother struggled to support my sister and me. She worked hard all her life and still does. She wasn't always there for us, which is understandable under the circumstances, because she had her own anger and hurt to deal with."

"That must have been so hard not having a father around. I can't imagine."

"Yeah, it wasn't easy. My father leaving us affected me a lot. At first I blamed myself; I thought I must have done something to make him mad and that's why he left. My grades plummeted and I had a hard time getting them to improve. My mother tried to help me and got after me for not trying harder. When she finally found out that I blamed myself for Dad leaving, she tried to explain it to me the best she could. I still struggled a lot but I didn't blame myself quite so much." He fell silent.

"How's your mom doing now?"

"She's had a hard life. I wish I could bring her some happiness. She deserves it for all she did for us."

"Do you have any idea why your father abandoned you? Did your mother ever tell you what made him leave?"

"No, she never divulged too many details, especially when it happened. I was only a kid, nine. I wouldn't have understood. When I was sixteen I asked her about it. That's when she opened up and told me stuff. She said he was having an affair with a young girl from work. When my mom found out she confronted him and he exploded. He basically told her that it was his life and she had no business interfering. As long as he was putting food on the table and paying the bills, he was doing his part and she had no right to question his activities. He planned to continue his relationship with the girl but was willing to stay married to my mother as long as she'd stop rocking the boat. He was willing to stay for us kids."

Tessa could feel her mouth hang in disbelief. "You're kidding?"

"Not one bit. Well, you can imagine how that went over with her. She was furious and demanded that he give up the other woman. He stayed another week listening to my mom insist that he change. Finally he told her he'd had enough, packed a suitcase and left. My mom told me she begged him not to leave, to give their marriage a chance. She reminded him over and over about his responsibility to us children, that we needed him."

"He didn't listen?" Tessa asked in shock.

"She told me that she cried and pleaded with him that Saturday morning while he packed his things. He didn't say a word the whole time and apparently refused even to look at her. After he walked out the door, he drove off in his car and we never saw him again. I don't remember that morning or where I was. I asked my mother and she said my sister and I must have been playing outside with friends from the neighborhood. The last memory I have of my father is of him yelling at me because I tipped my cup of milk at the dinner table the night before. Not a very good final farewell, is it?"

"No," Tessa said quietly. It was such a shocking story, she didn't know what to say.

"I don't even remember what he looks like. I have one blurry picture of him. I wouldn't know him if he passed me on the street."

Tessa said, "I don't know what to say."

"You don't need to say anything. Nothing you say will change the past." Pain oozed from his eyes.

Tessa felt pierced through by the knowledge. It was too much to take in at once. She held a new respect for this man sitting across from her. His painful past was more than what she could have imagined.

Finally she said, "My life has been very peaceful and normal compared to yours. My father would never leave. I know he loves us and is absolutely committed to us. It makes me feel guilty for having had it so good."

"Never feel guilty, only thankful."

"I am, very. But I'm so sorry for you, Cody."

"Well, that's not where my story ends, thank God!" The pain in his eyes left and a deep peace replaced it.

Tessa was intrigued by the sudden change.

"God's done quite a work in me. I'm thankful for that."

"What about your sister? How did she handle it?"

"She struggled a lot too. I remember her crying all the time. Choey's two years older than I am but boy was she a baby. I guess everyone responds differently to life's challenges. She would crawl up on Mother's lap and cry for hours. My mom allowed it and would often cry with her. I was more angry than sad. I wanted to find my dad and beat him up."

"Was your mother able to stay in the house that you had?"

"Actually, no. We lived in a beautiful two-story house in a nice area of the city. It wasn't paid for and my mother couldn't afford the mortgage. She sold it and put the equity into a small one-story home. She managed to get a fairly good job working for a travel agency. Night courses helped her to learn what she needed for the business. After years of hard work, she was eventually promoted into management. I'm very proud of her." The approval on Cody's face was obvious.

"You've told me before that you lived a rough life before you became a Christian. What did you mean by that?"

"This conversation sure seems to be one-sided doesn't it? When is it going to be your turn?" He gave her a lopsided grin.

"There's not much to tell. My life's been fairly mild and uneventful compared to what you've been through."

He nodded, sighed and said, "Okay, let me think back. I guess when I was around twelve or thirteen, I started hanging out with these guys from school that introduced me to booze. I remember my father having a beer now and then when he lived with us so it wasn't new to me. I started drinking heavier as the years went by. We started getting into harder liquor and eventually I was getting drunk at every party we had.

"My mother noticed me coming home drunk. It really upset

her but at that point she had lost control. She was too busy working, couldn't watch what I did so I had the freedom to come and go as I pleased. By the time she realized what was happening, it was too late to turn things around but she still tried to speak some sense into me. At that point I didn't want to hear it. I became really hooked on alcohol. I got a job to support my drinking. I worked evenings and weekends at a lumber store. I'd load stuff for customers, stock shelves and whatever they needed me to do, then blow my paycheck on booze."

"It sounds like you were forced to grow up fast. You didn't have much of a childhood."

"You can say that again."

"Was it just drinking that controlled you during those years?"

"I wish I could say yes. My friend, Percy, offered us, me and my friends, some marijuana. I must have been around fifteen at the time. Well, it went from that to harder drugs. We experimented with a lot of things. I eventually became very addicted. It got to the point I knew I couldn't get away from it. My job couldn't support my habits anymore so I started selling drugs to help out with the cost of my lifestyle."

Cody stopped and studied her carefully. "Are you sure you want to hear all this? I can stop anytime."

It was hard to hear but Tessa wanted to know. "Please keep going."

"Okay." He took the last sip of his hot chocolate, leaned back, folded his hands on the table and continued. "I dropped out of school when I was seventeen. I couldn't keep it all together anymore. My mom was furious when I quit. She knew something was wrong; I just wasn't myself anymore. She often asked me if I was doing drugs but I always denied it. By the time I was twenty I was either drunk or stoned most of the time. I couldn't hold a job and was finding it hard to get enough money together to support my habits. I started stealing from my mother. She eventually kicked me out of the house even though it was very hard for her to do. She cried while she told me I couldn't live with her anymore.

"I have to admit the guys I hung out with were some pretty shady characters. I was part of them and she couldn't handle them coming around the house. She said that if I'd get myself together and live right, I could come back anytime. I felt sorry for her and wanted to change my life but it was too out of control. I wanted to please my mother but couldn't. I felt completely hopeless the day I left her home."

The waiter came around to ask if he could get them anything else. They both decided on another round of hot chocolate. Cody and Tessa were in a corner booth and as they talked, the restaurant slowly emptied. Tessa enjoyed having the place almost exclusively to themselves.

"Where did you go after you left your mother's?"

"I moved in with a friend but that didn't work out for long. The landlord kicked us out shortly after I moved there. We were pretty desperate so we went to a shelter for a while but they didn't want us there on a long-term basis. I then moved in with my sister. She was living with her boyfriend at the time. He wasn't too impressed with me, didn't really want me there and he let me know it. She tried to help me; checked out drug rehabilitation centers but I wouldn't co-operate. I eventually found a job and started making money again. Somehow I managed to keep the job even though I was still heavily drinking and doing drugs. I was still selling on the side so I could keep up my habit. The job helped me get my own apartment. It was a dive of a place and mouse-infested but I hardly noticed, being stoned most of the time. At least I could live on my own."

His story shook her but she had to know more. "It's just so hard to imagine you that way, knowing the way you are now. How did you ever get out of that lifestyle?"

"Well, it's very interesting how that all came about. I was at a very low point in my life and I couldn't see any way out. I was totally bound to my addictions. I remember it was a Saturday night. I had worked all day and when I arrived at the apartment, my drug suppliers were there to meet me. I hadn't paid them in a while and kept putting them off. There was no money to give them that night either. I had just spent the last of my money on some liquor for the weekend. To put it mildly, they weren't too impressed." He grinned crookedly at that. "They barged in and beat me up terribly. I was a mess."

"It sounds horrific!"

He shrugged and went on. "I cleaned myself up the best I could and sat in my apartment all evening, feeling like my life was spinning out of control. I couldn't cope anymore and began to contemplate ways to end it all."

Tessa placed a hand over her mouth.

"There was a gun I kept stashed under my bed for emergencies. I went to get that and considered suicide that whole evening. I knew I was a huge disappointment to my mother and sister and I was completely disgusted with myself. Hopelessness just took me over that night. Praying wasn't something I'd ever tried before. That evening I cried out to God and told him that if he was real and if he cared at all about my life that he should send someone that could help me. I also remember telling God that I wanted it to be very clear that it was him. I prayed that around nine that evening. At nine-thirty there was a knock at my door."

Just then the waiter came back with their refills of hot chocolate. Tessa felt annoyed at being interrupted at such a crucial moment. He set down the steaming mugs of hot chocolate; they thanked him and he left.

Cody gripped the handle of his mug and began again. "Well, I wasn't expecting anyone over that night. I went to the door and opened it cautiously, hoping it wouldn't be those two thugs again. There were two guys standing outside my door but I didn't recognize them at all. They were dressed in jeans and t-shirts and one of them had long hair. The one with the long hair must have been around my age and the other guy was around thirty. They asked if they could talk to me about God."

"No way!"

Cody grinned, nodded and continued. "I was a bit shocked at first but I agreed. They told me how much God loved me and how he sent his son, Jesus, to earth to die for me and how he was raised again from the dead to bring me eternal life. They explained how all men and women are born in sin and we're all headed for hell without a savior. It was God's great love that made a way for us to escape hell and to receive salvation through Jesus Christ. They said that if I'd accept him as my Lord and Savior, I could one day live eternally with him in heaven. They showed me John 3:16 and other scriptures from Bibles they were carrying."

"That is so cool!"

"You know, I had never heard about salvation my entire life. I didn't know that I was a sinner headed for hell. No one had told me anything like that, ever. My family never went to church. My mother never discussed religion and I never bothered with it. I stood there in complete shock. I must have looked like a complete dork, my mouth hanging open, my eyes glazed, my face beat to a pulp." He grinned, then continued. "They asked if I wanted Jesus to be my savior and I said yes right away. I was so amazed that God had answered me so quickly that I didn't hesitate. I knelt down right there and they led me in praying the sinner's prayer. These guys were so excited! I don't know if they ever had such a quick response in their door-to-door ministry."

Tessa chuckled and Cody joined in.

"After I prayed with them I felt like a thousand pounds rolled off my back. It was an awesome feeling. These guys invited me to come to their church the next day, gave me directions and asked if I needed a ride. I told them that I could find my way there."

"Did you go?"

"I did," Cody said with a twinkle in his eye.

"What was the church's name?" Tessa sat on the edge of her seat.

"It's the church I'm in right now, Church on the Move. I found out that the younger guy, Bryan, who came to my door, had accepted Christ a few years earlier and he came from a situation similar to mine. He had been hooked on booze and drugs and someone had come to his door and told him about Jesus. He got dramatically saved. The thirty-year old guy, Chad, was the pastor of the church and he had also come out of addictions and became a Christian in his early twenties. He was radical in his faith. He went to Bible School shortly after his salvation and started a church right after that. The church he started is down where the drug addicts live and a lot of the members are ex-druggies."

"Had you never been to a church service before?" She felt such intrigue at his amazing story.

"Never. I didn't know what to expect. They started with some singing. They had a few musicians at the front who sang songs I'd never heard before. They had an overhead projector set up with the words up on the front wall. Even though I didn't know any of the songs I enjoyed listening to them sing. They were very exuberant and sang like they meant it. They clapped and some raised their hands in the air. I had no idea why; it was all very new to me. Chad stood up to preach his message and everything he said was like it was meant just for me; it hit me so hard. When he was finished, he asked if anyone wanted prayer. He invited people to come up."

"So, did you go?"

He smiled warmly and nodded. "I did go up. I thought, what could it hurt; I probably need prayer more than the rest. Others went up too. When Chad came to me, he laid his hands on my head. I felt electricity go through me as he prayed. I'll never forget his prayer; it was for total deliverance from every evil thing. He took authority over every demonic addiction and asked God to fill me with his Spirit. As I felt that electricity go through me, I knew that the addictions had left. It was the best high for me, a much bigger high than any drug or drink had ever given me. You know, I never craved alcohol or drugs after that moment. It was totally gone! Man, I love God so much!"

Tessa gazed at him in wonder. Enthusiasm shone from his entire countenance.

"He has done so much for me and I have a hard time being quiet about it. I've had to calm down a bit with some Christians I've come to know. Not all of them are that happy for me. Some actually get offended if I talk about God too much, which I have a hard time understanding. The church I attend is full of people like me and I can talk freely there but our church gets together with other churches for some events and I've met people who get uptight at my excitement. I don't know what you think about all this but if we're going to spend a lot of time together and get to know each other, I want you to know where I'm coming from."

"I'm awestruck with what you've been through and how God answered your prayer. I never knew that you were so bound with addictions."

"I suppose I've only told you bits and pieces before."

"It's awesome to hear the whole story! Looking at you now, it's astounding what God has done in your life. No wonder you're so enthusiastic about him. How long has it been since your life changed so dramatically?"

"Well, I became a Christian when I was twenty and I'm twenty-four now so I guess that makes it four years. They've been the best four years of my entire life. God brought me tremendous healing. His awesome love has healed the hurt that my father's lack of love inflicted. God's love was what helped me finally forgive my father and let my pain and anger go. It has totally transformed me. When I look back to what I was like four years ago, I don't even recognize myself. It's all because of my Heavenly Father and I can't help but talk about him. He's the reason that I'm still alive." A smile tugged at the corners of his lips.

"I can definitely understand your love for God better now. I still can't relate to it completely. I've always been thankful for a Christian home and a godly upbringing; it spared me a lot of pain and turmoil. I do wish I could feel that kind of love and appreciation for God though. That's something I'm lacking and I envy that."

"So what was your upbringing like, Tessa?"

"You don't want to hear about it; it's too boring."

"Oh yes I do. You're not getting off the hook that easily. Come on, spill the beans."

Tessa leaned back in her chair and released a sigh of resignation. She didn't know exactly what to tell him or where to start but she had to say something, so reluctantly she started.

"Well, as you probably already know, I was raised by Christian parents. I have two brothers, Mac and Joe." She went on to explain her normal childhood, her parents' constant love and encouragement, her years of Sunday school, church and activity involvement. It all seemed so boring compared to what she had just heard.

Cody listened intently, eyes locked on hers, completely engrossed in her story.

"As a kid I went to church camps during the summers and as I got older I went as a cabin leader. I sang in the church choir for many years. Last year I let that go because I was too busy with school and work. I once even tried teaching a Sunday School class but couldn't tolerate the kids. They were an unruly bunch and I couldn't handle them. I guess teaching isn't one of my gifts. Once I started college, I kind of dropped out of the church scene for a while. I still attended occasionally but haven't been very involved for quite some time."

"You don't know how blessed you are." Cody looked completely sincere.

"I know how lackluster it must sound to you."

"Oh, no! It actually sounds safe and wonderful. I sometimes wonder what it must have been like being so protected. And what I'd be like now without all the junk of my previous lifestyle."

"Well, you do have quite the testimony."

"I think I'd rather have the godly heritage and background you have."

Her forehead crinkled skeptically. "Are you serious?"

"Absolutely!"

"It's hard to imagine that. You'd trade your amazing story for my boring one?"

"It's not so much about the story as the upbringing. I don't believe you know how blessed you've been. I have a lot of issues from the past to deal with. You've been spared that."

"I guess so," she said with a shrug.

Cody shifted the conversation. "How did you do in high school? Somehow I imagine you breezing your way through."

"Not exactly! I did get some good marks but I had to work my butt off. If I had goofed off, I'm sure I would have flunked a course. School was okay even with the hard work. I had some great friends I hung around with and that's what made it fulfilling for me. I've told you about Luke and Richelle, haven't I?"

"Yep. They're the ones you met with the other night, aren't they?"

"Yes. Well, they're the ones who made high school memorable for me. We had some amazing times together! I missed them a lot when we went our separate ways after graduation. The rest you already know about so, as you can tell, my life hasn't been that scintillating."

"Oh? Even meeting Cody Fields wasn't that thrilling?"

"Well, that has added some new dimensions of exhilaration to my life."

Giving her a playful grin, he checked the time on his phone before continuing. "It's getting late. We should go soon but there's one other thing I'd like to talk about." He looked at her for approval.

"Sure, what is it?"

"We've been seeing each other for two months, right?"

"Yes."

"I'm sure you've noticed we haven't held hands or kissed."

"Well... I was wondering about that. I didn't know if you wanted just friendship or if it was going to turn into something more." Finally, she'd find out what his intentions were.

"Before I became a Christian I had a reputation of taking advantage of girls right, left and center. I dated them for one purpose and one purpose only. It was the way I lived my life. After I became a Christian and learned what the Bible teaches about sex, I changed my ways. I found out that sex before marriage, in God's eyes, is sin. I made a commitment to him that I wouldn't do it again. I made a firm decision to wait till marriage and promised to keep myself pure before him till I married the woman that was meant for me."

This seemed like way too much information. Tessa could feel her cheeks heat up and knew she was blushing.

"I don't mean to embarrass you but I really need to say this."

So he had noticed her discomfort. "It's okay. Go ahead."

"Since my vow in this area, I tend to be very cautious not to do anything that would tempt me to break that promise to God. I lean toward caution to the point of scaring girls away, although you haven't run off yet."

What should she say after such a confession? Her mind whirled with possible answers. Finally, she said, "I have to be honest with you, Cody. I've often wondered why you weren't interested in anything physical. I thought maybe you weren't really attracted to me and yet you kept asking me out. It confused me and I wasn't sure what to think."

"It's not that I'm not attracted to you. It's quite the opposite." He laughed. "You're gorgeous and if I was the old Cody I would have had you by now, dumped you and moved on to someone else."

That fact didn't decrease her discomfort and she felt her cheeks warming again.

"I care about you a lot. I'd love to hold your hand and kiss you. It sometimes takes all the self-control I have not to. My goal has been to establish a friendship first. Dating should be for the sole purpose of finding a life partner. That's my purpose in dating now and I want to do right by you."

It shocked her to hear him say it. "'Wow!' is all I can say!

Most of the guys that I've dated have been like the old Cody. I've never met anyone like you before!"

"I hope that's a compliment."

"Yes. That's one of the reasons I like you so much. You treat me with so much respect. The respect actually confused me, it was so foreign! But I appreciate it more than you know. I'd like to continue seeing you." The words popped out before she could stop them and they surprised even her.

"Thanks, the feeling is mutual." He gazed at her with intense admiration and reached over to take her hands. "I'm glad we talked these things through. I'm looking forward to getting to know you even better. Do you think you can handle my extreme spiritual zeal?"

"I think I'll get used to it. Do you think you can handle my calmer approach to God?" Tessa threw back.

"I love you the way you are."

He said he loved me? Is he serious? He actually loves me?

Cody smiled brightly and said, "Let's get going." He got up, came around to her side and pulled back her chair for her.

It was definitely a unique experience.

Tessa thought over his words as he paid for the bill and they walked out. She wished she had asked him about his confession of love but the moment had passed and it would be awkward bringing it back up.

As they left the restaurant, Cody reached over, a warm glow in his eyes and took her hand in his. Tessa smiled shyly and took his hand willingly. This was a turn of events she had been wondering about and actually longing for.

CHAPTER 8

The following week of work flowed smoothly. Tessa's nerves were more settled and Les Jones no longer had to keep an eye on her, which was a huge relief. Knowing he was watching was intimidating. She knew what she was doing. Waitressing wasn't new to her.

Going back in time, now that was a different matter entirely. Tessa felt more comfortable as the week progressed and the discomfiting memories of the mansion faded somewhat.

By Saturday things seemed back to normal. The time travel was a fainter memory. The only disconcerting issue was Martha's lack of confidence in her. The woman didn't like her a great deal, of that Tessa was sure. Martha pinpointed only the negative and reminded Tessa of all she was doing wrong. Tessa wasn't sure the woman had the capacity to be positive. She tried to avoid the woman as much as possible.

To have a week's reprieve with no visit to the mansion was wonderful. The angel had warned her that more was on the way but she was extremely grateful for the break. It still made her jittery when her mind wandered back to the memories but the normalcy of the week had afforded her some peace of mind.

The bell above the door rang and Tessa looked up to see Richelle walk in. She wore a black leather mini skirt, tight red t-shirt and black leather boots that stopped just below her knees. Her short, blond hair was in its familiar bob but flipped out at the ends. Quite a few heads turned when she walked into the restaurant, which was the typical response. Richelle knew how to dress to get the looks.

Tessa gave her a wave. Richelle smiled and waved back. After finishing up the bill for the last table, taking it to her customers and settling up, Tessa headed to the door.

She gave Richelle a hug and said, "Hi! How are you?"

"So-so I guess." She looked despondent and her eyes were slightly bloodshot.

"Tough day at work?"

"No more than usual. I've had something on my mind all week and I really need to talk."

"Okay, that's cool. I just finished up and I'm done for the day." Tessa looked around for the hostess and spotted her toward the back by the drink machine. Turning to Richelle, she said, "I'll get Patrice to seat you at a table for two. I'll hang my apron in the staff room, get my things and join you."

"Sounds great."

Tessa spoke to Patrice then hurried to gather her things. Entering the dining room, she glanced around and saw Richelle seated by the window at a small table. She went and poured two glasses of diet coke before heading over.

"Thanks, Tessa. You read my mind." Richelle took a few sips of her drink.

After a taste of her own diet coke, Tessa asked, "So what's up? You don't look like you've had a very good day."

"I've had better weeks, I can assure you."

"Are you talking about the old mansion and what we saw there?"

"Yes...no. Well, it's sort of related. You know that Luke took me home that night, right? You stayed and we left."

Tessa nodded.

"Well, it was pretty late by the time he got me home. I had Luke drop me off a block from my place so Charlie wouldn't know I was with him. When I walked up to my apartment building, Charlie was waiting for me outside. He was upset when he saw me because he doesn't like me walking by myself at night. He yelled at me for being so stupid. It made me mad, him speaking to me like that. I just blurted out that Luke gave me a ride home. It was dumb!"

"Oh no! What did Charlie say?"

"He was furious! He accused me of cheating on him, trying to hide stuff from him. I kept telling him that the three of us were all together that night and that nothing was going on between Luke and me. Well, he didn't believe me. He kept asking me what we were doing till that time at night." Richelle looked completely distraught.

"I didn't want to tell him because it was such a strange evening that I didn't think he'd believe me anyway. I told him that we just hung out together and talked. It wasn't good enough for him and he kept pressuring me about what else we did. I finally broke down and told him about the old mansion and what happened to us there."

This wasn't good and it couldn't end well. The more people that were involved, the more complicated the whole situation would become.

"So he wanted me to prove it to him."

Tessa was sure she tasted bile making its way up her throat. She took a sip of her drink, swallowed hard and said, "So what did you do?"

Richelle fidgeted with her cup, swirling the straw around the cubes of ice, her eyes betraying her agitation. She wiggled in her seat, too upset to relax.

Tessa tried to remain empathetic.

"He insisted that I take him to the mansion and show him the time change. So that's what I did. Sunday afternoon I took him to the old house but nothing happened. I mean, nothing at all. There was no time change and the house was the same as it's always been. There was no snow, no guy in a trench coat, no Mary, no people, no nothing!" Her voice began to rise in volume.

People were starting to look over in their direction and not because of Richelle's mini skirt!

"Calm down, Richelle!" The last thing Tessa wanted was to draw attention. Martha was already glaring their way. She certainly didn't need that woman breathing down her neck.

"How can I calm down? Charlie has moved out, saying that he can't stay with someone he can't trust!" Richelle was clearly beside herself.

Tessa reached over and took her hand. "It'll be okay. I'll help you figure this out. Just calm down and tell me everything."

The physical contact did wonders for Richelle. She took a deep breath, looked Tessa in the eye and continued in a much calmer voice. "You know what happened at that old mansion. You know what we saw! I feel like I'm going crazy this week but I know what we saw. What am I supposed to do? I can't lose him!" A tear slipped from her eye and trickled down her cheek.

Tessa squeezed her hand. "I don't know. I just wonder why nothing happened when you and Charlie went over there. Isn't that a bit strange?"

"Completely!"

"Maybe the time shift only happens at specified times. I don't know what to say, Richelle. How can I help?"

"I thought maybe if you'd talk to Charlie he'd believe me. Or maybe if we'd go to the mansion altogether it might happen again. I don't know! All I know is that I want Charlie back. This whole thing is messing up my life!" Tears now flowed from her eyes and her mascara was starting to come undone.

It was amazing how the mansion had simultaneously messed up both of their lives. Tessa handed her a napkin; Richelle dabbed her eyes carefully.

"We'll find a way to fix this. But don't worry. Do you know where Charlie is right now?" Tessa asked.

"He usually works at his dad's shop on Saturdays. I don't know if he'd still be there. It's already four-thirty." Richelle pulled away and checked her cell phone.

"Why don't we go and see? Do you have your car here or did you take the bus?"

A sliver of hope gleamed in Richelle's eyes. "I have my car. It's parked out front. Are you sure you want to do this? Charlie can be pretty rude when he's upset. But I'll love you forever if you'll do this for me."

"I can't promise that it'll change anything but I can try." Tessa had no great affection for Charlie except that Richelle was so attached to him. She considered him a brute of a guy with few social graces. She definitely wasn't looking forward to this exchange. There was a myriad of other things she'd rather do after work.

"Thank you, thank you so much!" Richelle stood and headed for the door.

Tessa released a nervous breath, stood up and followed her. Richelle's small, white Honda was parked by the curb. She had saved for over a year to buy it. Richelle was very proud of it and preened it nearly as much as she did herself. Tessa couldn't remember ever seeing it dirty.

Richelle's meticulous care of everything around her reinforced the appearance of perfection. Her nearly obsessive-compulsive habits demanded flawlessness at all times. This difficulty and imperfection in her relationship with Charlie was throwing Richelle into a tail spin, the likes Tessa hadn't seen before. She only hoped she could say something that would steer Charlie in the right direction and bring some reconciliation between the two. Uttering a silent prayer, they arrived at the garage and pulled in.

Richelle had told her of Charlie's career choice and the dynamics of his and his father's relationship. The garage belonged to Charlie's father, with Charlie helping him out on weekends. His father had taught him the ropes and Charlie had taken some courses on car repair, giving him further advantage in the business. Fine carpentry was Charlie's first love, though. After establishing his carpenter license, he went to work for a local finishing carpentry company, Carter Construction. They specialized in cabinets and built-in entertainment units. But on weekends Charlie helped his dad.

According to Richelle, Charlie enjoyed both occupations but had chosen construction over the car repair business. His father had been disappointed but had come to terms with his son's decision.

When the two girls pulled up in front of the shop, Richelle looked at Tessa nervously. Tessa gave her a thumbs up before heading inside.

The possibility of Charlie's rage exploding didn't stem Tessa's nervousness. Self-control wasn't one of his finer qualities. Sweat beaded her brow as Richelle walked up to the front desk.

"Hi. Is Charlie here?"

"Do you want Charlie Kendal or Charlie Glidden?" The overweight, middle-aged woman wore a top two sizes too small, emphasizing her liberal curves, her rolls hanging copiously over her waistline. Her name tag read, "Maxine."

"Charlie Kendal, please." Richelle glanced around nervously for any sign of him.

"I'll go see if he's still here, dear." Maxine stood, walked through a door and into the shop beyond.

A minute later Charlie appeared in the doorway and walked briskly up to Richelle. "What are you doing here? Everything that needs to be said has already been said. So what do you want?"

"Charlie, please." Richelle's face twisted in pain. She looked ready to break down in tears. "I want you to come back. I was telling you the truth the other night. Tessa was with us and she's here to confirm what I told you. Please listen to her, okay?"

Begging wasn't Richelle's style. It sounded foreign coming from her pretty, painted lips. She must be really desperate to stoop this low and like him a great deal to endure his mistrust of her.

Tessa cleared her throat. "She's been telling you the truth. Richelle, Luke and I were all together that night. We met at Michael's Mocha Shop after dinner. We had coffee and a short visit then drove over to the mansion. Everything Richelle told you about that old house is true." She waited to see his response.

Charlie stared at her suspiciously and finally said, "Alright." His eyes held doubt as he nodded his head and looked from Tessa to Richelle and back again. "Okay, tell me what happened in that house that night. Tell me all the details and I'll see if it lines up with Richelle's story."

Tessa didn't like Charlie one bit. Whatever Richelle saw in him, she couldn't imagine. The guy was brash, loud, jealous and suspicious...and the list could go on. Tessa didn't have time. She was here for the express purpose of helping Richelle. Her focus needed to stay clear, divulge the necessary points and leave the rest unsaid.

"Is there another room where we could talk?" Tessa didn't want Maxine listening in on their conversation. The woman was already watching intently from behind her desk, listening to their every word.

Charlie led them to the back of the shop into an office and, after they entered, he closed the door. He leaned back against the mahogany desk, clasped his hands in front and stared at Tessa with a scowl. No offer to sit in the padded chairs was made, so the girls stood facing him.

Tessa told him all the details. It took her a good half hour to re-tell the story. She told up to the point when Richelle had left that night. When she was done, Charlie remained quiet and deep in thought. He studied his hands. After what seemed like an eternity to Tessa, he finally looked up.

"You actually expect me to believe this pile of dung?"

"Luke can verify the entire story!" protested Tessa angrily.

"Oh yes, Luke!" Charlie's eyes darted to Richelle. "By the way, where is Luke? Have you been keeping him company this week?"

"Please, Charlie, don't do this. I haven't seen him at all this week. He's a friend and that's all he is to me. That's all he'll ever be to me. You're the only one I'll ever love."

That seemed to soften him somewhat. His eyes took on a lighter hue and he grew quiet again. Finally he said, "Either you two have put your heads together and come up with this well-devised, cockamamie story or there really is something to it. It's a little too strange to believe. And why didn't it happen when I went there?" He turned a hard gaze on Tessa. "Can you explain that?"

"I don't know. I don't understand all of this either. All I do know is that Luke and Richelle were with me that night. When they were ready to leave I stayed. It wasn't because they didn't want me with them; they asked me to join them. Curiosity kept me at the mansion. Luke and Richelle had both seen enough. I can vouch that there's nothing going on between the two of them. In fact, Richelle was actually quite angry with Luke before we went to the house. She threatened not to go if he didn't stop irritating her. I can assure you that they have a completely innocent relationship." Tessa hoped this would be enough to assuage his doubts.

Charlie confronted Richelle. "What was Luke irritating you about?"

Richelle looked immediately uncomfortable. Tessa knew why. The irritation had been over Luke's negative evaluation of Charlie. It would be interesting to see how Richelle covered this one.

"Luke has a way of irritating me no matter what he says. Tessa is our referee. She comes to our rescue and keeps us from strangling each other."

Charlie actually grinned at that.

Richelle didn't waste any time. "I want you to come back to me. Please say yes!"

Charlie then shook his head. "I don't know. I need to think about it. I've had this kind of thing happen to me before and I don't take too kindly to having you doing things behind my back."

"I didn't mean to, honest...!"

117

He held up a hand to stop her. "Give me a day to think this over and I'll give you a call. Is that fair enough?"

"Yes, Charlie, that's fair. I'll be waiting." Her eyes pleaded with him. "I want you back more than anything and I would never do anything to hurt you. You have to know that."

"I have my doubts. I need time to think things over." He still looked immovable but the hard, cold stare from his eyes had softened some.

"All...right." Richelle looked completely out of her element. She was no longer in charge and she floundered because of it. She took a step toward him. "I love you, Charlie, and I don't know how I'd live without you."

Tessa restrained a smile at the amusing display of desperation.

Charlie walked around her, opened the office door and escorted the girls out. He stood at the front door and Tessa could see him watching them as they entered the car, started up and pulled away.

"Thanks, Tessa. You don't know how much I appreciate your help."

"I just hope it made a difference. Charlie still seemed very upset. I don't know if he believed me."

"You should have seen him when he found out that Luke had taken me home. I thought he was going to hit me."

"Are you sure this is the guy for you, Richelle?" asked Tessa anxiously. I don't want to upset you further, but if he gets angry enough to want to hit you, you should not be with him."

"Oh, I don't think he'd actually do it. He gets extremely jealous but he's not violent. I'm in love with him, Tessa, and I can't change that. He's my whole life and I absolutely can't live without him. This has been the most miserable week of my life and I have to get him back somehow."

Tessa noticed Richelle turn toward The Eating Place.

"Could you drop me off at my house? I don't need to go back to the restaurant."

"Oh, I'm not thinking straight, am I? Sorry about that." She turned the Honda around and headed towards Tessa's neighborhood.

After parking by the curb Richelle turned and said, "Could I ask you a favor?"

"Sure, ask me anything."

"If Charlie insists on going back to the old mansion to check out our story, would you be willing to go with us?"

The uneasy feeling returned and Tessa's stomach began to churn again. "I guess so, as long as it doesn't interfere with my work schedule. Just give me a call."

"Thanks again, Tessa. You're a true friend."

Tessa got out and Richelle drove off. She walked toward the house and sat down on the front step. Thoughts of Richelle crowded her mind. She didn't know why they had become such good friends. They were as different as night and day and held some very different values. The life that Richelle was living would not be an option for Tessa. Her parents had drilled godly principles into her. Living common-law was frowned upon in the March home. Although Tessa didn't agree with Richelle's lifestyle she still valued her as a friend.

Richelle saw nothing wrong with living with Charlie. Her parents struggled to get along and her mother had encouraged her to get to know the man before making anything permanent.

Tessa met Richelle in tenth grade. A few months into the school year, Richelle had moved into the area and they ended up in most of the same classes. She could still remember how Richelle looked the first time she saw her. She was excessively thin, not very developed at the time and very nervous. During one lunch break Tessa noticed her sitting alone and decided to sit with her. Richelle's initial appearance of shy quietness was dispelled when she revealed her true self. After only a few questions, Richelle had opened up and given her a full update on her life. Tessa opened up then and shared some things about her life as well.

The connection was made and a routine was formed; they sat together every lunch and got to know each other quickly. It didn't take long to discover how close they lived to each other; they just ended up taking different routes to and from home. Soon they spent evenings in each other's company, jointly tackled homework after school in the library and walked home together.

Although Tessa had other friends in school, they faded in importance after she met Richelle. She and Richelle became fast friends. Even though they didn't agree on religion and faith, Richelle was fun to be with and she was the most giving person

Tessa had ever met. True and faithful friends were hard to find.

By the time they reached eleventh grade, Richelle was fully developed and receiving plenty of male attention. Tessa could have dressed to get more looks but she chose not to. She knew she was good looking, although not as stunningly beautiful as Richelle, but didn't let it bother her. Their friendship was worth more than surface issues.

Luke had moved to the area early in their eleventh grade. Tessa noticed the new kid sitting by himself often at lunchtime. He threw Richelle looks now and then but she didn't notice. Tessa pointed him out to her and suggested showing him some friendliness. Being game, they'd walked over and asked if he wanted company. With his agreement secured, their threesome friendship started. At first he was interested in more than just friendship with Richelle but they soon found out how incompatible they were. They had fun as friends but that's as far as it went.

Luke didn't live far out of the way so they started walking home as a threesome and over the year they became close friends. There were others that he hung out with but he always considered Tessa and Richelle his special friends. Being a natural sports enthusiast, he tried out for every sports team in high school and was especially talented on the football team.

Thinking about their friendship brought back some sharp as well as sweet memories. Tessa knew it was her effort that had started their threesome relationship and she was so thankful for it. Both friends had brought such enjoyment and support into her life. It was so entertaining to sit and listen to Luke and Richelle banter back and forth – at least when it didn't turn into a fight which needed her refereeing. She was glad they had kept up their friendship over the years. It wasn't easy with all of them going in different directions but it was definitely worth the effort.

Suddenly the door behind her opened and she turned and saw her brother, Joe, step outside.

"Oh, you're home! Luke called a few minutes ago and I told him that you weren't around. He wants you to call him back as soon as you can." He took a step toward her and then said, "What are you doing out here all by yourself?"

"I'm just thinking about things. What did you do today?"

"Not a whole lot. I hung out with some friends earlier. I

actually studied for one of my exams. Can you believe that?"

"That is a shock! When's your exam?"

"On Monday. I have two of them on Monday. I thought I'd better be prepared. I sure hope I pass tenth grade."

"I'm sure you will. You're not actually worried, are you?"

"No, not really but I don't want to take a chance." He grinned crookedly. Joe was sixteen and school wasn't his favorite thing. Baseball season was well under way; he'd had a game last night. Spending time with his friends and being involved in sports ranked higher than studies. "I just have to apply myself and I know I'll do fine. Well, I'm heading out." He jumped the steps and landed on the walkway. Turning to face her, he walked backward and said, "I'm going to see a movie with Ralph."

"Have a good time."

"Will do." He then ran toward the sidewalk and turned left. Ralph lived a few houses down.

Tessa stood, walked up the two steps, opened the door and entered the house.

She punched in Luke's number and waited for him to answer. "Hello?"

"Hi there, Luke! What's up?"

"I'm so glad you called, sweetheart."

She grinned. Luke and all his terms of endearment. They always made her smile.

"I have a situation here that I want to discuss with you," he said. "I spent some time with Darren today and I happened to mention to him about the mansion and all that happened there. Well, he insisted that we go and check it out. You know Darren, he's terribly curious."

Oh no! Not another one! Why are they involving other people? This is making everything so complicated. I don't like it, not one bit!

She pushed down the feeling of panic and forced herself to listen calmly.

"Well, we went over there but nothing happened – nothing at all. I wanted to know if you've been back there since last Saturday."

"No, no I haven't."

"So, what do you make of it?"

This is just like Richelle's experience and is too weird!

"Tessa, are you there?"

"Yeah…I'm here. I don't know what to make of it."

"Do you think it has something to do with just the three of us? Is that why it didn't work for Darren?"

"I'm not sure."

"It has to have something to do with it," Luke said, sounding frustrated.

"It could be a timing thing. Maybe it'll only happen at certain times."

"I don't know. I find it super strange."

"Going back in time is strange, Luke!"

"I know, but so far it's only happened when we three are together. I'm just trying to figure this out."

"I've wracked my brain too and I don't understand it"

Luke said, "We should go there again, just the three of us, to see if it happens again. Are you up for it?"

"What do you mean? Now?"

"This weekend sometime. I don't have anything else planned."

"Well, I do. I'm going out tonight with Cody to a youth concert in the park. It was cancelled last week and they rescheduled it for tonight. Cody is very excited about it and I'm not backing out on him."

"Whoa! Are you two getting serious or what?"

"I made Cody a promise, that's all."

"I don't know. It's sounding serious to me." His chuckle tickled her ear. "Well, what about Sunday? Do you have any time to spare then?"

"I'm going to church in the morning. Maybe the afternoon or evening would work. You'll have to check with Richelle to see if it'll suit her."

"I can do that. I'll call her as soon as I get off the phone with you. Then I'll get back to you."

Tessa hung up the phone and hoped Richelle would say no. She was in no mood to go back to the mansion so soon.

CHAPTER 9

Twenty minutes later, the phone on the counter rang and Tessa hesitantly picked it up. "Hello?" she asked, carrying the phone to the kitchen table. Pulling out a chair, she sat cross-legged and twirled a piece of her hair around her index finger.

"Hi, it's me." Richelle's enthusiasm was unmistakable.

"Did Luke call you?"

"Yeah. I told him the only way I'd go again was if Charlie could come with us."

"What'd he say?"

"He didn't like it at first. He told me about his fiasco with Darren. He believes the time change will only happen with the three of us together. I didn't tell him I took Charlie there too. The last thing I need is Luke knowing about my problems with Charlie right now. He doesn't think much of Charlie as it is and I don't want him having any more ammunition. He'll just rub it in my face."

"I don't think Luke would do that. He does care about you, you know?"

"It's hard to tell sometimes."

She couldn't disagree. "So did he consent to Charlie coming along?"

"He did eventually."

"Have you passed it by Charlie?"

"No, not yet. I'll call him tonight and invite him."

Tessa felt sudden trepidation over going back to the unknown. "I just don't know if it's time to go back."

"What do you mean? If it could help Charlie and me get back together I think it would be superb timing. Luke's up for it, I'm ready to go back and the only one stalling is you. Please say yes. It's a very easy decision, if you ask me."

"You make it sound so painless." And yet the anxiety she felt wouldn't budge. "Why don't you wait to hear from Charlie and get back to me? Then we'll be able to plan something more concrete. We don't even know if he'll agree to this plan."

"Luke mentioned you were heading out tonight. What time should I call you back?"

"Well, how about if I call you?"

"Sure, sounds good to me. I'll talk to you later. Gotta run. Bye!"

Tessa pushed the "off" button and gazed at the phone resting in her hands. This pressure to go back drove her peace of mind out of reach. The angel had given clear instructions concerning visiting the mansion. There would be some kind of sign. Not that she knew what that was. Come to think of it, the instructions he gave were rather vague. Could the indication possibly be pressure from her friends? Was that the sign?

An uneasy feeling wrapped around her heart. Surely the signal would bring a complete knowing and a guarantee of direction, even a settling peace. Serenity was crowded out by this disturbing uncertainty she felt.

Silently, she prayed that it would be easy for her to discern the right timing and that the sign would be clear. Tessa slowly straightened her legs, returned the phone to its base and walked to her room to prepare for her evening with Cody.

~~~~~

It was just before eleven when Cody dropped Tessa off at her house. She walked through the front door with a smile. The evening had been more enjoyable than she'd imagined it could be. The bands that performed in the park had been very good. The crowd of youth had testified to that with their wild dancing, shouting and carrying on. Her brothers attended the event too but she hardly saw them in the huge crowd that filled the grounds. They'd been with their friends from another youth group in the city.

Being with Cody was becoming comfortable and she liked what she saw in him. He was very good with the youth and they respected him. "My youth," as he called them, were from the downtown district, the rough part of the city, and most had a lot to overcome. They were loud, rough, came with enough baggage to fill a train and yet respected and listened to whatever Cody told them. His way with them had caused her esteem of him to grow.

Cody had taken her out to eat before they headed to the park so, at her request, he took her home right after the concert.

Richelle would be waiting for her call. Tessa pulled her cell from her purse and punched in the number.

Richelle answered, "Finally! I've been waiting endlessly!"

"I called as soon as I stepped in the door."

"I know; it's just that I've been so impatient. Charlie called me tonight." She sounded breathless with excitement. "You'll never believe it!"

"What?"

"He told me that he loves me and wants to give us another chance. He wants to go over to the mansion with all of us and see if anything happens."

"And, what if nothing happens?"

"Tessa, don't say that!"

"Hypothetically."

"He did mention that if nothing happens, we're through."

"Well, then I hope for your sake we go back in time."

"I'm crossing my fingers already."

"Where should we meet and when?"

"Why don't we meet at Michael's Mocha Shop again?" Richelle waited for Tessa's response. "Are you still there?"

"I'm still debating whether this is the right time to head back to the mansion."

"Why would you say such a thing? Charlie wants to come and I need to prove to him that I wasn't lying. There's no better time than the present, Tessa. Please be a friend!"

She sighed in resignation, "All right, we'll go."

"Thank you, thank you! You don't know how much this means to me."

"Okay, tomorrow afternoon at Michael's. That'll work for me. Why don't we meet at three?"

"Sure, I'll call Luke and Charlie and let them know. Thanks a lot, Tessa. You're a life saver."

~~~~~~

The coffee shop was quiet. Besides the four of them, only two others sat at a table to the side, talking quietly. After ordering drinks, they found a table for four close to the window.

Tension filled the air, with Charlie and Richelle sitting on one side and Luke and Tessa on the other. Charlie refused to look at Luke, ignoring him entirely, keeping his eyes glued to his black coffee. Luke looked equally as uncomfortable. Once in a while Charlie stole a look in Richelle's direction, as though he were monitoring her faithfulness, watching her eyes. Richelle carried most of the conversation but even then it was sporadic and awkward. Tessa tried to keep up idle chatter with her but the strain between the guys was thick enough to cut with a knife. It made amiable discussion nearly impossible.

Luke finally said, "Well, I'm in the mood for something sweet and fattening." He pointed to a sign on the front counter. "Do you see that sign? They have fresh angel food cake with whipped cream and strawberries. It looks delicious and I'm going to get some." He stood and said, "I'm offering to buy today, so who else wants some?"

Tessa was sure she heard bells ring while Luke made his announcement and she looked around to see the source. She'd never heard that sound in this coffee shop before. Maybe they'd installed a new bell over the door.

No one spoke.

Richelle was the first to respond. "No thanks, I'll pass."

Charlie refused to reply or even look at him, glaring into his cup of coffee.

Tessa, did you want some angel food cake?"

Swinging around to face Luke, she said, "I heard it again."

"What are you talking about?" He looked impatient.

"Bells. I'm hearing bells ring."

"Looney tunes," whispered Charlie from his side, a crooked smile barely visible from his bent head position.

It was plenty loud enough for Tessa to catch. She glowered at him. He purposely kept his gaze fixated on his mug. A good kick under the table would wipe that stupid smile off his face. She resisted the urge.

Luke said, "When did you hear bells ring? I haven't heard a thing."

Turning to him, she said, "I don't know." She felt confused. "You didn't hear them?"

"No. All I hear is that sign calling to me." He pointed to the scrumptious picture of the cake.

She looked at the door again. No one new had entered the establishment in a while.

Richelle said, "Maybe it's someone's cell ring-tone."

"Mine's set on strum," admitted Tessa. "Does someone have theirs set to bells?"

"Nope," declared Luke.

Richelle shook her head and Charlie refused to respond.

Tessa said, "Angel food cake, huh?" Bells immediately rang again. "There, they just rang again!" She looked at Luke; surely he would have heard it this time.

He shook his head. "Nope, darling, not a thing."

Charlie chuckled quietly. Richelle told him to hush. Tessa felt like a fool. Luke stared at her with a dumbfounded look.

"What's going on here?" asked Tessa. "Someone's trying to pull my leg, right?"

Luke held up both hands. "Honestly, no. I wouldn't do such a thing."

"Yeah, right!" declared Richelle. "Luke would never do such a thing!"

"Stop with the sarcasm, Richelle," demanded Luke.

"You have a bell and you're ringing it, right?" Tessa asked Luke.

He looked at her. "No, I don't and I'm not."

Tessa released a frustrated sigh and thought things over.

Luke and Richelle were getting into a word war again but Tessa ignored them. She glanced at Charlie who was listening to the two and their verbal jousting with some surprise, his face registering revelation.

I think I've got it.

"Say it again."

They all looked at her.

"Say it again."

"What?" asked Luke.

"The cake name."

His face twisted in bewilderment. "Angel food cake?"

"There, I heard the bells again!" Tessa felt triumphant.

"So, you're telling me that whenever I say angel food cake you hear bells ringing?" Luke wore an incredulous grin.

The bells rang once more. Clear understanding flooded her at that moment. This was the sign. It was time to go back.

Luke asked, "What's this about, Tessa?"

"Oh, it's nothing important."

Richelle said, "Tell us, Tessa."

"Not now." She stood and grabbed her purse. "I need the ladies' room."

"Tessa!" shouted Richelle in frustration.

"You can't leave us high and dry like this," protested Luke, his palms held out in petition, as Tessa walked past him.

Smiling sweetly, Tessa ignored them and walked on. Richelle and Luke were perpetually curious. It would do them good to wait. Tessa needed to process what was happening first. What if she was wrong? She didn't want to divulge anything prematurely.

When Tessa returned, Luke was devouring his cake while Richelle sipped at her soda and Charlie downed his coffee. Richelle gave her a curious look but didn't pursue the bell subject, for which Tessa was grateful. After the cake had disappeared into Luke's cavernous stomach, they quickly made the decision to head on to the mansion.

The empty house was a mere two blocks away so they decided to walk over. The sun shone through the overhanging branches of the century-old trees, making dappled shadows on the sidewalk. It was another beautiful spring day and Tessa gratefully breathed in the fresh spring air. It ended up being a quiet, peaceful walk. Tessa was relieved to be outdoors, away from Charlie's mocking gaze and the tenseness back at the coffee shop. Richelle and Charlie led the way and Tessa was thankful for it. She didn't need him snickering at her from behind. Trying to like him was growing increasingly difficult.

They came to the decrepit house and after standing and studying the undermined ghost of a thing for a minute, they walked through the gate. Luke and Tessa took the lead with Charlie and

Richelle following. As Luke and Tessa passed the old oak tree everything changed around them and they were back to January 1946, with snow blanketing the scenery. Tessa heard Charlie gasp behind them. This time he was seeing what they saw.

"Interesting," whispered Tessa.

"What is?" asked Luke.

She looked at him, surprised he had heard her. "Oh nothing." She waved a hand around. "This."

He nodded. "It doesn't get old."

Luke still didn't know everything about Charlie's earlier visit here and she wasn't about to spill the beans. That was Richelle's job.

Tessa scanned the grounds for the angel in his black trench coat but he wasn't around; at least he wasn't showing himself yet.

Slowly they walked toward the mansion, the atmosphere tingling with excitement of the unknown.

"Does anyone know what this is about?" Charlie asked. "Why does it happen when the three of you are together? There must be some reason for it."

Luke answered, "Well, from what I can gather this seems to only occur when Tessa graces us with her presence. Do you have any idea why, Tessa?"

Tessa stopped short and stared at him. "What? You think this has to do with me?"

"That's all I can figure."

His words froze her inside. She had never come to that conclusion before.

So I'm the pivotal person here? This happens because of me? This is way too personal!

Fear danced up her spine and her throat tensed. Before she could get a grip on the terror pulling at her, she heard a noise from the street. Everyone turned to look in that direction. An antique car – antique to them but shiny new in 1946, came to a stop in front of the gate. The back door opened and Mr. Hardington stepped out. He turned to help Mary exit from the back. The driver stepped out from the car and opened the back door on the other side. Mrs. Hardington appeared and hurried over to take Mary's arm to assist her to the house.

Mr. Hardington turned for a moment and spoke to the driver.

"Edward, please drive the vehicle into the back garage."

"Yes, sir." Edward drove off.

The front door of the house opened and a servant, one the three friends hadn't seen before, held the door for Mr. and Mrs. Hardington and their daughter. Tessa and her companions stepped off the path to let the Hardingtons pass. Standing in the piled snow, feeling the chill on their legs, they kept their gaze on the threesome entering the mansion.

"They didn't see us at all. Why?" Charlie stared at the front door, awestruck.

"Didn't I tell you?" asked Richelle. "They can't see us. We're not really here with them. To us, it appears that we are. We can see everything that took place back then, but they can't see us. If you get in their way, they walk right through you." She turned to Luke. "Isn't that right, Luke?" Suddenly Richelle looked relieved, more confident and relaxed. She even gave a small chuckle.

"Don't remind me. That's one experience I don't care to recall."

Tessa said, "It's like we're here but we're not here. We can see everything but we can't interact with them."

"This is psychedelic!" exclaimed Charlie.

Tessa asked, "So, are you all ready to go on in?" Without waiting for a response, she turned and headed toward the house.

The others followed her up the steps, across the deck and into one of the side doors. They saw William and Elizabeth Hardington standing in the foyer discussing something. Off to the side, close to the stairway, stood Mary, well-dressed, with her hair curled and pinned up. She looked very fatigued, her face turned to the floor, her body swaying gently back and forth. However, except for her despondent stance, she looked quite normal.

The servant who had opened the doorway walked away, carrying the coats the Hardingtons had shed.

"I believe Mary will be cured in no time. This past week we have seen so many improvements. Even the doctor was very encouraged." William looked a lot more hopeful than he had a week ago.

"Dear, I feel we shouldn't rush Mary too much. She still needs to rest and recuperate fully. The doctor said she'll need a significant respite."

"What do doctors know anyway? They always try to impress people with their so-called knowledge." William pointed to his daughter. "It's quite clear that Mary has improved and perhaps within a week she'll be able to start at the bank. Wouldn't that put the doctor to shame?" He chuckled and turned to Mary. "What would you say, Mary, about starting with me at the bank soon? Giving you another week to recuperate should be plenty of time."

Mary's head jerked unnaturally, snapped to attention and she stared wild-eyed at her father. A horrible, wounded scream erupted from her and her violent head-shaking began again. Bringing her hands up to the sides of her head, it looked like she was attempting to shut out her own noise. Her intense shaking caused her hair to come undone, pins letting loose and making a clicking sound as they hit the floor. Strands of hair cascaded around her shoulders. The shaking was also throwing her off balance. She was about to fall when William reached her and took a firm hold.

William and Elizabeth both called out for their servants to help. A handful of servants appeared almost immediately and when they saw what was happening, quickly helped to assist Mary upstairs.

"I'm calling the doctor. He needs to get over here immediately! I don't know what he's been doing but so far it hasn't helped at all! He has some explaining to do!" With that, William turned and walked briskly into his study.

Elizabeth started up the stairs to see to her daughter, who was being accompanied to the second level ahead of her by the servants. She looked overcome by discouragement as she walked slowly but deliberately to the top floor.

Tessa spoke up as the other three continued to watch Elizabeth ascend the stairway. "Why don't we go to the sitting room for a while? We can come back and see what happens when the doctor arrives."

The others agreed and followed her to the expansive room off the foyer. There was no fire blazing in the fireplace today, making the room feel cool, drafty and much too large. The couches had lost none of their appeal so they sat down. Quietness filled the space for a few minutes, everyone lost in thought. Charlie was the first to speak.

"So what's up with this family? Do you know any of their

relatives that are living in our time? And why is this happening? I don't understand the reason for this time change thing."

Luke gave him a hard stare. "You sure are full of questions all of a sudden. Back at Michael's Mocha Shop, you wouldn't even look at me, never mind speak to me. What's up with you?"

Oh no! Here goes!

Charlie's eyes turned dark. "Hey, I thought you were messing around with my girl. That's something I don't take too kindly to. When I found out you had taken her home the other night and she came home so late, I had my suspicions. No one messes with Charlie Kendal or his girl!"

"Oh…! So that's it." Luke grinned. "Well, I can assure you there's nothing going on with the two of us. Richelle and I are friends and that's all we'll ever be. So just take a pill and relax. You're too uptight, Charlie."

Charlie's face turned red.

"Hey," said Luke, "can't you see Richelle adores you? She'd do anything for you. She loves you, man. In fact, she told the two of us that the other night."

Tessa gazed at Luke in amazement. He was actually defending Richelle to Charlie. It was such a rare occurrence, a sign of true friendship, that she could do nothing but stare at him.

"You did?" Charlie turned to look at Richelle seated beside him, his fury subsiding.

"That's what I've been telling you, Charlie. You just don't seem to hear me."

"Well, I love you too, Doll!" The two of them embraced and kissed.

Luke said, "Okay, that's enough, you two. If you want to keep that up, then head on home. We don't need a show."

Just then Tessa thought of something. She turned to Luke and asked, "Do you remember the last time we were in this room? You were telling us about Mary's diary and what you read in it. You never did finish telling us about it. Mary's scream interrupted our conversation. What did you find in her diary?"

"Oh yeah, that's right." He leaned back into the couch, lifted a leg, rested it on his other knee and said, "Well, she wrote about her grandmother, Eunice. According to the entry date she wrote it a few months back. Surprisingly, she was terrified of turning out like her grandmother. She'd had a string of nightmares about losing her mind and turning crazy. Apparently her grandmother went a little cuckoo as a young mom. With two small kids and her husband working out of state, rail construction or something, she didn't cope well. The strain of it all apparently pushed her to the limit and she suffered a nervous breakdown. The two children were placed with relatives for a while."

Luke's gaze shifted to a spot across the room and he looked deep in thought.

"Did she write anything else?" asked Tessa

Luke turned and locked eyes with her. "Yeah. I read a few of her entries. Mary wrote about when her grandfather, William's father, passed away. William was in his twenties, newly married, doing well in business and supplied funds to care for his mother in her own home. As the Hardingtons increased in wealth and moved to a much larger house, Elizabeth began to insist they take William's mother into their home and care for her. William was very opposed to it at first but after constant begging from his wife, he finally gave in.

"Mary wrote in her diary that it dramatically affected her. She was ten at the time and had rarely seen her grandmother. The questions she asked her parents brought only veiled answers. Apparently her grandmother would rant and rave over insignificant things and let out these unexpected screams that would send chills down her spine. When they'd invite guests over her father would lock Eunice into her bedroom so she wouldn't embarrass them."

"That's so cruel," stated Richelle. "I may not like my mother but I wouldn't do that to her!"

Luke chuckled. "Apparently, according to Mary, Eunice hated being locked up. She would pound on her door and scream to be let out. William then began to sedate her with sleeping pills before guests would arrive just to keep her calm." He shook his head in wonder. "This is quite the family, isn't it?"

Richelle said, "I'll say! It looks like Mary really is taking after her grandmother. That's horrible. She's so young and has her whole life in front of her. She doesn't need this."

Tessa stared at her friend. This was the first sympathetic thing Richelle had uttered about the situation. It surprised her. She could actually feel empathy growing in her own heart as she learned more about Mary.

Luke said, "I can't imagine having dreams of going crazy! How terrifying would that be?"

Tessa nodded. "It would be awful! And now it's coming true. I sure hope she snaps out of this." Sympathy for Mary started to overwhelm her.

Richelle said, "I hope so too. It sure would be an awful thing to live with for a whole lifetime."

Commotion in the lobby drew their attention. Someone was knocking on the front door and they heard footsteps. The four of them hurried to the lobby. A servant pulled the door open and a man entered.

"Hello, James. How are you this evening?"

"I'm well, sir. Here let me take your coat, Dr. Maxwell. Mr. Hardington is in his office. Just follow me and I'll announce you."

"Oh, that won't be necessary. I'll announce myself. Thank you, James."

James nodded and carried the doctor's heavy winter coat to another room. The doctor walked briskly to the office door, knocked and, after William's invitation to enter, went on in. He left the door slightly ajar so the four intruders walked over to the office to listen in on the conversation.

William filled the doctor in on Mary's condition and let the doctor know how upset he was that things had regressed.

After clearing his throat, Dr. Maxwell said, "I warned you that recovery time could be extensive. I have seen only a few others in Mary's condition. I've read quite a few case studies, though, and in every one there's an extensive recovery time. You can't be too impatient, Mr. Hardington. What Mary needs right now is a lot of love, care and a tremendous amount of rest. I have read about a specialist in mental illness that works out of a hospital in Chicago. If there is little or no improvement in Mary's condition within the next week, I might suggest taking her there for further testing. I've heard that they have come up with new systems of treating psychosis. These methods are very new so I don't have a lot of documented proof to show their effectiveness but I have researched the procedure thoroughly. If you are willing to allow Mary to go in a week's time, I could arrange it for you."

Discouragement filled William's eyes at the doctor's words. "I don't know if Elizabeth and I could handle sending our daughter off to Chicago. She's the only child we have. How could we bear to part with her?"

"What you could do, if you don't mind my suggestion, is rent a room or a house close to the hospital for Elizabeth. That way she could be close to her daughter and give her some moral support. She wouldn't be able to be with her during the procedures but she could spend time with her between and after them."

"What kind of procedures are you talking about? Are they safe? They won't harm my daughter, will they?"

"The treatment is called electroconvulsive shock therapy. An Italian doctor, Ugo Cerletti, came up with the invention. It's been tested repeatedly and Ugo has had tremendous success in treating schizophrenic patients and also those with severe depression. It has helped many patients return to a more normal state of mind. Since its inception in 1938, this method of treatment has spread quickly in the medical arena. Just within the last year I've been reading articles sent out by the Psychiatry and Mental Health Department and they name this procedure as one of the most effective in treating mental illness."

With a shake of his head, William said, "I don't believe my daughter has mental illness. She's been under tremendous stress and I believe that all she needs is more rest. I don't appreciate you suggesting that she's suffered a mental lapse!"

"I can understand your concerns about not putting a label on your daughter at this time but you do have to agree that her behavior has not been normal. I'm only saying that if things don't improve within the next week or if Mary regresses even further that there is an option available to you."

"Alright. I don't want you to do anything yet, Dr. Maxwell. I want to give Mary another week's reprieve and if there's no change at that time then I'll agree to your arrangement. I want the best for my daughter and if this procedure is something that will facilitate her recuperation, then I'd be willing to consider it."

"I'll come back next week to check on her again. I'd like to go upstairs and see how she is right now." The doctor waited for William's approval.

"Sure, why don't you go on up. Do you remember where her room is?"

"Yes, I do."

The four friends heard chairs moving. Tessa was the closest to the door and peeked in to see the two men shaking hands.

"Thank you, Doctor. I appreciate your willingness to come out on such short notice."

"Anything for you, sir. Now I'll go check on Mary."

The four moved to the side as the doctor exited the office and headed up the stairway.

"Do you guys want to go upstairs and see what's up with Mary?" Luke asked.

"Not me. I don't want to listen to any more screaming. It's too unnerving!" Richelle shuddered.

Tessa had no desire to listen to any ear-shattering noise either. She suggested, "Why don't we stay down in the sitting room for a bit and see if anything else happens?"

"Yeah, I'll go for that." Richelle followed Tessa.

"You know, I just started on this adventure and I'd love to explore this house." Charlie looked at Luke. "Why don't you show me around?"

"Sure, I could do that. We'll see you girls later." They turned and headed off to explore.

As Tessa took a seat on the couch she said, "Things are sure turning around. Charlie's even speaking to Luke now."

"It's astounding! I didn't think they'd ever warm up to each other."

"Maybe 'warming up' is too positive of a description yet," chided Tessa.

"Okay, I guess you're right. They're leaving the glacier fields behind. How's that?"

"It's a start."

They grinned at each other. Richelle wore a contented expression. Tessa was glad for her but her thoughts veered towards the Hardingtons' difficulties. Mary's problems seemed far from over. She wondered how much of Mary's life they'd be allowed to see.

"Isn't this a strange thing, Tessa? Don't you find this like totally bizarre?"

"What? Do you mean this whole experience or Mary's situation?"

"All of it. Why is this happening? I'm thinking you know because it only happens when you're with us. Do you have any clue?"

It irritated her to have Richelle draw that conclusion. "I only know a little." Maybe this was the moment to divulge some information. "Do you remember the man in the trench coat?"

"Yeah. What about him?"

"Well, the other night after you and Luke left he showed up and talked to me. He didn't give me a lot of information but he did tell me who he was." Tessa filled in the details for Richelle.

"An angel? Are you serious?"

Tessa nodded.

"Wow! An angel appeared to you? Do you believe in angels?"

"I always knew they existed but I didn't know God would send them to unimportant people like me. I guess I don't know a whole lot about them. From what he said, this message from God is going to be progressive and I have to figure it out as I go. To tell you the truth I'm not that comfortable with all this supernatural stuff. It makes me nervous!"

Richelle clapped her hands. "Well, I think it's exciting! I had no idea God did stuff like this! My image of him was that he was somewhat of a bore, outlawing anything fun, demanding and hard to please. Religion has never been a top priority for me. My parents aren't religious by any definition and I think they're pretty decent people. They're nicer than a lot of Christians I've met, except for you, of course." She gave a lopsided grin. "You're wonderful!"

"Thanks."

"No problem." Richelle lounged back, her legs crossed.

"This time travel stuff and an angel appearing are totally new for me. It's taking me a while to adjust to it," said Tessa.

Richelle lifted her arm and let her hand drop at the wrist. "Oh, I've totally adjusted. This whole week I was itching to come back. When our visit here without you became a debacle I thought that was it, that it would never happen again. I was devastated. I mean Charlie's response was part of my despondency but I desperately wanted to go back in time again."

Tessa shook her head in surprise.

"What?" asked Richelle.

"I dread coming back."

"But why?"

"It still totally freaks me out. I like normal life better."

"But where's the adventure in normal?"

Tessa shrugged. Normal was comfortable, predictable.

After a few minutes, the guys returned and plopped down on the couches. Charlie sat beside Richelle and took her hand in his. The smile on his face was a telltale sign of his changed attitude.

Charlie was the first to speak. "This house is amazing! These people are, were, whatever – they're loaded. The furniture, flooring, artwork, paintings, light fixtures and everything looks expensive and high-end all the way. I can't believe people actually live like this or maybe I should say, lived like this."

Luke said, "I have to agree with Charlie, this house is amazing! Did you girls know that there's another type of sitting room on the other side of the house? It looks more like a den for the old man. It has hunting trophies on wall shelves, a deer head mounted above the fireplace and a moose head on another wall. All the furniture is made of leather in there. It definitely looks like a man's room. Right across from here on the other side of the foyer is a huge dining room. The table's made of solid wood and it's beautiful and massive. I bet you all of our families could fit around it and there'd still be room. It's amazing!"

"Didn't you see that the last time you went exploring?" asked Richelle

"No, I didn't get that far that night. There's so much to see in this house. I spent most of my time reading Mary's diary and exploring the top floor. Why aren't you girls interested in looking around?"

Richelle retorted, "For one thing, we're not as snoopy as you are. Secondly, we're more interested in the emotional, relational stuff. Don't you care that Mary might be going through electric shock treatment? It sounds horrible to me!" She shuddered.

"We don't know that she'll be going through that. Maybe in a week she'll have snapped out of it and everything will return to normal."

Tessa said, "I don't know. It looks to me like she's dealing with some major mental stress."

Luke stared from Tessa to Richelle. "What have you two been

discussing in here? You both look depressed."

Richelle said, "We're not depressed. We're just contemplative. Tessa told me some heavy stuff. This whole time travel isn't just an adventure for us; it seems this has a lot to do with Tessa."

Tessa wished Richelle would have left that out of the conversation. She wasn't ready for a group discussion on it.

Turning to her, Luke asked, "What's this about?"

At that moment they all heard commotion in the foyer.

The interruption well-timed, Tessa jumped up and headed to the foyer. The rest of them followed her.

Dr. Maxwell was on his way down the stairs and calling for his coat. James came scurrying down a hallway and told the doctor that he'd be right out with his things. The doctor set his medical bag down by the door and waited for James to return. Mr. Hardington must have heard the commotion as well because he appeared from his office.

James returned from the left side hallway with the doctor's coat and boots, which he handed to the man then quickly disappeared down the hallway again.

The doctor pulled on his boots and while he slipped into his coat, he said, "Mary has regressed again, William. The bright color she had in her cheeks earlier at my office is gone. She looks pale and extremely drained. Did anything occur that would have set her off again?"

"I don't know. I don't understand what's happening with her at all."

Richelle whispered, "Why doesn't he just admit it? I wish I could tell the doctor how controlling and pushy he is. He's the one who has strained her emotions to the max and he's still pushing her to start work at his stupid bank!"

Tessa shared Richelle's viewpoint, her blood pressure rising to prove it.

Luke said, "You sure have changed your attitude, Richelle. You didn't have much sympathy for Mary the other night."

"I hate when men try to control others. It makes me so angry."

"Oh you do?" Luke said sarcastically, his eyebrows raised.

Richelle returned the comment with a dirty look.

Tessa stifled a laugh.

Charlie remained oblivious to the exchange; his eyes were

riveted on Mr. Hardington and Dr. Maxwell.

"Give me a call tomorrow and let me know how Mary's doing."

The doctor left and William walked down the left side hallway. It became quiet in the foyer as the four visitors waited for a sign of any continued action.

Luke interrupted the silence. "Well it looks like the fun is done for today. I believe we've seen what there is to see. I'm ready to go. How about the rest of you?"

Richelle said, "I wish we could stay longer and that there was more happening. This visit is way too short."

Tessa disagreed. "I'm ready to go."

Luke headed to the door and the rest followed.

CHAPTER 10

It was quiet and peaceful as they walked back to Michael's Mocha Shop. Charlie looked somewhat shell-shocked over what he'd witnessed.

At the shop Richelle and Charlie said good-bye and left. Luke and Tessa stood on the sidewalk and watched them drive off. Checking the time on her cell phone, Tessa noticed it was only four-thirty and she had nothing planned until the evening.

Turning to Luke she asked, "Do you have time for a coffee, tea, pop, whatever? I have something on my mind and I'd really like to discuss it with you."

"Sure, sweetie, I'd love to."

They walked into the shop, ordered some coffee and took a booth toward the back. For a time they both sipped their hot drinks, their thoughts preoccupied with the events of the afternoon. Luke eventually peered curiously at her and broke the silence.

"So what's on your mind, beautiful?"

She smiled at his free-flowing pet names for her. They always made her feel treasured and special. This time with him meant a great deal to her after their long separation. Releasing a contented sigh, she said, "Do you remember what Richelle said at the mansion about this whole thing being about me?"

"Yeah. Is this a good time? Do you want to talk about it?"

"I'd like to if you don't mind listening for a while."

"I don't mind. Go for it."

Tessa took a deep breath and began. She told him about the angel and all that he'd said to her, explaining that the time travel was about a message that God was trying to get through to her. As she continued, Luke began to squirm, his discomfort increasing.

"Does this bother you?"

"Honestly, I've never given God much thought. I've never needed God; always managed fine without him. My take on it is

141

that people believe in a deity because they're weak. Not you, of course, but a lot of other people." He grimaced before continuing. "It seems a lot of people use 'God' as a crutch. When I'd hear them talk about angels and things like that I thought it was a bunch of hocus-pocus. I'm just not sure about all this angel stuff."

Tessa nodded in understanding. "It was hard for me to believe at first too. If the man in the trench coat hadn't told me he was an angel, I would have avoided the time travel. Going back in time makes me really uneasy and I'm still suspicious about it. I was perfectly fine with the way my life was going and to be completely honest, I'd prefer if this weren't happening. It's messing up my theology too and my neatly-made plans. I don't know why God would send an angel to me. I mean, who am I?"

"It does all sound a bit far-fetched." He shook his head slowly. "But after what we've seen at the mansion, I guess anything is possible. If the guy in the trench coat is an angel, he's the rudest angel I've ever met!"

"And how many have you met?"

He shrugged. "None."

"Till now."

Luke stared at her, deep in thought, bewilderment in his eyes. Finally, he said, "That angel was so obnoxious! He refused even to answer me that one night or shake my hand! Would an angel sent from God be that rude?"

"From what I've heard over the years in church, angels are very intense beings and when they bring a message they aren't doing it just to fill time. They're on a mission and don't waste words. They demand obedience and if a person doesn't receive that message or doubts that it's from God, the Bible records that punishment comes."

"Then this is serious stuff we're dealing with."

She released a nervous breath. "I would never have asked for this in a million years!"

"You could stop going."

"And that would help how?"

"Would an angel chase a person?"

She shrugged and felt nearly as ignorant as Luke appeared to be. "I don't believe I can walk away from it."

"You could try."

"Would you be okay just walking away and never going back?"

Luke squirmed. "I want to go back."

"Why?"

"It's exciting, adventurous! I've never been close to experiencing anything as amazing as this before."

"So it's the thrill of it that entices you."

"Definitely!"

"What if this didn't involve me? What if God was trying to get a message to you? Would you still find it exciting?"

He made a face and finally said, "I don't think I'd walk away. The pull of excitement would be too much to resist."

"See? That's my dilemma. I was totally satisfied with my life the way it was. Now I know that God has something else for me or wants to direct me somehow, it scares me. I don't know exactly how it all fits into my life. The variables on how this experience will influence my future make me skittish."

"So you believe God is showing you stuff to redirect you?"

"That's what I don't know. If he is, I'm not sure I want my life to be redirected. It makes me upset just talking about it!" Just sharing her feelings was causing her temperature to rise.

"This is so strange. Angels, huh? Maybe it's just a hallucination that we're all having at the same time. Have you ever seen an angel before?"

"Well, that was one of the reasons I wanted to talk with you." She hesitated for a moment before continuing. "This has happened to me once before."

"You're kidding!"

His shocked expression would have made her laugh if she wasn't so distraught.

"No, I'm not."

"Was it the same angel?"

"He looked exactly the same. It was a man in a black trench coat and he was wearing a hat. I never stuck around long enough for him to reveal who he was."

"When did that happen?" Luke scooted to the edge of his seat, curiosity oozing from him. It gave Tessa the courage to continue.

"I was sixteen, toward the end of grade ten. I met Richelle at the beginning of the school year so we were good friends by then.

She desperately wanted to move out on her own, get out from her parents' rule. She asked me to move in with her so that she could afford it. Money wasn't a huge issue for her because she worked weekends and some evenings. I also had a weekend job. We thought if we both pooled our money, we could rent an apartment or a small house together. Well, she found something listed in the paper that looked good to both of us. It was a small house on Target Street and it was only $250.00 a month, with utilities included. Richelle saw it in the paper on a Sunday and asked me to take a look at it Monday after school. She was scheduled to work."

Tessa took a sip of coffee and then continued. "I called the owner and he told me the house was empty, that I could pick up a key at his office and then return it when I was done. His office was only a block from the house. I believe it was early April and I was hoping we could rent it starting the first of May."

As Tessa retold the story, it felt like she was reliving it, with all the emotion and fear attached.

"After my last class that day, I took the bus over to the rental office, picked up the key from the receptionist and walked a block over on Target Street.

"The houses along the street were all tiny, just like I'd envisioned, and the mature trees along the street reached for each other overhead. A stiff wind whistled around me so I wrapped my insulated hoodie more tightly over my shoulders and hurried along till I noticed the right house number.

"Stopping to assess it from the sidewalk, the light green, one-story home with darker green shutters wouldn't have been my first pick in house colors but it looked the perfect size for the two of us. The yard needed some tender loving care, something I was sure my mother could help with.

"Heading up the walk to the front door, I felt a lot of anticipation. I positioned the key into the lock and it suddenly grew darker outside, as though someone had switched off a light. Swinging around, I looked at the sky and studied it carefully. There was a good amount of cloud cover. I couldn't remember seeing that before. It was impossible to see the position of the sun but, with the minuscule amount of light still left, it looked close to dusk. Glancing at my cell phone, it showed four-thirty, much too early for such a dark sky.

"I thought that was super weird but I figured that maybe some clouds had just drifted across the sun's path. I unlocked the door and stepped inside. Just inside the foyer, a barrage of voices drifted toward me and I stopped in shock as a chill raced down my spine. The owner had told me that the house was empty. I thought maybe someone had broken in.

"Still standing in the doorway, I contemplated my next move. Finally, I decided at least to look around the corner to see who was there and what was going on. My gut instinct told me to run but my curiosity egged me to look. I pushed the fear aside and forced my body to move.

"Cautiously, I peered around the corner and what I saw brought on a wave of confusion. The room was fully furnished with couches, coffee tables and a television on a stand filling the space. From my vantage point it appeared that the entire house was furnished. A quick look back at the entrance confirmed that. There was a doormat and shoes to one side.

"The noise level rose and I glanced back into the room. I noticed three people, a man, woman and a child. The little boy was about five years of age and he was sitting quietly in a corner playing with some toys. He looked up nervously now and then at his parents, who were in the throes of a heated argument.

"The man (I eventually heard his wife call him Mark) complained about his wife spending too much money on clothes for their son, Riley. He was furious, claiming she was spending money they didn't have.

"The wife, whom Mark called Chondra, insisted that she wasn't wasting their money on useless things. Their son, Riley, needed a new outfit for the new school year and she'd bought a few groceries. Their cupboards were getting bare.

"Mark yelled at her for buying clothes, insisting that Riley already had a pile of clothes. He actually told her that if she did the laundry more often she wouldn't have to buy him more stuff.

"Chondra argued that most of Riley's clothes were getting too small for him. At that point, Mark looked extremely agitated, insisted that they were struggling to make ends meet and said she needed to ask before spending the last bit in their account. Chondra apologized, suggesting that she go look for a job to help out.

"At that, Mark became really angry. He reminded her of how

sick she'd been the year before and declared that she wasn't strong enough to work. Chondra attempted to convince Mark that she could handle an office job or something not too strenuous. With Riley starting kindergarten in a few weeks, it would be a perfect time to get a job, plus it would relieve the financial stress they were under.

"Mark refused, reminding her that they couldn't afford for her to get sick again. Riley needed her and the cost of her hospital care the last time she'd been sick had strapped them for cash.

"Chondra suggested she search for a job with health and dental benefits which would alleviate their financial distress. At that point Mark had heard enough and snapped that he was done discussing the matter, that he could provide for his family! He turned and stomped toward the door.

"I quickly backed into the foyer so I wouldn't be seen. Just then Riley let out a strange sound and I heard a thumping noise from the room I had been watching. Chondra let out a terrified scream and began calling for Mark to come back. I peeked around the short wall in the foyer again to see what the commotion was. From what I could tell, Riley was having a convulsive attack of some kind and thrashing wildly on the floor.

"Chondra was beside herself with worry. I heard her say, 'Riley, Riley, talk to me! Please, Riley, stop this and talk to mommy!'

"Mark looked distressed and said he'd call 911 and told Chondra to keep a close eye on Riley to make sure he didn't hurt himself! He ran toward the doorway where I was standing. For some reason I froze where I stood and couldn't force myself to back away and hide again.

"As he came toward me I asked Mark if I could help him but he acted like he didn't see me. I flinched and closed my eyes, knowing he'd collide with me. When I felt nothing, I tentatively opened my eyes again and saw Mark standing down the hall, the phone to his ear, punching in a number. How he managed to get past me without touching me, without knocking me over, completely confused me. It wasn't even possible. I'd been directly in his path. I stared at him while he talked frantically into the phone piece.

"With confusion swirling through my mind, I walked back into the living room. Chondra was on the floor, Riley's head on her lap, trying to contain him so he wouldn't hurt himself. Tears poured from her eyes and she kept begging him to speak to her.

"I didn't have a clue what was going on, how this was happening and why they couldn't see me.

"Movement in the corner caught my eye. Looking over, I saw a man in a black trench coat. He stood quietly, holding a hat in his hand, his eyes fixed steadily on me. I stared back, not knowing what to make of it.

"First Mark wouldn't even acknowledge my presence and now this man wouldn't stop looking at me. I felt both fear and anger in that moment.

"I focused on the man in the corner and said, 'Why don't you help them?'

"He told me, 'I haven't been sent to help them.'

"'Then why are you here?' I asked.

"'To deliver a message,' he answered.

"I couldn't believe it! That guy sure had a lot of nerve! These people were in serious trouble and he came to bring a message?

"I decided that I was going to try and help them if it was possible. I turned toward Chondra and asked if I could help. She didn't even look up. I asked over and over again and even raised my voice but she refused to respond. I felt so puzzled over the whole bizarre thing.

"Mark came back into the room and hurried over to Chondra and Riley. I moved out of the way when he drew near. Not once did he make eye contact.

"Mark told her that the ambulance was on its way and asked about Riley.

"Chondra responded, 'I don't know. He's still the same. What's happening, Mark? Why is this happening to him?' Tears flowed in a steady stream down her cheeks.

"'I don't know,' Mark said. He lifted a hand to his forehead and rubbed. He looked as upset as his wife except for the tears.

"Riley had calmed somewhat but still lay unresponsive in his mother's arms. Mark turned and walked past me without acknowledging my presence. I felt dumbfounded as I watched him walk over to the window to watch for the ambulance.

"I knew I couldn't take much more. It was too bizarre.

Glancing over to the corner, I saw the man in the trench coat standing motionless with his eyes still locked on me. I didn't know what his problem was and I sure didn't care about his stupid message!

"Having endured all I could take, I turned and headed for the door. Once outside, I closed and locked the door as quickly as I could with a shaking hand. I ran toward the sidewalk and the sky grew visibly brighter as I did. In my fear to get away, the light change hardly registered.

"I hurried away from that house and headed back to the office to drop off the key. I gave the receptionist some excuse of why the rental wouldn't work and left. Entering a house that was reportedly empty and ready to rent only to find it occupied with ghosts terrified me. Getting away - anywhere but there - was my only goal.

"As I boarded the bus home, I hoped I could give Richelle a believable excuse why the house wouldn't work out."

There! She had finally shared it. After all these years of secrecy, it was out and it brought huge relief. The look on Luke's face made her a bit nervous, though. She had no idea how he'd respond.

"Wow! I don't know what to say."

"I don't know if there's anything to say. I ran from that experience and I would have run this time too if the angel hadn't made his identity known."

"You wouldn't have gone back that second night if Richelle and I hadn't pressured you to, would you?"

She shook her head. "When it happened that first time, years ago, I thought that man was so insensitive and uncaring. He just stood there in the corner and didn't seem to care about what that family was going through. The way he stared at me seemed so rude and made me feel completely uncomfortable. Knowing the house was empty, I thought maybe it was haunted. It frightened me terribly! I didn't understand it at all."

"Do you understand it now?"

"I don't know much more except that this angel is trying to get a message over to me. I suspect he was trying to tell me something back then too. I was too spooked and afraid to wait around for it then. If only this whole angel directive were easier to decipher. I wish he'd come out and tell me what this is all about instead of 'tiptoeing through the tulips.'"

"Why do you think he's being so secretive?"

"He told me he could only show me what he's told to show me."

"Who's telling him what to show you?"

Tessa smiled at that. Luke looked completely dumbfounded. She couldn't blame him really. "God," she said softly.

"So God tells the angel what he's allowed to show you?"

"Yes."

"Why not tell you straight out?"

"That's what I don't get." She shrugged. "Maybe I wouldn't catch on if it was all dumped on me at one time. Perhaps I have to see things in bits and pieces to understand the whole thing. I really don't know."

Luke was silent for a while. "This is very heavy. I can't remember us ever having such a deep conversation. I have to be honest; it's a bit overwhelming. I liked it better when it was just an adventure and we were going back in time. This angel and God business is too much for me."

"Does that mean you won't go back to the old mansion with me again? I don't want to go alone and I'd miss the company."

"I don't know. I'll have to think about it. Having an angel messing with my life doesn't create much appeal."

The silence stretched on for a few moments.

Luke finally said, "It seems like it's you that the angel is targeting so if I'd go back I could just go for the fun of it. I won't have to get involved in the 'message from heaven.'" He used his fingers to denote the quotations.

Tessa smiled. "You can't stay away, can you?"

"It has a strong pull."

"I'm glad it does. I don't think I'd have the courage to go alone."

"You could ask Cody to go with you?"

"Actually, I haven't even told him about our experience at the house."

He looked incredulous. "Why not? He's your boyfriend, isn't he? Or did you call it quits?"

"No, I didn't call it quits. We're still seeing each other. I don't

149

know why I haven't told him. I guess I'm unsure what he'd think of this kind of thing and I don't know him very well yet. I don't want to scare him off. He might think I'm a total kook and stay away."

"To tell you the truth, if I hadn't been with you and seen what you saw, I'd think you were a total nut case. Maybe it's better if you don't tell him. Look what happened when Richelle told Charlie. He totally freaked out on her and she almost lost him over this thing. That wouldn't have been a total loss, mind you."

"Luke, don't be cruel."

"I'm not cruel. That's my compassion at play. I don't like Charlie at all. He's a complete control-freak. Richelle deserves better."

"Well, she loves him so you have to be careful what you say to her." A thought came to her. "By the way, how do you know about Charlie going to the mansion with Richelle?"

"He told me while we were investigating the house together."

Tessa nodded. "Oh."

"Do you like him?" Luke asked.

"Don't ask me such a question! I don't want to answer that." How could she admit how little respect she had for the man?

"Come on, Tessa, out with it, do you like him?"

"I can't say that I like him much. He's quite rude and brash and has to have things his way. I feel sorry for Richelle sometimes. She does say though that he treats her well and that he'll do anything for her so there must be some good qualities about him. I just haven't seen much of that side. Of what I've seen, he's seems very demanding when he's with her."

"Yeah, that's exactly what I meant. I wish I could speak some sense into her. She doesn't take advice from me, though. Maybe you could talk to her."

"I'm sorry, Luke. I've tried to hint that maybe he's not the one for her but she's totally taken with him. There's nothing I could say that would change her mind."

"Maybe you're right. We should have seen through his character long ago and warned her."

"She wouldn't have listened then either. Taking advice is not one of her strong points. Making her own way is her style."

"Our stubborn Barbie Doll."

"She is a stubborn one!" Tessa agreed.

"With Charlie in the mix, it's affecting our friendship and I hate it. The three of us used to do everything together and now I have to sneak around Charlie and try not to upset things where he's concerned. It's ridiculous," Luke said.

"Let's hope he settles down and can accept you without suspicion. I'd hate to see you two have to part ways because of Charlie. That would be terrible!"

"It would irritate me to no end! The three of us have been friends for a long time. I don't want it to die out. I think the ball's in Richelle's court on this issue; she's letting Charlie control her right now." He looked despondent.

"He did notice the innocent banter between the two of you tonight."

"You actually think it'll make a difference?"

"It might."

"He still has an issue with jealousy."

Tessa nodded. She sure hoped Richelle knew what she was getting herself into.

Luke gazed at her affectionately. "Well, darling, I have to get going. If you ever want to go back to the mansion, give me a call and I'll let you know then if I'll go with you."

He stood, waited for her to join him and they walked to the door together.

"I'll do that, Luke. Thanks."

"Do you want a ride home?"

"Sure." Cody would be by her place later to pick her up. A ride would give her extra time to get ready.

CHAPTER 11

Another week had come and gone and Saturday morning was busier than usual. The line of customers was steady and as soon as a table emptied and cleared, another group was soon seated. Tessa scurried from one table to the other, trying to keep up to the constant demand.

Around eleven there was finally a break in the stream of people entering the restaurant. The hectic pace slowed and Tessa could finally keep up without too much trouble. Tessa and Tabitha stood together at the drink machine chatting while filling orders.

Martha came by and with a stern expression said, "Tessa, I suggest you go and check on your customers. Joan just seated someone in your section and they are waiting!"

"Yes, I'll get on it." She sighed heavily.

When Martha walked on, Tabitha rolled her eyes. "What's got into her this morning? Why doesn't she take a pill and relax?"

"I don't know. I was just out there a minute ago and there was no one there. I swear Martha hates my guts."

"She does pick on you a lot, doesn't she?"

"She's made it her second career."

Tabitha grinned at that.

Tessa positioned the tray of drinks on one arm and said, "Here I go."

As noon approached, a steady stream of customers kept Tessa busy. The lunch hour rush stretched far into the afternoon but caused the day to fly by in a blur of activity. Her shift ended at five and just as Tessa finished off her last table, Richelle walked into the restaurant. Joan, the hostess that day, seated her at a small table in the corner and informed Tessa that her friend was waiting for her.

After getting a drink, she headed to the table. "Hi Richelle! Can I get you anything before I sit down? I got myself a milkshake. I can get you the same if you'd like."

"No thanks. I had something on my way over here. I need to talk."

"Sure. What's on your mind?" Tessa slipped into the seat across from her and took a long sip of her strawberry milkshake.

"Do you remember when we went to the party at the mansion and I saw a girl there that I recognized?"

"Yes, I do. Why?"

"Her name was Nancy, remember?"

"Yes, now that you mention it, it's coming back to me. She's the one that interrupted Richard and Mary's dance. She's the one with the crush on Richard."

"Well, I know who she is."

Tessa felt incredulous. "Are you serious?"

"I want you to walk over to my parents' place with me and I'll show you who she is." Richelle smiled mysteriously.

"Now? I just finished work."

"So did I and I've been on my feet all day too. But it'll be fun to walk over there together, just like we used to every day after school."

"Where's your car?"

"I let Charlie use it today. His car broke down. He took me to work this morning and I took the bus here."

"Did you bring decent shoes to walk in?"

"Yeah, I changed after work. What do you say?"

"Okay, I'll go with you." Tessa finished her milkshake and they headed out.

The two friends talked about their day as they walked. Tessa felt a chill in the air but the sun was shining and it helped to warm their backs. Richelle's parents lived only two blocks from Tessa's parents. It was virtually the same route she took every day. They arrived at Mr. and Mrs. Randall's home, knocked and after a moment Richelle's mother came to the door and opened it wide.

"Hi there, Richelle! How come you're here again so soon?"

"Too soon, huh?" she retorted to her mom.

"Of course not. But you were just here last night."

"Well, I'm here again."

Richelle's agitation with her mother showed at times. Tessa wondered if they'd ever have an amicable relationship.

"And, Tessa, I haven't seen you for so long. It's so good to see you again."

"Thank you. It's good to see you again too, Mrs. Randall."

The woman was in her early fifties with blond hair like her daughter but with silver streaks throughout. Even at her age she was a fine-looking lady. It was obvious Richelle had received her beautiful features from her mother. Walking toward her, Mrs. Randall gave Tessa a big hug. She had always felt welcome in their home and Mrs. Randall was like a second mother to her.

"I'm sorry I haven't come around more often. My life has been super busy with school and I just started working full time a few weeks ago."

"Oh you don't have to apologize. I know how busy you've been. Richelle has told me what you've been up to so don't worry about it. Come on in you two; I'll put the kettle on and make some tea."

They settled down into the family room and waited for Richelle's mom to bring out the tea. Mrs. Randall came out shortly carrying a tray with three china tea cups, sugar, milk and a bright orange pot of tea. Pouring the tea for them, Mrs. Randall sat with them as they fixed their drinks to their liking. As they chatted, the realization hit Tessa how long it had been since she'd been over here for a visit.

Mrs. Randall appeared thrilled to have Tessa in her home again and chattered on about trivial things.

During a lull in conversation Richelle piped up with a question. With Mrs. Randall, one had to jump in to get a word said. "Mom, do you remember the pictures we were looking at last night?"

"Yes, dear, they're in the study with the rest of our albums. Why are you asking about those?"

"I'd like to show Tessa some of them if you don't mind."

"You're more than welcome to but I don't know why she'd like to look at our old family pictures. But if that's what you two girls want to do, help yourselves." She looked puzzled but didn't question her daughter any further. Richelle didn't appear eager to go into more detail.

Mrs. Randall gathered up the empty cups and placed them on the tray. "I'll leave you two to do your thing. I need to run out to the grocery store. If you need to leave before I get back, just lock the door on your way out. I have a key to get back in. Okay?"

"Sure, Mom. Thanks for the tea."

"Yes, thank you, Mrs. Randall."

With that she took the tray and left the room. Richelle disappeared into the study and came back a few minutes later carrying a pile of photo albums in her arms. Carrying more than she could handle, one nearly fell.

"Whoa, do you need a hand with that?"

"No not at all, I'll just let them all crash to the floor!"

Tessa went to her. "You don't have to be so sarcastic."

"Just give me a hand, okay."

She grabbed a few and carried them to the coffee table in front of the couch. They both sat and Richelle grabbed an album and leafed through it.

"Nothing in this one." She placed that one to the side and grabbed another one. Scanning through it quickly, she tossed it with the discarded pile and went on to the third. Then she found what she was searching for. "Here, look at this. This is the girl from the party, Nancy."

Looking at the photo, it displayed a girl seated on a chair and Tessa estimated her to be in her twenties. It was a formal pose but it was definitely the girl from the party or at least someone that looked very much like her.

"Who is she? Is she your relative?"

"She's my grandmother. And get this; her name is Nancy Parker. My grandmother knew Mary and she was there that night. I wish we could ask her about that house, the family and whatever happened to them."

A stab of hope flooded her. "Is she still living?"

In exasperation Richelle said, "No, she passed away two years ago."

"That's too bad."

"I never had much use for my grandmother. That may sound bad but I never liked being around old people much. Now I would love to talk to her and ask her some questions. She could tell us so much."

Tessa placed her chin in her palms, her elbows resting on her knees, deep in thought. She couldn't help but feel disappointed.

Lowering her hands, she said, "This is so fascinating. For some reason your grandmother is involved in all of this. So, it's not possible to discuss this with her but I'm wondering if the angel's message is for you too. I mean, your grandmother was involved so maybe there's something for you at the mansion too."

Richelle shrugged her shoulders. "I don't know."

She gazed at Richelle thoughtfully. "I also wonder if Luke will have some connection in all of this. The three of us have always been together when the time change happens so maybe all of us have a part in this somehow."

"You're getting too carried away! You're suggesting that this angel has a message for me too? He's never paid me the least attention so I don't know how you can think that he has anything to say to me. I'm just in this for the excitement. The realization that my grandmother was there has some appeal but it's only a passing fascination, I'm sure."

"I wonder if your mother would know anything about the old mansion. Has she ever said anything about it?"

"No, I can't remember her ever mentioning it. She never talks much about the past. I think she'd rather forget it ever happened."

"Maybe we should ask her when she gets back home."

"I don't know if that's such a great idea."

"Why not?"

"I've asked her stuff about her upbringing before and she always avoids it. I don't think she's ever given me any straight answers. She's extremely evasive."

"I wonder why?"

"Why don't you ask her when she gets in?"

"I might just do that."

They looked at some more pictures of Nancy. A wedding picture caught their eye. The bride and groom were standing together, the man at Nancy's side being of medium height. With a balding spot at the front of his head, he looked a few years older than she. He was moderately good-looking and appeared vaguely familiar as well. He wore a suit, vest and tie and Nancy had a beautiful white wedding dress.

Their stance in the pose looked odd. They stood a bit apart and their expressions were serious, almost sad. What an abnormal bridal couple they were.

"They don't look extremely happy, do they?" asked Tessa.

"I've always thought the same thing. My mother said that back then it wasn't customary to smile for pictures. The more serious the pose, the more natural it would look. I'm not sure if I believe her."

There were other pictures as well. There was one of Nancy with a baby and some other pictures with Nancy and two small children.

"How many children did your grandmother have?"

"That's all she had, just the two of them. She had two girls, my mother, Ann, and her sister, Amy. My mother was the oldest of the two."

"Do you keep in contact with your aunt?"

"Not really. She lives in California with her husband. They have one child and he's a lot younger than I am. Aunt Amy moved out there when she was in her twenties and she's seldom been back to visit. My parents and I have been there to visit a few times. It wasn't enough to develop a close relationship."

"So I guess talking to her is out of the question."

"I'd say so."

They could hear some commotion at the door. Richelle's mother was home. Tessa and Richelle stood and walked to meet her. They helped carry the few groceries to the kitchen and placed them in the cupboards. When they were done, the three of them stood in the kitchen and chatted.

"Should I put on the kettle for more tea?" asked Mrs. Randall.

"No thank you. I've had enough," said Tessa. This was her opportunity. Hopefully Mrs. Randall would open up to her. "I have something I'd like to ask you, if you don't mind."

Ann Randall leaned back against the cupboard and crossed her arms. "Sure, Tessa, you can ask me anything."

"It's kind of personal and it has to do with the pictures Richelle and I were looking at. If you don't want to answer my question you don't have to."

"Well, why don't you ask and I'll decide," she said with a smile.

Richelle pulled out a chair from the table, sat down and crossed her legs, curiosity filling her eyes.

Tessa stayed standing. "Okay, first of all I'd like to ask you about an old house. Richelle and I have walked by – an old mansion among all those beautiful houses on Young Street. There's one there that's deserted and falling apart. We were wondering if you know anything about its history."

"Why would you want to know about that old thing?"

Richelle spoke up. "It's just that we've often wondered about it."

Anne looked contemplative for a moment as she studied a spot on the floor and then slowly raised her eyes to lock with Tessa's gaze. "My mother mentioned it once and said she was somewhat familiar with the family. She said they were having some problems and couldn't hold things together. The house began to fall into disrepair and they did nothing to stop its downward spiral. They eventually moved out and it's been empty ever since. I wish the city would tear it down because it is such an eye sore."

"I wonder if it belongs to anyone. Would the city have the right to tear down a building that doesn't belong to them?" Tessa felt concern for the old mansion and she knew it was only because she'd seen the people who once lived there, the beautiful home it had once been and perhaps the potential it still had.

"What they should do is give the owner a notice to fix the place up within a certain time period and if that doesn't take place they should demolish it. It's time, in my opinion, to get rid of that old place."

Richelle said, "I bet it would take a boat load of money to repair everything. Maybe the owner can't afford to fix it. But it is a shame to let such a beautiful house rot away."

Ann stared at her daughter in disbelief. "Beautiful? That house is anything but beautiful! It's a horrible eye sore and needs to come down."

"Well, I agree that's it's awful to look at right now. If I look at the houses surrounding it, I can only imagine how stunning it must have once been. I'm sure it has the potential of looking grand again." Richelle glanced at Tessa and winked.

Tessa forced down a chuckle. So Richelle was also feeling an attachment for the old house. They both had a special bond with it, now that they had seen its former magnificence.

"With potential and a pile of money, maybe yes. If it hasn't been fixed yet, I don't know if it ever will be. It's been decaying for many, many years." Anne turned away, opened the dishwasher and began to clear out the clean dishes.

She was losing interest in the conversation.

"I'd like to ask you another question, Mrs. Randall."

She turned in surprise to face Tessa once more. "Sure, what is it?"

"It's about your parents' wedding picture. Was it customary for the bride and groom to stand apart from each other and look sad for pictures?"

An uncomfortable smile twisted her lips. "I don't know why you'd want to know about that. I can't tell you a lot about their wedding day because I wasn't there. I know only some of the customs then, what they've told me. Their marriage wasn't the smoothest, if that's what you want to know, and it started out with difficulty too."

Tessa could see how discomfited she was. "I'm sorry if this is inappropriate. You don't need to talk about it if you don't want to."

"Did Richelle put you up to this?" She glared at her daughter accusingly.

Richelle raised both hands, palms up and shook her head.

"Richelle!" Tessa said with exasperation.

Ann eyed them both curiously for a moment before answering. "Okay girls, I'll tell you. I know Richelle has often asked about her grandparents and I've tried to keep it from her. Let's go and sit in the family room, shall we?"

They walked over to the other room and as Ann Randall sat down she picked up the open photo album with the picture of her parents' wedding photo. She remained silent for a moment as she studied it.

With a deep sigh she began. "My mother's name was Nancy Parker and she married a man by the name of Henry Stephens. My parents' marriage was always a struggle. I questioned my father once about all the tension between them. He actually opened up and told me. He said that he'd been on the rebound from a woman that he loved dearly but couldn't marry. Then Nancy came along. Although he didn't love Nancy when they married, to him it seemed like a reasonable thing to do at the time. He was getting up in age and wanted to settle down. She was a nice girl from a good family and he thought they would fall in love, given some time.

"Apparently, according to him, my mother couldn't have the man she truly wanted either and she settled for him. He believed she agreed to the marriage to seek revenge. I never understood what he meant by that and he never explained. He always believed that things would improve between the two of them but their relationship just seemed to get worse over time. The home I was raised in wasn't a pleasant place to be but my parents stayed together through the years. I do have some good memories. I prefer to forget the bad ones. It's easier for me if I don't talk about those difficult years."

Richelle looked stunned. "Wow, I never knew that Grandpa and Grandma weren't happy together. They were never lovey-dovey with each other but very few old people are."

"Well, now you know, Richelle. I don't want you to think less of your grandparents because of the problems they had. They were good people and they did their best for us. They weren't always happy but that's not a crime."

"It explains a lot about this wedding picture, that's for sure." Richelle studied the picture again.

"Thank you for sharing that, Mrs. Randall. I know it's not easy to talk about difficult family matters."

"You're welcome, dear. It actually feels good to finally get that out. I've kept it quiet for too long. I feel relieved that Richelle finally knows."

"I'm glad you told me too, Mom. You should have told me a long time ago. I could have handled the truth."

"My concern was that knowing the truth would cause you to lose respect for your grandparents."

"I do respect them! I think I respect them more now that I know they weren't perfect."

A light of understanding filled Ann's eyes.

Richelle stood and grabbed a few albums. "Anyway, I'll put these photos back and then we should go."

Tessa stood to help her. They left shortly afterwards.

They waited at the bus stop together where Richelle planned to catch the bus back to her apartment.

"You know what my mom said about my grandmother?"

"Which part?"

"She said my grandmother married Henry as a revenge thing."

"Yeah, I remember that."

"Remember the Henry from the mansion – the young man Mary was in love with? My grandfather could be that same man. He was on the rebound from a woman he couldn't marry. I wonder who Nancy was trying to take revenge on."

"That's right. In the wedding picture, your grandfather did resemble Henry from the mansion. I thought he looked familiar but he did look a fair bit older. I wonder how this all fits together?" Tessa felt amazed at the connection.

"Do you want to go back to the old house this weekend and see if we can find out anything else?"

"I have a lot planned this weekend, Richelle. I don't think that's going to work out."

"Okay. Just let me know when you're going. I want to come with you."

"All right, I'll do that."

The bus pulled up, Richelle left and Tessa began her walk home, pondering over what they had just learned. She wondered how it all connected. Even though the thought of going back was intimidating and still brought on anxiety, the urge to figure out the mystery was growing stronger. She couldn't deny its pull.

CHAPTER 12

Two days later

The trees showcased new, green foliage with hardly any movement and Tessa marveled at the stillness of the air as she strolled along the sidewalk. She took a deep breath of the spring air. To her it seemed as though an early summer had pounced on the landscape almost overnight. With the rain they'd had and the sunny, warm weather they'd enjoyed the last few days, the grass had turned a bright green. Tender new blooms, crocuses and tulips enhanced various flower beds in the neighborhood as she passed through. She absolutely loved the sights and smells of spring. Today it brought added enjoyment since she had the day off, plus the weather was perfect for walking. The winter chill had finally gone and the warmth of spring was making a happy return.

Tessa reached the entrance to Fairview Park. City workers were busy digging holes for the flowers that were sitting to the side in their store-bought containers. Their quiet scratching in the dirt was calming. No lawn mowers were out yet, something she was thankful for. The roar of those motors always took away from a peaceful walk in the park.

Even with the subdued feel of the place, her mind wandered back in time to the lives of the occupants of the mansion. She had no desire to spoil a perfectly good day by dwelling on the past so she pushed the thoughts aside.

Fairview Park was located only a few blocks from her parents' home and it spanned an area of six blocks. It had a small lake in the center, fed by a stream that meandered through the city. Encircling the lake ran a walkway, with pathways joining it from other areas of the park. The green space had plenty of biking trails, play areas for children as well as picnic spots and benches scattered around for those who wanted to take it easy.

On the lake, ducks floated lazily across the water, plunging their heads beneath the surface in search of a morsel of food. Two graceful swans glided over the water as if on glass and their reflections appeared as clear as crystal. A large weeping willow on the far side made a perfect backdrop, its image mirrored in the still water. Various trees surrounded the lake, some full of blossoms, adding a burst of color to the scene. The fragrance of the flowers wafted toward her as she passed beneath them and she breathed deeply.

Lots of people were out enjoying the warm weather, some biking, some walking and even a few on roller blades. As she passed the playground she noticed it buzzing with the noise of little ones thrilled to be outside. The mothers looked just as grateful finally to get their bundles of energy outdoors after a long winter.

There were numerous dogs on leashes, the owners tagging along. Tessa had once wanted a dog but her mother insisted it was too much work so they opted for a cat. Muffin fit in well with their family. With her white fur and mostly brown legs, the name suited her well. She was twelve years old and the most relaxed and lovable cat Tessa had ever met. The members of the March family led busy lives and the cat didn't mind time alone. Now that Muffin was getting along in years, she had become even more docile and stationary. Thinking of her brought a smile.

After finishing one loop around the lake and starting on her second, Tessa let her mind wander to the old mansion. She wondered what Mary was going through, or had gone through. It was hard to keep the past and present separate. She hoped Mary wouldn't have to go through the electric shock treatments. It seemed so "Dark Ages" and it was hard to fathom how it could possibly help anyone.

Mary's life had been filled with great potential. Except for the redirection of her love life, her future had seemed quite bright. For her exciting course to be so quickly snuffed out seemed unfair. It was difficult to understand. Tessa realized that her initial irritation with Mary's emotional turmoil had quickly changed as more information came to light. Now she was curious how Mary's future would pan out and what, if anything, it had to do with her.

She wished the purpose would become clearer because it took up far too much of her thought life. Her mind was constantly consumed with the past and it was irksome not being able to find out more quickly. Why would a message from God be this suspenseful and drawn out?

Finishing her second loop around the lake, she found an empty bench to relax for a few minutes.

If only I could make sense of this all.

A young girl riding her bicycle, equipped with training wheels, peddled down the path toward her. Tessa guessed the girl to be around three years old. Her young, pregnant mother was racing on foot to keep up. There was a slight decline and the bike sped up. With her protruding belly, the young woman ran awkwardly and breathed heavily. Concern played across her features. There was no way she could keep up.

"Slow down! Wait for mommy! Angel, do you hear me?"

Ringing of bells filled the air around Tessa. Leaning forward, she wondered whether the bells she heard were real or imagined.

Paying no attention to her mother, the little girl instead picked up speed, her face lit with pure delight. The exhilarating ride was too much fun to spoil by obeying.

"Angel, slow down!" yelled the mother.

Tessa knew she hadn't imagined the bells the second time. Realization sank in. It was time to go back to the mansion. She sat for a minute longer watching the little girl slow to a stop, the young mother finally catching up with her and scolding her. With a huge grin of pleasure, the girl looked at her mother with the innocence of youth. Her mother let out an exasperated sigh, gave up the scolding and the two continued down the path and out of earshot.

Tessa contemplated her next move. Richelle had asked to be there for the next mansion visit. Perhaps she should give both Richelle and Luke a call and let them know what she was up to.

Should I go now or wait till the evening?

A few phone calls should clear up her dilemma. Luke might be working and the same might be true of Richelle, although Richelle had most Mondays off. Tessa started her walk back home.

An empty and quiet house greeted her. Her parents were both working and her brothers were in school. After starting another load of laundry, she called her friends. Neither of them answered and she didn't feel like leaving messages.

Tessa felt torn. It was time to go back but she sure didn't want to go alone. It gave her chills walking into that house, even when her friends were with her. Going solo would be completely overwhelming.

Going this afternoon would be best since she and Cody had plans in the evening. She decided to wait a few hours and give her friends another call.

A few hours later, after all her laundry was done and put away, she tried calling again. Still no answer. Frustration gnawed at her. Why couldn't they be home? She was sure Luke was done his shift by now and where was Richelle? She couldn't wait any longer. The day was ticking away and time was running out.

Tessa headed out, walked to Young Street, stopped in at Michael's Mocha Shop for a diet soda, drank it quickly and continued on.

When she finally arrived at the mansion, she stood nervously on the sidewalk, just before the gate and faced the decrepit estate. Studying it for a few minutes, deep in thought, she didn't notice a man approach on the sidewalk. Shuffling of feet notified her and the suddenness of the sound made her jump.

"I scared you." The stranger chuckled.

"Yes. That you did."

He pointed to the house. "It's pathetic looking, isn't it?"

"I suppose it is."

"The city is planning to tear it down this summer sometime. I just read it in the paper. It's about time because it's an awful blot on the street."

Looking back to the house, his words felt like horrible news to her. "I wish they'd restore it instead. It has so much potential."

"I don't know what you're looking at, but potential is not what I see! It's a fire hazard! Any kid could go and light a fire in there and it would be up in a ball of smoke."

Tessa turned back to him. The man looked amused.

"It's a dangerous place! Anyway, have a good day, Miss." With that he walked on.

Considering the information he'd brought, Tessa didn't know what to think. She used to have similar feelings – that it should be demolished, its ungainly view removed from the neighborhood – but her outlook had done a dramatic one-eighty. It had somehow become personal. As ridiculous as that seemed to her, it was true.

Knowing the people who had lived here and what they'd gone through made the house valuable. It distressed her to think of it being destroyed.

The words begged for a voice. "Please, God, don't let them tear it down!"

After a steadying breath, Tessa pushed on the gate, which groaned in protest, and entered the yard. She walked slowly toward the big oak tree and, as she passed it, everything suddenly switched over to 1946. The change in temperature sliced through her thin sweater, bringing a chill. Her shoes disappeared under a layer of snow. Quickly, she ran along the walkway, up the side steps and through the side doorway.

As she entered, she rubbed her arms to warm herself. The place was quiet and appeared deserted. Walking to the middle of the foyer, she surveyed the entrance area then noticed some movement on the steps. The angel stood halfway down the stairway, gazing at her. He began to descend, wearing his customary black trench coat and holding his black hat in his hands. Deliberately, he headed her way.

His expression was somber as he came to a stop before her, yet Tessa detected a small smile glowing in his eyes. "It's good that you came."

"I'm glad you were here to meet me. I almost didn't come. I don't like being here by myself. It makes me nervous."

He nodded. "You came just in time."

"But the house looks empty so why was I summoned?"

"You'll soon see. Why don't you follow me and wait for the Hardingtons to return home?"

Leading the way to the right side of the foyer, he stood with his back to the wall and Tessa joined him.

A minute later they heard the front door open and watched as William and Elizabeth Hardington entered. A servant came scurrying from the left side hallway to retrieve the Hardingtons' coats and boots. Their movements were slow and deliberate and their expressions grim.

"Elizabeth, why don't you go and instruct some of the staff to pack some things for us. I'll only need a few items but you and Mary will need an extensive amount for your stay. I'll need to make some arrangements at the bank and I'll call some business associates in Chicago to find a house for you to stay there."

"How soon will we be leaving, William?"

"As soon as all the arrangements are made. The sooner we leave the better it will be for Mary."

"I just wish there was another way."

"I do too, Elizabeth. I want the best for her."

Tears began to flow down Elizabeth's cheeks and William walked over, embraced her and let her cry on his shoulder for a while.

"It will be okay, dear. The doctor said that this procedure has been very successful for many patients and he's sure that it will help Mary. We need to trust him."

"It's so upsetting that she hasn't improved any this past week. I'm praying that this procedure will work quickly and that I'll be able to return with Mary soon."

William pulled away, his features hardened. "I don't believe prayer ever helped anyone. Our only hope is this new treatment."

"How can you say that, William? We've always believed in God and in prayer. We've gone to church all these years. Why are you turning your back on God and the church now?"

Anger flashed from his eyes. "That pastor said nothing of help. He kept babbling on about the irrelevant. He even hinted that I repent. With that kind of a pastor, I don't need him or the church!"

She looked distraught. "Does this mean we're never going back to church?"

"That's right, so get used to it. If you want to pray, go right ahead, but don't expect me to join you." William headed to his office and slammed the door shut.

Elizabeth stared at the closed door in shock. She whispered a prayer, "Lord, please help us!" then headed down the left hallway, her back slumped in discouragement.

Tessa and the angel were alone again. She looked at him to see if he'd give her any direction. He put up his index finger as if to say, "Wait." Momentarily there was a knock at the door and a servant hurried to open it.

A young girl walked through and into the foyer. Her eyes darted back and forth nervously. She looked familiar, someone Tessa had seen the night of the party, but she couldn't remember her name.

"Who may I say is visiting, miss?"

"I'm Hilda. I have a gift for Mary. Is she here?"

"No, Miss Hilda, but I'll go and get Mr. Hardington."

"That's not necessary. I'll leave the gift with you and you can see that Mary receives it."

"I insist on letting Mr. Hardington know about your visit, Miss Hilda."

"Oh, all right then." She looked completely uncomfortable and fidgeted anxiously as she waited.

The servant knocked on the office door and William appeared, walked over to Hilda and welcomed her.

Hilda said, "I'm sorry I haven't been here sooner. I heard about what happened to Mary but I didn't have the courage to come. I couldn't bear to see her that way."

"I understand. I'm sure Mary, in a right frame of mind, would understand too. She's not here though; she's at the hospital. We took her there today since it was hard for us to keep her sedated. She's having a difficult time."

"What will happen to her?"

"She needs more help than the doctors here can give her. We're sending her to Chicago for a while. There are doctors there that can offer her the treatment she needs. I'm confident Mary will return soon and be back to her normal self."

"That's what I'm hoping for, sir." Hilda's jaw twitched tensely at the silence that followed. "Well, I brought Mary a small gift." She handed him a wrapped box.

"Thank you. I'll give it to her when she's in a better state of mind. I know she'll appreciate it." He held the small box almost reverently before returning his attention to Hilda. "Perhaps you could inform me about something. I've been a little surprised that none of her friends have come to see her or even asked about her, except for you, of course. Why is that?"

She couldn't meet his eyes and her hands fidgeted again. "They've all heard about Mary, sir, so I don't know what to say. I guess they feel unsure about what they'd say to her. They feel badly for her, as I do."

"Why wouldn't her church friends at least drop by or leave a letter, something to show they cared? Doesn't it seem a bit odd to you?"

"I'm sorry, sir. I don't know why they wouldn't reach out."

"Has Pastor Reed said anything about our situation?"

Hilda looked immediately distraught. "I'm not sure what you mean."

"Has he mentioned our family?"

Her hesitancy to answer was obvious. "He did mention your struggles."

"What did he say?"

"He...he mentioned that people have to reap what they sow."

"And he was referring to us?" Mr. Hardington's face turned red with the question.

Sheepishly, she nodded.

"What else did he say?"

Reluctantly she met his eyes, her hesitation showing. "He...he suggested that...that the congregation give you space to repent."

This statement made his face turn a fiercer shade of red. Visibly controlling his emotions, he simply nodded.

"I'm sorry, sir! I didn't want to say anything."

"That's all right. I asked." He breathed deeply and slowly exhaled, reigning in his anger. "Thank you for making an effort. Mary would be pleased."

Hilda fell silent for a moment and then asked, "What's going to happen to Mary? Is she going to be okay?"

"We're taking her to Chicago for some special treatments. Our doctor is very hopeful that they will be successful. The initial treatments will span a few weeks. If they work as well as we're hoping, Mary should be back home within a month."

"Could I come and see her then?"

"We would love to have you come. Give us a call in a few weeks."

"Thank you, I'll do that. Now I must be going."

"Thank you for coming, Hilda." He opened the door for her and she left quickly.

Red faced, William headed back to his office, cursing under his breath, and closed his door with a slam.

Tessa looked at the angel beside her. "How could the church be so cruel and uncaring? It just doesn't make sense."

"God has instructed me to share that bit of information with you. You already know how controlling William has been in regard to his own daughter. His desire to manipulate things has also affected church affairs. He's a wealthy man and his wealth speaks, which has given him a lot of influence in church interactions. His money has enabled him to get his way.

"Reverend Reed has often attempted to tell William that he needs to stick to banking and let him, as the pastor, decide church matters. The reverend's frustration over William's manipulating ways came to a head. This situation with Mary offered him the perfect opportunity to put William in his place, but he's been terribly hurt and it will affect his family for a time."

"It's such a heartless thing to do. The Hardingtons are already hurting because of Mary's condition and then to distress them further through rejection seems unthinkable."

"There are too many things that happen on this earth that are unreasonable. God is full of mercy and desires to bring healing to such hurt and rejection."

Tessa soaked in the information. She glanced at him, curiosity tugging at her. "Why are you telling me all this?"

"You need to know."

"But why do I need to know?"

The angel moved from the wall to face her. With a sober expression he said, "You prayed and asked for it."

Immediate confusion and anger filled her at the angel's statement. "I never asked God for this! How can you say I asked for this?" She tried to think of when she had ever made a request even remotely related to what she was experiencing.

"Do you remember when you were fifteen? It was in the fall when your church had a special speaker?"

"I'm not sure. That's a long time ago."

"The speaker's name was Alcott Spenser. He talked about fulfilling God's plan for your life. He explained how God had taken him from being satisfied in his work, to being dissatisfied, to a revelation of God's plan for him and then finally fulfilling that purpose. Alcott challenged everyone not to seek after their own desires but after God's best for them. You prayed then and this is what you said. 'God, please help me to fulfill your plan for my life, my destiny. Show me what your plan is.'"

Although the angel spoke the words, Tessa heard them in her own voice, loud and accusatory in her ears.

"Do you remember now?"

She could feel the blood draining from her face and nausea stirring in her gut. Her legs felt like jello beneath her. The memory of that service, the speaker and her prayer returned. "God heard me pray that?"

"He hears every prayer and remembers every petition. People forget but God never forgets a prayer that's been uttered in sincerity. This..." The angel moved his hand to show the house. "...is part of the fulfillment of your prayer."

Her legs gave way and she slid down the wall to the floor. She sat cross-legged, rested her elbows on her legs and placed her face in her hands. The impact of the angel's words had sapped her strength. After a few minutes, she finally lifted her eyes to see if he was still around. He still stood in the same position, looking at her with the same intense expression.

"How will this impact my life?"

"Only you can decide that. I've been sent to bring a message and help you see God's plan."

"I wish this wasn't so baffling. Why doesn't God come right out and tell me what I'm supposed to do instead of dragging things on like this?"

"I'm sure he has his reasons. I have to be going now. I suggest you stay a while. There's someone you need to see. I've been instructed to tell you not to be afraid. There are others of my kind here with you and they will not leave you."

With that, the angel walked toward the main entrance and vanished into thin air.

Tessa stared at the spot for a long time, transfixed by what she'd just seen. She pinched her arm and flinched. No, she wasn't dreaming but it was feeling more and more like she was living out a science fiction movie.

Long fingers of fear gripped her throat, threatening to choke her. She pushed the sensation away. It was so hard to believe that she was actually here, angels were real and that this was even possible. There was no physical sign of any other angelic presence. She would have to go on in faith.

Hopefully she'd understand all of this soon so her life could return to normal. Then again, she didn't know if her life would ever be normal again after all she'd witnessed here. Her once-confident self was becoming a bundle of raw nerves. For crying out loud, she was being led around with the sound of bells! How peculiar was that? And to think it all had to do with God's direction for her life.

She had been so busy pursuing her own dreams, she hadn't taken the time to find out God's plan for her. But then again, maybe her plan was God's plan. Maybe he only wanted to add another dimension to her life that she would never have considered before. She hated feeling so uncertain and the accompanying aggravation was wearisome.

Tessa stayed in her position on the floor a few more minutes, contemplating her choices. Dodging this whole "message from God" thing seemed a viable option. It was throwing her life into chaos, a position she wanted to avoid. Her curiosity came a very close second on the list. Staying and finding out what this was all about was a tempting alternative. Being torn in two directions vexed her.

The foyer was empty and quiet and the house seemed asleep. Faint noises down the hall toward the kitchen told her the servants were still about and busy. At times she could hear William's voice softly through the office door.

Why did the angel tell me to wait? There's no one to talk to here. Should I go looking for someone? Do I wait here and they'll come to me?

Noise from the top floor alerted her but looking up she saw nothing. Shuffling, groans and strange sounds filtered down. Every hair on her body stood on end and fear started tap dancing around her heart.

Slowly, Tessa stood and headed to the staircase. She was nervous about walking through the house on her own but her inquisitiveness prodded her up the stairs. At the top of the steps, she scanned the landing. There was no sign of anyone.

What do I do now?

She headed down the left hallway since she was familiar with that side of the house. She passed a few rooms then suddenly stopped in her tracks. A door to the left was standing wide open with light spilling from the room. This was the same room that had been closed the night of the party. It was the room from which Luke, Richelle and she had heard knocking.

Could this be the grandmother's room?

She remembered Luke telling them that Mary's diary had described the grandmother as being crazy. It didn't give Tessa any more incentive to continue down the hallway. From her position, she couldn't see into the room; all she saw was light spilling into the hall. Standing still for a few minutes, she tried to decide whether to walk past or investigate.

Footsteps alerted her but before she could move away, someone appeared in the doorway. The elderly lady shuffled to stand there, her hands extended to the sides, bracing herself on the door frame and began frantically to look back and forth down the hall. She looked ancient, wrinkles lining her face and neck. It was hard to judge how old she actually was.

She wore a stained nightgown and slippers on her feet and her white hair was pulled back into a messy bun, loose strands sticking out in every direction. Thoughts of Richelle and her beautician skills came to mind. With the light coming from behind the old woman, it made her look almost angelic, as though she were wearing a halo, but there was a wild searching in her eyes that canceled that observation. The old lady grunted and groaned but kept looking back and forth down the hall.

Tessa shook her head in wonder. She knew Luke had mentioned this lady's name from Mary's diary but she couldn't remember it.

Suddenly, the old lady turned piercing eyes straight to Tessa, honing in on her, refusing to let go of her gaze.

Goose bumps mottled her flesh and terror seized her mind. This lady shouldn't be seeing her. No one else could so why was this old hag looking straight at her?

Tessa moved over a few steps but the old lady didn't break eye contact. When she moved, the woman's eyes moved with her. Tessa decided to walk past the room to see what the old woman would do. Gingerly, she moved down the hall, keeping her eyes locked on grandmother. Eerily, the woman's eyes stayed with her, her head turning as Tessa moved.

The urge to bolt came with force and Tessa turned back toward the stairs, prepared to do just that when the woman spoke.

"Wait! Come in here!" She didn't really say it but stated it like a command. Then she turned and walked into her room.

With fear dotting her flesh with goose bumps, Tessa stood in complete shock for a minute, not sure what to do. She absolutely did not want to go into that room, especially not with a crazy woman, but what if this was the person she was supposed to see? Could that be possible? Greatly apprehensive, she walked toward the room and glanced in. It looked safe enough. Entering cautiously, she noticed the old lady sitting in a rocking chair by the window. The woman once again turned toward her and pointed to another chair located across from her.

It was a large bedroom, bigger than most Tessa had seen in the house. There was a queen-sized bed on one side, in shambles. The blankets lay crumpled on the floor, one pillow scrunched up on the middle of the bed and a few others thrown about the room. Clothes were lying about and empty plates and cups covered a lot of the furniture. A door on the far side led to a bathroom. With towels strewn about the floor, it didn't look too clean in there either.

The old lady sat in a small living room area with chairs and a bookcase that lined one wall. There were more books stacked on the floor than there were in the bookcase. A number of plants that had seen better days stood on stands close to the window. Most were dry and dying, uncared for and unattended.

Tessa looked at the woman and wondered if that was how she felt.

The furniture was all of good quality and the room was beautiful, although the mess everywhere detracted from the room's charm. Insufficient light made the space dark and dingy. Two floor lamps were the only source of light and thick curtains were drawn tightly over the two windows located in the room.

"Sit down, sit down!" barked the old lady.

Surprised, Tessa jumped.

The woman again pointed to the chair across from her, impatience on her face.

Tessa sat down quickly, not knowing what to expect. She asked the first question that came to mind. "Why can you see me?"

"What a stupid question! I'm not blind. I may be crazy but I'm not blind." She cackled loudly, amused by her own admission. She then bent forward, cupped a hand around her mouth and whispered, "Do you want to know a secret?"

Tessa felt on edge, unsure whether to stay and carry on a

conversation or bolt for the door. She reluctantly answered, "All right, you can tell me."

"God is alive." She giggled and held her belly. "Isn't that a wonderful secret?"

Tessa smiled at the absurdity of the conversation but decided to answer politely. "Yes, he is." Hopefully this strange chat would end soon so she could leave. This uncanny situation was causing her a great deal of discomfort.

The old lady bent forward again, cupped her hand around her mouth and whispered, "Do you want to know something else?"

"Sure, whatever."

"You're on target." She grinned the biggest grin Tessa had ever seen on anyone. Many of the woman's teeth were missing and others were black and rotten; it wasn't a pretty sight.

She cringed involuntarily and her forehead creased in bewilderment as she thought on the old lady's statement. "What do you mean?"

"Ohhhh! You forget so quickly, do you? No, no, no, this will never do!" The old lady jumped up, scooted behind her chair and paced back and forth. "This will never do, this will never do." She kept repeating it over and over. Frequently, she hit her forehead with the palm of one hand as she continued to pace and chant her disappointment. "This will never do, this will never do!"

I'm on target? What does she mean by that? I don't get it!

Suddenly it hit her. That's where she had her first time travel experience. That first house had been on Target Street. But how would this old lady know about that? She stared at the woman's bizarre antics, not knowing what to make of them.

Tessa decided to disclose what was on her mind and see what effect it would have. "I was on Target Street and I saw a little boy having a seizure."

The old lady stopped dead in her tracks, stared at her and suddenly looked more like a mad scientist than a crazy grandmother as she scurried back around her chair and sat down on the edge of it. "You're on target." She stared wild-eyed at Tessa. "You're on target."

Her skin crawled with the freakish tension in the room. "How do you know about that?"

"Because there's a plan, there's always a plan."

"A plan for what?"

"Do young people know nothing? Young people know nothing, they know nothing, they know nothing! Why do young people know nothing?" After calming down slightly, she stared intensely at Tessa but gave no explanation.

Tessa shook her head in confusion before speaking. "What I do know is that we're having this talk and I don't know why."

"Because there's a plan. I already told you that." She looked upset but Tessa was also agitated with this seemingly senseless conversation.

"What kind of plan?"

"A plan for deliverance!" she shouted.

Noise from the doorway demanded their attention. Mrs. Hardington stood there with a scowl on her face.

"Eunice, what is all the shouting and yelling about in here? Would you please quiet down?"

She didn't waste any time responding. "Can't you see I'm talking to this fine young lady? Why are you interrupting me? Get out, get out!"

"Eunice, there's no one in here but you, so quiet down. Your voice is traveling through the whole house and it's becoming a nuisance!"

"I will not have my daughter-in-law interrupting my conversation with my guest. I want you to leave my room now!" Eunice's voice rose to a screech as she ordered her daughter-in-law out.

"Well, if you can't keep quiet, I'll close your door." Elizabeth seemed accustomed to her mother-in-law's outbursts. She didn't flinch or seem bothered by the rebuke as she backed out of the room and closed the door after her.

"No respect, no respect. I don't get any respect around here. Now where were we?"

Tessa focused her gaze on the crazy lady before her and wondered why she was speaking to someone whom everyone believed had lost her marbles. She pushed the thoughts away and reminded Eunice of their conversation. "You were telling me about a plan for deliverance."

"Oh yes, deliverance! You tell me the plan." Eunice's eyes bulged as she stared at her expectantly.

Tessa didn't know what to say that wouldn't upset this old grandmother. Her thoughts traveled to her own grandmother who was a bit younger and certainly wasn't crazy. They were close, she and her sweet granny, and Tessa loved to visit her. She'd had no preparation for dealing with this kind of woman, where the least bit of agitation set her off.

After struggling to find the right answer, she finally said, "I haven't been given the plan. Maybe you know the plan."

Eunice pointed a gnarled, wrinkled, index finger straight at her. "How could I know the plan? I've been praying for deliverance and you have the plan!"

"I don't know what you're talking about. I haven't been given any plan. I think I should leave." Tessa moved as if to get up but before she could stand, Eunice burst into heart-wrenching sobs. Staying seated, Tessa watched the woman cry her heart out. There was a handkerchief lying on an end table beside her so she reached to pick it up but her hand went through thin air. Clearly the table and handkerchief didn't exist in real time.

Eunice, as if sensing Tessa's intent, reached for the handkerchief and wiped her face but kept up her wailing. After what seemed like an eternity, Eunice finally calmed somewhat and began to speak, her voice breaking at the effort.

"I've prayed...and prayed for...all these years. I asked God...to send someone...to help us." The weeping began again for a brief moment. She finally let up and continued. "And now, Mary, our dear Mary. How can this...happen to her?" More sobbing. "Deliverance is what...we need and...God promised me...that he'd send someone." She swatted at her face with the handkerchief and wiped at her nose furiously before continuing. "I was sure...you were the one...he sent to help us." With tears streaming down her face she looked at Tessa. "Will you help us?"

Talk about pressure!

"I don't know how."

"You'll know. I promise you...that you'll know. When the time is right you will know the plan." She smiled a semi-toothless grin through her tears. Eunice wiped her face the best she could, with her now-drenched handkerchief, then suddenly stood.

Tessa watched her walk around the room picking things up – a few books, a pillow, a cup lying on its side on the floor, a dead leaf from a plant – but not putting them anywhere in particular. Her arms were soon full but she seemed confused as to how they had gotten that way. After walking over to a corner, she threw them down into a heap and then started pacing back and forth across her room, mumbling to herself. The wandering woman looked lost in a world of her own.

She's forgotten all about me. I suppose our little chat is over.

Tessa stood, walked to the door and opened it. She looked back at Eunice Hardington, who was still pacing back and forth and mumbling nonsense words. It looked like such a sad way to finish the last of a person's days, mixed up and alone. Yet Eunice had spoken fairly intelligently about some things and she seemed to know things she shouldn't and couldn't possibly have known. It was rather threatening and brought on another wave of anxiety.

Stepping out, Tessa closed the door, wandered back downstairs and crossed the quiet foyer. As she gratefully exited the front door, she noticed big snowflakes descending from the cloud-laden sky, coating everything with a fresh, new blanket of snow. It was a pretty sight, seeing the branches of the trees holding a layer of white fluff. She stopped and took in how the snow transformed everything to look clean, pure and white. The gentle fall of the flakes resting wherever they landed had a peaceful effect on her frayed nerves.

If only her mind could absorb their peace. There were too many questions and unknowns. Having a break from all the troubling thoughts would be so welcome. Instead, after her little visit with Eunice, her mind was bombarded by more uncertainty and increasing confusion. After releasing a deep sigh, she walked down the pathway toward the big oak tree, switching back into the present.

Just like that, birds were singing in the tree behind her and she could hear people cutting grass a few yards down the block. She shielded her eyes from the sudden glare of the sun hovering in the western sky, slowly starting its descent to the horizon.

A tremendous sense of relief flooded her as she stepped on the sidewalk heading toward home. Perhaps time with Cody tonight would keep her mind occupied with other things. Eunice's words still rang loudly in her mind. She realized then it would be nearly impossible to enjoy the evening. Eunice had seen to that.

CHAPTER 13

Two and a half weeks passed after Tessa's last visit to the old house. Her life had been fairly uneventful since then. She'd decided to hold off telling Cody about her time travel, although the temptation was often there to do just that. Keeping it from him caused her some guilt. There were so many questions. How would she tell him? What would she say? Would he understand? Would he even believe her?

It was such a personal thing to her. It was God's way of getting a message to her. But more than that, she was terrified that Cody would consider her a complete quack. She didn't think her heart could handle his mockery.

Mary had dominated her thoughts the last few weeks. Just imagining Mary going through electric shock treatments sent chills through her body. Tessa found herself praying for success even though she was completely aware that it lay in the past. It was long done.

If only she knew what had happened to the girl, how her life had turned out. Maybe there was still a chance she'd be shown the whole story. If only it was a book she was reading, she could continue to the end. With days and weeks between episodes, the story was dragging on much too long.

There had been no further sign to go back and the long break was a relief. After all, the last visit had emotionally drained her. It had taken her days to recuperate and be able to function normally again. The more she had prayed about her talk with Eunice, the more apprehensive she became. Trusting God in this whole mess wasn't easy for her.

Luke and Richelle had been upset about her solo mansion visit but had acknowledged her attempts to contact them. She'd promised to take them along the next time. They were completely intrigued by her conversation with Eunice Hardington. She told them as much as she could recall. They concluded together that there probably wouldn't be much action at the mansion for a while with Mary being in Chicago. Luke and Richelle were disappointed but Tessa was relieved that there'd be no pressure from them to go back any time soon.

As soon as she walked into her house she could smell something wonderful cooking on the stove. Heading to the kitchen, she saw her mother cutting up some romaine lettuce at the counter.

"Hi Mom! What are you making?"

"Hi there, dear! I'm making lasagna, Caesar salad and garlic bread. Are you staying for dinner?"

"I think you just talked me into it. Cody hasn't called, has he?"

"No, he hasn't."

"He told me a few days ago that he wanted to go see his mother and sister this weekend. They live about an hour's drive from here." She backed up to the counter and hoisted herself up. Swinging her legs against the cupboards, she turned and watched her mom.

Dianne frowned. "Why wouldn't he take you along to meet them?"

"We've only been seeing each other a short while. And he's planning to stay at his mom's overnight and head back tomorrow. He said he'd take me sometime for a day trip. His mother really wants to meet me."

Dianne stopped working, turned and raised her eyebrows. "It's sounding serious!" A hint of a smile played at her mouth. "How serious is it?"

Tessa shrugged. "I do like him a lot."

"It's not more than that?"

"We've only been dating…," she mentally calculated, "five months now. Give us some time! We're still getting to know each other."

"I'm glad to hear it. I wouldn't want you to rush into a relationship too quickly. It's good to take it slowly and find out what his character is. I like this boy, though; he seems like a nice young man." She turned back to the cutting board.

"Thanks, I think." She rolled her eyes. Her mother always gave her opinion about her boyfriends, regardless of whether it was welcome or not. "I'm going for a shower and then I can help with dinner."

"Okay, that's fine, dear."

The evening was quiet with just the family. Tessa seldom saw her brothers lately. They were both so busy with sports and friends that it wasn't often she was able to enjoy their company at the dinner table.

After the food was consumed, they stayed at the table and talked, catching up on each other's lives. The phone rang and Mac stood to answer it. He soon came back to the table and handed it to Tessa. She took it, got up and headed to the living room.

"Hello?"

"Hi, Tessa."

"Oh hi, Cody! Are you on your way to your mother's?"

"Yeah. I just started out but I miss you already. Why don't we get together Sunday night? I should be back in Chelsey by then."

"I'd love that! I'll be looking forward to it."

"All right, have a great weekend."

"I will. Enjoy your time with your mother."

"I will but I'll be thinking about you the whole time."

It made her smile. "Bye, Cody."

"Bye."

She pushed the "off" button and held the phone in her hands. She pondered how their relationship had changed over the past few weeks. They were more intimate with each other lately. There were still doubts but the more she got to know him, the more she liked him. He was sweet, considerate and always treated her like a lady. He was definitely a rare breed and she wasn't going to let him go anytime soon.

The phone rang in her hands and it shook her from her daydream. Wiping the smile from her face, she chided herself for acting like a love-struck schoolgirl and lifted the phone to her ear.

"Hello, this is the March residence."

"Hi. Tessa?"

"Oh hi, Luke. Yep, it's me. What's up?"

"Well, I have a favor to ask."

Feeling immediately hesitant, she asked, "Like…what?"

"Well, I met this girl. We've been dating a few weeks now. I kind of told her about the mansion thing. She's very curious and wants to check it out. I was just wondering if you'd go with us."

Frustration welled within her. "Luke! Why did you tell her about the mansion?"

"Richelle told Charlie about it. You didn't seem so upset about that."

"It's just that this whole mansion thing isn't a tourist attraction! That's not what it's meant to accomplish. It's not a good idea to be showing everyone this house."

"I'm not asking for everyone, just my girlfriend. What would it hurt? It's not like the Hardingtons know the difference. I'm just asking for one extra person. Come on, Tessa, say yes."

Anger boiled inside her. "Why don't we advertise, sell tickets, do tours and make money while we're at it?"

"Hmm. I think you're onto something."

"Luke!"

"Just kidding. Come on, Tessa. Don't be mad."

"I am mad!"

Silence reigned for a few moments.

Tessa exhaled heavily. "What's her name?"

"Who?"

"Your girlfriend? Or have you forgotten about her already?"

"Now, don't be mean. I know I go through girlfriends rather quickly but this girl is very sweet and she's quite the looker too."

"So, what's her name?"

"Now, what was it again?"

"Luke!"

He chuckled and said, "Janaye Howard. Her name is Janaye Howard. She actually went to the same high school we did. I can't say I remember her from high school. She's two years younger than the two of us. I was focused on girls my own age at that point. You'll like her a lot. You just need to get to know her. So what do you say?"

"Why don't the two of you go on your own?"

"I tried that with Darren. Nothing happens without you there."

"Why does she want to see it?"

"Probably the same reason the rest of us want to see it. It's exciting. I mean, who ever heard of going back in time for real. Come on, Tessa, why are you stalling?"

"I don't know. I don't think it's time for me to go back and I don't want to abuse this thing. We're making it into a peep show instead of what it's meant to be. It's supposed to be a message from Heaven. Using it as entertainment just isn't right. I'm sorry, Luke, but I can't do it."

"Wow, you sure have changed! You're becoming so serious and intense. Do you have to be that way?"

"I'm sorry. I can't help what I'm becoming. This whole thing is on my mind almost nonstop. Maybe it is changing me. I never planned for that to happen but my answer is still no."

"Okay, Tessa. I guess I don't have any choice then. If you change your mind, let me know. Janaye and I will be at my place for a while. Alright?"

"I should say, unless God changes my mind for me, my answer is no."

"Well, let's hope he gets involved. Hey, I know! I'll pray about it."

Tessa laughed at that. "Okay, Luke, you do that. It'll be a first."

"It just might be."

"Bye, Luke."

"Bye, Tessie."

Tessa grimaced as she hung up. She hated being called Tessie and Luke knew it. He must be more upset with her than she thought. "Oh well, he'll get over it."

She put the phone away and helped clean up the kitchen. When that was done, her parents headed to the family room and Tessa decided to join them. Her brothers had disappeared after dinner. They were probably downstairs playing some video game. Her dad switched the T.V. to the local news channel. It was always his first choice and since he usually controlled the remote, that's what they watched.

Dianne looked at Tessa and asked, "Have you heard about this"

"What?"

"They're talking about this run-down house on Young Street. It's been deserted for years and the city council wants it torn down."

"Yeah, they think it's simply a fire hazard and an eye sore," her dad added.

Dianne said, "The neighborhood has registered a lot of

complaints lately and the council has felt pressured into making a decision. Your father heard something on the radio about it." She turned to him, "What did they say again?"

"The city council voted and the decision was made to tear it down. They're throwing ideas around right now. One idea is turning that lot into a park. I think most of the neighborhood was pleased with that suggestion. There's some aversion to it, though. Some people want the house restored to its former condition and sold to a responsible owner. The neighbors surrounding the deserted mansion don't want a park right beside them. It would bring noise with it and would infringe on their privacy. They're pushing for restoration."

Tessa felt relief that there was opposition to the vote.

Her dad continued, "There's another group that offered to buy it and turn it into a bread and breakfast place but that was turned down by the surrounding community because it would create too much traffic on the street."

Dianne said, "Wasn't there something strange about the council? What happened with that? Remember, Harvey, you told me about it?" She sat cuddled up close to him and looked up into his face. He bent over and kissed her gently on the lips before he answered.

"Yes, I remember. One of the most influential members of the council resigned shortly after the vote was made. They hired someone else in his place within a week. As soon as they hired this new guy, he began to push hard for restoration. He must have been quite persuasive because the council reversed their decision and now it's all up in the air again. They want to campaign the neighborhood one more time to see what the public consensus is and vote again. I don't know why this has to be such a prolonged process."

"It's all about politics," said Tessa.

Her dad grinned and nodded.

Dianne asked, "What was his name, Harvey? That new guy. It was strange, wasn't it?"

"Yes, it was unusual. Let me think. I have a hard time remembering names." He fell silent, deep in thought.

"Well, dear, you let us know when you remember." Dianne patted his hand and turned to Tessa.

She couldn't hold back her opinion another second. "I hope they choose to restore the old house. It would be a shame to tear down what used to be such a beautiful home."

Her mother said, "I didn't know you cared about that old thing. Didn't it always frighten you? I remember you telling me Luke once asked you to go with him to explore it and you refused."

"I know, but that was a few years ago and I have grown up a bit since then," she said with a raised eyebrow. "Doesn't that mansion belong to someone? Have they tried to find the owner?"

Her dad looked at her quizzically. "I don't know. I haven't heard anything about any owner. Maybe the city just took over since it's been empty so long. I'm sure the property taxes are in arrears. If they are, the city would have taken it over."

"Are they allowed to do that?"

"I'm sure they have by-laws stating what happens in a situation like this one. They haven't said much about it that I can remember."

Dianne sat up a bit straighter. "Oh, wasn't that councilor's last name native? It was Feathers or something like that."

"Oh yeah, now I remember. It was Featherwing, Gabriel Featherwing. He sounds more like an angel instead of a councilor." He chuckled.

Tessa froze, not knowing if she had heard correctly. "Did the doorbell ring?"

Dianne looked at her. "No, I didn't hear anything. Did you hear the doorbell?" She glanced toward the entrance. There was a large glass window in their front door so it was easy to see if someone was there. "I don't see anyone."

"I thought I heard the bell. It must be nothing." Tessa shook her head in confusion.

Dianne said, "Isn't that quite the name? Gabriel Featherwing! Wouldn't it be amazing if he really were an angel in disguise? I wonder if God ever intervenes in a situation like this, although I don't believe he cares much if that house stays standing or comes down."

Harvey was focused on the next bit of news being broadcast and didn't bother answering.

The sound of bells was slowly fading around Tessa's head. At her mother's mention of an angel, the bells had come back in force.

Tessa glanced toward the door but she already knew she'd see no one there. Sinking into the couch further, the thought of visiting the old mansion tonight distressed her. Not an ounce of desire moved her in that direction but if she truly meant what she'd prayed to God, about wanting his will, then she had to go.

Her parents were glued to the television, watching some news item. Tessa reluctantly stood and started out of the room.

Her mother noticed and said, "Dear, where are you going? I thought you were staying home tonight."

Thinking on her feet, Tessa said, "I'd love to spend a quiet evening at home but Luke called me earlier and he wants to get together. I need to contact him and see what time he wants to meet."

Disappointment in her eyes, her mother smiled sadly and said, "Oh, all right. Have a good time."

Having the whole family home was something her mother loved. Tessa was sorry to disappoint her. Heaving a big sigh, she headed to the phone.

~~~~~

When Tessa arrived at the mansion, Luke and Janaye were waiting for her at the front gate. The first impression she had of the girl was one of surprise. Janaye didn't fit the typical look that Luke usually chose. She was pretty but not strikingly stunning. She was dressed modestly and had an innocent aura about her. Luke introduced them and Tessa had to admit she liked the girl immediately.

She couldn't resist asking, "So how'd you two meet?"

"Janaye works in the office where I work."

Janaye said, "Yes, Luke is quite the charmer. He wanted to date me the first week he was there. I didn't know him from a hole in the ground, so I said no. He wasn't really my type."

Her openness was refreshing. Tessa liked her even more.

"It took a bit of time but eventually I swept her off her feet. She couldn't say no." Luke grinned boyishly.

"Well, getting flowers every day for a week and all those sweet cards made it hard to ignore him. Everyone in the office was talking about it. Luke was the center of the office gossip. It was becoming a joke."

"So that's what all the snickering was about every time I passed the accounting area. I just thought all the girls had a crush on me."

"You are so vain!" Janaye punched his arm.

"No, I'm just very sure of myself. I was very sure I wanted to date you."

Janaye batted her eyes at him and smiled. "It doesn't hurt that you're kind of cute too."

Tessa shook her head. "Okay, I can tell that something is going on here. This is fairly serious after only two weeks."

Janaye nodded and smiled in pleasure. "When Luke told me about this mansion thing, I insisted on seeing it. It sounds completely intriguing!"

Tessa looked at the two love birds and said, "So, are you two ready for this adventure?"

"We're ready!" Luke opened the gate and held it for them.

As they walked toward the big oak tree, Janaye grabbed Luke's arm nervously. "When will we switch over to the past?"

"It always happens on the other side of this tree." He looked as excited about going back as he had the first few times, with no hint of reservation on his face.

The three of them switched over to 1946 and stood on the cleared pathway with snow piled on both sides. Janaye caught her breath and started shivering.

It still amazed Tessa how they could feel the cold even though she knew the snow didn't really exist. To prove her theory, she bent down, reached into the snow bank and her hand went right through it like there was nothing there. Her hand hit the grass beneath and it actually felt warm to the touch. She stood, pleased with her discovery. Perhaps the cold they felt was psychological. The sight of the snow brought on the sensation of chill more than the air temperature around them, although she had to admit the air did feel cooler than what a June day should.

Luke and Janaye kept walking but he turned back to look at her. "What are you doing back there?"

"Just testing out a theory."

"And what theory is that?" He gazed at her quizzically.

"Throw a snowball at me and then you'll know."

He looked at her in disbelief. "Okay. Don't get mad. Remember, you asked for it." He bent down to the waist-high bank of snow beside him. As he applied pressure, the non-existent snow failed to hold him and he went tumbling over and disappeared beneath the bank. Only his feet protruded onto the pathway, with the snow remaining unaffected by his fall.

Janaye screamed and Tessa couldn't help but laugh.

"That looks so hilarious, Luke! You should see yourself. We can only see your feet." She struggled to gain control of her giggling fit.

Luke maneuvered onto all fours and slowly appeared above the snow bank. Janaye's shocked face only added to Tessa's laughter. This was turning out to be good fun!

"Are you okay, Luke?" Janaye asked, a smile edging her lips, as he stood to his feet.

Tessa held back her chuckles and said, "Luke's fine. Did he tell you about the time a servant in this mansion walked right through him?"

Janaye's eyes looked stunned as she shook her head.

"We can see everything like it actually was back in 1946 but we're not really back there. We can see the snow but we can't feel it."

"This is so weird!" Janaye said. "You two scared me with that trick." She looked at Luke accusingly. "Did you plan this ahead of time?"

"No!" He turned wary eyes to Tessa. "I owe you one."

"Oh, don't be mad. You didn't get hurt."

"My pride did!" He said as he brushed bits of grass and dust off his shirt and pants. He turned to her and said, "Are we ready to go now?"

"You are mad at me."

"I never get mad. I just get even." He started up the walkway, then turned and looked back at them. "You know what I just thought of?"

"What?" asked Tessa. She was still struggling to wipe the smirk off her face at the hilarity of seeing him sprawled beneath the snow bank.

"We could use this outdoor trick thing on Richelle. One of us could hide under the snow and the other one could lure Richelle here. Boy, could we ever scare her out of her wits."

"That would be so mean! It would be fun but she would be so mad."

"She'd get over it."

"Oh, just like you're over what I did?"

"It might take some time but she'd forgive us."

"I don't know, Luke. That's like playing with this whole thing again. This is a message from God, not an amusement park."

"Oh? It didn't look like you minded playing with this time travel a minute ago."

"I didn't plan it; it just happened. It was a spur of the moment thing."

"You have a double standard, girl!"

It did seem that way. Tessa didn't know how to answer.

Janaye saved her. "This whole experience is a message from God?"

"Didn't Luke tell you that?"

"I didn't want to freak her out about God and all." He suddenly looked impatient and took a few steps up toward the landing but when he noticed Janaye still standing, wanting to discuss it with Tessa, he stopped and waited.

"That's awesome. How do you know that it's a message from God?"

"An angel appeared to me here and told me. He revealed that he was sent to show me some things."

"Wow!"

"He often shows up when we come here. I apparently have to figure out what God wants me to do by the things that I see here. The angel doesn't even know the complete message. He just shows me what God tells him to each time I come."

Janaye's face filled with amazement. "That is so exciting! I've gone to church my whole life and I've never heard that angels actually appear to people. I mean they did in the Bible but to people we know? This is totally awesome!"

Tessa was surprised to find out Janaye was a church girl and even more surprised that Luke would have picked someone like her.

Janaye asked, "Do you think we'll see the angel today?"

189

Tessa glanced toward the house entrance to see if she could see him. "I don't know. We'll have to see if he shows up."

"Okay, you two, let's go in." Luke took the steps of the landing two at a time.

They entered through the left side. In the foyer an eerie silence greeted them. Standing in the center, none of them knew what to do first.

Tessa felt strongly that she needed to check out Mary's room. She didn't know what was waiting for her there but she couldn't ignore the feeling. "I'm going up to Mary's room first."

Luke said, "I'd like to see if Mr. Hardington's around. Did you two notice the boots by the door? Someone's here and I want to find out who it is. The office door is open but it looks empty. I think I'll check the den first. Janaye, do you want to join me?"

"Yes, I would love to." She looked up at him with a smile, hooked her arm through his and they walked off down the hallway together.

Tessa released a nervous sigh, slowly ascended the stairway then walked along the hallway toward Mary's room. Passing Eunice's room made her nervous but she had no choice. She walked soundlessly, not wanting to draw the old lady's attention again. As she approached, she was grateful to notice that Eunice's door was closed.

She continued on to Mary's room. The door was opened a crack and with a little push, it opened farther. As she entered the room, she noticed it was in perfect order, with the bed made and everything in its place. The makeshift clothesline that had held the new office digs for Mary had been removed. Tessa walked over to the closet and opened it to see if they had been placed inside but didn't recognize any of the clothes that she'd seen hanging on the makeshift clothesline the night of the party. Perhaps they had been put away till Mary improved. They had certainly upset her the night of the party.

The evening gown that Mary had worn that night hung between the folds of two other gowns. Reaching out to touch it, Tessa's hand went right through it. Thoughtfully, she pulled her hand back. Beautifully tailored suits, jackets with skirts, filled the closet space and she guessed that many of them had been outfits Mary had used for university. They would have been more practical than some of the gowns hanging here. Not one pair of pants could be found.

"I sure am thankful I didn't live during her era," Tessa said, closing the closet doors and turning to face the room.

The window seat on the other side of the room looked inviting so she headed that way. Seating herself on the cushion, grateful that it still existed here, she looked out the window. Tessa could see the next door neighbors' house from this vantage point. Their structure was grand and spectacular, with a good distance between the two properties, a stone fence separating the yards. A large tree, just outside Mary's window, heavy with a coating of snow, nearly blocked one side of the window. It was a pretty, winter-wonderland view, which could have been on any current Christmas card. The scenery mesmerized her for a time.

After turning to scan the room once more, she noticed a nightstand on either side of the bed, a pretty lamp on each one. The lampshades were covered in white Battenberg lace and ruffles graced both the top and bottom. The stands were yellow to match the yellow bedding.

The drawer of the nightstand closest to her stood ajar so she sauntered toward the bed and started to sit down. As she did, she realized the foolishness of such a move. What if the bed wasn't even here? She placed her hand down onto the bed and her hand disappeared, stopping on the mattress below. The bed still existed but the bedding was no longer there. Tessa shook her head in amazement. Such strange happenings were still awkward for her. As she sat down, the bed held her, although she sank deep into the bedding.

Turning her attention from the bed to the nightstand, she touched it and after feeling solid wood, opened the drawer and spotted a book inside.

Could this be Mary's diary? The one Luke snooped in?

Reaching inside, her hand penetrated right through the diary and touched the wooden bottom of the drawer. Disappointment was her initial response until she remembered what Luke had told them. He'd managed to manipulate the book with a hanger.

Lifting herself from the bed, she bent down to the floor and felt for what she knew would be here somewhere. Hopefully there was nothing on the floor that would harm her. Any broken glass from the window was probably close to the window sill. Thoughts of spiders crawling around caused her some agitation but her desire to find the discarded hanger carried more pull. After feeling around at the side of the bed and finding nothing, Tessa stood and turned to the bed.

Maybe Luke tossed the hanger onto the bed. She leaned over and touched as far as she could reach but it produced no results. Frustration hounded her. Where would he have left it? She tried to think like her brothers. What would they have done? Where would they have tossed it?

The only idea that came to her was that they would have absently carried it to the door, then realized what they still held in their grasp and chucked it onto the floor on their way out. With that knowledge, Tessa headed to the door, got down on her hands and knees and felt for the object. It didn't take long. A little to the left, beside the doorway, her hand felt it, a thin metal length of hanger.

Picking it up and getting back to her feet, she headed to the other side of the bed. Standing in front of the nightstand provided a better view. It would also be easier, from this vantage point, to manipulate the pages. Hopefully it would work to open the book and turn the sheets from its present location.

Positioning herself carefully, she used the hanger to hook beneath the cover and lifted it. It worked! The cover moved and then, with a careful direction, it swung over and flopped open. She felt like cheering. Delicately, so as not to tear any of the pages, she flipped them over a few at a time until her eyes fell on an entry that looked interesting.

The date was recorded as July 2, 1945. Tessa read:

Today has been a difficult day for me. I've been in school now for almost two years and have taken an equivalent of over three years of business management. I need a repose so badly! I talked to my father about giving me the summer off to rest. He has refused my request, insisting the foolishness of such a decision. He believes it would be for the best if I just continue right on through till I'm done. It will mean summer school.

Well, I don't believe that's the best for me. My schedule is overwhelming and I realize I won't be able to handle much more of this. Even begging for him to reconsider this unreasonable pace was useless. Immovable is how I would describe him and I hate him for it! Guilt and hatred vie for dominance when I think of my father. If only he could see my distress. The only thing he is willing to acknowledge is his own viewpoint. I feel so very tired. If only I were a bird, I'd fly away to a deserted island and rest. I shouldn't complain. My father is giving me an amazing opportunity. There is so much to be thankful for. If only my heart could grasp that.

A career should be a dream come true. It would be that if I were taking nursing. My father insists that I become a bank manager, joining him in his work.

He refuses to consider my wants. My desires are changing lately. Now what I desire more than anything is to marry the man I love and be a wife and mother. A few of my acquaintances are engaged and a few are married. I envy them. Marrying Henry will be out of the question if my father has his way.

Ever since Henry returned from the war, dreaming of a life with him keeps me going. We'd live in a nice house, surrounded by a white picket fence. We'd have two children and I know the names I would choose for them. The girl we would name Beth after my mother. The boy would be Luke, a name I've always loved.

Daydreaming is an escape, helping me forget about my life for a few moments, providing a spell of peace.

When the day's entry was done, Tessa closed the diary and stared at the cover for a long time. That Luke's name was mentioned in Mary's writing astounded her. Was there a possibility that he was somehow related to this family? Maybe Mary did eventually have a son and if she did name him Luke, perhaps he would have named his son after himself. Tessa knew her mind was wandering to the brink of impossibility but there was a slight chance that there could be a link.

She tried to think back to what Luke had told her about his family but she couldn't remember him ever talking about his father. It had been a rare occasion that she'd ever been at Luke's house while they were in high school. When the three of them got together it would usually be at either Richelle's or Tessa's place. Luke avoided inviting them over and now she wondered why. She needed to have a heart-to-heart with him.

Luke lived about three blocks from her house while they were in high school. Now, during the summer, he was renting an apartment but it seemed odd to her. Why wouldn't he have moved in with his mother for a few months? Tessa didn't know what their relationship was like but living with his mother would have saved him money, something he needed for his next year of university.

Tessa closed the drawer of the nightstand, placed the hanger so it rested on top of the piece of furniture and exited the room. Heading down the hall, she descended the stairs and searched the foyer for any sign of Luke and Janaye. It was deathly quiet there. The two of them had headed down the left hallway earlier so she went in that direction. Partway down, voices filtered toward her.

A large set of dark wooden doors to the left caught her eye. They were imposing and impressive. Did they lead to the den Luke mentioned? Pulling on one of the doors, she opened it a crack and looked inside. Mr. Hardington was seated on a leather couch discussing business with a gentleman she hadn't seen before. The gentleman looked dwarfed by the big leather chair opposite Mr. Hardington. On the far wall was a huge fireplace, logs burning within, and a deer head mounted on the space above it.

Pulling the door open farther, Tessa squeezed inside and looked to her left. Luke and Janaye were here, their backs hugging the wall. Both of them turned to her as she took up a position beside them.

"What's happening?"

Luke said, "Shhh! Just listen."

William spoke. "So how do we go about doing that?"

"Well, I have some contacts in Chicago. I've been keeping in touch with them this past week and it seems there are some incredible opportunities. There are buildings that we could buy for a very good price. I've also hired an architect to give us ideas on renovations and inquired with some contractors regarding quotes on cost."

"How soon can we move on these deals, Alfred?"

"As soon as you say the word, sir."

"Well, then move on it now. It's the right time to expand and check out other markets. I believe we're ready for it."

"It's an exciting time, sir. Do you know who will run the bank in Chicago?"

"I myself will run it."

Alfred looked confused. "But, sir, what about the responsibilities you have with the bank here in Chelsey? You can't just abandon it."

"It will not be abandoned. Provisions are being made. You will be one of the top executives here and I will depend on you to make sure things keep running smoothly."

"Well yes, certainly, but how will you run the bank in Chicago? Managing it long distance would be difficult. Are you planning to move your family there?"

"That's exactly what I have in mind. Things have been difficult for us here and I think a new start would be refreshing for the family."

"This is truly a surprise." Alfred didn't look pleased with the information. "Who do you have in mind as manager for the bank here in Chelsey?"

"I'm not ready to reveal that yet. I have some ideas to consider and some people in mind. I'll let you know when I've made my final decision."

"Sir, I have a lot of experience and know I could handle the job. I hope that you keep me in mind in your decision-making."

William stood, signifying the meeting was over. Alfred stood as well, quickly gathered his papers and placed them into his briefcase.

Walking to the door, William opened it wide and said, "Have a good day, Alfred. My butler, James, will see you out."

"Just remember, sir, that I could handle the job." His eyes shone with anticipation. Or maybe it was greed.

William nodded but refused to answer. "Good-bye, Alfred," is all he said.

Alfred left and William returned to the couch to look over some papers that covered the coffee table. He appeared lost in thought.

Luke pointed to the door, the girls nodded, and they walked quietly out of the room and closed the door. As they entered the foyer, they watched James see Alfred out and head back down a hallway to his other duties.

Tessa looked at Luke. "So what was that all about? William Hardington is starting another bank?"

"Yep. I'm not sure how Mary plays into all of this. Don't know if she'll move with them."

Tessa was confused. "I wonder why William would consider moving his family all the way to Chicago. Wouldn't that be harder on Mary? She'd be separated from her friends and all that's familiar to her."

Luke said, "I don't know what he's thinking. It does seem like a good business decision, though. It's always good to expand if it's a money-making proposition. I'm not sure if it'd be good for Mary or not."

Janaye said, "From what Luke's told me, Mary's gone a little loco so would she even know the difference? Does it really matter where she lives?"

"I think it does," insisted Tessa. "She's had enough upheaval in her life the last while. Having a stable environment would help in her recovery."

Luke nodded and the conversation stalled. He finally said, "Anyway, I think I'm ready to go. Are you two pretty ladies ready?"

Janaye stepped closer to Luke, slipped her hand into his and said, "I'd love to see the rest of the house."

"Tessa, did you want to stay with us and give Janaye a tour?"

"I guess it wouldn't hurt. Let's go."

During the quick tour, Tessa realized how large the house actually was. Many of the rooms she'd never seen before. Janaye was amazed at how beautiful it was. The last room they looked at was the sitting room and while they were there Luke demonstrated some of the strange things about their time travel experience. While Janaye studied the room, Luke went over to the grand piano and walked right through it. When she noticed him standing in the center of the piano, she let out a high-pitched scream.

Luke laughed loudly, came to stand beside Janaye and explained what just happened.

Pushing against his arm, she said, "Don't do that to me! You scared me."

"But isn't this cool? Who has ever gone back in time and experienced things like this? I love being here."

Tessa said, "You've forgotten quickly how it feels to be the one fooled. Remember the snow thing?"

A sly glint flashed from his eyes. "I haven't forgotten. I'm the one who usually does the practical jokes around here. Try to remember that."

Ignoring him, Tessa turned to Janaye and pointed to Luke. "You'll have to keep an eye on that one."

Luke only shrugged in reply.

"He is a strange one." Janaye gave him an adoring look. "But I won't trade him in quite yet."

"I'm thankful for that!" He gazed at her tenderly and placed an arm around her shoulders.

Tessa turned and walked toward the foyer. "I'm ready to go."

Luke and Janaye followed and they headed out the front door.

CHAPTER 14

On Monday, Luke was already waiting when Tessa arrived at JACY'S restaurant. She'd called him and said they needed to talk. Scanning the restaurant, she noticed him sitting at a booth toward the back and headed that way. Luke stood to embrace her and gave her a kiss on the cheek before they took their seats.

"Hey, beautiful, how are you?"

"I'm great. Should you be hugging and kissing me now that you have a girlfriend? The word might get around that you've been seen with another woman." She gave him a mischievous smile.

"Janaye better not be jealous like Charlie or else she's out of here! I won't put up with that kind of foolishness."

"It looked like the two of you were getting along well the other day."

"She's great, isn't she?"

"I really like her."

He looked pleased with her admission.

A waitress approached, holding an order pad and pen and asked what she could get them. Tessa ordered a Diet Coke and Luke decided on a coffee and a piece of apple pie with ice cream. The waitress left quickly.

Gazing at Luke for a moment, Tessa finally broke the quiet and asked about his job. He told her how pleased he was and the opportunities he'd been given. They'd even offered him a job for the following summer and a full-time position after he finished university.

Tessa said, "I'm happy for you. And to top it off you found yourself a girlfriend there. You're doing pretty well this summer."

"No complaints, no complaints." He grinned widely, looking pleased with his accomplishments. "And how about your job? Do you enjoy it at The Eating Place?"

"It's about what I expected. It's hard work because I'm on my feet all day and it's a very busy restaurant. It keeps me out of trouble, I suppose." She told him about some of her challenges and her coworkers.

During her dialogue, the waitress brought them their drinks and the pie. Luke dove right in and finished in no time. Tessa finished talking and watched him eat. After coming up for air, Luke wiped his mouth on his napkin.

Tessa said, "That was quick. You must be hungry. Should I call the waitress back to take another order?"

"The idea is tempting but I better stop at one piece." He took a sip of his coffee, set it down, looked at her and asked, "So what did you want to talk about?"

Tessa told Luke about the diary entry she'd read and her possible theory. Luke sat quietly, his forehead furrowed in thought, his smile gone and a forlorn look clouding his eyes.

"I wish I had a father and a family line that I could look back on. I don't have a father; I mean I know I have a father somewhere but I don't know him and have never seen him. He's never been part of my life."

"I know that your mother raised you. Was she ever married?"

"No. I've always gone by my mother's last name. Her maiden name and the only name she's ever had is Owens."

"I guess you never talked about your family much."

"There was never much to talk about. I didn't want people feeling sorry for me. My life was my life and I just dealt with it. Talking about it wasn't going to bring my father on the scene so I just kept quiet."

"Do you know what happened between your parents? Do you know anything about your father?"

Luke's face revealed how hard these questions were on him. He went from leaning forward over his coffee to slouching back into the seat, his hands clenched tightly. "I don't know, Tessa. I don't know if there's any point in discussing this."

"It might help to share it with someone who cares about you."

The way he looked at her, the sadness in his eyes, almost made her cry. Suddenly, she realized how little she really knew Luke and the pain he carried. She knew virtually nothing of his past.

Luke let out a deep sigh, stared into his coffee mug and finally lifted his gaze to look at her. "You really want to know about my past?"

"I think it would help for you to talk about it."

"Who would it help?"

"Maybe it would help you, or us to know each other better. I'm not exactly sure. I thought you might want to get it out instead of carrying it inside."

Luke smiled. "You've suddenly become a psychiatrist?"

"No! Only a friend who cares about you."

Nodding, he said, "Well, remember you asked for it. If this bores you to tears, don't blame me." He waited a moment as if expecting her to change her mind.

Patiently, she waited.

Leaning forward again, his arms resting on the table, he finally began. "I've asked my mom about my father. He was her boss. It was her first job right after high school. She was his secretary and he made advances. Aware that he was married, she initially resisted his attention. With all his wooing, constant compliments and kindness, she began to soften. That he was the typical tall and handsome dude also played in to it. My mom said I look a lot like him." With a crack of a smile, he raised and lowered his eyebrows a few times.

His attempt at light-heartedness made her smile.

The smile vanished and he continued. "My mom fell in love with him and they eventually started an affair. He made all sorts of promises; he told her that he'd divorce his wife and marry her. For about two years they spent a lot of time together but he still wouldn't divorce his wife. Eventually the hard facts began to hit her: he wanted both worlds, his wife and family and a girlfriend on the side. I think he had a few kids with his wife." Anger flashed from his eyes and he said, "He sounds like a real jerk, doesn't he?"

"I'd say!"

"My mom told me that his wife eventually found out about her and wanted the affair to stop. He wasn't willing to give my mom up so he ended up leaving his wife and kids and moved in with my mother."

"How long did that last?"

"Well, a few months later she got pregnant. Once he found out he started treating her differently. He became distant and aloof. He didn't want her to work anymore so she quit her job. That's when the excuses started about having to work late. When I was born he didn't even come to see us at the hospital. There was some reason for that too. Excuses became the norm. Shortly after that, my mother found out that he had a new mistress. She kicked him out and never saw or heard from him again. End of story."

"Wow! What a horrible, awful man."

"I've hated him for a lifetime and don't even know him."

Compassion filled her. "I'm so sorry, Luke."

"Don't worry about it, beautiful. I try not to think about him. It ruins my day to waste time on him."

"Did your mother ever mention his name?"

"Let's drop it okay, Tessa? I don't want to mention the jerk's name."

"All right." The look on Luke's face told her he was through with the discussion so she willingly dropped it.

They sat quietly for a while, both lost in their own thoughts. Luke finally spoke up.

"With what you told me at the beginning about Mary's diary entry, I don't think there's any way I could be related to the Hardingtons. I don't know of any connection at all. My mother's family is originally from New York. My mother, her brother and their parents moved to this area when she was in high school and then, when I was two, my mother moved away from here. We moved to Minneapolis for a while because she wanted to forget all the pain of her relationship with my father.

"Working at a grocery store there as a cashier, she worked her way up to a manager's position. The grocery store owners were opening new stores all over the place and an opportunity opened up for her back here in Chelsey. I'd just finished tenth grade and she asked me about moving back here. Being offered a store manager position here with a substantial raise really intrigued her. I told her to go for it. It was an amazing opportunity for her. With me being in high school, she was concerned about moving, but I didn't care. I just wanted what was best for her and it worked out okay for both of us."

"Your mother must be very special to you."

"She's all I have. I have relatives on her side. I have an uncle and grandparents. My uncle is married and has three kids. I know my cousins but not that well. They grew up here and I grew up in

Minneapolis. My mom is very dear to me; she's the sweetest mother anyone could have. I guess I've always been very protective of her and she tends to be a bit overprotective of me."

"Is that why you didn't move in with her this summer?"

"That's part of it, but another reason is that she's been seeing someone and I didn't want to get in the way. She never had a boyfriend all the years I was growing up. I can remember a few guys showing interest in her but she always refused. She wanted to focus her attention on raising me and now that I'm in university, she's trying out her single wings again."

"I hope she finds someone wonderful who will truly love her."

"I hope so too. If anyone ever hurts my mother again, I'll kill him."

"Oh, Luke, you wouldn't do that!" But then, the fierce look in his eyes didn't lie.

"I'd be tempted to. My mother deserves a decent guy. I know she hasn't done everything right either. I mean she technically broke up someone's marriage. If my father hadn't pressured her for a relationship I don't think she ever would have fallen for him. She can read the character of a person very well now and she's very choosy about men."

Tessa could tell he was proud of her. His love for her was obvious.

Tessa said, "I'm going to change the subject."

"Go for it."

"Have you heard from Richelle lately?"

"I called her Sunday. I made sure she answered the phone before I revealed who I was. I don't need Charlie breathing down my neck again. I told her about us going to the mansion on Saturday and she was furious about being left out."

"Oh-oh! Now I'll be in trouble. You shouldn't have told her."

"She would have found out eventually anyway."

"That's probably true. I just didn't think of calling her. I only thought of it later when I got back home. I'll have to head over there and have a talk with her."

Luke was grinning from ear to ear. Trouble should have been his second name. It would suit him.

"I have to run, Tessa." He stood and threw a twenty-dollar bill down on the table.

Grabbing the bill, Tessa said, "It can't be that much."

"The waitress can keep the change."

The tip was a good ten bucks. "Come over to The Eating Place more often and sit in my section, would you?"

Walking out of the restaurant, they said their good-byes, hugged and went different directions.

Tessa decided to take the bus to Richelle's apartment and appear unannounced. A block from her destination, she exited. Stopping at a florist first, she bought a few carnations and a card before heading on.

The apartment building was old and didn't have any security system up front. She walked through the entrance, up the stairs to the second floor. In one hand she held the flowers and card and knocked on the door with her other. She heard footsteps inside and the door swung open. Charlie stood before her with a surprised expression but he offered no welcome.

"Is Richelle here?"

"Yeah, I'll get her."

It didn't take long for Richelle to appear and, when she saw Tessa, a scowl creased her pretty face. Crossing her arms, she said, "I know why you're here. You're here to make up and those flowers are not going to help. So just take them and give them to your mother or somebody else. I don't want them!"

"Richelle, please don't be mad. I totally forgot to call you. I wasn't planning to go Saturday night and I didn't do it on purpose. Then I heard the bells again when my parents mentioned the word angel and something about the city council. It was a real spur of the moment decision! Please forgive me, okay?"

"I don't know if you deserve it."

Richelle could be so stubborn at times.

"Well, I don't know what else I can say. Here take these, I don't want them." Tessa held out the carnations but Richelle kept her arms crossed, a scowl still twisting her flawless face.

Slowly Richelle's anger subsided and, with a sigh, she reached out and grabbed them. "Okay, I forgive you." Turning, she walked into the apartment.

Tessa wasn't sure if she was invited in or not so she waited.

Richelle swung around and said, "Are you coming in, or what?"

"You didn't invite me in!"

"Well, I am now, so come in!"

"Okay." Tessa shrugged her shoulders, partly in frustration at her rudeness and partly in relief that the apology was over.

Richelle could be volatile when offended and Tessa didn't always know how to respond.

The T.V. was on and Charlie was in the big armchair, watching a baseball game. Richelle waved her into the kitchen and, after pouring two cups of coffee, they sat down at the kitchen table.

"So what's up? What happened at the mansion the other night?" Richelle still looked a bit upset but at least she was willing to converse and Tessa breathed deeply in relief before speaking.

After filling in the details of the visit, Tessa explained her possible theory on Mary's diary entry. "After talking to Luke, I don't think there's any connection there. I thought I had stumbled onto something important, but I guess I was just jumping to conclusions. I so desperately want to understand how everything fits together and make sense of it all."

Richelle said, "Well, don't let go of that yet. It might be a connection to something."

"I find it both interesting and frustrating. Looking into the past and putting the pieces together like parts of a puzzle is fascinating. I just wish it were a faster process. It's dragging out too long for my taste."

"I think the suspense of it all is what makes it so exciting. I wish we could go back in time every weekend."

Tessa shook her head. "That's too often for me. I think of it constantly as it is; it's mind-consuming. I wish there was a switch I could turn to 'off' some days."

"I still wonder if there's a connection between the three of us that's more than just friendship. My grandmother was involved in all of this, I recognized her at the mansion. It could be that we're all linked to the place somehow. It makes me so curious that I can hardly stand it!"

A unique thought crossed her mind. "Richelle, I just thought of something."

"What is it?"

"You moved here in tenth grade, didn't you?"

"Yes. Why?"

"Where did you move from again?"

"From Cincinnati, Ohio. My father's company transferred him here. He's into computer software and they needed some experienced leadership people for their branch here in Chelsey. I don't remember him ever asking me if I wanted to move. It was the pits leaving all my friends!"

"What I'm getting at is your grandmother was at the mansion in 1946. Did your family originate from this area?"

"Oh yeah, as a matter of fact they did. My mother moved to Cincinnati to go to university there. That's where my mother and father met, married and settled down. My grandparents stayed in Chelsey all their lives. And then we moved back here when I was in tenth grade."

"That explains that. I was wondering how your grandmother could have been at that mansion."

Richelle talked about the move, how hard it had been on her and discussed the start of their friendship. As she talked, Charlie came into the kitchen and got a beer from the refrigerator.

With his back to the counter, he opened the can and it popped. "What are you talking about?"

With a smile, Richelle said, "Hi, sweetie! We're reminiscing about our friendship; how it all started."

"How did you two meet?"

Richelle filled him in.

"I wish I had a good friend like that from high school. All I remember is a lot of tense moments, fights and a lot of blood. I won most of them." He smiled crookedly. "I guess I was a bit of a bully. It's not much to look back on. At least I won the majority of the fights. That's something to be proud of."

"Oh, my tough Charlie!" Richelle said with admiration. She turned to Tessa and said, "He's not that tough when you get to know him. Inside, he's a softy."

"Hey, don't give away my secrets. I'll have to kill you if you do." He walked behind her and pulled her ear.

Grabbing his hand, she pulled it to her mouth and kissed it. "You'd miss me too much and you know it."

With a boyish grin, Charlie walked back to watch the game.

After he'd gone, Tessa asked, "You really love him, don't you?"

"No, you really think so?" she said sarcastically.

"Do you think you'll marry him?"

"If he asked, I'd say yes right away."

"Do you ever talk about marriage?"

"I've told him that I'd love to marry him but he doesn't like to talk about it. It's almost like he's afraid to discuss marriage. He seems to be happy with this arrangement so I don't want to rock the boat, if you know what I mean. By the way, how are you and Cody doing?"

"Great. He really is a wonderful guy. There are so many great things about his character. The more I learn about him, the more I like what I see."

"Sounds serious. Have you told him about the mansion thing?"

"No, and I'm feeling very guilty about it. I mean Charlie knows about it and now Janaye knows and both of them have been there. I haven't even mentioned it to Cody. I want to tell him the next time we're together."

"Really? You haven't told him?"

"No." Her guilt felt heavier with the admission.

"I'm shocked! Do you think he'll be upset that you've kept it from him?"

"I hope not. I don't think so. He's not easily upset about things."

"Will you take him over there?"

"I will if he wants me to."

"Can you imagine how many people could be there the next time we check out the mansion? If the three of us go with our sidekicks, we'll be six in all."

Tessa's uneasiness crept back. "Is it getting too out of hand, do you think?"

"Well, like you said about the diary entry, there could be a purpose in us all being there. Maybe our sidekicks fit into the picture somehow too."

It seemed a bit implausible to Tessa and she grimaced.

"All I'm saying is that it could be possible. When are you going to tell Cody?"

"We haven't spent much time together lately. He was away last weekend. I thought of telling him Sunday night but it didn't work out. I'm planning on telling him this coming weekend."

Tessa looked at the time and stood. "I have to get going."

After saying goodbye, promising Richelle she'd be included on the next mansion visit, Tessa left the building and walked over to the bus station. Beautiful soft pastels colored the western sky as the sun descended on the horizon. The sunset was mesmerizing, an amazing tapestry of color and light. What an awesome artist God was to paint such a scene for her at such an unexpected moment.

Is that what God's doing with my life? Does he want to paint a picture on my heart? What if that's what he's trying to do but he can't because I'm too busy slapping my own paint around?

That imagery bothered her and she shook her head at the disturbing thought. The bus approached and came to a screeching halt. Tearing her eyes from the kaleidoscope of color, she got out her bus pass and boarded.

CHAPTER 15

After a hectic day and too many run-ins with Martha, Tessa made it home in record time, her agitation contributing to her speedy pace. Walking into the house, Muffin, their cat, opened lazy eyes, stood and stretched on the living room chair he usually occupied and meowed at her. Stepping toward him, Tessa rubbed his fur until he seemed satisfied.

She headed to her room to prepare for her date with Cody. Anticipation filled her as her thoughts flitted to the evening ahead – and it was more than just the planned dinner and show. It had been a while since they'd been alone, the two of them, and she missed him more than she had imagined possible. These feelings were new for her. Shaking off the frustrations of her day, she took a quick shower with a cheerful hum, got dressed and did her hair.

Later, after dinner and a movie, Tessa and Cody decided to head over to Michael's Mocha Shop. It took them fifteen minutes to drive there but Tessa didn't mind. It gave them time to debate their views on the movie.

When they arrived, they ordered coffee at the counter then found a booth. They both sipped their hot drinks. Cody gazed at her in noticeable approval and, although she enjoyed it, his intense gaze also brought some discomfort. She dropped her eyes and focused on the whitened coffee in her cup.

"Do you know how beautiful you are?"

She looked up in surprise and smiled. "You're embarrassing me, you know?"

"I'm serious, Tessa. You're always beautiful but tonight you look especially gorgeous with the sundress you're wearing and your hair up like that."

Swallowing and feeling nervous, she said, "Thanks. You don't look so bad yourself."

"Is that supposed to be a compliment?" he asked with a

chuckle.

It made her smile. "I admit that was kind of lame. Let me try again."

He waited.

After clearing her throat, she said, "You're a very handsome man and I love to be seen with you."

He nodded. "Not bad!" He stood then, reached over the table, placed his hands on either side of her face and planted a soft kiss on her lips.

Warmth radiated from her middle upwards and she was sure her face was turning a bright pink. The unexpected kiss had taken her off guard but it had also brought a flutter to her middle that she couldn't ignore. As Cody took his seat again, Tessa looked around to see how much attention that had drawn. No one really saw or cared. They were all too involved in their own conversations. She met his eyes and saw a mischievous twinkle there.

"You surprised me."

"You don't like spontaneous kisses?" He looked a little disappointed.

"Well, I do. I don't like drawing attention." With a shrug, she smiled, "I guess I can get used to it."

"We've hardly seen each other. I've missed you. We need more time together. I know we're both busy but we have to make time for us."

Tessa nodded. With work and time travel it was hard to fit him in. A stab of guilt thrust through her.

"You seem really preoccupied lately. Is there something on your mind?"

Stalling for a minute, she finally said, "I suppose I do have a lot on my mind." She had to be sure she understood. "Why do you ask?"

His eyes registered concern. "Sometimes when we're together it's like you're not really with me. Your mind seems to drift and you don't really engage in conversation. It worries me a bit. I mean, if you're not sure about our relationship, please say so. I don't want to fall head over heels in love with you just to find out that you don't care for me. Honesty would be good here. I need to know where you're at and how you feel."

This was her opportunity to reveal the truth. She felt overcome by nervousness but knew he deserved an explanation. "I'm sorry if I've given you the impression I'm not interested. It's true that I've been very preoccupied but it's not because I'm not enjoying your company. My feelings for you are growing. In fact, I love being with you and think we get along very well."

"Well, I want to let you know right now before we go any further that I am definitely in love with you. You're the girl for me. I've been praying about us – that I'd know if you're the one." He smiled. "I've known for a few weeks now, without a doubt, that you're the girl for me." Lifting both hands as if in surrender, he said, "Not that I want to apply pressure or anything; it's just that I thought you should know where I'm coming from."

Shock and pleasure pounded in her chest. She stared at him wide-eyed. Amazement over his confession flooded her and she was at a loss for words. Finally, she said, "Wow! You're full of surprises tonight. I wasn't expecting that and don't know what to say."

"You don't have to say anything. That's not why I shared what I did. But, if you have any doubts about us, now's the time to let me know."

She shook her head. "I don't have a single doubt, Cody. Just give me some more time to get to know you."

"I can do that." He smiled. "Now, what's been on your mind lately?"

Tessa pushed aside her feelings of apprehension. "I need to share something with you. I just don't know how. Something's been happening for a number of weeks. It's so hard to explain." Her hands felt damp and she rubbed them on her dress nervously. "To me it's very personal and I needed to understand it first before telling you. To be honest, I still don't understand it all but I know it's time to let you know."

Cody's eyebrows reached for each other. "This sounds fairly mysterious. What's it about?"

Starting from the beginning, she told Cody the story, the whole time-travel mansion experience, angel and all. Drawing from courage she didn't know she possessed, she even told him about Charlie and then Janaye tagging along to see it. Although Cody remained absorbed till the end of her story, he didn't respond like Charlie or Janaye had. A strange look filled his eyes and he sat quietly studying his coffee mug.

"So, what do you think? Do you believe me or do you think I'm a total nut case?" A nervous giggle escaped.

Cody looked deep in thought but kept his eyes averted. Tessa's anxiety increased at his unexpected silence, causing her to fidget with her cup, spoon and napkin, not sure what to make of the surreal moment.

Finally he lifted his eyes to hers and said, "Why did you wait so long to tell me? I mean, Charlie – is that his name?"

"Yes."

"Charlie and Janaye were welcomed to go before you even told me? Why is that?" His eyes betrayed hurt.

That is what Tessa had feared. She had hoped Cody wouldn't be upset. But now, here they were in this difficult conversation and she felt at a loss how to explain it to him.

"I don't know what to say except that I didn't know when was the best time to tell you. It wasn't my choice to invite Charlie or Janaye; my friends pressured me into it. If it had been my decision, only the three of us, Richelle, Luke and I, would have been privy to it. I didn't want anyone else to know until I figured out the purpose of the time travel. I'm sorry I didn't tell you sooner; I wanted to but it never seemed like the right time. I was afraid it might strain our relationship and didn't want to upset you."

"I am upset." The hurt in his eyes attested to that.

Her heart fluttered in consternation. "Will you please forgive me?"

With a nod of his head and a troubled sigh, he said, "What choice do I have?"

She felt like a complete heel, an idiot. Why did she keep it from him?

"Yes, I forgive you, Tessa. I'm still not sure why you didn't tell me sooner but hey, whatever, I'll get over it."

"I'm really sorry."

"Yeah, I know."

The pain in his eyes made her guilt feel heavier.

"The old mansion you're talking about is the one on Young Street, isn't it?"

"Yes," she said, relieved that he was shifting the conversation somewhat.

His head bobbed in understanding. "There's something I haven't told you. I didn't know if it would mean anything to you, but now it might. Our church is looking into buying that house."

"Are you serious?" The change of subject felt wonderful, like a breath of fresh air.

"You know that we minister to a lot of street people and some of them are hooked on alcohol and drugs. They're really bound to their addictions and a lot of them feel so hopeless. Many of them attend our church. Our pastor has wanted to help them in a practical way for a long time. Just recently our church has grown in numbers. There are some new people that have a heart for the down and out and they have the money to do something about it. Now there's an opportunity to actually help these people on the street. Our church wants to turn that house into a rehabilitation and deliverance center. Right now we're looking into the legal aspects of buying it. There's a lot of red tape involved but one man on the city council is very supportive. He's doing his best to see that the council votes in favor of this."

"So how's that going to work? You'll turn this house into a rehab center and do what with these people?"

"Well, it's going to be much more than rehab. The pastor's shared some of his ideas. He's researched other rehabilitation ministries so he has some understanding of how it should be done. Pastor Chad wants to minister to both men and women but it wouldn't be practical to house men and women in the same place – too distracting for those trying get free. He wants to start with a home for women and then eventually open another one for men."

"Do you think the neighborhood will accept this proposal?"

"That's another concern we'll have to contend with. We're praying for God to smooth the way for us."

"That's amazing for a small church like yours to have such a big vision."

"I find it very exciting! My pastor believes that it's the Word of God that will set these women and men free. You know, God sends his words and heals us. So the focus will be on the Word of God. He believes that renewing their minds and way of life will be the answer."

"I think it's wonderful. It's a pretty big vision."

"It really is."

"Would you consider working in the men's facility, you know, when it's operational?"

A thoughtful expression crossed his face. "I hadn't really considered that. I don't know. I think I'd find it extremely fascinating."

Something Cody said triggered a memory. "That guy on the city council, isn't his name Gabriel Featherwing?"

"Yes, that's it. How did you know?"

"My parents heard about him and were discussing him one evening. Did you know that the city council had decided to tear the house down and put a park in there?"

Cody shook his head.

"Well, apparently Gabriel Featherwing replaced another city council member that resigned and he had the whole decision reversed in a matter of days. It sounds like God has his hand on that house."

"Interesting! Perhaps God placed him there and maybe this Gabriel fellow will pave the way for our idea."

Tessa nodded.

Cody said, "I wonder why God is so interested in that mansion when it seems like so much sadness has happened there. Why even bother with it after all these years? It makes me wonder what God's up to. Do you know what he's trying to show you there?"

"I know it has to do with his plan for my life. He's trying to redirect me in some way. It's like a big puzzle that I have to piece together. I wish it were a faster process because I think about it constantly and, to be honest with you, it's messing up my summer."

Cody grinned.

Seeing his positive attitude returning was encouraging. Perhaps his disappointment in her had abated.

Cody said, "For some reason God wants to save that house and do something with it. You'll have to keep me informed on what God shows you there."

Gazing at him, she realized again what a great guy he was. A twinge of guilt prodded her to make a suggestion. "Would you be interested in visiting the old house with me sometime?"

"If that's what you'd like."

His calm, unemotional response was so foreign. It was

completely opposite to the way everyone else had reacted to the idea of time travel and it confused her. Maybe she had hurt him more than she realized. Perhaps his aloof reply was proof of that.

"I would love to have you join me!"

"Well then, I'd be happy to accompany you the next time you go. Just let me know and I'll be ready."

Feeling relieved, Tessa said, "I'll do that."

Cody moved to get up. "Let's go, beautiful. I'll take you home."

Tessa relaxed. It was nice to hear him call her beautiful. Knowing of his love for her, that term of endearment meant a great deal. When Luke called her beautiful she knew it was merely an expression of affection and close friendship. Hearing it from Cody was different. Their relationship was moving faster than she'd anticipated and it both thrilled her and caused some nervousness. She hadn't been prepared for his confession tonight. To admit to love was a serious thing!

As they drove, Tessa's mind was occupied with their earlier conversation. When they arrived at her house, Cody exited the vehicle, walked around the car and opened the door for her. Stepping out, she waited as he closed it and faced her. The desire in his eyes was like a balm. Moving toward her, he took her in his arms and kissed her with deep passion. Desire soon raged between them. It was at that moment she knew all was forgiven. She allowed her frame to melt into his loving embrace. After a few moments, Cody pulled back, his eyes dark, his breathing intense, and his smile melting her heart.

"Can I see you tomorrow?"

"Yes," she said breathlessly, her heart racing wildly.

"I'll miss you!" He placed a light kiss on her lips.

"I'll miss you too!"

Cody finally pulled out of the embrace and watched as Tessa walked to her front door. He got into his car and drove off, Tessa watching from the front window till the car disappeared around the corner.

Now she knew where things stood. He loved her! He really did! She felt giddy with the realization and grateful he had been so honest, her heart still fluttering with the intensity of their embrace.

If only every area of her life would become as clear and

definite.

CHAPTER 16

Cody and Tessa arrived at the abandoned mansion just before the arranged time so they waited on the sidewalk at the gate. A minute later Richelle's white Honda pulled up to the curb and she and Charlie got out. Only Luke and Janaye were missing. They had agreed to meet them here.

When Richelle and Charlie joined Cody and Tessa on the sidewalk, they all made introductions. This was the first time Cody had met the two.

During church that morning, the pastor had mentioned angels a number of times. Ringing bells had distracted Tessa from paying much attention to anything else he said. After lunch she'd contacted her friends and they all made room in their schedules to come. There'd be six of them on this visit today. Tessa didn't like that their numbers were growing but she couldn't force anyone to stay away.

Two weeks had passed since Tessa had been here and she was sure Mary would be back from Chicago by now. On the drive over, Tessa filled Cody in on as much as she knew about the occupants of this house. She felt impatient to discover how Mary handled the treatments and scanned the sidewalk for any sign of Luke.

"Where's Luke with his new girlfriend? What's her name again?" Richelle searched the sidewalk in both directions.

"Her name's Janaye and I don't know where he's staying. He said he'd be here at four o'clock sharp." Tessa looked at her cell phone. It showed four-fifteen. "He must be running late."

Someone was calling from down the sidewalk and they all looked in that direction. Janaye was hurrying toward them.

"Hi there, everyone. I'm Janaye Howard, Luke's girlfriend." She held out her hand and shook everyone's hand. "Luke is going to be a little late. We were ready to come when something came up. He told me to go on ahead to let you know he'll be here soon."

Tessa nodded and said, "All right then; I suppose he'll catch up with us." Opening the gate, she led the way down the path toward the mansion.

As they passed the tree, everything switched over to 1946. Tessa reflected that it would now be into March of that year. It still felt chilly and there was still snow everywhere but the air didn't have quite as much bite, for which she was grateful. She acknowledged that it truly did feel cold and it wasn't only psychological as she had formerly thought. The hot summer air that had surrounded her earlier was gone.

The piles of snow were about the same height as before. A few more weeks and a lot of this snow would be gone.

Richelle, dressed warmly today, not her usual summer attire, but in Capri pants, a t-shirt and sweater, stepped beside Tessa and the two stood viewing the yard. That Richelle had come prepared for the cold made Tessa smile. She'd come set for the weather herself and wore a jacket over her summery clothes.

Richelle said, "I'm so excited to be back here finally. It's been about a month for me."

Tessa said, "That's a long time! I'm curious about how Mary's treatments went."

Suddenly Richelle screamed, "Tessa!"

Tessa jumped. "What?" She followed Richelle's pointing finger.

"Look at that! There's a hand sticking out of the snow! Someone's buried in the front yard under the snowbank!" Her horrified look would have been funny if the situation wasn't so serious.

Suddenly Tessa knew what was happening and held back an urge to laugh. A few yards ahead to the left of them from the top of the snow bank protruded a limp, lifeless hand that hung from the wrist.

"Who could it be?" Richelle said in panic, her eyes jerking in Tessa's direction.

Tessa shrugged but couldn't wipe the smirk off her lips.

Understanding slowly began to dawn on Richelle's face and, with narrowed eyes, she mouthed soundlessly, "Luke?"

Tessa nodded.

As the others stopped and watched, Richelle walked down the

path to where the hand protruded. "Tessa, what should we do? What if the Hardingtons killed Mary and buried her in the front yard till they can find a way to get rid of the body? I am so scared!"

Shaking her head, Tessa watched as Richelle hammed it up. Tessa turned back to take in the guys. Cody and Charlie looked dumbfounded by the whole thing. She turned back to see how this would play out.

Richelle braced herself, swung her right leg back and kicked it forward into the snow bank as hard as she could. A loud, wounded yelp echoed from the pile of snow and the hand quickly lowered and disappeared. Richelle swung back once more and kicked. It found its mark again. Luke's cursing poured from beneath the snowbank. Janaye burst out in laughter and Charlie began a silent chuckle. Cody smiled but it was clear he didn't fully understand what was going on.

Richelle swung back a third time and kicked, but she connected with air and it sent her off balance. Tilting back, she fell on her bottom and yelled. It didn't take long for her to jump back to her feet and begin running through the piles of snow in search of Luke, yelling at him the whole time.

Luke was trying to get away as fast as he could. From time to time, where the snow was sparse, they could see him crawling, trying to escape her wrath. Richelle saw him too and took after him. He was losing ground fast. As soon as he realized it, he scrambled to his feet and ran, with Richelle in hot pursuit. Around the side of the house, he suddenly tripped and disappeared from view beneath a mound of snow.

Richelle didn't stop in time, tripped over him and went down right after him. Neither of them could be seen but the rest could hear the two scuffling beneath the snow, Richelle yelling and hitting him and Luke begging for mercy.

"Okay, Richelle, stop, stop!" Luke finally jumped up and ran back to the pathway, laughing hysterically and completely out of breath.

Racing after him, Richelle came up behind him, jumped on his back and grabbed him around the neck. Being held in a headlock, there was no easy way for Luke to disentangle himself from her fury. It was amazing how strong she could be when out for revenge.

The four onlookers roared with laughter.

"Richelle, stop it. I'm sorry, okay?" Luke could hardly get the words out because of his uncontrollable laughter.

"You haven't begun to feel sorry! I'll make you regret this till your dying day!" She finally let go of his head but punched him hard on the arm before she stepped away.

"Ow!" He rubbed his arm and looked at her. "You can't stay mad at me for long."

"We'll see about that." She looked less upset now that she'd vented her anger.

Luke was still laughing and so were the others. "That was so hilarious. You really believed that someone was buried in the front yard." He let out another raucous laugh and doubled over to grab his aching stomach.

"You better stop laughing!" Richelle glanced around suspiciously at those still chuckling. "Were you all in on this?" Anger flashed from her eyes.

Tessa said, "No. Last time we were here, Luke mentioned he might play a trick on you but I had no idea he'd actually go through with it."

Richelle glared at Janaye. "Did you know?"

Everyone's eyes turned to her.

She looked immediately remorseful. "I'm sorry, Richelle."

Luke piped up, "Hey, it was totally my idea and I just asked Janaye to help me out. The fault is mine." A smirk still played on his lips. He didn't look very apologetic. "It sure was fun, though." He chuckled again.

Richelle started to laugh. "I can't believe you did that. How long did you lie under the snow waiting for me?"

"Not too long. You would have seen me from the sidewalk if I'd been there before the time change. I was hiding by the house behind those bushes and when you all started past the tree I scooted on my belly, beneath the snow, over to the side of the path and stuck my hand up. It worked out better than I'd hoped." A permanent smile was pasted on his face.

"Just wait, Luke; your turn is coming." Richelle gave a warning nod.

"Oooh, I'm so scared."

"You'd better be!"

Charlie asked, "Why did the two of you both go down like a load of bricks? Did you both trip on something or what?" He looked amused. At least he wasn't mad at the exchange between Richelle and Luke.

"I should have known that big limb was there because I saw it lying in the yard before I switched time zones and hid by the house. I totally forgot about it when Richelle chased me. I tripped over it first and then she fell and landed right on my gut. I didn't know better than to get out of the way," he said, rubbing his middle. "Did you hurt yourself, Richelle?"

"No, a big lummox cushioned my fall so I'm okay! I was more shocked than anything. I was so focused on paying you back that I went down punching."

"Yeah, I noticed." Luke still rubbed his one arm.

"Okay, enough of fun and games. Let's go into the house and see what's happening." Tessa turned and led the way. Cody grabbed her hand and squeezed as they walked into the house together.

Cody said, "Those two are quite the pair!"

"It's never dull with them around. They do need supervision though. They can get really out of hand sometimes."

The six of them gathered in the foyer around the table which held the massive floral arrangement. Today it was filled with predominantly yellow and purple mums, scattered with white lilies, white snapdragons, baby's breath and a pile of greenery. The expansive, high-ceilinged room was completely silent. The large crystal chandelier above them, a work of art in itself, glittered with light, making dappled markings on walls and floor. Tessa looked down and could vaguely see her reflection in the shiny marble tiles. The entrance area really was magnificent.

"This place is amazing!" Cody's jaw hung open and his face looked awestruck by the beauty of the place.

"It is, isn't it?" said Tessa.

He shook his head in wonder. "It's hard to believe that a mansion that looks so run-down on the outside, at one time looked this good on the inside."

Tessa said, "I know. It astounds me every time I step into this place."

Silence lingered for a moment, as each was lost in thought.

Richelle finally broke the quiet. "Wasn't Mary supposed to be back home by now?"

Tessa said, "I think so. I remember the doctor saying it was a four-week treatment depending on her response to it. I sure hope she's back."

"What should we do?" asked Richelle. "I've been itching to come here and now we're here, just standing around. Shouldn't we check out the house? Do something?"

"Look up there." Charlie pointed to the upstairs landing. "Is that Mary?"

He judged accurately. With her face looking pale and drawn, her frame as thin as a rail, Mary descended the right stairway in a housecoat, tied tightly around her and slippers on her feet. The housecoat looked four sizes too big; she was drowning in it. As she neared the bottom of the steps, Tessa could see the slightest sparkle of life in her eyes, something she hadn't seen in her the last few visits.

Mary walked slowly and deliberately, gripping the railing as though her life depended on it. When she reached the bottom, she breathed a big sigh of relief. Elizabeth Hardington must have heard the sound because she appeared from the sitting room.

"Mary! Are you coming to join me? I'd love to have you sit with me."

"Sure, Mom." Her words came out in a whisper.

Elizabeth held Mary's hand and helped her to the sitting room. Following at a good distance, the six visitors slipped into the room and stationed themselves against the wall next to the door. Mary and her mother sat down kitty-corner to each other on the couches. An open book lay on the end table, face down, between the couches, probably abandoned by Elizabeth before she entered the foyer and approached Mary. On the far wall a fire blazed in the hearth, casting a warm glow on everything in the room.

"Isn't it good to be home?" asked Elizabeth.

"Yes, Mother, it's very good to be home." Mary sat quietly, gazing into the fire. With the large couch dwarfing her, she seemed to appear even smaller and frailer.

"Would you like something to drink? I'll get Esther to bring out some tea and biscuits."

"No. Not right now. Give me some time."

"Sure, dear."

Mary glanced nervously toward her mother. "Where's Dad?"

With a melancholy expression, her mother said, "He's in the den looking over some business papers." She paused and said, "You know your father has some wonderful plans for you, dear."

A weary look crossed Mary's face. "I don't want to hear any more of his plans." Tears formed quickly and spilled from her eyes.

Elizabeth leaned forward. "Please, dear, don't cry. I didn't mean to upset you. We love you so much! You know that we both want only the best for you. I know the treatments were difficult. Oh, I would have taken your place if I could have. It broke my heart to see you after each one. It was the most traumatizing thing I've ever had to go through. I was so tempted to take you and leave, get you away from that place. But I also wanted you to get better. I was completely torn over the whole thing."

Mary nodded sadly. "I hardly remember any of it except the intense pain I felt the last few times." She looked off into the fire, her eyes dazed.

"At the beginning, there was no improvement and you looked so awful after each treatment. I was terrified that I would lose you." Elizabeth's eyes grew moist and a tear trickled down her cheek. "But after the second week, you slowly began to improve."

With a nod of her head, Mary glanced down at her hands in her lap. "I'm sorry I put you through so much, Mother. I never meant to be such a problem."

"Oh, Mary, don't ever apologize. I'm just so glad you're getting better. The last week of your treatments I was so thankful to see the positive results. You were communicating and more back to normal. It was very encouraging."

With a frail voice, Mary said, "I don't like to think about it. I wish I could erase the last few months of my life. How will I ever show my face in this city again? Everyone believes I'm crazy. Maybe I am. I just don't want to end up like Grandma." She looked frightened and utterly weary, like she'd been carrying the weight of the world on her shoulders.

"You won't end up like your grandmother! We did for her what we could. You are much stronger than she is."

"Why won't Daddy arrange for her to have these electric shock treatments? It might help her too."

"We did ask the doctor. At her age there are too many risks involved. There are other methods of controlling behavior for elderly people, like sedatives."

The side door opened from the kitchen. Esther entered, walked toward the two and said, "Hi Mary. We are all so glad to have you back again."

Mary nodded.

Esther then turned her attention to Mrs. Hardington. "May I get you anything?"

"Yes, bring us some tea and some fresh biscuits, muffins or whatever you have."

"Of course. I'll be right back." Turning to Mary once more, she said, "It really is good to see you up and around, Miss Mary."

"Thank you, Esther. It's good to be home."

Esther turned then and left the room.

Mary's gaze rested on the blazing fire in the hearth and Elizabeth studied her folded hands in her lap. Slowly, Mary turned her eyes, filled with a mixture of sorrow and curiosity, to her mother.

"Mother?"

Elizabeth met her eyes.

"What exactly happened at the party that night? I don't remember much. Did I make a fool of myself in front of all our guests and friends?"

With a shake of her head, Elizabeth said, "Oh no, Mary, you didn't. All the guests had left and nothing happened until you had retired to your room. Of course they all know about your difficulties but they never saw you in that condition."

With a sigh of relief, Mary said, "I'm so thankful for that." Then she said, "I've heard Dad talk a lot about Chicago lately. Is there something he's not telling me?"

An uncomfortable look settled into Elizabeth's eyes and her hands fidgeted nervously. "He is planning something but now is not the right time to discuss it. Oh look, here comes Esther with our tea." Her eagerness to change the subject was not lost on the onlookers.

The door closed behind Esther and she came toward them with

a tray in her hands, setting it down on the rich mahogany coffee table between the two.

"I'm sorry, Mother. I feel exhausted right now. I think I'll go to my room and rest for a while." Mary tried to stand but was having difficulty finding the strength.

Quickly, Elizabeth rose to help Mary then turned to Esther and asked, "Would you assist Mary upstairs to her room?"

"Yes, of course, Mrs. Hardington. Come, Mary, hold on to my arm."

Clinging to Esther as though afraid she would fall, Mary shuffled along beside her and walked slowly out of the room.

They could hear the two scuffling, working their way up the stairs together. Tessa and her friends stayed in the room for a while, not knowing what to do next. Taking her seat again, Elizabeth reached for her book and began to read. Soon footsteps in the foyer sounded and grew increasingly louder, causing all six visitors to turn their eyes in the direction of the doorway. Mr. Hardington walked in, scooted around the couch and sat in the place Mary had just vacated.

He cleared his throat and said, "I saw Mary going upstairs with Esther. How's she doing?"

With her book still in her hands, Elizabeth said, "All right, I suppose. She's so thin and weak. She'll need time to get her strength back."

"She'll get strong quickly now. She'll have a lot of time to rest." He smiled reassuringly. "I want to discuss my plans with you and see what you think."

"You mean you want to *tell* me your plans so I'll be prepared. Isn't that right? I never seem to have a say in your decisions."

"That's not true. I always consider your thoughts in my negotiations. How you feel is very important to me."

"You'll have to forgive me, William. I'm still upset about Mary and all that she's gone through, even though I know it was for the best. She's improved a great deal. But, a move now would be too much for all of us and I would like you to reconsider. I feel strongly that I need to be here in our own home with Mary and help her recover. Too many changes for her right now would be detrimental. The doctor in Chicago said so."

"I agree totally. She needs to stay here where she's

comfortable."

A look of confusion crossed her face. "So you're saying that you've changed your mind about moving to Chicago?"

"No. I'm starting up a new bank there and I will be managing it. At first I'll commute between Chicago and Chelsey to make sure everything keeps running smoothly. I will soon discuss my plans with the man I have in mind to run the bank here. Right now we will stay in this house until Mary has regained her strength. It's important for you to be here for her and she likewise needs you."

"So, what are you planning after that?"

"Well, I do want us to move to Chicago eventually. I'll be doing a lot of traveling for a few months to work on all the arrangements. As you know, we've bought a building that we will renovate into a bank. The plans and schedule are being worked on as we speak. I'll be going back within the week to make some other business provisions. I also want to contact some real estate agents to look for a suitable home for us."

"Oh, William, that's what I've been trying to tell you. I don't want to move! This is home for me. You're asking me to leave all my friends, everything familiar and start over again. It overwhelms me!" She looked frantic.

Surprise filled his eyes. "Haven't you realized yet that we don't have any friends? How many of our acquaintances have dropped in or contacted us since this thing with Mary happened? I'll answer that for you. None! No one cares! As for me, I'm done with this city and our so-called friends. The only people who have shown any concern at all have been my business associates."

Elizabeth studied her hands, wringing them incessantly. She looked distraught, like a trapped animal with no way out. "I just wish we could give them another chance. Our friends probably don't know what to say to us. It's not like they've abandoned us."

"The church has discarded us and the pastor has encouraged the congregation to have nothing to do with us."

With suspicion in her eyes, she looked at him and asked, "How do you know this?"

"Someone told me. I'm sorry, Elizabeth, it's true. I wasn't going to tell you. I knew it would upset you. As for me, I can't stay in this city."

She looked stricken.

William spoke apologetically and tenderly. "It'll be okay. I've met some wonderful people in Chicago. You can even find a church there if that would make it easier for you. We'll make an effort to get together with my business associates and their wives. We'll make some new friends. It will be a new start for both of us."

Her whole countenance fell in discouragement. "How soon did you want us to move?"

"I'd like to be relocated within six months."

Halfheartedly, she nodded. "At least I'll have time to adjust to the idea."

"I knew you'd see the positive in it. It will be a good thing for both of us. Well, I need to work on a few more things in the office." William reached over to pat Elizabeth's hand, rose and left the room.

Tears filled Elizabeth's eyes, rolled down her cheeks and spilled unhindered unto her blouse before she reached for her handkerchief. Drying her face, she studied the fire for a few minutes before lifting her book from her lap. Her tears still flowed and occasionally she wiped them away.

Luke motioned to the door and the six of them walked back into the foyer and gathered in front of the large round table. Luke leaned back against the table and crossed his arms while the others gathered in a semi-circle around him.

"Did you notice what William didn't say?"

Richelle asked, "What do you mean?"

"He didn't mention Mary at all in the moving plans. I'm just wondering what he's planning to do with her now."

Tessa said, "But he did say that it would be good for Mary to stay here and regain her strength."

"Yes he did. But in talking about the move to Chicago, he said it would be a new start for the two of them. There was no mention of Mary moving."

Richelle said, "Do you think he's still hoping Mary will manage this bank here?"

"I don't know," replied Luke.

Charlie said, "I can't imagine he'd expect her to run a bank with her mental issues."

Tessa took offence at his blunt and heartless assessment.

Janaye asked, "Do you think he'll want her to stay here in this house all by herself?"

"I don't know. He didn't say what he's planning to do with his mother either."

Cody asked, "His mother is the woman upstairs who's a little crazy, right? Tessa told me about her."

"Yeah, she's the one," said Luke.

"I don't know if she'd be able to handle the move either, in her condition," declared Richelle.

Charlie said, "This place is depressing. If I'm ever in the mood for a downer, I'll know where to come."

Richelle answered him. "It's really not their fault that life sucks for them. To be honest, there is some positive now, compared to a few weeks ago. At least Mary is over the worst of it. I actually feel encouraged by what I've seen today."

Tessa nodded. "I agree. It looks like she's on the mend and that's wonderful news."

"Well, it sounds like their church people sure haven't helped them at all. It about sums up Christians, I'd say." Charlie sounded bitter and cynical.

Cody's eyebrows shot up. "It's obvious their church made a mistake in how they handled this whole thing, but if the Hardingtons turn away from God, they're turning away from the biggest help they have."

Charlie sneered. "So what are you saying? You're a Christian?"

"Yes, actually I am. Without God's help in my life, I'd be dead right now. I was ready to commit suicide, blow my brains out with a bullet, when I called out to him. I was in a mess, at the end of my rope and my life wasn't worth living. I bargained with him. I told him that if he was real, he had to show me clearly and help me."

"I'll tell you what happened," said Charlie, his voice filled with disdain. "Nothing!"

Cody smiled and shook his head. "Within half an hour, someone knocked at my door."

Charlie smirked. "God?"

"No, but God sent these two guys." Cody related his story.

When he finished, Charlie's lips twisted in scorn as he mocked, "Aw! How sweet!"

Cody ignored him and continued. "I didn't hesitate; I accepted Jesus as my Savior right then and there – the best decision I've ever made in my life. I was so weighed down with every kind of sin imaginable and life for me had become complete misery. When I asked Jesus into my heart, the heaviness and depression left like that." He snapped his fingers. "Life became worth living and it's been an absolute adventure ever since."

Charlie didn't respond. He actually looked somewhat uncomfortable.

Tessa said, "Well, I'd have to agree with Cody. God has brought a lot of adventure into my life the last few months. This whole time travel thing is God's message to me. Perhaps God is trying to get all of our attention since we're all here. He does make life exciting."

"So you're a Christian too?" Charlie looked downright annoyed.

"Yes. I agree with Cody. God has made life worth living."

Charlie grunted. "Worth living, huh? The only reason my life is bearable is because of Richelle."

Richelle took a step toward him and slipped her hand into his.

Cody said, "It doesn't have to be that way. The peace that God gives is available to anyone. Accepting Jesus Christ as Savior is open to everyone. He is the Prince of Peace. The Bible says that God so loved the world that he gave his only son so that whoever believes in him will have eternal life. That eternal life is available for anyone who will accept Jesus as their Savior."

Luke fidgeted and looked upset. "This is turning churchy. Shouldn't we get going?"

Cody turned to him. "Have you ever accepted Jesus Christ as your Savior?"

"Look, church boy, I get along fine the way I am! I don't need a crutch to get me through life, so lay off!"

"Well, you certainly can't say that God doesn't exist. Just look around you. This is God's doing and he's showing you clearly that he does exist and that he cares a lot about you. He wouldn't have you here in this house in a time travel experience if he didn't care about you. God is not a crutch; he's a necessity."

Charlie retorted, "Whatever. It's time to go." With that he headed to the door, Richelle's hand still in his. She followed along willingly.

"Wait!"

They all heard the deep voice at the same time and turned to look. It was the angel in the trench coat. He stood at the bottom of the stairway, his face serious and intense, holding his hat in his hands in front of him. There was a soft glow around him and his dark hair and trench coat were being blown around by an invisible wind.

Tessa could feel a draft in the room and her arms broke out in goosebumps.

The angel said, "Now is the time of God's favor, now is the day for salvation. I encourage you not to ignore it."

"What's that supposed to mean?" Luke looked spooked and ready to bolt for the door.

"Salvation is found in no one else but Jesus Christ. There is no other name that has been given that can save you." With that, the angel turned and headed up the stairs, becoming increasingly transparent as he ascended until he completely disappeared from view.

"I'm out of here!" Luke rushed for the door and Janaye turned and followed him.

Charlie wasn't far behind, with Richelle in tow.

Cody and Tessa looked at each other and smiled with amazement. This experience was becoming more interesting all the time.

Cody said, "I think God got their attention. What do you think?"

"I'll say. I think they'll have something to think about for a while."

"And they'll have a decision to make."

"I know what I'll pray about tonight." Tessa said as they started for the door.

Cody nodded.

They left the porch steps and walked into the yard. As they passed the tree and switched back into the present, they could see Richelle and Charlie already in their vehicle, pulling away from the curb. Luke and Janaye were walking back to the coffee shop, where they'd left his car.

CHAPTER 17

One week later

The drive to Detroit Lakes sped by. After navigating expertly through the city, Cody pulled up to a small, one-story home and parked behind his mother's vehicle in the driveway. Tessa glanced at the time on the dashboard. It was well past noon and she was hungry. Cody's mother was making lunch for them and Tessa hoped she was a good cook because, at the moment, she felt like she could eat a horse. They'd started out right after church and hadn't stopped till now.

They walked to the front door, hand in hand. The house was modest, but pretty, with beige siding, white shutters and a large bay window to one side. Two large trees in the front yard shaded the grass beneath and a simple concrete walkway headed from the driveway to the three steps leading to the front door.

Cody knocked and walked right in, Tessa following him inside. Turning to her, excitement in his eyes, he said, "I can't wait for my mom to meet you!" He scanned the front room and yelled, "Hey Mom, we're here!"

She appeared from a doorway and hurried toward them.

Tessa judged she was close to her own mother's age. Mrs. Fields was a fine-looking lady with dark brown hair, a few strands of gray throughout, which she wore in a short, stylish cut. She reached for Cody and gave him a hug.

Pulling back, she said, "It's so good to see you again, Cody. Did you have a good drive?"

"Yes, perfect." He smiled brightly.

Turning to Tessa, she said, "And this must be Tessa. I'm Beth Fields." She moved forward with open arms. After embracing, Mrs. Fields pulled away and said, "You're as beautiful as Cody told me. Welcome to my humble home."

"Thank you. Cody has told me a lot about you too. He's very

230

proud of you."

"Not as proud as I am of him. He has come a long way, my Cody." She reached up to pat his cheek. "Choey should be here any minute. She's coming for lunch too."

"Awesome!" Cody wrapped an arm around Tessa's waist and squeezed, then planted a kiss on her cheek. "I can't wait for her to meet Tessa."

"She's been waiting for this," said Beth with a smile, "impatiently, I might add!"

"I'm looking forward to meeting her too," admitted Tessa. It was surprising, but she felt very relaxed. Mrs. Fields was warm and easy to talk to.

Cody gazed into Tessa's eyes and she smiled up at him.

Beth said, "I'm looking forward to getting to know you, Tessa. Cody has told me so much about you. I can assure you, all he's told me is good."

She chuckled at that.

They heard a knock at the door; it opened and in walked a petite young woman with hair the same shade of brown as Beth's. The young woman threw her purse onto a chair, screamed and ran toward Cody, grabbing him around the neck.

"Hey, little brother." She pulled away and said, "So you finally brought your girlfriend home for us to check out." Turning to Tessa, she said, "It's so good to finally meet you." She held out a hand and they shook. "I'm Choey. Cody has told us a lot about you and I've been so impatient to get to know you. I kept telling him to bring you down for a visit so we could be introduced. Finally he brought you! It's taken him forever!" Reaching over, she gave Cody a shove. "I didn't know if he ever would. Brothers! They never listen. He was taking his sweet time and the curiosity was killing me!"

Coming up for a breath of air for a second, she continued. "Wow! You're beautiful, Tessa." She turned to Cody. "You did good!"

Words came easily for the girl; she was a real talker, hadn't stopped since she stepped in the door and as they walked on into the kitchen, Choey kept up her chatter, with no let-up in sight. Tessa didn't have a chance to get in a single word.

While Choey chattered, Tessa studied the interior of the house.

It was small but cozy, the kitchen compact but sufficient with an eating area big enough for them to sit in comfort. As they stood inside the kitchen, Tessa noted the table was set and Mrs. Fields was busy setting the food onto the table. She had made roast beef with all the fixings and, by the aroma filling the house, it was obvious she was a wonderful cook.

"Everyone sit. The food's ready."

Cody prayed for the meal and they all dove in as though famished. The spread proved to be delicious. After eating, Beth served tea and coffee and presented a raspberry cheesecake for dessert. It was better than anything Michael's Mocha Shop could offer; in fact, better than any cheesecake Tessa had ever eaten. It melted in her mouth. When they finished lunch, they relaxed around the table and talked.

"So, Tessa, you're a waitress, right?" asked Choey.

"Yes, but just for the summer months. I'm starting my new job in September. I took Business Administration in college and that's what I really want to do. I've already been hired by a law firm but they don't need me until September. One of their main accountants is retiring. She's planning to quit in November so she'll train me for a couple of months then I'll take over. I'm very excited about starting there. Being a waitress is okay but it's not something I want to do for much longer."

Choey nodded. "I've tried waitressing before. It's a hard job, very exhausting being on your feet all day. I couldn't handle it. The social aspect was great but it was hard work. I've attempted other jobs but none of them have panned out. Working at a grocery store as a cashier was the same – being on my feet all day. So far I haven't found anything that I'd really like to do long-term. I don't have a lot of physical or emotional strength. That kind of narrows the options."

Cody said, "Well, you're just a late bloomer, that's all. You'll find something eventually."

"Don't, Cody. Stop humoring me. There's nothing positive about my life. I've made a mess of things. I can't seem to keep a job and my marriage has been a failure. My husband left me. At least my son can't leave me; he's too young."

Tessa didn't know what to say. It was an awkward moment.

Choey turned to her and said, "I'm sorry. You didn't come

here to listen to this."

"Cody told me he has a nephew. What's your son's name?"

Her eyes lit up. "He's the light of my life. We call him Joey."

Cody said, "I call him Joe-Joe. He's my little man."

Choey frowned at him, "Don't interrupt your older sister. Anyway, Joey is nine and he's growing up so fast. He'll be starting fourth grade in the fall. You won't be able to see him today because he's with his dad this weekend. Maybe you'll have a chance the next time you come."

Tessa asked, "Is he involved in any sports? I have two brothers and they are always playing some kind of sport."

"No. He has some physical restrictions so he's never been able to participate in a lot of activities. But there are other things that he can do. Reading is something he loves and he's very creative. Drawing cartoon figures is his passion. He makes up his own characters and puts them into these cartoon strips with script, narration and everything."

"He is amazingly good at it for his age," inserted Cody.

Choey continued, "They are hilarious! He has such a sense of humor."

Cody nodded.

"He makes my life worth living and I've never been sorry I had him, even though it's a challenge being a single mom. I don't know where I'd be if not for him. He's the sunshine in my life. Anyway, you'll have to meet him, Tessa; he's absolutely adorable and the sweetest kid anyone could ever have."

Beth said, "I have to agree with my daughter. Joey's a very talented and sweet boy and I'm very proud of my grandson!"

That was the first Beth had spoken since the after-lunch chatter started. She seemed content to listen, surrounded by her children, the dishes left untouched. With a relaxed smile, her eyes lit up with warmth at the mention of her grandson.

Later, they spent the afternoon playing games and getting to know each other better. Tessa was thankful she felt comfortable around this family so quickly. It was easy to see that they loved each other. They treated each other with kindness and it felt safe to be there with them.

For dinner they ordered in pizza and ate it in front of the T.V., watching a movie that Choey had rented, a romantic comedy. It kept the evening light and fun. Shortly after that, Cody and Tessa said their good-byes and started back to Chelsey.

With the lights of Detroit Lakes behind them, Cody broke the silence and asked, "So, what do you think of my family?"

"They're wonderful. Your mother is very sweet and giving. Choey's extremely talkative but she's easy to be with," Tessa said with a grin.

Cody laughed out loud. "That's an understatement. She can't stop jabbering but, hey, she's my sister and I love her."

"At least it's never quiet for very long."

"You've got that right." Cody stared out at the road, deep in thought. He broke in, "She deserves some happiness."

"It sounds like she's had a difficult time with her marriage and with her son's problems. How is she handling all of it?"

"She's had her share of grief. She used to live in Chelsey with her husband and Joey. When they separated, she moved to Detroit Lakes to be close to Mom. Her husband, Mark, is still in Chelsey but I seldom see him. He does make an effort to go and see Choey and Joe-Joe though and I'm glad for that."

"Your sister said that she has a hard time keeping a job. How does she support herself and her son?"

"Mark is taking care of that. He's really a great guy. I've always liked him, still do. Mark and Choey had a lot of financial struggles and then with Joey's problems, it put a lot of strain on their marriage. They've been separated now for about a year. We're still hoping they'll get back together."

"How can Mark support himself plus another place for Choey and Joey? If they struggled financially before it must be very hard for him now."

"Well, it was very hard at first. My sister moved in with my mom for a while. Mark found a much better-paying job a few months ago and he encouraged Choey to move into an apartment. He didn't want to be coming to my mom's house to see Joey and I can understand his point. He seems to be doing much better financially now. Mark and Choey just need to work on some of the other issues in their marriage and I think they'd be great together."

"Has your mother always lived in Detroit Lakes?"

"No, only for a few years. When I was finished high school she moved. She wanted to live somewhere that was pretty and peaceful. It's a bit of a tourist town in the summer months but she loves the beauty of the lakes and I guess it brings her some peace of mind."

Tessa nodded and her thoughts ran toward his sister once more. "Choey doesn't seem to have a lot of self-confidence. Do you know why that is?"

"She's always had this negative view of herself. I keep trying to build her up but she refuses to believe anything positive. For some reason, she can't see how special she is. I think my dad leaving when he did was harder on her than she's willing to admit and she needs some emotional healing. What she and my mother both need is Jesus in their lives. I've tried to talk to them about receiving him but they keep refusing."

"I would think that after seeing what God has done in your life, they would be interested in what changed you."

"My mother has never been religious. She insists she's always managed well on her own without help. I've tried to share the gospel with her but she tunes out when I do. My sister refuses to talk about God, even calls herself an atheist. If she could only know the love that God has for her, it would totally change her outlook. She's had a lot of struggles and has tried for too long to solve them her own way."

"Well, from what I've seen God do for Luke, Richelle and Charlie, I know that he can speak to Choey. He can reveal his love to her."

"That's what I've been praying for. I've been praying that God would send someone to her that she would listen to because she certainly won't listen to me."

Tessa simply nodded.

~~~~~

The following week flew by in a whirl. Before Tessa knew it, it was Friday and another busy day of work. Her shift was nearly done and she felt impatient to leave. It was becoming a consistent pattern; she seemed to feel that way a lot lately.

As she carried a platter filled with steaming plates of food, she wondered if that's the way it would always be. Would she always feel this way while working full time? Did it come with the territory?

Martha had been easier on her lately. Les had noticed the unfair treatment and had a talk with Martha. It was still obvious to Tessa that she didn't like her. The woman didn't waste an opportunity to point out her mistakes or slip-ups. It was irritating but Tessa tried not to let it bother her or show. Ignoring her seemed to work the best and Martha was trying harder to be civil.

It was late afternoon and, besides the one table with the full orders, there were a few couples sitting in her section having dessert and coffee. There was also a table of businessmen having a meeting and, as she served them some more coffee, she couldn't help but overhear their conversation.

"John, that's not how I remember it. He said the merger was going to take place next week and everyone was agreed on it."

"I was there, Ted, and I don't remember everyone being in agreement. Raymond Taylor was very opposed to this merger. He was fighting it with everything he had and he has a lot of say in that company."

"Are you sure? My secretary, Phyllis Arnold, was there taking notes and she has nothing in the minutes of any opposition. I wish I had been there myself."

"You should have been. It was an intense meeting."

Tessa filled Ted's cup last and, as she lifted the coffee pot away from his mug, he spoke up.

"Thanks, angel. My cup hardly empties before you're back to fill it. I appreciate that. I wish my secretary was as dependable as this angel waitress. Are you sure you don't have wings? What's your name?"

Tessa pointed to her nametag. "My name's Tessa."

"It should be Angel or Angela. It would suit you."

She smiled and said, "Thanks for the compliment."

As she walked away, she heard John speak up. "Okay, Ted, enough of your clowning around, let's get back to business."

The guys at the table all laughed, while the sound of ringing bells faded around her head.

It's time to go back!

Her evening plans would need some adjusting. Instead of a relaxing evening, putting her feet up and having Cody over for popcorn and a movie, she'd be heading over to the abandoned mansion. Her mind churned about whom she would call and how to organize the evening.

~~~~~

Cody parked next to the curb, got out and walked around to open Tessa's door. After offering his hand and helping her out, they walked hand in hand to the gate. It was just the two of them on this visit. She'd tried contacting both Luke and Richelle but had no success.

The sky was overcast and a few sprinkles began to spot the sidewalk and moisten their faces as they walked through the gate and into the yard. As they passed the tree and switched over to 1946, the drizzle gave way to big snowflakes that dropped around them like falling fluffs of cotton. The white filtered atmosphere brought back memories of their last visit. Remembering Luke and Richelle's humorous escapade caused Tessa to giggle.

"Are you thinking about last time?"

"Luke and Richelle tend to have this effect on me."

"They are quite the pair, aren't they?"

"There's never a dull moment with the two of them together."

"I wonder why those two never paired up. They'd look good together."

"They can have fun but they would never make it as a couple. They're too similar and fight like cats and dogs. They'd end up tearing each other apart. They need a referee most of the time." Tessa pointed to herself. "As long as I'm around they can survive each other. I don't think I'd like to tag along to a marriage like that."

Cody chuckled. They ascended the steps to the landing and entered through the side entrance. Tessa expected a quiet, still house as usual but, when they came around the corner, they immediately saw Mr. Hardington exit his office. He called for a servant and one soon came hurrying from the right side hallway.

"Yes, Mr. Hardington?"

"James, I'm expecting a young man. His name is Richard Ridgefield. Will you please see him to my office when he arrives?"

"Yes, sir, I'll do that."

Mr. Hardington retreated back into his office and closed the door.

Cody and Tessa walked further into the foyer and stood close to the large round table in the center. A new batch of fresh flowers rested in the massive vase on the table, a mixture of red roses, white carnations, purple irises, baby's breath and green fern leaves placed throughout. The strong aroma filled the air around her and bewilderment hit her at being able to smell the flowers she knew didn't really exist. She reached out to touch one of the perfect red roses but her fingers passed right through the delicate petals.

Turning her attention toward Cody, she asked, "Do you want to wait here until Richard comes or do you want to look around?"

"Well, we'll probably hear the knock on the door when he gets here. I'd like to see how Mary's doing. Why don't we go look for her?"

"Sure. She's often in the sitting room. Let's go check."

The two of them walked over to the room and looked in. It was vacant.

"She's probably upstairs," said Tessa.

They headed up the stairway, sauntered down the hallway and stopped in front of Mary's closed door.

"What should we do?"

Cody took the initiative, opened it and held it for Tessa.

She shook her head. "No, you go first."

He walked in and Tessa followed slowly.

Mary was sitting quietly on her bed, cross-legged and looking comfortable in a flannel nightgown. She looked slightly better than she had two weeks ago. There was more color to her cheeks and they had filled in some, although she still looked very thin. With her hair hanging loose, she was busy studying a book that lay in her lap. A few strands escaped, obscuring her view. Lifting her hand, she tucked the wandering tresses behind her ear. Her hair behaved for a while but it didn't take long for more to come loose and screen her vision. She finally grabbed her hair into a bundle with one hand, held it tightly, picked up a pen with her other hand and started to write.

The book looked like Mary's diary. Curiosity plagued Tessa over what Mary could be writing. She turned to Cody and noticed him watching Mary intently.

"What are you thinking?" She whispered, even though she knew Mary couldn't hear.

"It's amazing how beautiful she is. How old would she be now? This is happening in 1946, right?"

"Yes. How old would that make her?"

Cody said, "Old, really old! That is if she's still living."

"I know. It's really quite unbelievable."

"And yet, here we are, watching her."

It really was fantastical. If Tessa hadn't already been here numerous times, she would also find it hard to accept but it had become her summer norm.

Mary was deep in thought as she studiously entered her daily musings. She finished her diary entry, set the book on her nightstand, scooted off her bed and walked toward the door. As Mary walked toward them, Tessa was struck at how stunning the girl looked, with her long hair wafting back from her face and her big brown, mesmerizing eyes.

Confusion suddenly slammed into Tessa with a force that shocked her. Mary suddenly looked familiar. Tessa couldn't remember thinking that before. Of whom did she remind her?

After Mary left the room, Tessa walked over to the nightstand. Cody followed her. She looked at the diary and sat down on the bed and sank down beneath the bedding. Cody grinned and sat down next to her.

"Why don't you pick it up and read it?"

Tessa placed her hand above the diary and let her hand fall through it till her hand touched the nightstand beneath it. "As you can see, the diary's no longer here but I know how we can still read it."

"How?" Curiosity filled his eyes.

Reaching over to the side of the diary, Tessa felt for the hanger that she'd placed there the last time, within access and easy to find. She held it up and said, "This is present in both time spaces so I use it to turn the pages of the diary."

"That's brilliant," he said, nodding.

"Luke's the one who figured that out."

"Then he's the brilliant one," Cody said with a grin.

"Hey! What does that make me?"

"Gorgeous and smart!" Cody said, leaning in for a kiss.

She liked his answer and the kiss was an added bonus. She turned to the diary and, using the hanger, opened the cover. It didn't take long till she found the last entry. Tessa and Cody put their heads together and read.

I'm feeling stronger every day. I'm still being medicated. It leaves me feeling sleepy a lot of the time. I hope that soon I'll be able to stop taking them. I still feel very tired but I do feel stronger than I did at first.

None of my friends has made any attempt to come and see me. I wish I would hear from Henry for I miss him so! I wonder if he'd even want me now. Everyone believes that I've lost my mind but I know that I'm not crazy. I know now that the stress of my life caused me to lose my mental capabilities for a while. If only Henry would come visit and ask me to marry him. I'd elope with him if that was the only way. I don't want to go through life without him.

I know Father is up to something but I'm not certain what it is. It's fairly obvious when he's planning and strategizing. He gets very intense and secretive at those times. That's how he's been lately. Something's afoot and I know he's busy preparing. I've asked Mother but she won't give me any direct answer. Maybe I should go straight to him and ask. I wonder if he'd tell me.

That's where Mary's entry ended. Tessa closed the book with the hanger and placed it back beside the diary.

Cody looked contemplative. "I wonder if Mary went to ask her father."

"Should we go see if she's getting anywhere?"

"Sure, let's go."

Quickly, they headed down the hall, descended the stairway and walked toward the office. The door was open and they could see Mary seated across from her father's desk. It was unusually quiet in the room. She was sitting silently and appeared to be waiting for him to finish what he was working on.

Mary's father finally looked up from the paperwork on his desk, irritation in his eyes, and said, "I'll be done soon, Mary; just give me a minute."

"I'm in no hurry."

The massive armchair Mary sat in made her look small, unimportant and frail. Her father sat in a similar chair on his side of the desk but he looked rather commanding. Mary gazed around her father's office nervously, her hands fidgeting in her lap.

"There that's done." William moved the papers to a stack on another table and turned to face his daughter. "Now what did you want to ask? I'm expecting someone shortly so you'll need to make it quick."

She straightened and said, "It's just that I've noticed some unusual happenings lately and I was wondering about it. Your intensity level has increased. It always does when you're working on a new project. You're planning something, aren't you?"

He smiled approvingly before answering. "You're very observant, Mary, and yes, I am making some plans. I think at this point it would be better if you didn't know. You need to concentrate on getting better and that's the only thing that you need to concern yourself with. Overwhelming you with my agenda would not be in your best interest." He lifted both hands, palms toward her. "Not that they will upset you but you need to get better first."

Staring at her father, mistrust in her eyes, she said, "I wish you would tell me; I don't like being left out. I'm part of the family too. I know I've had my struggles but I could handle the truth."

"No, I'm not discussing them with you right now. It would not be wise." His eyes held deep conviction, or maybe it was simply stubbornness.

Tessa could see the fight leave Mary's face.

She fell quiet for a few seconds then said, "I'd like to ask a favor."

His face softened. "What, dear?"

"Could you please allow Henry Stephens to come over to the house so I could speak with him?"

His jaw twitched in displeasure. "Now, Mary, you know my thoughts about that boy. Why would you ask such a thing when you know how I feel about him?"

She looked desperate. "Father, I love Henry! I've always loved him and I know he loves me. I want to marry him. If you would accept Henry as a possible son-in-law, it would bring me so much joy. Please, Father, reconsider your decision."

"It's totally out of the question. He's not good enough for my daughter. There is a wonderful man for you, Mary, someone of whom we can all be proud. Just be patient and you'll see that things will work out just fine."

Mary leaned forward. "Why don't you ever listen to me? Why don't you care how I feel? Please, I'm begging you; just let me see Henry and let me talk to him."

"The answer is no! Now I'd like you to leave. I'm expecting someone very soon and you need to make yourself scarce."

Her eyes grew watery with disappointment and a trickle of tears began streaming down her cheeks. Soon deep sobs tore from her chest, filling William's office with her grief.

William looked stricken with remorse. He stood, came around the desk, knelt down in front of her and took her hands in his.

"Dear Mary, I'm sorry that I seem so harsh on this matter. If you only knew the good things that are coming for you, you wouldn't be crying. I love you, Mary, and I will make sure that you are taken care of."

She tried to regain her composure. "If you truly...love me...you'll...let me see Henry."

Hesitantly, he nodded. "I'll think about it, okay?"

Her face brightened but her tears still flowed. "Yes, please do, Daddy."

He patted her hand and nodded once more. "Okay, now go on."

Mary took the handkerchief that her father handed her and wiped her eyes. She exited the office and slowly started back up the stairs, gradually disappearing from view.

Cody and Tessa left the office to wait. Tessa's heart felt vexed for Mary. Understanding William's motives was beyond her. If only he weren't so harsh and demanding. Mary needed some tender loving care and received precious little of that. It made her wonder what William had up his sleeve this time.

"Wow, I didn't realize how controlling William is. He sure does try to govern every area of Mary's life, doesn't he?" Cody looked shocked at the display they'd just witnessed.

"He dominates everyone around him."

"Wouldn't it be great if Mary would elope with Henry?"

"Yeah, it would. But I know she won't."

"How do you know that?"

Tessa told Cody about what she'd learned about Henry and Nancy from Richelle and her mother.

"Wow, so Richelle's grandmother was involved with this family somehow. That's amazing! So Nancy marries Henry out of revenge?"

Tessa nodded.

"I wonder why anyone would marry someone out of revenge. That's the stupidest thing I've ever heard of."

"From what I learned from Mrs. Randall, her parents had a difficult marriage."

"I'm not at all surprised to hear it."

A knock at the door interrupted their conversation. James appeared and rushed to open it. A tall, handsome young man entered and Tessa recognized him as Richard from the party. He carried himself with an air of confidence and egotism that was hard to miss. Setting his briefcase down, he took off his coat and handed it to James without greeting the man or thanking him for his service. He actually made a point of ignoring James entirely except for allowing the man to deal with his outerwear.

Tessa felt appalled at his arrogant behavior, which caused her to dislike him even more.

Picking up his briefcase, he allowed James to show him to William's office. As soon as he was through the door, Cody and Tessa sneaked in directly behind him. They watched as William came around the desk to shake Richard's hand.

Richard sat down in the chair Mary had occupied moments earlier and Mr. Hardington turned to close the door before returning to his position behind his desk.

"I'm glad you came, Richard. I have an offer for you that I don't think you'll be able to refuse."

"Well, from what you hinted at the other day, you raised my curiosity."

"I know you've almost completed university and I'm willing to offer you a career option that I believe is very generous. One I encourage you not to turn down."

Cody whispered, "Now there's some pressure."

Tessa nodded in agreement.

"Does it have to do with your bank, sir?" asked Richard.

"Yes it does," William said, a hint of a smile on his face. "I don't know if you've heard this yet but I'm starting a new bank in Chicago."

"No, I hadn't heard that. When will you be opening it?" Intense expectation shone from his eyes.

"We're starting renovations on a building as we speak. It should take about six months to complete." William paused, as if to increase the suspense.

Richard jumped in immediately. "So did you want me involved in that bank or did you have something else in mind?"

"You do understand that all that we're discussing today is confidential?"

"You can trust me, sir. I'll keep everything to myself."

"I will be managing the bank in Chicago. Mrs. Hardington and I will be moving there when the time is right. What I have in mind for you is a management position at the bank here in Chelsey. I'd like to train you and show you the ropes. You would take on the role of Assistant Manager for now until you've had some experience. Then, if things work out, you would move into the position of Manager. What are your thoughts on this opportunity?"

Richard looked a little flabbergasted at the huge prospect laid in his lap and he stuttered to find the words. "I… I… I hard, hardly know what to say, sir. This is substantially more generous than I thought." He placed a hand over his heart. "I'm honored that you would trust me to this extent. I know that I can do the job! This is what I've been training for and I would be thrilled to work for you." His tongue was operational again and the words flowed now with self-assurance.

"I'm pleased to hear it. I have a lot of confidence in you. You have a commanding presence and I believe that you will gain respect in the banking field. There are some other men at the Chelsey bank that are eagerly hoping for the position I've offered you. I will be placing one of them in as Manager for now but I won't tell him of my future strategy, at least not yet. You'll need to keep my plans in complete confidence and blend in. When the time is right, we'll make the switch. I'll take care of the details."

"This is truly an exciting venture! Mr. Hardington, I want to thank you for this wonderful opportunity. I won't let you down." He stood to shake the elder's hand. "Sir, I do have a question though," he said, sitting back down.

"Yes, what is it?"

"What about Mary? She was supposed to have the position of Assistant Manager, wasn't she?"

"Well, that has changed. I've realized over the last few months that she is not capable of the job. I'm sure you've heard about her difficulties."

"Yes sir, I have, and I'm so sorry to hear about that. How is she doing now?"

"She's improved a great deal. We took her for some treatments in Chicago. It was a difficult process for her but it did cause her to snap out of her mental lapse. She's getting stronger every day and her mother and I are very thankful for that. Although she's very thin and needs to put on some weight, I'm confident that will come in time."

"I'd love to see Mary soon if that would be all right with you."

A look of pleasure spread across William's face. "Nothing would please me more. She needs a strong and stable friend right now and I can arrange to have you see her. Let's give her some more time to recuperate and then we'll arrange it."

"I'd like that, sir."

After discussing a few more items related to Richard's new upcoming position, William stood, signaling the meeting was over. Richard gathered his briefcase and opened the door to the foyer. Tessa and Cody followed them. After calling for James, he appeared, carrying Richard's coat and boots. William waited to see him out and, before leaving, Richard turned and thanked him again for the opportunity.

James closed the door as William retraced his steps back to the office. William looked unusually cheerful.

"What do you think about that?" asked Cody.

Tessa shook her head in disgust. "He's up to his old tricks again, manipulating and totally running Mary's life. I bet he's playing matchmaker. He's going to destroy her. I feel so sorry for that girl."

"It does look like he's setting the two up, that's for sure. Do you know how Mary feels about him?"

She filled him in on Mary's disdain for Richard.

Shaking his head in disbelief, he said, "I never knew that the problems in this family went so far back."

"What do you mean?"

He looked suddenly uncomfortable. "Well, what I mean is that everyone knows there were problems here or else this house wouldn't be vacant now. It's just interesting to see what brought it about."

"I have a feeling that the pieces are coming together quickly now and I'm so looking forward to seeing the whole picture."

Cody nodded.

Tessa glanced around after a few moments and said, "It looks like the action's done for today."

"Are you ready to go?"

"Yeah, I'm ready."

Cody held the door for her and they exited the house, walked across the landing, down the steps and toward the big oak tree.

Tessa glanced out toward the street and expected to see Cody's car by the curb but it wasn't there. What she did see was an old-fashioned car slowly making its way down the street. The driver tried to speed up but swerved on the slippery, snow-covered street then gradually disappeared around a curve up ahead.

They walked past the large oak and switched back to the present. Cody's car suddenly appeared right where he had parked it and raindrops hit their faces as they ran for cover.

After getting a bite to eat at a fast food restaurant, Cody dropped her off at her house and walked her to the door. Taking a step toward her, he took her in his arms and kissed her passionately. Her heart beat wildly as he pulled away.

He walked down the path, toward his car, turned back and waved. "See you soon." The look of love in his eyes was enough to light up the night.

The car roared to life and she watched it disappear down the street. With a sigh of contentment, she turned and walked inside. To have shared this time travel with Cody by herself was exhilarating. It made her feel closer to him than ever.

CHAPTER 18

After Sunday lunch, with dishes done, Tessa sat on the couch and randomly flicked through T.V. channels. Nothing grabbed her attention. Being distracted didn't help. Preoccupation with the fact that Cody hadn't called since Friday night consumed her thoughts. He never went this long without calling her. She'd gone to church with her parents that morning.

Why would he leave me hanging all weekend? Doesn't he want to see me? I thought he said he'd call. Maybe I should call him.

She decided to wait a minute more, flick through a few more channels, maybe find something that would interest her. The ringing of the phone brought her head around.

"I'll get it." She jumped up, ran for the phone and pulled it from its base. "Hello, this is the March residence."

"Hi there, sweetheart."

"Cody! What have you been up to? I was just about to call and check on you."

"Aha! You were missing me, weren't you?" His voice was light and sounded like heaven.

"Yes, I was. So what's up?"

"There's been an interesting development. I was going to call last night and take you out but something came up. I got a call from Charlie."

"Really?"

"Yeah. He admitted he's been absolutely miserable. God has been on his mind the past two weeks. I asked him if he wanted to get together and talk and he jumped at it. He came over to my apartment last night. After a good discussion and answering a lot of his questions, he accepted Christ."

The news hit her with full force. "Are you serious?"

"I'm very serious."

"You said Charlie, right, or did you mean Luke?"

"Charlie."

"Wow!" Although disappointment filled her that it hadn't been Luke, she pushed it down and continued. "I would never have expected Charlie to respond that way!"

"Well, he responded all right. This morning he came to church with me. I think he really enjoyed the service. He wants to come back next Sunday and mentioned bringing Richelle with him. He tried to talk her into coming today but she turned him down."

"Wow, I hardly know what to say. I hope Richelle will join him soon. I don't know how she can resist God's love after what happened at the mansion. She hasn't called me all week. I am so surprised about Charlie, though."

"After church we went for lunch and had a very interesting talk. We both opened up about our past. He's had some similar issues to mine. His mother left when he was young and his father raised him. With his mom abandoning him, he became angry and blamed God. Avoiding God felt safe to him, but God came and met him. Charlie seems truly grateful and I'm thrilled."

"I don't blame you." She could hardly process the whole thing. Charlie was the last person she'd imagined turning to God. She'd thought his brash outer shell was impenetrable. Or perhaps her reaction was fueled by her longing to see Luke accept Christ.

"I have a question," said Cody.

"What?"

"Do you want to go back to the mansion today? I have this uncanny feeling we need to go back."

"But I haven't had a sign and besides, we were just there two days ago."

"Angel."

"What did you say that for?" She felt immediate frustration at being prodded into something she wasn't sure she wanted. Amusement followed the anger.

"Did you hear bells ringing?"

"I'm not telling you," she said with an edge. But she grinned at his eagerness to return to the adventure they both shared. Although she felt some nervousness at the prospect of going back, Cody's desire to venture to the mansion increased her own desire slightly.

"Come on, tell me, Tessa. Did you hear bells when I said 'angel'?"

"Yes."

"All right. I'll come pick you up and we'll head over there."

She remained silent for a second as she allowed the evident direction of her day to settle in. "Should I call the others?"

"Sure, they can join us if they want to."

~~~~~

They met Luke and Janaye on the sidewalk in front of the mansion. Tessa had called Richelle and invited her, told her Charlie was also welcome, but she had declined the offer. She explained that she and Charlie needed some time to talk things over. By the tone of her voice, it was clear she was upset about something but didn't go into detail. Tessa could only imagine what the two needed to work out.

The four went to the mansion, switched time zones, walked into the house and gathered in the foyer. Almost immediately, they saw Mary appear from the left hallway and walk meticulously across the foyer. She wore a dark green, knee-length dress that hugged her slim frame. Around the scooped neckline was a dainty off-white lace collar. Her shoes were two-inch heeled, classic pumps in the same shade of off-white as her lace collar. A pearl necklace and matching pearl earrings graced her pale skin. Her curled hair was partially pinned up by a dazzling diamond-and-pearl-studded clip.

She looked stunning but more than her outward looks, her eyes glowed with youthful energy and joy. Her walk was graceful and model-like. Even with her very thin frame, she really was striking.

Stopping by the mirror in the entrance, Mary turned to take a look, pinched her cheeks to bring some color to her pale complexion then turned and headed toward the sitting room.

Elizabeth appeared from the right side hallway and approached Mary with open arms. "Oh, my dear, how beautiful you look."

"Thank you, Mother. Do you think he'll be pleased?"

"I don't know of any young man who wouldn't be."

They embraced and Elizabeth kissed Mary's cheek.

"Could you tell James to see my guest into the sitting room when he comes?"

"I'll do that, dear. You go and have a seat."

Mary went into the sitting room and Elizabeth went to find James.

The four friends looked at each other with puzzled faces.

"I wonder who Mary's all dolled up for." Luke looked curious.

Tessa filled him in on what happened there Friday. "Mary asked her father if she could see Henry but her father is also going to arrange a visit between Richard and Mary. By Mary's striking appearance, I would venture to say it's Henry she's expecting."

"This could be interesting."

While they waited for Mary's guest to arrive, they stayed in the foyer and talked. Ten minutes later there was a knock on the front door and James hurried to open it.

Henry entered, removed his winter coat and boots and handed them to James. He wore dark casual pants and a white shirt, simple but smart. As James ushered Henry past them, Tessa could smell his cologne and she smiled at his efforts to impress the woman he loved.

"He smells prepared, doesn't he?" Luke smirked as Henry entered the sitting room.

"I don't think he's here for a business meeting, that's for sure," said Tessa.

The four observers followed quickly, slipped into the room behind Henry and settled against the wall.

As Henry approached Mary, she rose from her place on the couch. She smiled pleasantly and held out her hands to him. He reached out for them, held them warmly and placed a kiss on her cheek. After releasing his hold, they both took a seat. Mary returned to her previous spot and Henry purposefully took a different couch, kitty-corner to her. Her smile faded, a look of concern replacing it, but she visibly shook it away and a timid smile returned.

"I'm so glad you came, Henry."

"How are you doing, Mary? You look wonderful."

"Thank you. I'm doing much better now. I've been through a very difficult time. I'm sure you've heard." She waited and he nodded slightly. "I've improved tremendously and I'm getting stronger every day."

"You look terrific. You're a bit thinner than the last time I saw you but you're still as beautiful as ever." His eyes shone with approval.

Glancing down at her hands, her cheeks blushed a soft pink and a smile of pleasure curled the edges of her lips.

Henry asked, "Why did you want to see me?"

With pleading eyes, she returned his gaze. "Well, I've missed you so much and I wanted to speak with you."

"What's left to say?"

"Things have changed for me, Henry. I don't believe my father will expect me to manage the bank now. He knows that I don't have the emotional endurance to handle that position."

"How does that change things for us?"

"I don't know exactly. All I know is that I don't want to live without you. I've missed you so. You've been on my mind day and night. I want to spend the rest of my life with you and I'd even be willing to elope if that's the only option." Desperation filled Mary's voice.

A cloud of confusion crossed his face and he paused before he answered. "What makes you think your father has changed his mind about me? You yourself said that you wouldn't be able to break your father's heart and marry me. Has his opinion of me altered in any way?"

"I don't know." Her hands were clasped tightly in her lap and her knuckles were turning white. "My father wanted me to help manage his bank and I didn't want to destroy his plans and dreams."

"And marrying me wasn't part of the plan," stated Henry simply.

Mary shrugged. "I also thought that I'd be consumed with starting a career. I was hoping that my father would leave the decision about marriage up to me, given some time. But now, I don't believe he'll trust me to make that decision on my own, especially with what I've gone through."

"So, he would even stoop to arranging a marriage partner for you?" Henry looked incredulous.

"I don't know for sure. I don't want to take that chance. It's you I want to marry and my father won't listen to me."

"What do you want me to do?"

"I want us to elope and get married."

Henry's lips twisted with a sad smile. He shook his head and his shoulders slumped. "When your father called me and asked me to come see you, I had hoped that he had changed his mind concerning me." His thin smile disappeared, replaced with an unhappy understanding.

"Mary, what you're asking me to do is separate you from your family for the rest of your life. You're also asking me to set your father's wrath against me for the rest of my days. I don't think you realize the stakes. You're suggesting that I bring tremendous strife to your family. That would only end up causing you great pain."

Mary's lip started to quiver and she struggled not to cry. "I was so hoping you'd be pleased."

Henry stood, went to her, sat down beside her and took her hands in his. With a tear trickling down her cheek, she turned to look up at him. He tenderly wiped her tear away.

"My dear Mary. I love you and always will, but I can't marry you like this. It will cause you and your family too much pain. If I married you, I'd do it right."

She couldn't control her tears any longer and they spilled freely down her cheeks. "I'm sorry, Henry. I wanted to show you that I was strong and...here I am...crying like a...baby."

"I will talk to your father and see if he'll relent. I'll ask for your hand in marriage and ask for his blessing. It can't hurt to try. If he absolutely refuses, then we'll give up this dream of ours. Okay?"

"No! I'll never give up, Henry. I won't accept no for an answer. I can't live without you!"

"Mary, please be reasonable."

She started to cry uncontrollably. "How can I be...reasonable? I know my father...will forbid it...even...before you ask." Her crying grew louder.

Henry looked bewildered, as though unsure of how to proceed.

A noise at the door alerted them both. Mary and Henry looked to see her father walk into the room.

"What's happening in here? Why is Mary so upset?" William's anger and disdain immediately filled the room. "What have you been saying to her?"

Henry stood quickly. "I'm sorry, sir. I didn't mean to upset her."

He looked stern. "Well, you have distressed her frail emotions and I need to ask you to leave." He pointed to the door.

Mary jumped up and cried out in alarm, "No! I don't want him to leave! Daddy, it's not his fault!" The tears still flowed unhindered down her pale cheeks.

Henry said, "Mr. Hardington, would I please be able to have a word with you alone?"

William stared at him with an intensity that would make an insecure man look away. After a pause, he said, "Well, I suppose it wouldn't hurt to give you a few minutes. Follow me to my office."

Henry turned and gave Mary a smile before he followed her father out of the room. As the two men left the sitting room, Mary hurriedly brushed the tears from her face, placed her hands together and closed her eyes as if in prayer.

The four friends scooted out and followed the two men to the office. William closed the door after he had let Henry in. They were stuck outside. Tessa felt intense disappointment. Stepping toward the door, Luke placed his ear against it. The rest stood around and listened intently. Perhaps they'd overhear some of what was said behind the closed door.

"Do you hear anything?" asked Tessa.

"I can't hear a thing. They're keeping their voices down," Luke whispered in a frustrated voice.

All four moved closer and strained to hear but the two men inside spoke quietly, their voices low and indiscernible from their side of the door. They eventually stepped back into the foyer and waited.

Luke glanced at Tessa and held her gaze.

"What?"

"We could just walk in. They'd never know the difference."

"No," Tessa said, shaking her head. "I can't. It makes me too nervous thinking of walking in on them."

"They won't see us. They won't see the door opening and closing."

"I'm not going in there." She crossed her arms for emphasis. Mr. Hardington's harsh style was intimidating, even though she knew he wouldn't know the difference.

Luke shrugged but didn't press the issue. He placed an arm around Janaye's shoulders and waited.

Tessa breathed a sigh of relief. Cody reached for her hand and gave it a squeeze. She looked at him and smiled.

Ten minutes passed before the door finally opened and Henry and William walked out.

"I'll see you to the door." William headed immediately in that direction.

"Sir, if I could make a request?" Henry hadn't moved from just outside the office door.

"What is it?" William looked impatient as he swung around to face him.

"If I could please let Mary know where things stand. I feel she needs to hear it from me."

William stared at him with icy eyes, trying to decide whether to grant the petition. Finally he said, "Maybe that wouldn't hurt, as long as you don't upset her further."

"I'll try not to, sir."

William waved him on and retreated back into his office. Henry walked over to the sitting room door, glanced in cautiously and walked in. The four friends followed.

Mary sat on the couch, her head resting against the back of the seat, her eyes closed. A throw cushion was clasped in her arms and she held it to her chest as if it were a lifeline.

Henry walked toward her and her eyes fluttered open. She gazed at him with expectation as he took a seat beside her. Taking the cushion from her hands, Henry placed it to the side, took her hands in his and studied them. He worried his bottom lip with his teeth and looked hesitant to speak.

Mary stared at him, her eyes searching his face for the answer. "Henry? What did my father say?"

Slowly he shook his head.

"No, Henry! No!" Despair and sorrow contorted her pretty features.

"Now listen, Mary. I promised your father that I wouldn't upset you, so please don't cry."

She struggled to hold back the tears and breathed heavily to contain the pain etched on her face.

"Please try to be strong. You know that I love you and I always will. You will always be my first love. In time you'll meet someone that you'll fall in love with. I will too. We have to be positive. This isn't the end of our lives, even though we may feel as though all hope is gone."

"I can't breathe, Henry."

"Please don't cry."

"I can't breathe." Her face looked ghostly white. "I don't want to cry but my whole world is falling apart. What am I supposed to do without you?" She fell into his arms, her cheek against his chest and he enfolded her with his arms.

A deep, heavy sigh escaped his lips. "We'll make it somehow, my love." His lips brushed the top of her head. "We can still be friends."

Soft cries filtered from Mary as she leaned against his chest. "No we can't. We'll never see each other again."

Falling silent, they both seemed to realize this would be the last time they'd be alone.

Her voice came soft and devastated. "Why won't you elope with me? It would fix everything."

"You know it wouldn't fix everything. It's nice to think that maybe it would but we both know the problems it would cause. I can't do that to you." He stroked her hair gently, placing light kisses on her forehead.

She calmed then and a strength and determination they hadn't seen before came over her. After a deep breath, she sat up and pulled out of Henry's embrace. With pain-filled eyes she gazed at him. "So what did my father say?"

"He told me there was no way he'd agree to having me as a son-in-law and made it abundantly clear that I wasn't good enough for you." Henry stopped there and gave a lopsided grin. "It's good I don't believe everything I hear. I personally think we'd make a wonderful couple. Your father told me he has certain plans for you and wants to see those fulfilled. I pleaded with him for quite some time, tried to explain how much I love you but he was as stubborn as a mule. I deliberated over the fact that I could make you happy, that this was your heart's desire as well but he refused to reconsider. He's a determined man and knows what he wants. I truly wish I were part of what he wants."

Reaching out a hand, Henry touched her cheek. "We'll survive, Mary. We're both strong and we'll carry on."

"Do you really believe that I'm strong?"

"You're extremely resilient. If you can endure a father like you have and come out like this, then I know you have great strength."

"You don't know what that means to me, Henry. I thought everyone would think of me as a weak woman, you know, after what I went through."

"Anyone who has to cope with a father like yours, go through treatments like you did and sit here and be so amazing, is tops in my book."

She smiled through watery eyes. "Thank you."

"You'll be fine. I have tremendous confidence in you."

"Will you write to me?"

"I would love to but I have a feeling the letters would be intercepted and it would end up causing more trouble for you. I think it's best if we say our good-byes now."

Mary lunged at him and threw her arms around his neck. Henry embraced her and they held tightly for a few moments. As they let go, tears flowed down Mary's cheeks.

"I'll always love you, Henry Stephens. I'll never forget you."

He wiped her tears away with his hand and brushed the moisture onto his trousers. "I love you too, Mary. Goodbye, my love." Slowly, determinedly, he stood and walked toward the door. He stopped, looked back one last time, gave her a sweet but sad smile then turned and left.

She stayed where she was, her tears still flowing but seemingly resolved to her fate. They all heard the front door open and close and he was gone. Her tears gradually subsided and a calm look of determination replaced her sorrow.

Tessa wiped tears from her own cheeks, looked at Janaye and noticed she was doing the same.

Cody and Luke looked at each other and shook their heads at the emotional display.

"Girls!" said Cody.

Tessa punched him lightly on the arm and then went back to wiping her face. "This is so sad."

Mary slowly rose from the couch and left the room. The four friends followed her to the foyer and watched her ascend the stairway and disappear from view.

"Wow, I'm a basket case. That was so sad!" Janaye's eyes were red from crying.

"I don't know how much more of this I can handle. So much misery has taken place here. I wish I knew what this has to do with me and the rest of us."

"Just give it time, Tessa. I'm sure you'll know soon." Cody was the only one that didn't look depressed.

"How can you be so positive all the time?" Even Luke looked upset by what had taken place, although his eyes were dry.

"Well, it's never over till it's over," said Cody.

"What's that supposed to mean?"

"There's always more hope than you think. There's hope for this family. I think that's what this whole time travel is about."

Luke looked angry. "Well, I don't feel hope. I feel like punching Mary's old man. What right does he have to ruin her life like this?"

"He has no right but he obviously thinks he does."

Luke said, "I'd sure give him a piece of my mind if I could. I'd tell him where to stick all his plans."

"Why doesn't Mary say something to him?" asked Janaye.

"She was willing to marry Henry in spite of her father's wishes. That took courage," said Tessa

Luke shook his head. "Now Henry's too chicken to go through with it."

"Or maybe too wise," suggested Cody.

"No, he doesn't have the guts to stand up to the bank mogul."

Janaye slipped a hand into Luke's and said, "This has really upset you today."

"Yeah well, whatever. I'm ready to leave. How about you?"

Janaye nodded and the two walked to the door.

Tessa glanced at Cody. "Did you want to go too?"

"I'd like to check on Mary first."

"All right, we can do that." She called after Luke and Janaye, "We'll see you later. We're going to stay."

Luke and Janaye said their good-byes and Tessa and Cody started up the stairs. They saw Mary's two-inch heels lying outside Eunice's door. Cody motioned toward the room. Tessa was in no mood to see the old woman again but Cody was already leading the way into her room and she didn't have the courage to speak up and possibly draw Eunice's attention. The door was ajar so he inched it open and walked in. Cautiously, she followed.

257

As soon as they entered, Tessa noticed Eunice in a chair with her back to them and breathed a sigh of relief. Mary was sitting on the floor facing her grandmother with her back resting against a chair. The old lady seemed better put together this time. Her dress looked fresh and wrinkle-free and her hair wasn't quite as disheveled. At the moment she almost looked normal. The two both sat quietly with Eunice's eyes locked intently on Mary. Mary's gaze focused on her fidgeting hands in her lap.

Cody and Tessa stayed close to the open door. Tessa reached over to slip her hand into Cody's. It was a little unnerving being in Eunice's room again and Cody's touch helped to bring some calm.

Scanning the room, she noticed there were still books scattered all over the floor. It looked a tad tidier than last time. Someone must have done some cleaning. Only one tray of empty dishes sat on a coffee table close to the chairs. Although the bed looked recently used and rumpled, the bedding was on the bed where it belonged. The curtains were spread wide and the sun shone in, warming the room. The windows sparkled with rays of sunshine dancing across them. Someone must have cleaned those recently.

Birdsong filtered through the glass, various birds flitting back and forth from the window to the tree just outside the room. The atmosphere of the room was drastically improved by the sun filtering in and the birds chirping cheerfully.

Even with the entertainment on the other side of the glass, Tessa felt impatient as the silence stretched in the room. After what seemed like forever, Eunice's voice broke the quiet.

"Tell me, tell me, tell me, child. What's wrong with my little girl?" Eunice reached up to scratch her forehead. The scratching continued unabated for some time.

Mary finally spoke. "Grandma, stop it. Stop scratching yourself. You're going to rub it raw if you don't stop."

She halted immediately, pulled her hand down and looked at it as though she had just discovered it. "Ohhhh!" She placed her hand in her lap and slowly lifted her eyes to lock with Mary's again.

"My life isn't worth living, Grandma. I have nothing left to live for."

"Life is good; life is always good. If not life, then death. Life is good."

"My dad won't let me marry the man I love. I don't know how

I can live without Henry."

"God will take care of you, my little girl. God is good, God is good."

"How can you say that, Grandma? Look at what your life has been like. Do you call that good?"

"My God is good and he will turn things around." Slowly Eunice stood, turned around three times and then sat down again.

"Grandma!" Mary said with exasperation in her voice. "You're not making any sense. I guess I should be used to that by now. I don't know why I came in here. Going through my own mental lapse, I thought maybe we'd be able to relate to each other better somehow. I don't know what I was thinking."

Mary started to get up when Eunice spoke again.

Her eyes danced wildly. "Take note of it, Mary. God will turn things around." She twirled her index finger around in the air three times. "It may take some time but God will turn things around."

"All right, Grandma. I love you." Mary walked over to her grandmother, bent over and kissed her cheek. Then she dejectedly headed for the door and exited the room.

Eunice turned around in her chair to watch Mary leave. Tessa and Cody were going to exit the room right after Mary but Eunice called out frantically.

"Aha, aha! There it is, Mary. There it is. Do you see them? Do you see them?"

Cody and Tessa both stopped in their tracks and dodged to the side as Mary stuck her head back into the room.

"What are you talking about, Grandma?"

Eunice frantically pointed to Cody and Tessa. "Can't you see them, Mary? There's hope, there's hope, there's hope!" Her voice grew in volume as she ranted and shook her index finger in their direction.

"Grandma, you need to calm down. I'll go and get Margaret to give you your medicine." With that Mary pulled back and disappeared from view.

"No, no, no, no! You don't understand! Come back, come back." The woman slowly lost her focus. Her eyes no longer locked on the two of them but began looking back and forth on the floor beside her as if she had dropped something. Getting down on all fours, she began looking under the chair for some lost treasure.

Tessa turned her gaze to Cody. He watched the old lady intently and began shaking his head in disbelief. With an incredulous grin he said, "What next!"

"She's as crazy as a loon. I should have warned you."

Cody motioned for her to follow him and they walked out into the hallway and toward Mary's room.

"I'd still like to check on her, if you don't mind," Cody said.

"I wouldn't mind checking on her myself."

"All right, here we go." He turned the doorknob and led the way into Mary's room.

As soon as Tessa entered she could feel the difference. There was a tangible presence of sorrow, a heaviness that surrounded her, pressing her.

Mary lay face down on her bed, still wearing her outfit from her encounter with Henry. Sobs tore from her soul and penetrated the room. She looked so broken, lost and hopeless as her deep grief escaped her lips. The girl's desperate wails were almost more than Tessa could bear.

Tessa wept silently for the brokenhearted girl before her. William's heartlessness was difficult to understand. It made her angry to think about it. Why would he take such a firm stand against Henry? Why oppose the man that Mary truly loved? If only William could see his daughter now in this state, perhaps he would change his mind and allow her some personal choice and a chance of joy for her future.

Cody slipped his hand into hers and nudged her toward the door. She willingly agreed and they exited the room together. As they walked down the hall, she could feel the heavy spirit of sorrow slowly dissipate from her mind and soul.

"I couldn't take watching that much longer," Cody finally said.

"I know what you mean. I feel so sad for her. It seems so unfair and cruel of her father to treat her this way. I don't understand him at all."

"Maybe there's more to his story than we know."

"Even if there is, I don't think it would excuse his conduct." She felt so angry at him. If only there were a way to help Mary, she would.

They made their way down the stairway to the main floor, exited the house, crossed the yard and, as they passed the old oak, switched over to the present.

Cody finally spoke, "That old lady amazes me. It's like she knows things and speaks with some intelligence. I think she actually saw us! That was so freaky! But then she totally flipped out again." He looked dumbfounded by the experience. "Didn't you tell me about her? You met her before, right?"

"Yes, I had a conversation with her one day." She chuckled.

"What? Really?"

"When you headed for her room I did not want to go in there!"

"Why?"

"Because she acted really weird the first time I saw her. She actually saw me and talked to me. There were things she knew about me that she couldn't possibly have known! No one else in this mansion can see me except her. When you walked into her room today, I felt terrified. I didn't want her to notice me or talk to me again. I was so scared!"

He laughed and then grew serious. "I find her very fascinating. I would love to sit down with her and pick her mind."

"Not that there's much to pick."

Cody chuckled at that.

"You'll have to do it on your own time because I don't want to go back into that room again." A thought came to her. "You know what? Today she saw both of us. She said as much too. Remember when she asked Mary if she saw us? It was plural. She very clearly said 'them' – 'Mary, do you see them?' That's what she asked. I wonder what that means."

"Maybe time will tell."

At his car, he held the passenger door for her and closed it after she slipped in. While Cody walked to his side, she took another look at the mansion. She had an uncanny impression that things would move quickly now, like puzzle pieces scurrying into place. It reassured her that she didn't have to go it alone. She had friends more than willing to join her in this adventure.

Cody started his car and pulled away from the curb.

Tessa touched his arm and said, "Thanks for joining me here today. I wouldn't want to do this time travel by myself."

"Hey, by your side is where I love to be." He took her hand and kissed the back of it. "And don't forget, I'm the one who instigated this visit."

"I'm glad you did." A warmth of belonging flooded through her.

CHAPTER 19

The restaurant was slow and Tessa and Tabitha each decided to make a milkshake and sit at a booth till business picked up. It was a good thing Martha wasn't working today or this would not be happening. She'd have them hustling and bustling about, cleaning or doing some random errand.

After taking a long sip of her milkshake, Tabitha sighed heavily and said, "Our summers are so short and it's depressing to think that fall will be here soon." Her eyes suddenly lit up and she said, "Hey, maybe I should move south and get a job. I could enjoy some real heat that way."

Tessa frowned and asked, "How far south are we talking?"

She shrugged. "How about Texas or Florida?"

"I don't know. The winters might be nice down there but the summers would be brutally hot."

"I'd get used to it."

"I suppose so. Let me know if you do move. You'll be my winter vacation spot. I'll provide the airfare and you'll supply the room."

A frown replaced Tabitha's cheerfulness. "Oh yeah, that's true. It would be like running a hotel. My family would always come to visit. I know them too well! They'd be hanging out at my place constantly!" She shook her head. "But that way I wouldn't get too lonely. We're very close, you know. I would just have to set things straight right from the start. If they want to eat, they buy the groceries, they cook and I don't make beds."

Tessa laughed. "It sounds like you have things covered."

She nodded in agreement and glanced over to the entrance. "Look, Tessa, isn't that your friend?"

Glancing over, she saw Richelle talking to Joan, the hostess. Joan pointed Richelle toward the booth and she headed their way.

Richelle wore a short, yellow sundress with a white border

around the neckline and hem which looked stunning. She had white, four-inch heels and large, silver hoop earrings. Her blond hair was newly cut and styled in a short bob with every strand impeccably in position.

A few interested eyes from Nina's section turned in Richelle's direction as she passed tables and approached. She was a vision of perfection and yet oblivious to the stir she made. Her eyes exuded unhappiness and her lips were pursed in a pout. She never could hide her feelings well.

Stopping at the table, Richelle completely ignored Tabitha, stared at Tessa and said, "Could I talk to you alone, please?"

Her rudeness was a bit shocking. "Richelle." Tessa lifted a hand toward Tabitha sitting across from her. "This is my coworker, Tabitha." Then she turned to Tabitha and said, "And this is my friend, Richelle."

A sheepish look crossed Richelle's face as she turned toward Tabitha and held out her hand. They shook politely, Richelle looking as stiff as a board.

"Nice to meet you," said Tabitha.

"Uh-huh." Turning back to Tessa with an impatient gesture, Richelle said, "Please, can we talk?"

"Well, technically I'm still working. I'm sitting here because it's been so slow today. I get off at five but if you give me a minute, I'll ask Les if I can get off early."

"Thanks." She looked desperate.

Tessa went to find Les. He granted her request so she returned and found Richelle waiting at the entrance, pacing impatiently in the small area. With no clue that all the males in the room were focused on her, watching her every move, Richelle was in a world of her own today.

"It's arranged," said Tessa. "Did you want to talk here or go someplace else?"

"I'm way too antsy to sit! Why don't I drive us to the park and we can walk around the lake?"

"Okay. Let's go."

Richelle drove Tessa home first so she could change into shorts and a t-shirt. Richelle had brought a change of clothes along so she also changed at Tessa's house then drove to the park. The parking lot was nearly empty. As they exited the car, the warm summer breeze blew their hair about.

It was a beautiful sunny day and the breeze brought some welcome relief from the heat. Tessa could feel humidity in the air and she knew the frizz job it would make of her hair. It was always a struggle controlling her curls during the summer months, the humidity playing havoc with her preferred style. So she grabbed a hair band from her pocket and whipped her hair into a pony tail.

They walked quietly for a while, enjoying the sights and sounds of the nearly deserted park. Tessa was surprised Richelle didn't unload immediately; she was acting very jittery.

"This is so much better than working!" admitted Tessa. "I love walking here. It's so peaceful today."

Suddenly Richelle stopped, turned toward Tessa and said, "I'm so upset!"

Tessa stopped and looked at her. "About what?"

"I'm sure you've heard that Charlie went to church with Cody." Anger laced her voice.

"Yes, Cody told me."

"Then I suppose you also know that Charlie has become a Christian!" she said with venom.

"Yes, I also know that."

Her eyes looked tormented. "He's not the same Charlie anymore. He's completely different and I don't like him. I want my old Charlie back. He's reading the Bible all the time and all he wants to talk about is God. He keeps asking me if I want to become a Christian too. I hate it!"

"It's not so bad being a Christian."

"Don't start on me too, Tessa! I can't handle any more pressure right now."

"I'm a Christian, remember?"

"So what?"

"It's not such a bad choice."

Richelle glared at her. "Stop it or I'm leaving!"

"Let's keep walking." Tessa started down the path. Richelle kept pace. Tessa asked, "So what's so bad about Charlie's decision? It might even soften him some."

"That's the thing. He's too nice. I'm not used to him that way and I don't know if I even like him this way." Her forehead crunched in confusion. "That sounds dumb, doesn't it?"

"A little," Tessa agreed.

Richelle put a hand to her forehead. Tessa had never seen her like this before.

"There's more, isn't there?"

"Yes. Charlie moved out today," she said in a broken voice. She appeared on the verge of tears as she continued a slow pace down the path.

Tessa fell silent for a few moments to allow Richelle to rein in her frail emotions. Finally, she asked, "Why did he move out?"

"Apparently, Cody had a little talk with him about how he and I were living in sin! He told Charlie that the right thing to do would be to move out and not live with me until marriage. Can you believe that? I am so angry! I hate Cody! He's ruining my life! If he were here, I'd strangle him!"

"Wow! Charlie is really serious about living for God."

Richelle turned abruptly and faced her. "What's that supposed to mean?" Her voice was becoming hysterical and her eyes accusing. "I'm the one hurting here and it's your boyfriend who's caused it!"

"Richelle, Cody didn't force Charlie to accept Christ. It was Charlie's decision. No one twisted his arm. Be honest, Richelle, have you ever seen Charlie so happy?"

"You're not hearing me! Do you even know how upset I am?" Her eyes were watery and threatening to spill their load. "I love Charlie. I just barely got over losing him once and now everything's in a tailspin again!"

"But you're not losing him. He still loves you. He loves God more, that's all."

"Oh, that's very reassuring!" said Richelle in a biting voice.

"I know it doesn't sound comforting, but it is. Charlie just wants to please God."

Richelle stared at her in bewilderment. "I have no clue what you're talking about. It sounds like gibberish to me. All I know is that Charlie's moved out and I'm alone." She turned away, threw her hands up in the air, let them drop and released a strangled sigh. "I can't handle this roller-coaster relationship. It's too hard emotionally and it's tearing me up inside."

"Would you consider going to church with Charlie on Sunday?"

She looked torn. "I don't know. I've never been to church except that one time I went to your church to hear you sing in the choir. I've been to a few weddings but that's it." Stopping close to the lake, she stood on a rock and looked out at the rippling waves. Finally, she asked, "Are you going? With Cody?"

She decided quickly. "Yes, I'll be there."

Richelle sighed deeply. "I can't promise. I'm still too upset to think straight." She stepped off the rock and continued strolling down the path.

Tessa felt encouraged by their conversation. She'd often invited Richelle to her church while they were still in high school. There'd always been an excuse for her to avoid it. Maybe now, Charlie would be reason enough for her to go.

They were coming around the lake for the second time and the heat was getting to both of them. Perspiration clung to their clothing. Tessa had switched the conversation to other things to try to calm Richelle's storm. She seemed more relaxed and less frenzied. Tessa was glad she could be of service once again. At least she was needed, even if she was a Christian.

Richelle finally said, "I need to go. Thanks for listening to me rant and rave again. I'm doing a lot of that lately, huh?"

"I don't mind so much. I can understand how this whole thing would be upsetting. I see it from a different viewpoint, that's all. Charlie's change might be positive, you know."

"I can't imagine how it could be, Tessa. I'm still too upset about him moving out."

"I know. Just give it time."

"I want to spend all my time with Charlie, not like this, agonizing over where we stand as a couple."

On that note, both girls entered Richelle's car. Richelle dropped her off at home and Tessa watched the white Honda drive away, praying Richelle would follow Charlie's lead soon. It was a prayer she had uttered over many years. To see change taking place was completely thrilling. As she walked to the front door, she prayed for Luke too. Those two had been her constant prayer requests for as long as she had known them.

~~~~~

The church was located in downtown Chelsey, a small rental space in a long strip of stores. As Tessa walked in with Cody, she could feel the warmth of the place. This church always made her feel that way. They'd come early and groups of people had already gathered and were talking.

Pastor Chad was on the far side talking to Charlie. Tessa shook her head at the strange sight. Never in a thousand years! He looked like a sponge, thirsty and dry, soaking up every word the pastor said. It made her smile.

Chad walked on to greet some other newcomer and Charlie noticed the two of them. He hurried over, wearing the biggest grin. It looked completely foreign on his normally stern face.

He came, holding both hands out, palms up. "I can't believe I'm actually in church! Charlie in church and I'm not even in a coffin! Can you believe it? I was sure I'd shut the door on religion forever."

Cody nodded and said, "God has a way of opening those doors. He has never stopped seeking after you. He's thrilled to start this new relationship with you."

"It just boggles my mind what he's done for me already! The peace is worth it all. I just never knew! I had no clue!" He looked overwhelmed.

Cody said, "The love of God is what totally did it for me. I suddenly felt so loved when I accepted him."

"Yeah. And who would have thought God could love someone like me?"

Tessa suddenly felt guilty for her past misgivings about Charlie. If God accepted him, she should do no less.

Charlie said, "I just wish I had found him sooner."

Cody said, "Be glad you found him when you did. You still have the rest of your life ahead."

Charlie nodded, looking grateful.

Tessa couldn't stop the question that had been eating at her since she saw him: "Charlie, is Richelle coming today?"

"I called her this morning but she wouldn't give me a straight answer. I offered to give her a ride but she said she'd come on her own, if she came at all. I hope she shows."

"I do too," admitted Tessa.

He nodded and Tessa felt amazed that the two of them

actually agreed on something.

The worship band was beginning their first song, signaling the service was about to begin so they headed to the front and sat down in the second row. As the music and singing continued, Tessa noticed Charlie glancing toward the back. She took a look too but there was no sign of Richelle.

The worship ended and Chad Casey stood, greeted everyone, gave the announcements then started on the message. He spoke on the love of God and, although it was old hat to Tessa, one look at Charlie told her that he was drinking it all up. He totally forgot to keep an eye out for Richelle. Since the message started, he hadn't looked back once.

Chad finished the service with a closing prayer and at that point Charlie stood quickly and left.

Tessa turned to look and noticed Richelle sitting on the back row. Charlie slipped in beside her to talk to her. Richelle shook her head in answer to whatever he'd asked and refused to meet his gaze. She glanced up, saw Tessa, gave her a dart-throwing look and averted her eyes to Pastor Chad.

Poor Charlie! He has his work cut out for him.

Tessa turned back to the front. When the service was over, everyone stood and moved.

Cody said, "I want to talk to Chad for a bit."

"Sure. Did you notice Richelle?"

"She came?"

"Yeah. Charlie's back there with her."

Cody looked. "She looks ready to bolt."

"I know. I need to catch her before she does."

Tessa hurried toward Richelle and Charlie. They were embroiled in deep conversation so she held back and let them finish. Richelle looked gorgeous in a bright, sky-blue miniskirt, white form-fitting t-shirt, sky-blue beads around her neck and white three-inch sandals. Her impetuous scowl distracted somewhat from her cute outfit and coiffed hair. Richelle finally glanced her way and gave her a disinterested wave. Tessa stepped forward and gave her a hug.

"I'm so glad you came."

"Yeah, whatever."

"Did you enjoy the service?"

"No, I hated it! There's too much pressure here. It's suffocating! Can we go outside?" she asked with a trapped, fierce look.

Charlie, standing beside her, looked despondent.

"Sure." Tessa led the way.

They stepped outside the front doors and stood on the paved walkway before the store fronts.

Richelle turned on Charlie with an accusatory gesture. "You told me you'd never step inside a church as long as you'd live. Why are you going back on that promise?"

"I never planned on breaking that promise. It just happened." He lifted his hands and let them drop. "I thought the only time I'd ever be in church was for my funeral."

"That's what I was counting on. How could you do this to me?"

"I never did this to you. I did this for me."

"But why?" She looked near tears.

"Because I learned that God loves me. I feel it for the first time and it's amazing!"

"You told me that all Christians are hypocrites! You told me that you'd never become one! Charlie, please change your mind!" Panic filled her voice.

He just smiled, with such peace shining from his eyes, it was uncanny. It only caused Richelle to look angrier.

Tessa didn't know what to say so she just listened.

"You're hurting me, Charlie. Christians aren't supposed to hurt others."

She's playing dirty! Wow! If pleading doesn't work, maybe a guilt trip will? Come on, Richelle, grow up!

Charlie sighed in exasperation. "Look, Richelle, I'm not going back on my decision. This God thing has changed me forever. If you only realized how much he loves you, how much he wants to have a relationship with you. Please, Richelle, accept Jesus as your Savior. It will be the best decision of your life."

Staring at him in disdain, she said, "No. Absolutely not! I can't believe you're even suggesting such an asinine thing."

"What did you say?"

"You heard exactly what I said, you big lug!"

"Just because you don't understand this, doesn't mean it's

270

stupid!" protested Charlie.

"It's the stupidest thing you've ever done," she yelled back.

Will I end up playing referee here too? This is ridiculous!

People exiting the church were starting to look their way. The two didn't care.

"You know, Richelle, I could just leave you be and never bother with you again."

She crossed her arms and stared at him with venom. "I'd be glad if you would."

He looked hurt. "You really mean that?"

She turned away and sighed deeply. "This is useless. Tessa, please talk some sense into him. Explain to him how he's ruining my life. Maybe he'll listen to you."

"I can hear you just fine, Richelle," said Charlie.

Tessa finally said, "I don't know what you want me to say."

She spat out, "Tell him to give up this religious nonsense."

"I can't tell him what to do. It's his decision, not mine."

Richelle stared daggers at her. "Well, then you're not much of a friend!" She spun on her heels, walked quickly to her car and got in. With wheels squealing, she took off in a cloud of dust.

Charlie looked completely flabbergasted, staring after her car in the distance. Tessa touched his arm in compassion. She never thought she'd be doing that anytime soon.

He turned to her and said, "I wish it had turned out different. She can be so stubborn."

Giving his arm a pat, Tessa said, "Just give her some time. God's not going to give up on her. He's going to do everything possible to draw her to himself. It often takes time."

Charlie looked a little encouraged. Cody walked toward them and, after some discussion, they decided to have lunch together.

They chose the family restaurant just around the corner which was known for its terrific fried chicken.

Once seated, the waitress came with her notepad. "Hi there. I'll be serving you today. If you need anything, just call me. My name's Angela." She pointed to her name tag. "Could I take your drink order?"

They gave her their beverage selection and she left to fill it. Cody gazed into Tessa's eyes questioningly and she nodded. Charlie noticed their secret exchange and his forehead scrunched in disapproval. Tessa knew she had to explain. Secrets would only strain the new friendship they had.

"I just got a sign."

Charlie's eyes narrowed in confusion.

Cody explained, "Tessa just received the signal that it's time to head back to the mansion."

"What signal? I didn't see any signal."

"Tessa hears the signal; she doesn't see it."

"So what is it?"

"Bells. I hear bells ringing," said Tessa.

Cody continued, "Yeah, when she hears the word 'angel,'- or today it was the waitress' name, Angela – she hears bells ringing."

"And...then...it's time to go back?" asked Charlie, looking bemused.

Tessa nodded.

"So when the waitress said her name, you heard bells ringing?" He looked skeptical.

"It's been like this from the beginning of the time travel."

Cody nodded to confirm it. "Did you want to join us?"

Tessa was thrilled Cody simply assumed he was joining her. He was treating them like a team. They both looked at Charlie and waited.

He grinned impishly. "I wouldn't miss it. Do you mind if I call Richelle and invite her along?"

Tessa said, "We wouldn't mind at all. I'll call Luke too and let him know."

CHAPTER 20

The six of them met at the mansion at two in the afternoon and entered single file. Since no one was around and no action looked imminent, they decided to go wait in the sitting room.

Most of them sat on the couches around the empty fireplace. Cody toured the room and studied the framed pictures on the wall, artwork, statues and figurines placed on beautiful sculptured wooden bases.

Tessa glanced toward Richelle and Charlie. Richelle still looked icily distant and refused to make much eye contact with Charlie. He kept looking at her with longing. Luke and Janaye were like two lovebirds, sitting close, he holding her hand and whispering sweet things in her ear. It was actually quite annoying. Tessa thought she preferred the icy distance instead of the overt romance.

Luke suddenly pulled away from Janaye and stood. He walked over to where Cody stood at the fireplace. A big clock hung up above the mantel, looking much like a miniature grandfather clock. It was a beautifully handcrafted wooden clock, stained a dark mahogany with detailed carving on its face. Tessa had heard it chime before. It sounded on each hour. Luke reached up to touch it but his hand went right through it, stopping on the brick beneath.

"Interesting," said Cody.

Luke grinned. He pulled his hand back and turned his attention to the articles on the mantel, studying them for some time. There were a number of pictures set on the wooden ledge along with some books held by bookends, candlesticks holding tapered candles and a few marble figurines. Luke gently reached out to touch them but his hand again passed through them.

Curiosity brought Tessa out of her seat to Luke's side. She looked at the pictures more closely.

"I wonder who this is." She pointed to one with a woman and a child.

Luke shrugged. "She's holding a little one. It could be Elizabeth and Mary."

Cody leaned in to take a look. "The kid looks like a boy. Maybe it's Eunice with William."

Luke responded, "Yeah, maybe. But look at this one. Doesn't this couple look like William and Elizabeth?"

"Yeah they do," said Tessa. "But how can that be? There are two children in the picture."

The three of them gazed at the photo in curiosity.

The picture was unquestionably of William and Elizabeth, just a lot younger and there were positively two children in the photo. The boy was about four years old and a baby girl lay in Elizabeth's arms, a bow tied in her short hair. She was wrapped in a blanket.

"I never knew they had a son," said Tessa in shock.

"What could have happened to him?" asked Luke.

Tessa turned and said to the others. "Hey guys, come look at this."

Charlie, Richelle and Janaye came and studied the photo.

Richelle blurted out, "They had two kids!"

"And look at this picture." Cody pointed to a framed photo of a seated, young teenage boy.

"I wonder if that's the same kid?" asked Luke.

"He sure has the same features," said Cody.

"I wonder whatever became of him?" asked Richelle.

Tessa said, "Maybe we'll find out…" A sound at the door stopped her.

William and Elizabeth entered the room. Elizabeth clasped her hands before her and wrung them in agitation. She sat down on the edge of one of the couches and her husband sat across from her on another. Making himself comfortable, William sank back into the backrest, a satisfied smile on his face.

The six felt conspicuous standing by the fireplace directly in front of them. But the couple had no clue they had any intruders. They stood still, ready to listen and learn. Not once did Elizabeth or William look their way.

"I'm very pleased with the arranged meeting this afternoon. This is what I've been hoping for and I do hope that Mary cooperates."

Frustration played in Elizabeth's eyes. "William, you know what Mary wants. Why do you oppose her every step?"

"I'm not opposing her, just orchestrating things for her. There's a big difference."

"I don't know that there is." She looked near tears.

"Elizabeth, dear, this is the best for her. Richard's a fine young man and I believe he'll make Mary very happy."

"Mary is in love with Henry. Why can't you see that?"

The smile vanished from his face, replaced by stern impatience. "I don't want you fighting me over this. I've decided and the issue is settled."

"It's because Richard looks like our own John. That's why you've chosen him, isn't it?"

A slight smile returned. "There is a strong resemblance, I have to agree."

"That's no reason to ruin Mary's life."

He looked exasperated. "I am not ruining her life. Richard is educated and comes from a good family. I like the boy and I believe Mary will soften to him."

"I think you're making a mistake. You can't make Mary fall in love with anyone. You could be arranging a difficult, unhappy and unfulfilling life for her."

"You worry too much, Elizabeth. We need to think positively on this issue. I believe Mary is stronger than you think."

"But, if she doesn't love him it…"

"Elizabeth, stop!" His volume shook the room.

She stared at him in shock.

"He's a fine man, a good looking man. There's no reason she can't fall in love with him."

"What if it's not enough? Please consider her feelings."

He stood then, weary of his wife's apprehension.

Elizabeth looked suddenly pensive. "I so wish our Johnny was still here."

William went to stand by the grand piano and pressed a few keys. The notes seemed to hang in mid air as though suspended. "I had so many dreams and plans for him. He was such a strong and vibrant young boy. I don't understand what went wrong."

"First there was the sickness, the spiked fever and then…." Her voice trailed off, she looked over at the mantel and studied the pictures sitting there. "We still have our dear Mary. We need to do right by her."

"That's why I arranged this meeting. I've talked to Richard and I believe Mary will be pleasantly surprised."

Elizabeth sighed wearily.

"Would you go let Mary know that Richard is on his way? Tell her to dress in her best."

She stood slowly and said, "All right, William, but I don't agree with how you're handling this." With that she left the room.

William walked over to the fireplace. The six friends fanned out to make room for him as he picked up the picture of the boy in his early teens. He studied it for a few minutes in silence.

With sadness in his voice, he said, "I miss you, John. I'd give anything to have you back with us again." He stared at it a moment more, set it back on the mantel and slowly turned and left the room.

Tessa finally broke the hush that engulfed the room. "That's why he's so determined about Richard. He's trying to replace his son with someone who looks like him."

"It's crazy!" declared Richelle.

"The man's losing it," stated Luke. "He's as bonkers as his mother."

Richelle said, "He always seems so unreasonable to me. He's controlling and manipulating but he's obviously hurting too."

Tessa turned to her and asked, "Are you feeling sorry for him?"

"I know it's stupid! I should hate him. He's damaged Mary so much with his control issues. But I do...I do feel sorry for him."

"I'd say they've seen their share of grief," said Luke.

Janaye spoke quietly, "I agree. I wonder when it will end."

No one knew how to answer.

Cody finally said, "Only God knows the answer to that."

Richelle stepped away in annoyance. "God, God, God! Richard better show up quick or else I'm leaving!" She walked rigidly to the doorway and out into the foyer.

"I'll go talk to her." Charlie left the room and followed her.

Suddenly music filled the room, echoing off the walls and saturating the space with an ethereal sound. Tessa scanned the room and noticed the trench-coated man at the piano, playing his heart out. The music was exhilarating, alive, flowing right through her. She heard an invisible band playing along, providing deep bass, pounding drum and sweeping guitar strings that were beyond anything she had heard before. She could feel the music pouring into every fiber of her being, vibrating deep inside and surrounding her completely.

She looked at Cody. He looked as awestruck as she felt.

The song was very familiar to her: "How Great Thou Art."

Charlie and Richelle returned and stood just inside the door. They looked completely mesmerized as they watched the angel tickle the ivory keys, his whole soul encompassed in his playing. The angel's trench coat was unbuttoned, revealing a white shirt beneath, black trousers, socks and shoes. His black hat rested on top of the piano and his dark hair moved as he poured his heart into the song.

The music seemed to have a power of its own, as though alive. The melodious sound waves flowed right through them and touched them to their inner core. It continued for about ten minutes while the six of them were held completely captive.

Tessa tore her gaze away from the angel for a moment and peered over at Luke and Richelle. They looked frozen in place, completely focused on the angel; they didn't even flinch. She would have thought they'd have both bolted for the door.

The music grew softer until the notes gradually faded away. The angel turned on the piano seat and gazed at Luke and Richelle, standing side by side. His stare was so intense that they both looked away. When they dared to look again, the angel slowly disappeared from the spot where he sat.

The atmosphere was charged with the heavenly visitation. There was a tangible presence in the air. Everyone was afraid even to move, for fear of breaking the blissful feeling. Eventually they began to look at each other, wonder mirrored in each face.

"I don't know how that could have happened." Luke appeared spooked but not enough to keep him from tentatively approaching the piano. He walked through and stood in the middle of it. "See, it's not even here so how could we have heard any music? How could the angel have been sitting on a piano bench and playing a piano that doesn't even exist? I don't believe it is God at all. There are probably ghosts haunting this house."

Cody jumped in immediately, "No, God is showing you clearly that he does exist, Luke, even though you're making up excuses to explain him away."

"I'm out of here." Luke hurried toward the door, looking shaken by the experience.

A knock at the front door stopped him in his tracks.

"Richard's here," said Tessa.

They all headed to the foyer and watched as one of the servants opened the door and let Richard in. With an air of utter confidence, he removed his coat, revealing a smart business suit beneath. Tessa had to admit he looked dashing and sophisticated. The man was handsome with his dark hair, good looks and impressive height.

"Is Mr. Hardington here?"

"Yes, Mr. Ridgefield, but I understood you were coming to see Miss Mary and not her father."

"Well yes, that's true. I was wondering if I'd be able to speak with Mr. Hardington first."

"I'll check with him, sir. Just a moment." The servant hurried down the left hallway, carrying Richard's coat with him.

Richard stayed at the door and looked around, his eyes glancing up to the top level for any sign of Mary, no doubt. He sported a grin as he gazed about arrogantly, his shoulders thrown back.

"He looks so cocky!" Tessa said, feeling disdain rise in her throat.

"Nothing that a little humbling won't solve," said Cody.

"What do you mean by that?" she asked curiously.

"Pride comes before a fall."

"It'd be nice to see him taken down a few notches." She felt immediately guilty for saying such a thing. "That sounded mean, right?"

Cody just smiled; so did Charlie.

After a few minutes Mr. Hardington appeared, walking briskly from the hall to the front door, irritation reflecting in his eyes.

"Richard, is there something you need help with?"

"I wanted to say hi, sir, and was also curious if there was anything more definite on the timing of the new job. I'm eager to start as soon as I can."

He smiled in feigned amusement. "As I said before, I'll let you know when the details are worked out. Until then we have nothing further to discuss."

"Yes, sir, I understand. I do have one other question."

"Yes, what is it?" William said with impatience.

"I was wondering if it would be suitable and appropriate if I proposed to Mary today. I know it's rather speedy but I don't see any reason to prolong something that I believe is destined to be."

William looked truly taken off guard. "Well, I, uh…it does seem rather sudden." He rubbed his chin with his right hand as he thought over the request. "But I don't see what harm it would do. It would definitely take Mary's mind off her troubles. With a wedding to plan, her days would be filled. What are your thoughts on the timing?'"

"I'm open to suggestions, sir"

"We can discuss that at another time. Go take a seat in the sitting room. I'll send a servant to get Mary and she'll join you soon."

"Thank you, sir," Richard said with a satisfied smile.

William walked off and Richard headed for the sitting room.

The six waited in the foyer for Mary. A new servant appeared. She was young, in her early twenties, but walked with a sense of confidence and wore the familiar garb all the servants wore. She ascended the stairs and walked down an upstairs hallway.

A few minutes later the servant girl reappeared. She was a petite little thing with pretty features and blond hair that was pulled back into a high ponytail. She walked into the sitting room and they overheard her speak.

"Mr. Ridgefield?"

"Yes."

"Mary is not quite ready. It will be a few minutes before she joins you."

Pausing, Richard replied. "I didn't realize the Hardingtons had such a pretty servant."

"Sir?'

"Would you care to keep me company while I wait?"

"I have duties that I need to fulfill, sir."

"A few minutes to keep a guest company wouldn't hurt, would it?"

"No, I suppose not." She sounded hesitant.

The six friends looked at each other in shocked disbelief.

Luke said, "He's a scallywag!"

"What an absolute jerk!" Richelle verbalized what they all felt.

The six of them hurried into the sitting room.

"This should be interesting," whispered Cody.

"I don't like this development," admitted Tessa.

Richard stood and said, "Please sit down. What's your name?" The servant girl sat down nervously, at the edge of the couch. Only then did Richard return to his seat.

"My name's Ruth."

"I don't believe I've seen you before. How long have you worked here?"

"It's been over a year now. I've been in the kitchen most of the time. I didn't enjoy it very much so they recently gave me other jobs."

"Well it's wonderful to have a pretty face around here to bring me messages." Richard smiled flirtatiously.

Ruth smiled and her cheeks turned a bright pink. She stood then and said, "I really do have to return to my work, sir."

"Oh, I didn't mean to embarrass you, Miss Ruth." Richard stood and walked over to her, took her hand and kissed it. "Thank you for gracing me with your presence."

She didn't say a word but hurried out of the room.

Richelle said in disgust, "If only I could talk to Mr. Hardington and let him know what this Richard is really like. He'd kick him out in a heartbeat."

Tessa said, "I wish we could."

They heard footsteps in the foyer and, a moment later, Mary appeared in the doorway. She was dressed in a conservative black and white checkered jumper with a white turtleneck underneath. She wore black two-inch heels on her feet and her hair was pulled back into a partial ponytail. A few shorter tendrils hung down onto her face and helped soften her look. Her overall appearance was tame compared to how she'd dressed for Henry.

Richard rose as she approached.

"Hi, Mary; it's so good to see you." He took her hands in his and held them up to his lips, kissed them then let them go.

"Hi, Richard." Her lack of enthusiasm was unmistakable as

she seated herself on a separate couch.

Richard smiled at her. He purposely moved closer and took a seat beside her. She scooted over an inch to allow a smidgen of space between them.

"I see you're doing much better."

"Yes, thank you. I feel much stronger."

"You look beautiful as always, Mary."

"Thank you, Richard." She struggled to keep eye contact with the scamp. Tessa couldn't blame her.

Mary looked away and asked, "Was there a reason you came to see me?"

Cody leaned over to Tessa and said, "He's just barely arrived and she's ready to cut to the chase already. Say what you came to say and get out."

Tessa nodded.

"You're a business woman at heart, aren't you?" asked Richard.

She stared at him with controlled impatience.

A twitch of nervousness moved his lips. "Yes, there is a reason that I'm here. First of all, I came to spend time with you. I want us to get to know each other better. I was hoping you'd be pleased."

"I don't know if pleased would be the word to describe how I feel."

"Then it's better than I had hoped. Great! What I propose is that we meet every Sunday afternoon. That way we'll get to know each other quickly."

Her eyebrows narrowed in confusion and apprehension showed in her eyes. "Why is it important we get to know each other quickly, Richard?"

He slipped off the couch and onto the floor to one knee in front of her. Panic filled her face.

"I love you, Mary. I know it hasn't been a secret. I've wanted you from the first time I saw you. I want to court you, but more than that, I want to marry you. Would you marry me?"

"Oh dear! Oh dear!" Mary stood with one hand to her heart.

She walked away, the color in her face draining till she looked as pale as death. Hurrying to the piano, she sat down on the bench, her hands brushing the keys. But she applied no pressure, no sound was made. Taking deep breaths and fanning her fingers back and forth over the ivory keys appeared to be her attempt to stay calm.

Richard stood, walked over to the piano and placed his hands on her shoulders. When he did, Mary closed her eyes tightly, as if by doing so she could make him disappear.

"That wasn't much of an answer, Mary. It wasn't exactly what I was hoping for."

Richard looked unsure of himself for the first time that day and it brought some satisfaction to Tessa.

Mary released an anxious sigh and opened her eyes. "You know I'm in love with someone else so how could you possibly think of coming here and proposing to me?" A telling look crossed her face. "It's my father, isn't it? He put you up to this, didn't he?"

"Mary, your father had nothing to do with this. He's not powerful enough to force me to marry anyone. I want to marry you. You know I've wanted you for a long time. That's no secret to you."

She finally turned to look at him. "But you know that he refused me the man I love."

"He did mention that Henry was completely out of the picture. It gave me more confidence in coming to see you today."

Her shoulders drooped in sorrow.

Richard moved to her side and knelt down once more. He took her hands in his and said, "Listen, Mary, how many other chances will you have at marriage, considering your mental lapse? What man would want to marry a woman who is mentally weak? I'm offering you a wonderful opportunity."

She stood immediately at the obvious insult and walked away from him again. Heading to the window, she nervously parted the curtains to look outside, finally turning back toward him.

"Then why do you want to marry me? If I'm so weak mentally, what's the appeal?"

"You're still beautiful and I think we'd make a great team together. I have enough strength for both of us. I could be a pillar for you." Richard appeared tentative of the outcome but he also looked hopeful.

Mary turned away and looked outside. "When would we marry?"

A look of relief flooded his face. "We'll marry as soon as possible. I'll make all the arrangements so that you don't need to worry yourself with anything. I've already looked at some houses to buy."

Her head shot back to face him and she shook her head in disbelief. "I didn't say I'd marry you, Richard!"

"But you asked when we'd marry."

She looked agitated and torn as she fidgeted with the curtains. "I don't know. This is all so sudden. How can I marry someone I don't even love?"

Richard looked stricken, or at least he made a good imitation of it.

Guilt suddenly escaped from Mary's eyes at the hurt she'd inflicted. "I'm sorry...but it's how I feel." She turned, walked to the couch and sat down, indecision plaguing her eyes.

Richard followed her at a distance and sat across from her, providing some distance this time. "Mary, please listen to me. I know you don't have great affection for me right now. I believe those amorous feelings can come eventually. Why don't you give us a chance? I believe you'll fall in love with me, given some time. Say yes and we'll start courting."

She looked overwhelmed and sorrowful as she gazed at him. "Do you even know how I feel?"

He shook his head.

"I feel like you and my father have manipulated this whole thing and are forcing me into this relationship."

"If that's truly how you see this, then perhaps I should leave and you can disregard my proposal." Richard rose as if to leave.

"No, wait." She looked utterly torn.

He sat back down.

"Maybe this will be my only opportunity for marriage." She studied her folded hands in her lap.

Patiently, he waited for her.

Finally, lifting her gaze, she said, "You're a fine man, Richard, and I know that you would take care of me." Her eyes averted nervously as she struggled to continue. Turning to him again, she said, "All right, the answer is yes."

"Yes, you'll marry me?"

"Yes."

"Wonderful!" He clapped his hands and breathed a huge sigh of relief. "You'll see that it's the best decision. I'm sure we'll be wonderfully happy together. I'll do right by you, Mary."

Mary nodded sadly.

"Then we'll begin weekly Sunday visits."

"Yes, that would be fine." The wind was out of her sails; her weak, tired smile said it all.

Richard moved closer to her. He eagerly discussed his plans for the wedding and their future together. Mary looked like a trapped animal. It was surprising that her disinterest and woeful face didn't dissuade him from his conversation.

Richelle motioned to Tessa for her to follow. Richelle led the way out of the room. In the middle of the foyer, she stopped and turned to face her.

"I can't believe that Mary's actually going for it. She is such a wimp!"

"But she hardly has a choice. What are her options?"

"I'd stay single if I were her. Richard is flirting with another woman already and that was before he even proposed!"

Luke and the others were coming to join them. He said, "We know he was flirting but she doesn't. He did admit to her that he loves her."

Tessa said, "That's true. If words mean anything, she'll believe him."

"This whole thing is making me sick!" Richelle didn't look well either.

Charlie said, "Come on, Richelle, I'll take you home." He took hold of her hand but she yanked it away angrily.

"I brought my own car remember, Charlie! We're not together anymore or have you forgotten?" It was clear her anger went deeper than just because of Mary's ill-fated decision.

"We don't live together but I still want to be with you."

"Well, maybe I don't." With that Richelle turned and walked out the door. Charlie dejectedly followed her.

"Wow, things are sure rocky on that front. What's up with those two?" Luke asked.

Tessa filled him in and he shook his head in disbelief.

"So Charlie became a Christian, did he?"

Tessa nodded.

"Is that why he's wearing that stupid smile all the time? I thought maybe he was high on drugs or something."

"Luke, don't!" Tessa chided him.

"He always was a strange one. He just got weirder." Taking hold of Janaye's hand, he said, "Come on, it's time to go."

Tessa watched the two leave. Janaye had become very quiet. Tessa wondered what was going on. Luke was definitely not acting his usual lighthearted self either. Perhaps knowing that Janaye was a Christian, he was growing uncomfortable with the increasing pressure.

Cody looked at Tessa and smiled. He reached over, took her into his arms and kissed her longingly. Pulling away, he said, "This time travel sure keeps things interesting."

Tessa looked up at him, smiled and said, "You can say that again."

"I don't know if Luke or Richelle would agree."

"Well, for them it's stirring things up."

He nodded.

"There's enough excitement in this place to last a lifetime."

"And to think it's all happening during your summer break."

She laughed. "At least it keeps me out of trouble."

He grinned. "Yeah, you're such a trouble maker."

"And don't you know it."

With a smile, he took her hand and they left the mansion.

CHAPTER 21

The salon where Richelle worked, Bristol Boutique, was located on Bristol Avenue. Sitting on the hydraulic chair, Tessa glanced about the salon, a large cape draped over her shoulders, Richelle snipping at her hair,

The place was tastefully decorated in mostly black and white, the stark contrast in colors bold and catchy. The chrome ceiling added an unusual punch and crystal chandeliers hanging from above gave it bling.

After the trim was complete, Richelle began the drying process. It always amazed Tessa how Richelle could get her hair so straight, simply by drying and yanking it around. Richelle was adept at using a brush and dryer to manipulate the hair into a sculptured masterpiece.

A few pictures were taped to Richelle's mirror. There was a big picture of Charlie and a smaller one of Lacy, her dog. A card sat on the counter in front of the mirror, a big heart surrounded by roses and the words, "To My Sweetheart" on the face. It was obviously from Charlie.

Richelle turned off the dryer and set it in its holder. Tessa pointed to the card. "From Charlie?" She looked at Richelle's reflection in the mirror.

Richelle met her gaze. "Yeah. He gave it to me on the weekend." Silence stretched for a few seconds. "I told him we're through."

Shock coursed through Tessa. She turned to face her: "No!"

"Yep. We're done."

"I thought you loved him?"

"I love the old Charlie. I don't love him the way he is now."

"Richelle! I can't believe you did that!"

"Oh, just chill. I'm going to see if he lets this Christianity thing drop. If he truly loves me, he'll give it up for me."

Tessa couldn't believe her ears. "Couldn't he say the same thing about you? Maybe he's thinking that if you truly love him you'll check out what Christianity is about."

Frustration showed in her eyes. "Look, if you came here to encourage me, you're not doing a very good job. I don't need this!"

"I'm just giving you a possible scenario."

"Well, I don't like that scenario." Richelle picked up the hot iron.

"I'm just saying it could backfire on you."

"I don't see how." She lifted a piece of Tessa's long hair and ran the iron through it, straightening it further.

"There are plenty of pretty girls at the church and I've noticed them eyeing Charlie. I just want you to realize the possible consequences of your decision."

"Tessa! Don't do this to me." She waved the hot iron above her head. "Just remember who has the weapon."

Tessa shook her head in exasperation. "Do you have to act so juvenile?"

Richelle actually grinned at that. Her grin faded quickly and she returned to her iron work. Finally, she said, "Why do you always have to be so reasonable, so reality-driven? I want to romanticize this whole thing. Like, Charlie could never love anyone the way he loves me." She caught Tessa's eye in the mirror. "Play along if nothing else, okay?"

"All right, Richelle. How about this?" She placed a hand over her heart. "I'm sure his love for you will outweigh his newfound love for God and he'll throw his eternal salvation away for you, the woman he loves."

A confused look filled Richelle's eyes. "I'm not sure I completely understood that. It sounds like a mixed message to me." She shook her head. "I don't think you're helping."

"Well then, let's change the subject. I'm your last client, right?"

Still wearing an unnerved look, Richelle nodded.

"At the restaurant today there was this family and they had the cutest, curly-haired, little girl. They didn't sit in my section but I overheard Martha talking to them. She asked them her name and they told her it was Amber but Martha kept calling her 'Angel' the whole time they were there. I'm sure you can read between the lines."

"You heard the bells again! You want to go back tonight?"

"I'd like to go sooner than that. I tried calling Cody but he's at work. I also tried Luke but he didn't answer. I have a feeling we need to go there soon and I don't think we should wait till evening. Would you go with me?"

"Sure, I'll clean up my station and then we can go. We can drive there in my car."

Richelle rushed through the rest of the straightening job but it still turned out silky and smooth. Tessa loved the feeling of her hair after Richelle finished. She certainly was gifted in making every woman who visited her salon into a beauty, that is, if hair was the only qualifying factor.

Tessa paid and waited at the front while Richelle tidied up.

As they drove to the house, dark clouds hovered overhead, threatening rain. Richelle parked by the curb and as she did, rain drops began splattering against the windshield.

They ran for the house and when they switched time zones, they ran through puddles of water, with partially melted piles of snow still heaped on either side of the pathway. A fair bit of water had accumulated on the path, making a messy entrance to the place. Doing some mental calculation, Tessa concluded it must be the middle of April 1946 and that spring had sprung.

They walked into the house and wiped their feet on the mat at the door. Tessa shook her head. The mat didn't really exist. Their feet were rubbing up against the hardwood floor.

Richelle looked at her and said, "Why do we always forget?"

"Everything looks so real!"

"It's hard to keep things compartmentalized. What exists and what doesn't."

"I know. I keep forgetting that some things aren't really here."

"It still seems so ethereal."

Richelle seemed more lighthearted, her issues regarding Charlie forgotten for the moment. They walked to the big round table in the center of the foyer. A new batch of flowers filled the huge vase on the table.

Richelle looked around the foyer and up to the top landing. "I don't see anyone. What should we do? Are you getting any direction from God or that angel as to what we're supposed to do?"

Tessa eyed her suspiciously. "Are you being sarcastic?"

"No, I'm serious."

"I thought you didn't believe in God."

"I believe there's a God, I just don't want him messing up my life."

Interesting!

She tore her eyes from Richelle, looked around and said, "I have no clue where we're supposed to go or what we're supposed to do."

"Hmph. And I thought you were the one in charge."

"I've never been in charge."

Richelle stared at her. "How do you figure that?"

"I didn't make this happen."

"But it happens when you come here."

"So?" Tessa stared at her.

Richelle stared right back.

Changing the subject, Tessa said, "I've never checked out the dining room. Why don't we go take a look?"

"That's the big plan, to look at a table and chairs?"

"Do you have any better ideas?" she shot back.

Richelle lifted her arms and let them fall. "Okay, let's do it."

They walked to the dining room, located on the left side of the house, where it was closed off by heavy, wooden double doors.

"Luke told us about this room. He seemed quite impressed," Richelle said, pulling at the door handle.

It creaked noisily as it swung open. They entered, closed the door behind them and scanned the room. Two bay windows were located in this large room, one facing the front to the street, the other facing the side yard. Thick white sheers covered the windows and sheer valances draped over the top curtain rods and cascaded down the sides. The window coverings shielded the room from outside light and made the room appear dark and dingy at first observation. The table in the center was huge, easily able to seat at least thirty people. The room was massive, with plenty of space around the table for numerous servants to maneuver and serve.

I wonder if they do a lot of entertaining?

All the furniture in the room, table, chairs, side server and china cabinet, were stained in dark cherry and varnished to a shining glow. Above the table hung two large crystal chandeliers that sparkled even with the small amount of light coming through the sheers. The overall effect was enchanting.

Tessa walked toward the china cabinet and viewed the pieces on the glass shelves. White china in gold trim was a beautiful contrast against the dark wood. There were elaborate crystal glasses arranged symmetrically on some of the shelves, as well as delicate floral-designed teacups and saucers.

She turned her attention back to the table and noticed, for the first time, an expansive rug beneath the table over the rich hardwood, spanning the entire length. With a cream-colored background, the overlaid floral design was in shades of white and gold, a few soft green leaves throughout, and the entire rug bordered in gold.

Around the edges of the room stood impressive, ivory statues of African animals, an elephant, giraffe, impala, male lion and a bald eagle. Large oil paintings hugged the walls with small spotlights placed above each for optimum viewing. The entire effect of the room was grand and breathtaking.

Richelle said, "We should have checked this out sooner. This room is amazing!"

"There's always so much happening here that it's hard to spend time sightseeing." A noise from the other room alerted her. It sounded like someone had knocked. She turned to Richelle and asked, "Did you hear that?"

"Yes. Someone's here."

The girls exited the room, gingerly stepping into the foyer and staying to the side. A servant girl hurried to the front door.

"Ruth," whispered Richelle.

Tessa nodded.

Ruth was medium height and, although not stunning, she was a very pretty girl with blond, wavy hair that hung past her shoulders. Her most striking asset was her eyes; they shone a light shade of aquamarine, like a Caribbean ocean, their intensity mesmerizing.

She opened the front door and Richard Ridgefield entered. As soon as he saw her his face lit up with pleasure.

"Why, how nice to be greeted at the door by a pretty face. It's wonderful to see you again, Ruth."

Ruth smiled and looked charmed, her cheeks warming with the

compliment. Shaking off her timidity and with a flirtatious twist of her lips, she said, "It's likewise pleasant to greet a handsome gentleman at the door."

He looked somewhat nonplussed, "Ruth, are you flirting with me?"

She grinned mischievously and said, "May I take your coat, Mr. Ridgefield?"

Smiling in amusement, he nodded and said, "Oh yes, I nearly forgot." He shed his coat and handed it to her, his demeanor suddenly changing. "Is Mary here this afternoon?"

"She left with her parents an hour ago. They went to see a theatrical production."

"Oh, really?"

Ruth nodded and held out his coat. "I suppose you want this back then, Mr. Ridgefield?"

He gazed at her with new interest. "I would prefer if you would call me Richard. No more of this Mr. Ridgefield nonsense, all right?"

"Yes of course, Richard." She gazed girl-like into his eyes.

"Could I spend some time with you, Ruth? I mean, that is…if you're not too busy."

"I do have duties to attend to."

"Of course, I realize that. But I did come all this way to see Mary. Perhaps if you could spare a few minutes of interesting conversation it would make this seemingly unnecessary trip worthwhile and not quite so pointless. Would you please humor me?" He gave her a charming smile.

"Well, put that way, I would love to."

"I think it would be wise if we went somewhere where we could be alone. We wouldn't want to create gossip, if you know what I mean?"

A shocked look crossed her face.

"I think it's wise for propriety."

"Of course." She looked thoughtful for a moment. "The guest room is available upstairs and no one enters it." A seductive smiled curved her lips. "Mary won't be back for a while. She'd never have to know."

Desire flared in his eyes and he gave her a knowing look. "That's perfect. Great minds think alike. Lead the way."

The two schemers made their way up the stairs and disappeared from view as they headed down a hallway on the top floor.

Richelle stomped her foot and said, "I can't believe this! He's cheating on Mary. What an absolute jerk."

Shock was mild to describe how Tessa felt. The situation had become appalling and her stomach churned sickeningly. "Ruth's not exactly a saint either. Things seem to be getting worse by the day and I was hoping things would improve for Mary. Richard is definitely not an upgrade for her!"

"My grandmother never knew how lucky she was. Richard was the man she wanted to marry. It makes me sick just thinking about it!"

"She wasn't the best judge of character, huh?"

Richelle shook her head. "I guess not! My grandfather was a good man. Henry was honorable and always treated my grandmother with respect. She never knew how good she had it. I don't know why she never loved him."

"Mary obviously recognized something good when she found it. It's too bad she couldn't have married Henry."

Richelle pointed upstairs, "Mary's in for a load of trouble with this guy."

They both shook their heads, staring up at the top floor. Tessa still felt sick to her stomach.

"Do you think we should check on them?" asked Richelle.

Alarmed, Tessa asked, "What? Do you mean walk into the guest room and see what they're doing?"

"No! What I'm trying to get at is maybe we're just jumping to conclusions. Maybe all they're doing in there is talking. We'll never know for sure if we stay down here. We could listen in at the door."

It made sense. Why pass on information that was only subjective guesswork? What if they were assuming the worst prematurely or judging erroneously? Maybe Richard was a truly great guy and they were painting him with the wrong brush. How would they know unless they got information first hand?

Tessa nodded and swayed her head in the direction of the stairs. They hurried up the steps and headed down the hallway they had seen Richard and Ruth take. Walking down the hall quietly, they listened for any telltale noises. As they approached the third door on the right, both of them stopped and listened. Richard and Ruth were definitely in there. Soft laughter and low voices drifted through the closed door.

They moved in closer, their ears against the wood grain of the door. The laughter and talking gradually stopped and was replaced by indiscernible sounds. Then the quiet gave way to moans, groans and the creak of a bed.

Richelle said, "Do you hear that?"

Tessa nodded. "I'm hearing birds and bees."

"Exactly! He's as culpable as they come!"

"So what do we do?"

"Keep listening."

Tessa moved her ear from the door. "I feel guilty doing this. We should stop them."

"How?" Richelle removed her ear and faced her.

She raised her arms and let them drop. "Walk in on them?"

"What would that help? They wouldn't see us."

"Bang on the door?"

"They wouldn't hear us."

It was hopeless. There was nothing they could do to prevent this.

They both jumped at a noise behind them. They swung around and saw the angel standing in the hall. His face looked stern.

"You scared us." That's all Tessa could think to say as her heart hammered against her ribs.

"Just remember that God's grace is greater than any sin." With that he turned, walked toward the stairway, but before reaching it, he disappeared into thin air.

Tessa felt shaken by the short but firm announcement. She glimpsed at Richelle who looked equally as spooked.

"Well, I don't want to listen to any more of this," Richelle said, pointing to the door. She turned and headed toward the stairs.

Tessa followed and about halfway down, heavenly music suddenly filled the house. It was different than the last time they'd heard a song here and not like anything Tessa had ever heard before. She recognized it easily – "Amazing Grace." There were no words, only music. The sound wasn't coming from anywhere in particular. Its intensity stayed the same as they descended; it followed them, projected directly over them and surrounded them continually. As Tessa headed to the sitting room, the volume of the music didn't differ.

Looking in, there was no one at the piano and yet the music continued. Richelle stepped in beside her and stared at her, discomfort and fear dancing in her eyes.

Tessa felt trepidation too but she refused to let it dominate her. She began to sing the words she knew so well.

"Amazing Grace, how sweet the sound that saved a wretch like me. I once was lost but now am found, was blind but now I see."

She hummed the rest and began to understand the significance of the song. God's grace was going to be extended to this family. There was no obvious indication when this would occur but she knew, deep inside, that at some point this family would seek him and he would offer them grace.

"What does 'grace' mean anyway?" asked Richelle, with an apprehensive gaze.

"Grace in the Bible means God's unmerited favor. Or in other words it is favor that someone doesn't deserve but God gives it to him or her anyway."

Richelle nodded.

The heavenly music still filled the room but gradually diminished in intensity, until it finally faded away.

"I'm glad that's over. It was freaking me out!" Richelle plopped down on a couch and deliberately changed the subject. "Have you ever thought how these couches might look now? They've been here for who knows how many years with no one looking after them. They look fine to the eye because we're seeing them in 1946 but they're still actually here in our time. They're probably filthy, dusty and gross!" She sat forward removing her back from the aged thing.

"You're right. They could be mice-infested!"

With a look of alarm, Richelle quickly stood. "That sure ruins taking a load off my feet. Remind me to bring a lawn chair next time."

Tessa laughed. "I'm sure the couches are okay. I haven't felt any creepy critters yet."

"I don't think I want to take that chance." Richelle walked around the room while Tessa sat down to relax.

They both heard a sound in the foyer and headed that way to see Richard and Ruth descending the stairway. Her hair looked tousled and she tried to fix it as she walked. Her cheeks were flushed and a smile curled the edges of her lips but Richard didn't look any worse for wear as he descended ahead of her. Confidence oozed from him, like he had just played some game and won. As he reached the main floor, he immediately headed for the sitting room.

"Richard."

He turned around to face Ruth. "Yes, what is it?"

"What are you going to do now?"

"I'm going to wait in the sitting room till Mary arrives."

"I mean about us."

"What do you mean us?"

"Are you still planning to marry Mary?"

A contemptuous sound escaped his lips. "Of course I'm going to marry her. You knew that before our little rendezvous. Nothing's changed. I do want to thank you for the entertainment while I waited. It was very pleasurable. Maybe we can do it again sometime." He went back and handed Ruth his coat. "Find a place for that, would you?"

She stood transfixed, a stricken look on her face as the color slowly drained from her cheeks. Mist filled her eyes and she looked suddenly lost, not knowing which direction to turn.

"Don't you have something you should be doing, Ruth? I suggest you return to your duties." With that Richard headed toward the sitting room. He stopped after a few steps and turned back toward her. "Oh by the way, let Mary know I'm here when she arrives. Thank you." Without waiting for a reply, he walked off.

As Richard passed them, Richelle stuck her foot into his path but he walked right through it and on to the sitting room.

"Ugh! How I'd like to hurt him!"

"He's completely selfish!" agreed Tessa.

Ruth still stood transfixed at the bottom of the stairway. A deep sigh escaped her lips and she shook her head in discouragement. "What have I done?" she whispered, turned and moved down the hall.

Richelle said, "I hope she fixes herself up before the

Hardingtons arrive home. It looks like she's been wrestling."

"Do you think she'll suspect anything?"

"Who, Mary?"

Tessa nodded.

"She's too naïve."

"I wish her parents could see through Richard's deceit and know what he's really like."

"William sees only what he wants to see. I have a feeling Elizabeth has her suspicions. She doesn't have the nerve to voice them though because William intimidates everyone around here."

After what she'd just witnessed, Tessa felt as though she had been vomited on. Richard was one awful young man and she detested being near him. Being in his presence wasn't easy and she didn't know how much more she could stand of him.

The two stood quietly for a while, not knowing how long it would take for the Hardingtons to arrive home. After a few minutes, they noticed Ruth appear from the left hallway. Her hair was neatly restyled into a ponytail but her eyes were red and puffy. She headed toward the sitting room but suddenly stopped. She clasped her hands nervously and bit her bottom lip. Uncertainty played in her blood shot eyes. With nervous steps, she finally continued on into the sitting room.

Tessa and Richelle followed her inside and stood to watch.

Ruth sauntered slowly toward Richard who was studying a newspaper. He didn't even notice her. Only after she cleared her throat did he look up in surprise.

"Ruth! Is Mary here already? I didn't hear the door."

"No Mary's not here. I.... I.... I want to make sure that this stays between us."

He looked at her condescendingly as a wisp of a smile formed on his lips. "Of course. I wouldn't think of sharing it with Mary or her parents." He chuckled in derision. "I had counted on a measure of common sense in this matter."

Relief flooded her face.

"And you had better keep your mouth shut! If you mess things up for me, it'll be the end for you."

"I wouldn't think of saying anything." She wrung her hands nervously at the threat. "I need this job."

"I think it would be best if you'd refer to me as 'sir' or 'Mr.

Ridgefield.' We need to keep up appearances, if you know what I mean."

"Yes, sir."

Her anxiety was as great as her flirtation had been a mere half hour ago. She was about to turn and leave when Richard suddenly grabbed her hand, smiled, lifted it to his lips, kissed it and let go.

"Ruth, when we're alone you can call me whatever you'd like."

Surprise lit her eyes but she didn't utter a word as she turned and left the room.

Richelle said, "Talk about mixed messages."

"He wants to lead a double life," said Tessa.

"That'll take some ingenious acting. He'd better hope he can pull this off."

Tessa shook her head. "I like him less by the minute."

They slipped back into the foyer, sat down on the steps and waited, deliberating over the time travel and their ideas of how it would end. Half an hour ticked by before noise at the door alerted them. Ruth appeared and headed to the door. The Hardingtons entered, discussing the performance they had seen. Ruth stood silently, ready to take their coats.

This was the first time Tessa had seen the three family members together in a moment where they enjoyed amiable conversation.

The Hardingtons shed their coats and passed them to Ruth's waiting arms. She left with the load and carried them down the hallway. Returning shortly, she waited while the Hardingtons continued to discuss the production.

The rare camaraderie between them was like a breath of fresh air.

William suddenly noticed Ruth still standing by patiently. "What is it?"

"Mary has a guest waiting in the sitting room, sir." She turned her attention to Mary. "Mr. Ridgefield is here to see you."

"Oh, thank you." She gave Ruth a distracted nod and then headed to the sitting room.

Tessa and Richelle followed her.

Mary walked around the couches and when Richard noticed her, he stood and greeted her with a kiss on the lips. Mary pulled back slightly at the intimate gesture.

"It's so good to see you. How's my bride-to-be?"

"I'm doing well." Puzzlement crossed her face. "Why are you here in the middle of the week? I thought we had agreed to see each other on Sunday afternoons."

"Now that we're to be wed, I believe that the more time we spend together the faster we'll get to know each other. I'm actually here to suggest a date for our wedding."

"Oh? And when would that be?" She didn't look thrilled at the news.

He waved a hand to the couch. "Why don't we sit while we discuss these things?"

Mary sat and Richard lowered himself close to her, taking her hand in his.

"I had a meeting with your father a few days ago and some new details have come forth. Have your parents explained to you what's about to happen?"

Mary frowned, confusion in her eyes. "No, I don't know anything."

"Then I suppose they've left it to me to tell. I suggested to your father that he share his plans with you. He thought it best if I tell you, now that we're engaged to be married."

She looked irritated. "I would have preferred hearing it from my father."

"I understand."

With a shrug she said, "But I do need to know what's happening."

"Then I'll tell you."

She sighed defenselessly.

He gave her a consoling smile. "I can see you're upset. I'm sorry that I'm the one to break the news to you."

"Please, just tell me." She looked weary of him already.

"Your father is opening a new bank in Chicago. He bought a building and the renovations are going along faster than anticipated. They have informed him that it will be ready within two months. He is planning to move there and manage it. In fact, he'll need to move there sooner to arrange the business end of things. Of course, your mother will be moving there eventually as well."

Horror filled her eyes. "Wait, wait, wait! What you're telling me is that my parents are moving to another city?"

"Yes, that's correct."

"And where will I be?" she asked, her voice rising hysterically.

"You'll be with me, of course. We're getting married, remember?" He chuckled softly.

"Will we move to Chicago too?"

"No. That's the exciting part. Your father has asked me to become part of the management team of the bank here in Chelsey. Initially I'll be in training but then he plans to promote me as Manager of the bank. It's an amazing opportunity for us, Mary."

"So where will we live and what will become of this house?"

"I think you'll be pleased with that as well. Your father suggested that after our marriage we could live here. That way it would be an easy transition for you. The shift to married life should be seamless and worry-free for you. You won't have your mother or father around but you'll be able to stay in the home you grew up in. You'll also have all the servants that you're accustomed too."

She sat speechless, trying to take it all in as Richard continued.

"So with everything moving ahead faster than originally projected, I feel that our wedding needs to take place sooner than what we'd initially planned."

"I didn't realize we had proposed anything concrete so far." Mary looked dazed.

"We hadn't. I'd estimated a courtship of four months but now I feel we should marry within the month."

"Within the month! I don't know, Richard." Shaking her head furiously, she said, "I'm still getting used to the idea that I'm going to marry you and now within a month! I won't be ready that soon!"

"Mary, we've known each other for years. It's not like we're starting from scratch. I do agree we haven't spent a lot of time alone but that will come. I don't see any reason to prolong the wait, especially with your parents moving away. You don't want to live here by yourself and you don't want to move to Chicago with them, seeing that you'll be marrying me."

She stared daggers at him. "Don't tell me what I want!"

Richelle whispered, "You go, girl! Just give it to him with both barrels!"

Tessa whispered back, "You're getting a little involved, aren't you?"

She shot a dirty look back and they both turned to watch the scene unfold.

"Think of it, Mary. It would be perfect timing to get married before your parents move away. I'm sure your mother would like to help with wedding preparations and they could both be part of this special time."

"I need to talk to my parents first before I decide anything. My first response is an absolute no! I will not be pushed into a wedding so quickly."

Richelle stuck up a thumb in support.

"All right. Why don't we call your parents in and discuss it altogether?"

"Right now?"

"Yes." He rose from his seat and walked briskly from the room.

He was gone for a few minutes and then returned with William and Elizabeth in tow. Elizabeth sat down beside her daughter and took her hand. William took a seat on another couch, lifted one leg and rested it on his other knee.

Turning to her mother, Mary asked, "Is it true? Are you moving to Chicago with Dad?"

"Yes, dear, it's true. I don't want to move away but my place is with your father. This is something he wants to do and I need to support him."

William, his arms stretched out, cradling the top of the couch, turned his attention to his daughter and explained the situation. "I know this might be hard for you, knowing what you've been through. But it's not like we'll be gone forever. We'll come back to visit and I still have the bank here in Chelsey. As Richard has probably told you, he will take over the management of this bank in time. We won't abandon you, Mary. Your mother and I promise you that."

"It's just such a shock for me, Dad!" Elizabeth patted Mary's hand in comfort. "How soon will you move?"

"I'll be moving in four to five weeks. Your mother will join me when she's ready. I'd like her to come as soon as possible; perhaps two to three months from now."

Elizabeth said, "I want to help plan your wedding and assist with all the arrangements before I move."

Anger flashed in Mary's eyes. "So you've all discussed the timing of the wedding before even consulting me?"

"No, dear," exclaimed Elizabeth. "We were only throwing around some ideas of what would work. If you're opposed to the wedding taking place that quickly we can wait. I don't know how involved I could be with wedding preparations from Chicago." She gazed at her daughter hopefully.

"This is all so sudden that I don't know what to say."

Richard said, "Why don't you take some time to think it over? I'll come by on Sunday and you can let me know your decision then."

"Yes, I do need time to think this through." Mary turned to her mother. "I would love to have you around to help plan my wedding. I just need time to digest all this information."

"Certainly, Mary, I understand." Elizabeth stood and motioned for William to join her.

As the two left the room, Richard moved closer to Mary's side. He draped an arm over her shoulder and squeezed her tightly.

"I'm sorry I had to drop all this on you today. It would have been so much nicer to talk about pleasantries and get to know each other better. We'll have plenty of time for that once we're married. I can't wait till the day. I've been dreaming of this for a long time."

Mary seemed to soften some as she looked up into his face. "Richard, you can be charming if you try. I hope your sweetness doesn't end when the marriage vows are said."

He looked offended. "Now why would you say such a thing?"

"I don't know you very well and it causes me great concern."

"You have nothing to fear. I'll take good care of you." He pulled away. "Now I must be going."

He stood and reached for Mary's hand to help her to her feet. Mary walked ahead of him out of the room with Richard following close behind.

Tessa and Richelle were right on their heels.

Mary walked to the door, called for Ruth, who appeared momentarily with Richard's coat. She looked nervous at being in such close proximity to her recent love tryst.

"Thank you. What's your name?" Richard gazed intently into Ruth's eyes.

He sure knows how to play the game! What an absolute hypocrite! If only Mary knew!

Ruth looked at him nervously, tongue-tied.

With a tone of agitation Mary said, "This is Ruth. She seems to have lost her voice. Ruth, show some manners in the presence of my guest."

"I'm sorry, sir. Yes, my name is Ruth."

Richard gave Ruth a wink and Mary was none the wiser.

Tessa didn't miss it.

"He has so much nerve!" Richelle said.

"He needs a good kick where it hurts!"

While Ruth looked on, Richard turned to Mary, grabbed her around the waist and gave her a sound kiss on the lips. Ruth turned quickly and hurried away. With a sly smile, he turned to watch Ruth's back disappear around the corner.

Mary said, "I'm sorry about her. She's still new as butler. James is sick today so she stepped in for him."

"Oh, I don't mind. Don't be too hard on her."

Mary opened the front door and Richard stepped outside but turned back and said, "I'll see you Sunday."

With a nod, she closed the door, then turned and ascended the stairs.

Tessa and Richelle watched her till she disappeared from view. Revulsion filled Tessa from all she had seen here this day. Her stomach reeled and the air felt weighty and oppressive. Mary's coming wedding felt more like an impending funeral. She mourned the day.

Without a word, Richelle headed for the front door and Tessa followed her outside.

CHAPTER 22

After a full day in each other's company, Cody and Tessa drove to Michael's Mocha Shop to meet Luke, Janaye, Richelle and Charlie. The curb in front of the establishment was full so they turned around, found a spot further down the street and walked to the coffee shop hand in hand.

That morning Cody had visited Tessa's church and joined the March family for lunch. Tessa's mom was thrilled to have him over for a meal. In the afternoon Cody and Tessa watched a movie with her brothers, Mac and Joe. They were getting more comfortable around Cody, their initial nervousness evaporating. Later she and Cody walked to the park but, because of the heat, they had to cut it short. After ice cream and a leisurely drive around the city, they decided to go for coffee and invite some friends. What better way for Cody to get to know her friends than to spend time with them?

Walking into the shop, they could see that it was as full as the parking situation had suggested but there was no sign of a familiar face. Although the place was packed, Tessa did notice a few people getting up to leave. The two waited till a few tables cleared then pushed them together to make room for six.

Tessa sat down and Cody went to the counter to order something for both of them. Facing the door, she saw Luke and Janaye enter. She waved them over.

Janaye said, "Hi, Tessa. Thanks for inviting us."

"Hi, guys. I'm glad you could come."

Luke kissed her cheek. "Hi."

She accepted it graciously.

"How have you been, Tessa?" asked Janaye.

"Great. And you?"

"Wonderful!" She gazed affectionately up at Luke. He stood a good four inches taller than she did.

He looked as handsome as usual, with his tall frame and dark hair. Even with the attention he drew from the opposite sex, he maintained a humble attitude, never using his looks as bait. His warmth of character was his strongest attribute and was what had drawn Tessa to him years ago.

Luke turned to her and said, "So what's this meeting about? Has anything come up at the mansion that I don't know about?"

"No, there's nothing new there. This is just to get to know each other better." She'd already filled him in on what happened when she and Richelle visited the mansion alone.

"I thought we did know each other." He looked a little bemused.

"We don't all know each other. I don't know Janaye that well."

Luke nodded. "We'll be back." He then led Janaye to the serving counter to order.

Charlie and Richelle were the next to walk through the doors. Richelle acknowledged her, waved, and they got in line to order.

Soon they were all seated, eating pastries, sipping coffee or soft drinks and started with small talk. Tessa was glad to see Richelle had come with Charlie. She hadn't talked to Richelle in at least a week and didn't know the current status of their relationship. Hopefully, her agitated emotions had calmed down some.

The conversation seemed a little strained at first but after a few minutes they became engrossed in discussing the latest developments at the mansion. Even though Tessa had revealed the events of her last visit over the phone with Cody and Luke, she and Richelle went over the details again. Charlie looked puzzled, as though he had not heard the facts before. Had Richelle not told him earlier? Was she withholding information from him on purpose?

Richelle said, "I really wonder who the relatives are now in our time."

Tessa joined in, "Yeah, I wonder if Richard and Mary's children or grandchildren are living in the city."

Charlie finally asked, "Do you know what Ruth's last name is?"

Tessa responded, "No, I don't believe it came up in any of the conversations. Why would that be important?"

"I thought maybe it would be helpful to figure this whole thing out. You know, a clue to these people's descendants."

Tessa said, "I was thinking the same thing this week. I feel this time travel is about us being sent to help them. We can't help Mary or the Hardingtons. They're probably dead and gone by now. But perhaps we're being sent to their children and grandchildren."

"Whoa! Whoa! Whoa!" said Luke. 'Who said anything about helping anyone?"

Richelle said, "Yeah. We're basically in this for the thrill, nothing more."

Their flippant attitude bothered Tessa but she couldn't really blame them. "I feel strongly this whole experience is meant for something significant. It's not just a thrill ride. I don't understand it all but I'm also certain it involves their future family. I don't know what else it could mean."

Cody said, "Perhaps we're all destined to help the future generation somehow."

Luke shook his head. "I don't think so. Every time the angel showed up he'd only speak to Tessa. She's seen the angel more times than the rest of us." He pointed at her. "Maybe you're meant to help this family but the rest of us don't feel that way. I go back for the excitement and that's it."

Richelle nodded.

Tessa felt annoyed. "But don't you feel some compassion for them?"

"Yeah, I feel sorry for them but hey, they've done it to themselves. They've made their bed and now they're going to have to lie in it. Literally!" Luke grinned at his pun.

"Don't you have a compassionate bone in your body?" Charlie stared at Luke accusingly.

"What's it to you? I've gone along with this whole thing because it brought some thrill to my summer. I'll be heading back to university in a few weeks and I'll be out of here and glad of it!"

Charlie grimaced.

Tessa said, "I don't expect anything from any of you. I'm just glad I had the company. If Luke and Richelle hadn't been with me, I would have walked right past the mansion without looking back. I never would have gone inside."

"That was our contribution." Luke leaned back and crossed his arms. "We offered you the courage you needed."

"Yeah, I guess. Without the two of you urging me on, it never would have happened. But, I don't know." She fell silent for a moment. "I still have a feeling you all have a part in this too, that's it's not just about me. Take Richelle for instance, she recognized her grandmother at the party right at the beginning. That wasn't just coincidence."

Richelle said, "Yeah, and I found out stuff from my mom that I never knew before."

"Exactly," Tessa said.

Richelle continued, "My grandmother married Henry for revenge. She wanted to marry Richard but couldn't have him, so to get back at Mary she chose Henry."

"That's totally stupid!" Charlie said.

"My grandmother never realized the amazing man she had. I remember her being resentful and miserable. I'm thankful she didn't marry Richard…not that I'm glad Mary got him because she didn't deserve that guy either."

"How about you?" Cody looked at Luke. "What's your take on the time travel?"

"Like I said, it's been an adventure and it made my summer memorable. How many people can say they've gone back in time for real?" He grinned. "It was cool but now it's almost over and time to get back to reality."

Charlie looked about to burst. "How can you say it was just an adventure? I was there when that angel spoke to us about salvation. It made me realize that I had been running from God my whole life. I had been blaming God for my self-centered, idiot of a mother. When that angel showed up, I finally realized I couldn't blame her or God any more. Choosing salvation was my choice and I figured out that waiting would be disastrous."

Richelle's face contorted in frustration. "Charlie! Just drop it, okay? Whatever happened to having a fun, light evening?"

With a derisive smirk, Luke said, "And what makes you think you'll be any different than your mother, Charlie? You yourself admitted she had issues. Do you think you're any better or any less selfish than she is?"

Charlie became thoughtful at that, then said, "I don't know. All I know is that my mother had problems. I'm sure I'll have my own set of struggles but if God is for me and I don't let go of him, I'll have a way to get through them."

"Do you know how corny you sound?" Luke said with disdain.

Charlie let out a chuckle. "I sure do, don't I?" He laughed out loud and it became contagious. Luke and Richelle were the only two stone-faced ones in the bunch.

"I don't see what's so funny." Richelle said.

"I don't either," admitted Charlie. "All I know is that my rage and resentment are gone and God loves me. For once I feel a semblance of peace. You can't beat that, not even with a great adventure."

It was amazing to Tessa at how dramatically a person could change in such a short time. She had to admit that she liked him a lot better this way than the way he was before. This mellower Charlie was actually a pleasure to be with.

Misery and anger flashed from Luke's eyes. "Well, hurray for you, Charlie! It must be nice to have so much peace."

Charlie shot back, "Hey, you can have it too. Jesus is the Prince of Peace."

With a roll of her eyes, Richelle turned to Tessa and asked, "Do you think we'll get the chance to see the wedding at the mansion?"

Tessa understood her desperate attempt to change the subject and saw the wisdom in it. "I don't know. They didn't get that far the other day. I don't even know if Mary's going to go for a quick wedding."

Cody included, "And the wedding would have to be held at the mansion for us to see it."

"I would love to see it," said Richelle.

"I want to see it too," admitted Janaye.

"I hope we can. Hey, I wonder if Nancy, my grandmother, will be invited. That would sure put a twist into the event."

Tessa shrugged and said, "I just hope Richard has enough sense not to flirt with Ruth at his own wedding."

"I wouldn't put it past him," said Richelle.

"You girls are throwing a lot of speculation into this whole thing. Shouldn't we wait and see what happens instead of running to random guesswork?" asked Cody.

"Don't be a stick in the mud," stated Richelle. "Half the fun is imagining what will happen next."

They bantered back and forth with all the possible scenarios of what could occur. The imaginings were growing out of control so Tessa decided to change the subject.

"Did you all know that Cody's church is planning to buy that mansion?"

"No! What are they planning to do with it?" Luke looked intrigued as he directed the question at Cody.

Cody explained the church's plans of helping street people and those hooked on substance abuse. "It has gone through now, despite protests from some of the neighbors about the type of people who would be living there. The city insisted our renovations would keep the house looking as good as the mansions around it. When they finally consented to our plans, they sold it to us for ten thousand dollars."

Luke said, "Ten thousand dollars? That sounds like a steal of a deal."

"Yes, but just think of the damage needing repair. Leaving a house for just one winter here in the north, with no heat, leaves a tremendous amount of damage. All the pipes are shot and need to be replaced; the wiring needs replacing, a lot of the inner walls are rotten and most of the flooring is ruined. Maybe we can save some of the hardwood but it will need refinishing and the roof needs major work. The front brick should be okay but all the wood siding is decomposing and rotting. The mansion hasn't been repainted in years. It was left to decay, exposed to the outside elements."

"That'll take a truckload of money," stated Luke.

"I know. The church will need to renovate the interior to suit what they want to use it for and the outside has to look refined. A rehabilitation center will need a lot of bedrooms so they want to divide some of the larger rooms into smaller ones. Ministering to as many as possible is the goal. There's a lot of work inside and out and the cost is phenomenal. If they hadn't sold it to us at such a reasonable price, there's no way we could have bought it." He looked energized talking about the project.

"What you need is an architect and engineer. I'd love to get into that kind of work. It sounds fascinating restoring an old, run-down mansion. It would be amazing to keep its 1940s appeal. Are you planning to modernize the place or let it stay in that architectural time frame?"

"I'm not sure. I haven't asked a lot of questions. I listen and take in what they're saying. I suppose I'm more enthralled at what will happen there when the renovations are done."

"Yeah, I'm sure it will be great." Luke was beginning to lose interest.

"So, who exactly will you be ministering to?" asked Charlie.

Cody explained about it being a women-only facility and the reasons why. "Our church has been looking around for another building to minister to men. They are very serious about offering this to both sexes. They've looked at a few buildings for a men's residence but haven't found anything suitable yet."

"Can they afford to do both right now?" asked Tessa.

"One of the wealthier men in our congregation came forward and donated a pile of money towards a male facility this past week. He has a grandson caught in addictions and doesn't want to wait a few years before a rehab center becomes available. He has a heart to see both men and women delivered. God is moving faster than we initially thought he would. We're just praying for God to send the right people to us who can help us with all the details. It will take a lot of manpower to make this vision come to life."

Janaye said, "That is so exciting! Our church has sometimes talked about doing something like that but nothing ever materializes."

"Well, not every church is called to do what we're doing. God put the dream in our pastor's heart and is now sending people with money and the desire to get it done. It's totally a God-thing and we're all really excited about it."

"Wow, so when I return from university in the spring, the mansion might be occupied?" Luke looked pleased. "It sure beats having a park there or an empty lot."

"And just think, guys, instead of so much despair in that house, people will go there and receive help. I think that's awesome." Richelle's eyes shone with hope.

Luke waved at a man who just entered; Janaye also noticed him and waved. Tessa estimated he was in his late twenties. There was a young woman with him, her arm draped through his. They acknowledged Luke and Janaye and made their way to their table.

Luke said, "Hey everyone, this is a guy from the office where

Janaye and I work. He and I have been working very closely on a number of projects this summer. This is Mitch Turner." Then, with a wave of his hand toward his friends, he said, "and these are all my friends," and introduced everyone.

Mitch said, "Hi everyone, it's nice to meet you." He pointed to the woman at his side, "This is my wife, Roselyn. We're out on a date. We have a sitter for the baby and finally have an evening to ourselves. It doesn't happen very often. So we'll let you be and find ourselves a table off in the corner. Enjoy!"

Everyone said goodbye.

Mitch grabbed Roselyn's hand and said, "Let's go, Angel."

The six friends watched them wander toward the back of the shop. Then everyone looked pointedly at Tessa.

Tessa nodded and said, "Yes, I heard bells. So who wants to join me at the mansion tonight?"

No one turned down the invitation.

CHAPTER 23

Just before nine that night they arrived at the deserted house. The heat of the day had subsided some but it still felt warm and muggy as they made their way through the lopsided, squeaky gate and wandered slowly toward the big oak. As they passed the large tree, switching time zones, puddles of water suddenly appeared, dotting the pathway to the house.

As all six of them walked into the foyer, they didn't initially notice anything, being too busy talking. Finally stopping and listening, they heard voices coming from the sitting room. They all headed that way and entered the room.

William sat on one of the couches with Richard seated on another, the two men facing each other. Business was being discussed.

"...will take place soon. My business partners in Chicago are eagerly waiting my arrival. So do you think you'll be prepared to take the position at the bank, Richard?"

"Oh yes, sir! I'm confident I'll fit right in there. Becoming the Manager is something I really look forward to. I know I'll be a great asset to your bank and am positive that I'll be able to meet all your expectations."

"Well, I certainly am hoping for the best. To have this new venture turn disagreeable would be unsatisfactory. Managing a bank is an immense undertaking. I have some very reliable men there right now who will teach and train you. They need to remain unapprised of my future plans. I don't want them suspecting their positions are threatened. If they begin to deduce you're there to replace them, their attitudes toward you could become problematic. Once you're well entrenched there we'll make the necessary transitions. They'll know in time. When I feel confident that you can manage that position, I'll transfer you over as Manager of the Chelsey Bank."

Richard's eyes gleamed in anticipation. "I'll keep our agreed arrangement under wraps. This opportunity you're offering is very exciting! I'll be completing my final exams this week and then I'll be ready to go to work."

"You can start as soon as you're ready." Noise at the door alerted them. William looked that way and said, "Oh look, here comes my beautiful daughter."

Mary walked into the room wearing a light yellow chiffon dress. With her dark hair and dark eyes, the light-toned dress made her fair skin look even whiter. She skirted the couches and took a seat beside Richard, purposely leaving a few inches between them. He reached over and took her hand.

"You look lovely tonight, dear."

"Thank you," she responded shyly.

"Well, I'll give you two some time alone." With a satisfied smile, William stood and left the room.

Richard closed the gap so their hips met, placed an arm around her shoulder and gave a light kiss on her cheek. Mary looked ill at ease with their close proximity.

"Have you made your decision yet?" asked Richard.

"And what decision is that?"

"Don't play games with me, Mary. You know the nature of my inquiry."

"You mean about a wedding within a few weeks?"

"Yes." His eyes bore into hers, full of anxious anticipation. "Well, what's the answer? Please say yes."

"I would prefer to wait – allow us time to get to know each other. I detest being pushed into this so soon."

Agitation filled his eyes but he remained silent, waiting for her to continue.

"But…I do want Mother to help me with the wedding plans. So…my answer is…yes."

He removed his arm from her shoulder and clapped his hands. "I'm so pleased you've agreed to an early wedding. You don't know how happy this makes me." Cupping her chin with his hand, he turned her face toward him and kissed her soundly on the lips.

No passion on her part was reciprocated.

Pulling away, a disappointed look in his eyes, he said, "I hope you won't be that cold and indifferent on our wedding night. You need to put some feeling into your kisses, Mary."

"I'm sorry. Our speedy courtship and looming wedding haven't given my feelings any time to catch up. You'll have to forgive me. I'm hoping the feelings will come in time."

"I certainly hope so. To have a wife who can't respond is somewhat distressing." He looked wary for the first time since their engagement.

Mary gazed at him. "You're a fine man, Richard. I see no reason why I shouldn't be able to love you." She then stood and faced him. "You'll have to excuse me for a moment. I'll be right back."

She left the room and the three girls trailed her. Walking down the right hallway, Mary headed to the end and into the back sunroom. The three followed her in and stayed close to the door. Wringing her hands, Mary paced the room, her eyes filling with tears. Eventually she stopped at an end table, which sat beside one couch, and picked up a hankie to dab at her cheeks. Her tears flowed off and on for a few minutes and she kept patting them away. After her tears subsided, she walked to the windows and gazed outside dazedly.

Tessa allowed her eyes to follow Mary's trajectory of the back yard. The snow was nearly melted back there and the beautifully manicured expanse, with trees and shrubs planted in various places, was now clearly visible. A curved walkway started at the house and ended at a gazebo with shrubs and plants surrounding the covered porch. The trees scattered throughout the yard were still leafless so the full beauty of the yard couldn't be seen. Surrounding the back yard on all sides was a heavy stone fence, giving optimum privacy.

After a few minutes of silently staring out the window, Mary burst out, "What am I doing? Why am I marrying someone I can't even stand being with?" Lowering her head, she studied the hankie in her hand. "I don't have many choices. I can't marry Henry and I don't think anyone else would want me." She folded her arms and looked outside again. "Except for Richard. The only reason he wants to marry me is because of Father's business proposition. It's a way to get ahead quickly and to become heir of the Hardington estate. Richard doesn't love me either," she said in disdain. "I can see it in his eyes. He says he does but I can see right through it.

He's a conniving, selfish, despicable man and I don't know how I'll ever live with him. I detest being in his presence. I know I don't love him and I'm positive he doesn't love me, despite his words of affection."

She paused, then said, "Perhaps we're well suited after all. Our feelings are mutual; we'll be on the same footing right from the start." A deep sigh escaped her pale lips. "I just hope we'll fall in love with time. To be stuck in a loveless marriage would be intolerable."

A tear trickled down her cheek. "I couldn't bear to live with that. Perhaps, at the very least, I'll come to respect him, given some time. I certainly hope so."

Talking to herself seemed to calm her emotions. She stood for a few more minutes staring at the still yard. Taking a deep, shaky breath, she turned toward the door. Leaving the hankie on the table where she'd found it, she exited the room with the three girls following.

Down the hallway, about halfway, Mary disappeared into a room for a few minutes. The three waited for her. She appeared shortly and continued on to the sitting room.

Janaye opened the door to the room Mary had exited and peeked in. Tessa and Richelle peered over her shoulder.

"Look at this massive bathroom!" Janaye exclaimed.

"This room is crazy!" Tessa said.

It was the largest bathroom she'd ever seen, at least in a home. Besides the usual items – toilet, vanity, sink and tub – there was a large open inner area, an elaborate make-up table and mirror and a sitting area tucked in one corner.

"Who would want to sit and relax in this bathroom?" asked Richelle.

"It's so strange," said Janaye.

Tessa only nodded. In the corner stood a small wooden table with a fresh bouquet of flowers in the center. A wing-backed chair graced either side. There was a rug beneath the whole sitting area. Beautiful paintings hung on the walls with strategic lights hung from the ceiling for effect. There were even a few plants placed about the spacious room.

Richelle said, "Who needs a bathroom this size?"

"They do, I guess," said Janaye, shaking her head in awe. "It's so wasteful."

"We should head to the sitting room," suggested Tessa.

Janaye left the room first and Richelle and Tessa followed her. When Janaye entered the sitting room, Tessa realized her chance. Reaching out to touch Richelle's arm, she asked, "What's happening with you and Charlie? I thought you two broke up."

"We're back together."

"He moved back in with you?"

"No, he refuses to do that but I've decided to give us another chance. What you said the other day made me think. I do still love him and I don't want to lose him to some religious floozy."

"I'm glad you're giving him a chance."

Richelle stared at her accusingly. "You always gave me the impression you didn't really like Charlie."

Tessa decided to be truthful. "I struggled to like him. I didn't think he was good enough for you. But now that he's changed he's easier to like."

"Do you really think so?" she asked skeptically.

"He's not as brash and angry and he can actually smile. I never knew he had the ability." She grinned.

Richelle smiled back and nodded. "He's nicer than you think."

They slipped into the sitting room and joined the others.

Mary sat alone in the room.

"Where's Richard?" asked Tessa.

Cody said, "While Mary was gone, Ruth came in here to see him."

"No! So where are they now?"

Luke said, "They both left together. We followed them into the dining room and they were all over each other in there, kissing and carrying on; it was ridiculous."

"Are you serious?" Tessa felt nauseous.

"It wasn't quite that severe," chided Cody. "They kissed and hugged but that's about it. Richard asked Ruth to find Mary's parents and invite them to join him and Mary in the sitting room. Ruth looked hurt after that and left fairly quickly."

Tessa glared at Luke and he shrugged his shoulders.

Richelle said, "I wish Mary had walked in on the two of them. He'd deserve that."

"I have to agree with you on that," said Charlie. "You know

what he told Ruth in there? After he kissed her, he said he wished Mary was as good of a kisser. Ruth looked quite pleased but her smile quickly vanished after he said he was heading back to the sitting room to wait for Mary." Charlie shook his head in disbelief.

Richelle looked a little sickly at the information. "So where is the two-timer now?"

"We saw him enter William's office. I guess he decided to invite the old man himself."

At that moment Richard entered the room and took his place beside Mary.

"Are you okay, dear?"

"Yes, I'm fine."

"I asked your parents to join us. I have some things I'd like to suggest with our upcoming wedding. I hope that doesn't offend you."

Mary didn't have a chance to reply because William and Elizabeth arrived. Elizabeth walked up to Richard and took his hand.

"I'm so glad to see you again, Richard. Welcome."

He gave her a hug. "Thank you, my mother-to-be."

She smiled. "It will be delightful to have a son-in-law as wonderful as you, Richard. You're a very polite young man. You just take good care of our daughter; she means everything to us."

He nodded in reply and Elizabeth took a seat beside her husband. They both turned their attention to the newly-engaged couple.

Richard began, "I'm glad you were able to come join us. I wanted to discuss some ideas I have prior to the wedding. The first thing I'd like to confer on concerns a dinner. I was wondering whether you would consider having dinner with our two families. Our two families getting together in an informal setting would give us the opportunity to become better acquainted. I'm well aware that you already know my parents but it might be a nice gesture."

Elizabeth said, "How wonderful! Yes, I'd love it. I'll begin preparations immediately. We'll have the dinner in our dining room; it's plenty big enough. How soon would you like it to take place?"

"I suppose we should first plan the wedding day. Then we can decide when to have the dinner. I'll just lay out my plans and then you can give your opinion. Nothing is written in stone yet."

William nodded in agreement.

"This is what I was thinking: we can have the dinner two weeks from today and the wedding in three weeks." Everyone fell silent for a moment. "If that's not suitable, the dates can easily be adjusted."

William's forehead furrowed in thought and his wife remained quiet and contemplative for a few moments.

Elizabeth said, "That would make the dinner and the wedding both on a Sunday. From my point of view, I believe the dinner date would work fine but I would prefer having the wedding on a Saturday instead. It will be difficult to get rentals and some of the services we'll need if the wedding takes place on a Sunday. For example, the flowers, the photographer, the food and the help we'll require for meal preparation and so on. I would suggest having the wedding the Saturday before, if you're agreed." She turned to face her husband. "William, what are your thoughts on this?"

"I see no reason why it wouldn't work. You go ahead and plan it and I'll show up." He sat relaxed and comfortable with a smug smile on his face.

Richard turned to his bride-to-be. "Are you all right with those dates?"

With a look of resignation, she said, "Yes, Richard, that will be fine. I don't know how I'll ever find a dress in time but I'm sure we'll come up with something." She turned to her mother with a look of desperation.

"Oh yes, the dress! Well, we won't have time to have one sewn. You could use my wedding dress. We'll have it altered, of course, so it fits you properly. You're so much thinner than I was. Would that be all right with you, Mary?"

"I've always loved your wedding dress. That would be fine."

Richard said, "Great! That went smoother than I had anticipated." Looking pleased with the arrangements so far, he continued. "I'll do whatever you need me to do. I can contact a photographer. I can also make the arrangements at my parents' church and ask the minister there to do the ceremony."

William's smile vanished and he said harshly, "No! We're not having the wedding in any church. You can ask the minister to come here and do the ceremony right in our own home."

Richard looked taken aback by the stern reply. "All right, sir, I'm sure that can be worked out. I'll contact the minister this week and see what can be set in place. Just let me know what other details you'd like me to look after and I'll do it."

"We have many servants that we can call on to fulfill the trivial details. My wife will plan the menu and the servants will look after the rest. Elizabeth is wonderful with details and could assist Mary in choosing the flowers. I'm sure Mary will have some ideas of the colors she wants."

"Yes, William, you're right," Elizabeth said. "I'll manage all the preparations with Mary's help. If I need you to do anything, Richard, I will let you know."

Mary listened in dazed acceptance.

"There's one other thing I'd like to discuss while we're all together. Will I need to purchase a home for Mary and myself? I know you had suggested, sir, that we would be able to live here in this house. When exactly will you be moving?"

"I would like you to move in with us right from the start if that isn't too offensive to you." He turned to his wife. "Elizabeth, are you agreed?"

Nodding, she said, "Yes, I would love that. We have plenty of room and we'd hardly notice another person around."

"Yes, I'll be heading to Chicago shortly after the wedding. Elizabeth will stay for a while longer. You'll have the house to yourselves before long."

Staring at Richard, Elizabeth said, "I will have to insist on one thing."

"Yes, anything."

"You have to promise to leave a room open for me to come and visit. I'll miss my daughter a lot and will need to come and stay often."

"Of course! We'll keep a room open for you all the time." Richard smiled at his in-laws-to-be. "Moving into this home right after the wedding is agreeable with me. I'm sure it will delight Mary as well." He turned, gave her a smile then faced her parents again. "Thank you for your generosity. I'm looking forward to calling you my parents-in-law."

"And we're looking forward to having you as our son-in-law," said William. He then stood. "Come, Elizabeth, let's give these two lovebirds some time alone."

She placed her hand on his arm and allowed William to escort her out.

Luke turned his head toward the door and mouthed, "Let's go." He led the way while the rest followed him into the foyer. William and Elizabeth had already wandered off to another part of the house and the entrance was quiet. They stood in the center of the large entry way and discussed what they'd witnessed.

Motion at the front door caught Tessa's attention and she glanced that way. The angel was walking determinedly toward her.

"Hey, guys?" she said, anxiety tap dancing against her ribs.

They turned to look at her and noticed the angel too.

He wasn't wearing his usual trench coat or hat but was clothed in a white robe that hung to his ankles and he shone as though he was lit from the inside out. There was a beauty about him that was indescribable, like the glory of a sunrise on a clear day. A warmth and electrical buzz radiated from him when he approached. As he drew closer, Tessa could feel her skin begin to tingle and a supernatural strength pulsing towards her. It was an uncanny and disturbing awareness.

They all moved back a step at the awesome and commanding presence stopping in front of them. His breathtaking appearance was overpowering. It appeared as though small lightning bolts or electrical currents were leaping from him, arcing out and then meshing back into him. This effect was constant and made him look as though he was continually sparkling, like an ethereal light bulb. His eyes blazed like a fire was burning from within.

With a piercing gaze, he scanned the group and made direct eye contact with each of them. "It is almost complete and you will soon know the full message. All of you need to return in two weeks and then you will know." His voice sounded like rushing water, like a whole multitude of voices combined. Slowly the effect of his words echoed away.

Fear hammered against Tessa's heart in the presence of such a powerful display but she desperately needed clarification. "We're supposed to come for the dinner?"

"You will know when it's time to come. Listen for the sign." The angel then slowly disappeared from their view right where he stood and a rosy glow remained in his place. This too slowly vanished.

The six friends stood transfixed in amazement. The surge of power brought by the angel lingered in the air.

"It never gets old, does it?" Janaye finally whispered in amazement. "I wish I could have been here from the start of this time travel thing."

"I'll have to come back for that weekend," said Luke, his face a shade lighter and a quiver to his lip. "I'll be heading to Minneapolis the week before to get my apartment set up for another year of university."

Tessa said, "Yes, please come back. I wouldn't want to figure this thing out without you and the angel did say that all six of us needed to come back in two weeks."

"That's true. He did say that, didn't he?"

Tessa looked at each one and noticed their awestruck faces. The angel had appeared in greater glory this time and the effect was clear. Everyone looked awe-struck by the experience. She could still feel heaven's power and force, which had left her knees weak. No wonder the prophets of old would fall on their faces at the sight of an angel.

Cody was the first to break the stillness. "I think we're done here for now."

Tessa looked at him and said, "Yeah, I think so."

"We should leave," said Luke, heading to the door as he spoke.

Everyone followed him, left the house, passed into the future and walked back toward their cars parked on the curb. They all promised to be available in two weeks and all made Tessa promise to tell them when she received the sign. After goodbyes were said, they went their separate ways.

As Tessa and Cody drove away from the mansion, she wondered what the final revelation would be and how it would affect them all.

Within a couple short months, her whole outlook on life had shifted. Before, there had been a feeling of complete contentment and satisfaction. Her life was good. If people struggled, she didn't really want to know about it and disconnected emotionally. Why should she get involved in others' problems? Let them deal with it.

Her outlook had been regrettably selfish, looking with disdain at those who couldn't maintain a well-balanced life. Her attitude had been less than admirable and she felt embarrassed now at her calloused approach.

It's so easy to judge people without knowing all the facts. God, please forgive me!

The mansion thing was still a mysterious puzzle but she felt more at peace and hoped the answers weren't too far away. Being redirected by heaven still felt uncomfortable, like being forcibly stretched, yet she could feel her heart slowly opening to new possibilities. She recognized a twinge of willingness to accept a divinely-altered future. It was a surprising realization.

CHAPTER 24

As Tessa totaled her last bill of the day, her thoughts wandered to Cody. She'd hardly seen him this week. They'd gone to the Wednesday night service at his church but there had been no time to talk. He'd picked her up after work and dropped her off at home immediately after. Disappointment crowded her thoughts.

Earlier today Cody had headed to Detroit Lakes to see his mother. Tessa was driving up to join him there after work. Hopefully they'd have some private moments together this weekend.

Cody hitched a ride there with his brother-in-law, Mark, who lived in Chelsey and had planned to go and see Choey and Joey this weekend. Cody offered Tessa to drive his car up when she was done work. He was planning to stay with his mother overnight and she'd invited Tessa to come and stay for the night as well. Beth Fields had assured her there was an extra bedroom for her.

Finishing up, Tessa stepped outside through the back door of the restaurant, and walked into the small parking lot reserved for the staff. She retrieved the keys for Cody's car from her purse. The sky was overcast and it brought welcome relief from the heat and calmed her frazzled nerves after an extraordinarily busy day. Gratefully, she sank into the driver's seat and started the engine. Feeling famished, she grabbed a granola bar from her purse and ate it rather quickly as she drove.

The hour's drive ahead would be relaxing and quiet, just what she needed after a hectic day. She hoped she'd stay awake with no one to talk to. She could always turn the music up or set the air conditioner cold enough to keep her shivering and awake.

As she left Chelsey behind, she felt excited for the weekend ahead. The two of them needed to talk and she prayed for an opportunity for them to be alone to delve into the matters of time travel and how it affected their future.

The clock on the dash display read seven-thirty when she reached Beth's house. Stuffing the empty granola bar wrapper into her purse, Tessa grabbed her small suitcase from the back seat and walked to the front door. Before she got there, it opened and Cody stepped out onto the landing, smiling.

"I'm glad to see you made it. How did the drive go?"

"Don't worry, Cody, your car is safe."

"I was more concerned about the pretty face behind the wheel," he said, wrapping his arms around her.

She let the suitcase drop and returned the embrace. After a long, intense kiss that sent waves of excitement through her, he pulled back and said, "You are a sight for sore eyes, a breath of fresh air and you taste better than honey on my lips, girl!"

Grinning with pleasure, she said, "Wow! I didn't expect that. My man is becoming poetic. Keep it up and you won't be able to get rid of me."

"Oh, so if that's all it takes to keep you then I'll have to polish up my poetic skills." He grinned impishly. "I'm so glad to see you, Tessa. I've missed you. It's been a hard week seeing you so little."

"It's been hard on me too. I've been looking forward to this weekend so much."

He leaned in and kissed her gently, the intensity growing as they folded into each other's embrace. He finally pulled back, letting her go, the desire in his eyes apparent.

"Ready to come inside?"

"I'm not sure. I think I like it out here."

He grinned, leaned in and kissed her again. "Come on." Picking up the suitcase, he led the way into the house.

Down the hall, he opened a door and Tessa followed him in.

"The guest bedroom?"

"Yep. This is where you'll hang."

It was a pretty room but a bit too girlish to be considered a guest room. The walls were covered with a floral print of pink and mauve carnations against a cream background, with light greenery surrounding them. The bedding on the single bed matched the wallpaper with the duvet in a mauve color, a bed skirt in cream and pillows in different shades of mauve and pink. The décor was quite outdated and yet it looked homey, despite the girlish feel.

"Isn't this where you usually sleep when you come to visit?"

she asked.

"Yes it is, but the pink flowers are a bit much for me. I hope you like pastels. This was my sister's room when she and Joey lived here for a time. I'm claiming the couch tonight. It's fairly comfortable."

Cody's mother appeared in the doorway wearing a pretty sundress and heels. Her dark, brown hair looked wonderful with new highlights accenting it, causing her to look younger than her years. Tessa admired her beauty and youthful look.

Beth Fields' big brown eyes gazed at her warmly. "Welcome, Tessa. I'm so glad you were able to come." She stepped forward and gave her a firm hug.

"Thank you for having me, Mrs. Fields."

"Please, just call me Beth." Looking at Cody, she said, "You'll have to excuse me tonight, dear, but I have a date. It came up last minute and I couldn't refuse. I'm sure the two of you will appreciate some time alone. We'll catch up tomorrow. I hope that's alright."

"That's fine, Mom. We're big kids; we can take care of ourselves. You go on and have a great time." He kissed her cheek.

"Thanks, sweetheart. I have cookies in the jar and there's lots of food in the fridge and pantry. Just help yourself to whatever you'd like."

"Go on, Mom, we'll be fine."

Beth left shortly after and Cody and Tessa settled on the living room couch and talked. It seemed like ages since they'd been alone. He asked about her job and she filled him in. There wasn't much new to say. Her job was the same as always.

"How's work at the insurance company? I know you've been really busy lately."

"Complaining?"

She held up index finger and thumb, a hair apart. "A little."

"It's been too busy. I know we've hardly had time to be together. I don't like that part but otherwise it's going well. My reputation with the clientele is building every day and I continue to garner prospective customers. God is really blessing my work and I'm very pleased with that."

A comfortable silence settled between them for a moment. "I want to tell you about something I've been considering."

"What is it?" asked Tessa.

"Well, it has to do with what my church is planning, ministering to those with addictions. They just found another facility for a men's drug rehab and are looking into purchasing it. They're also in the development stage right now with renovation ideas for the old mansion. I think they'll start with the actual restoration work in a few months. But they're also actively looking for people who are willing to take training to work at the homes when they're operational. It's been on my mind ever since I heard about it. It would be a fairly intensive training time but I'd like to go for it."

Tessa felt intrigued. "What's involved with that?"

"The church is looking into courses in the city that would be beneficial to drug rehabilitation centers. There are some recommended classes at the university that they offer on weeknights and Saturdays. They are also looking into getting some people from California to come and do training right at the church. In California there's a deliverance ministry similar to what the pastor wants to incorporate here. Apparently they've had tremendous success. Pastor Chad has already contacted them and they're interested."

"When would the training start?"

"The university courses start in September. I'm not sure when the Californian people would come. Those details still have to be worked out."

"So this is really going ahead?"

"Sure is. This is something I really would like to do. I realize it'd mean giving up the insurance business eventually. I'm not sure if I want to go into this ministry work full-time right from the start but I feel that eventually that's what I'll be doing."

This truly was a surprise. "Wow! That'll be quite a change for you."

"How do you feel about my decision, Tessa?"

"Well, it's your life. If this is what you want to do, then you should go for it."

"That's not exactly the answer I was looking for. I've told you before that I love you and I am definitely thinking marriage here. I want to know how you feel about it in regards to our future."

Our future! I like the sound of that.

"I think you working at the men's home is a great idea. If this is what you feel God leading you into, then I'll support that decision."

"I probably wouldn't make as much money in ministry as I do now." His questioning gaze held hers.

"Fulfilling God's purpose for your life is more important than money. If this is something God wants you to do, he'll take care of your needs."

"And what are your feelings about us?" Longing showed in his eyes.

"Well...I know I care about you deeply. I don't want to lose you." She smiled up at him.

"You know how I feel. I love you and want to marry you." With vulnerability he asked, "Do you love me?"

Tessa felt lightheaded. Did she love him? Could she say it wholeheartedly?

Cody said, "I don't want to rush you. I know you're the one for me and as soon as you're sure, we can make plans."

His directness shocked her and she felt a bit of uncertainty crowding her heart. It was suddenly hard to breathe. And yet there was something else, a warm glow that started in the pit of her stomach and filled her with a deep sense of belonging. He wanted her for his wife, to call her his own. It was a profound thought. Could this really be happening? She pinched herself then smiled at him.

"Are you going to say something or just smile at me for the rest of the evening?"

She chuckled. "It's just that I wasn't expecting this. You surprised me. I have very strong feelings for you and I believe I am falling in love with you. But, can I let you know when I'm ready?" She knew it was a lousy answer, not what he was anticipating but that's all she could promise for now.

He looked somewhat disappointed but nodded. Wrapping his arms around her, he held her tightly and she folded into him, reveling in the warmth and safety she felt.

Out of the corner of her eye she noticed something familiar. Turning her head to get a better look, she noticed a clock on the wall above the fireplace. It looked identical to the one she'd seen at the mansion. Shock shot through her at the thought. She remembered Luke attempting to touch it and his hand passing straight through it. The more she studied it the surer she became.

Cody gazed at her curiously. "Are you okay, Tessa?"

She pointed. "That clock on the wall. Doesn't it look exactly like the one we saw at the mansion a few weeks ago, you know, the one above their fireplace?"

A peculiar look shifted across his face and his suddenly nervous eyes made her shiver.

"Why are you looking at me that way?"

He shrugged uncertainly. "I didn't know when I'd have the chance to tell you. I knew I had to let you know soon but I suppose this is as good a time as any"

"What?"

"Well, I have to be honest, when you first told me about seeing things at that old mansion I wasn't interested at all in going there. I basically knew what was going on and didn't want to see it."

Tessa was completely astonished. "How could you possibly have known?"

"Because I'm related to them."

"No! You're not serious!" It suddenly felt like a load of bricks sat squarely on her chest. It was hard to breathe.

"I'm very serious." He squeezed her shoulder and then continued. "William and Elizabeth Hardington are my great grandparents. Mary Hardington and Richard Ridgefield are my grandparents. My mother's maiden name is Beth Ridgefield. She has one sister whose name is Laura Ridgefield. She married a Newburg so she's now Laura Newburg."

Tessa didn't know what to think. Cody's startling revelation caused her heart to hammer wildly.

"I didn't want to reveal this too soon. This whole experience for you was a message from God and I didn't want my information to give you a skewed view. Telling you too soon might have forfeited the purpose of the time travel. I wanted you to get the message first before I exposed too much. I didn't want to get in God's way."

Shock slowly retreated and a quiet relief began to filter down through her, calming her frazzled feelings. "I...I don't know what to say. This is amazing...incredible!"

"Well, it was extremely overwhelming for me when you first

told me about going back in time at that old house. It made me angry at first. For me it was like digging up garbage that needed to stay buried. I knew my family had dealt with some serious problems and I saw no reason to expose that. Generation after generation has seen difficulty and I didn't want to revisit it."

Tessa reached for his free hand and squeezed.

"God brought healing to my past and I didn't want to dig up anything more. I didn't see the purpose in re-examining my family history. When you told me about it, I was actually very upset that God was revealing it to you."

She nodded. "So how do you feel now that you've gone back and seen for yourself some of the things they've gone through?"

"Optimistic. I've felt hope for myself ever since I gave my life to God but this is different. I now know that God wants to bring restoration to every member of my family. He started with me when I called out to him for help and he answered miraculously. I know he'll do the same for any one of my family members and that encourages me."

"Remember what Eunice Hardington said the last time we saw her? I guess she'd be your great-great grandmother." Tessa grinned at the oddity of it. To actually see one's great-great grandmother was naturally impossible; at least she was sure it must be. "Eunice was talking to Mary and she told her that God was going to turn things around. Do you remember how she turned around three times?"

He nodded.

"Well you're the third generation down from Mary."

Understanding lit up his eyes. "That's right. Do you think that's what she meant?"

"It could be. God has definitely turned your life around."

"Then that must mean that change is coming for my sister, Choey, too. Emotional weakness is something she's dealt with all her life too, kind of like Mary. Her nervous breakdown happened shortly after Joey was born. She's doing much better now but she still struggles with fear of it happening again and her emotional instability caused a lot of problems in her marriage. I'm praying for a change there and for reconciliation for Mark and Choey."

Tessa and Cody talked for hours that evening about his family and what the time travel experience could mean for her.

A bit before eleven, Beth returned home. After making some coffee and serving cookies, she stayed up with them and talked. Cody attempted to squeeze out information on her date but she didn't divulge too much. She simply refused to discuss it with him.

Cody and his mother conversed freely with each other about different subjects and Tessa just listened. She felt so comfortable around Beth Fields. The older woman had a way about her, an open acceptance of Tessa that made her feel part of the family already. And now, looking at her, she knew why Mary had looked so familiar a few weeks back. Beth and Mary's eyes were nearly identical. Beth shared numerous traits with her mother, Mary.

~~~~~

The next day was bright and sunny – not a cloud in the sky. Tessa and Cody made arrangements to meet Mark, Choey and Joey at the lake. Beth declined, saying she didn't enjoy being in the hot sun. She did, however, make a delicious picnic meal for the five lake-goers and wished them an enjoyable day.

Cody parked his car in the public parking lot. He and Tessa gathered their gear, wandered across the asphalt and onto the sand beach. Cody pointed out the three sitting on a blanket close to the water's edge. As they approached, Tessa took note of Joey. He was a handsome nine-year-old boy. She looked for signs of the physical handicaps Choey had mentioned but they weren't apparent. Joey looked completely normal to her.

Mark, with his auburn hair and green eyes, looked somewhat familiar but she couldn't place where she had seen him. Joey definitely took after his mother in looks; his hair and eyes were a dark brown like hers.

Introductions were made before Tessa and Cody spread out their blanket on the sand. They swam, sunned themselves and played some beach games. It was a perfect summer day for the lake.

Tessa lay down on her back and propped herself up on her elbows to watch. Joey had brought his dog, Rex, a golden retriever, and the two of them were busy splashing in the shallow water. Mark and Cody went down the beach a few steps, throwing a

Frisbee back and forth. Choey was laid out beside Tessa on her large beach blanket.

Choey was uncharacteristically quiet at first so Tessa scanned the beach. It was filled to near-maximum capacity with people spread out on loungers, chairs and blankets as far as the eye could see. Some sun worshipers were busy slathering on sun screen, while others, already tanned dark from the sun's rays, lay carelessly taking in more of the solar warmth. The water's edge was a busy place, filled with little ones splashing and swimming, carefully monitored by their parents. Older children played with more freedom in deeper water.

Water skiers whipped around behind speed boats, showing off their skill, and many assorted tubes were pulled by other boats with screaming, wild-eyed kids hanging on for dear life. It was a cacophony of noise and a visual feast for the eyes. A slight breeze cooled off the high summer temperature and gave a bit of relief.

Tessa closed her eyes, tipped her head back and allowed the fresh air blowing off the lake to filter through her hair and cool her hot neck. A whoosh beside her brought her to attention. The Frisbee lay in the sand at her feet. She noticed Mark hurrying toward them to retrieve it.

"Hey, Tessa and Chondra, why don't you come join us?"

Choey opened one eye, looked at him and said, "I'm too tired to throw a Frisbee. This sun is wearing me out." Her eye closed again, making her point completely clear.

He looked at Tessa and she shook her head so he trotted back to join Cody.

He called her Chondra. Why would he do that? Her name's Choey, isn't it? Chondra. I've heard that name somewhere before.

Glancing over at Choey lying prone on the blanket, she decided there was no better way than to go direct. "I thought your name was Choey?"

Choey opened her eyes and peered over, shadowing her face with an arm. "Choey's my nickname. Cody has called me that since we were little. Mark always calls me by my full name, which is Chondra. I don't know why Choey has stuck all these years. When I was in high school I insisted that all my friends call me Chondra but I could never get Cody to call me by my full name. I tried often enough but he refused. I suppose he was too used to calling me Choey by then."

The memory suddenly came back with full force. Tessa knew! Chills raced up and down her spine in spite of the hot sun warming her body. Fear gnawed at her but she had to know the truth. "So, what about Joey? Is that his full name?"

"That's short for Joseph and it's actually his second name. Joseph and then Joey seemed to suit him better for some reason. I started calling him that when he was just little. His full name is Riley Joseph Trent. Cody loves to call him Joe-Joe but the rest of us call him Joey. When I'm upset with him, I revert to his first name. That way he knows mama's angry and he better smarten up." She grinned mischievously.

The information sank in like a stone thrown into deep water, hitting bottom. Tessa's body began to shake with the realization. Right now she was relieved that Choey or Chondra was talkative because it gave her time to digest this information. Now she knew why Mark looked so familiar. She was confused why she hadn't recognized Chondra. She inspected her intensely and then realized she'd seen her before as well.

The rest of the day was hard to enjoy, knowing what she now knew. The past and present being all so entwined and mingling together today was most unwelcome. This was her day off, a day for enjoying her boyfriend, the sun, sand and getting to know his family better. To comprehend that she knew them better than she intended made her wish she had never had that first time travel experience.

A talk with Cody was warranted but she was already dreading it. He'd been upset about her keeping the old mansion experience from him. How would he respond to her keeping her first time travel from him?

Mark and Cody finished throwing the Frisbee and walked over to them. Cody flopped down beside her, exhausted, and threw the Frisbee down on the sand. Mark went to get Joey and the two of them headed down the beach for a walk, with Rex running along beside them.

Cody stretched out on his beach towel and turned half open eyes to his sister. "So, Choey, what's happening with you and Mark?"

She gave him a quizzical and playful smile. "What do you

mean?"

"Well, Mark's here spending the weekend with you and Joey. Doesn't he usually just pick up Joey and do stuff with him?"

She shrugged in reply. Her unusually tight-lipped stance seemed odd.

"It looks like something's going on," Cody pressed.

"You are so nosy! Do you really think it's any of your business?"

"Of course it's my business! You're my sister, so that makes it my business."

"Okay, okay!" She inhaled deeply and released her breath slowly. "We've decided to give our marriage another go. Mark has asked me to move back to Chelsey with him. We haven't told Joey yet so don't say a word. This is a good time to move because Joey's on summer break. He won't have to switch schools in the middle of a school year, which will be good for him. He really misses his dad so I think he'll be really excited."

Cody nodded approvingly. "How about you? Do you still love him or are you doing this for Joey's sake?"

"Of course I love him. We just had some problems. We have a good grasp on our areas of weakness. We'll just need to work on those. I really hope it works out this time. I'm trying to be positive."

"Well, I'm thrilled, Choey. It'll be great to have you back in Chelsey and it will be good to have my brother-in-law back. I've missed Mark. You two belong together."

She gave him an endearing look. "I never knew you felt that way. That's so sweet."

"What about Mom? She'll miss you two when you move back to Chelsey. Do you think she'll end up moving back there too?"

"I doubt it. She loves it here. Did you know she's been dating someone?"

"Yeah. She went out last night with a mystery fellow. She wouldn't tell us who it was." He grinned and looked at Choey with interest. "Do you know him?"

"No. She won't tell me a thing."

Cody and Chondra talked and kidded back and forth. Tessa sat quietly, watching and listening to the comfortable banter. It was easy to see they were close.

When Mark and Joey returned from their walk, all five of them moved over to some picnic tables under the trees. They covered one of the tables with a tablecloth that Cody's mom had packed and then set out the delicious food she'd prepared. The meal tasted heavenly after hours in the sun.

Tessa loved the view of the lake at this time of day. The flaming orb in the sky was starting its descent, shimmering over the lake, which was slowly growing quieter. The boat traffic had lessened considerably and the beach was emptying.

"I love summer," she whispered quietly.

Chondra heard her and said, "I'll really miss this place. Joey and I come here often."

Tessa looked at her. "I don't blame you."

The look in Chondra's eyes told Tessa that she wouldn't miss it that much. Chondra's eyes wandered to lock with Mark's. She was trading a lake town for something better.

After the picnic meal, Cody and Tessa headed back to his mother's and spent some time with her before heading back to Chelsey.

As Cody and Tessa drove the hour's drive, she pondered how she'd share her newfound information. After a few minutes of agonized indecision, she finally found the emotional fortitude to tell him.

"Cody, I need to tell you something." Her hands felt damp in her lap.

He looked at her and nodded.

"I'm a bit nervous."

"Go ahead. You don't have to be nervous around me." His eyes smiled at her.

"It has to do with another time travel. It happened to me four years ago."

Turning his head, he stared at her in surprise for a moment before returning his gaze to the road. "Your life is filled with the unexplainable, huh?"

"I've never shared it with you but I know I need to now."

"Okay," he said cautiously.

She breathed deeply and released a quick puff of air. It helped calm her nerves. Slowly she divulged her time travel experience on Target Street. From the look on Cody's face, she could tell he was becoming distressed and her nervousness grew as she continued. As she finished her story, anxiety pushed her on.

"I didn't know it was your sister, her husband and child until today. I heard all of their names in that time travel experience but I never put two and two together. You called Chondra Choey and her son's name was Riley and not Joey. It threw me off. I know you're probably upset with me like you were when I didn't share the old mansion time travel with you. Please consider that I was sixteen and the whole thing frightened me so badly that I just ran in terror from it. I hope you can forgive me for that. I'm so sorry that I didn't try to help." She crossed her fingers in her lap and prayed he wouldn't be too angry.

He shook his head but remained quiet. After a short pause, he finally said, "This is truly amazing. God was trying to connect us. That he attempted to connect you with Mark, Chondra and Joey is astounding to me. He finally had to get the two of us together to do it."

"Yeah, I guess."

"He got it done too."

"You're not mad at me?" Her nerves still rattled with tension but she felt a little encouraged by his positive response.

"No, I'm not mad at anyone. I'm grateful to God for caring about my family. He cared enough to send someone to help us. I bet you Chondra will receive help from you, Tessa, because she'll listen to you. She likes you a lot and really respects you."

Shrugging her shoulders, she said, "I don't know."

"Whenever I try to give her any type of guidance, she gets mad. I have a feeling she'll take advice from you, though. Just maybe you've been sent to help her."

"But I don't know how to help her."

Deep sorrow crossed his face. "She's hooked on prescription drugs. Did you know that?"

"No, I didn't know."

"She's been on medication for a long time to calm her nerves and to keep her emotionally balanced. Her doctor has encouraged her to gradually diminish her dosage but she can't. She's tried. I've been praying for God to send someone whom she'll listen to."

Fear gnawed at her heart. "I'm willing to help if I can but God will have to show me what to do and what to say."

"He'll show you, Tessa," Cody said with confidence.

It helped to bolster her resolve. God would have to help her because she felt like a fish on dry land.

The rest of the trip was quite silent, their minds full of all they had learned that day. The afternoon spent in the sun also contributed to their tiredness. Tessa struggled to stay awake as the engine hummed around her; like a lullaby it wooed her toward sleep.

As they arrived at her house, the sun hugging the horizon, Cody asked if he could take her out for dinner during the week. She agreed and said it would be something she'd look forward to. He gave her a tender but passionate kiss and she didn't want to leave. It felt so right being wrapped in his arms. He finally pulled away, they said their goodbyes and she exited his car.

As Tessa stood on the sidewalk and watched Cody drive off, she knew in her heart he was the man for her; after today she felt surer than ever. It was becoming harder and harder to say goodbye to him. She did love him. The awareness hit her like a rainbow appearing in the sky. In fact, the sky was scattered with sunset color, the kaleidoscope display reinforcing the tremendous joy she felt.

CHAPTER 25

Although it was Saturday, Tessa's shift almost complete, and the week finally done, it still felt like the longest week of her life. Curiosity had plagued her over what would happen at the mansion. The two weeks were almost up. To be able to finally know the meaning behind the time travel, pulled at her and the slow plod of the days was agonizing.

According to her calculations, Luke should be back in Chelsey by now. He'd gone to Minneapolis to set up his apartment with his roommate but he'd absolutely assured them he'd be back to join them at the mansion. She was glad he'd be part of it. They were all equally interested as to how things would play out with the Hardingtons.

Her friends knew nothing of Cody's connection to the Hardingtons. It was his place to inform them and perhaps the visit to the mansion on Sunday would provide the right opportunity.

Tessa handed some steaming plates to a foursome sitting at one of her tables.

"Would any of you like fresh ground pepper?" she asked.

She ground the pepper mill over their plates, returned it to its place and headed to fill drink orders at another table in her section.

On Thursday she and Cody had gone out for dinner. Their conversation focused mainly on the mansion, time travel and what might happen on their next visit.

She smiled while filling glasses with fountain drinks, the liquid swirling around the ice at the bottom of each cup. Cody's enthusiasm only fueled her own. He was as eager about going tomorrow as she was. Having had her whole summer consumed with past events and how they played into the present made her anxious to know the final answers and bring some closure to this experience.

At just past three, Luke walked through the door of The Eating

Place. She saw him and headed that way immediately.

"Hi there, handsome! How are you doing?"

"Hi, gorgeous!" Luke gave her a kiss on the cheek and hugged her. "Cody's not jealous, is he? Just tell me if I need to watch my back. Actually, I'm leaving town soon so what am I worried about?" He gave her a mischievous grin.

She laughed at his rambling. "Cody's not jealous so don't worry." Waving toward the tables, she said, "It's slowed down some so why don't you sit down with me for a minute."

Tessa found an empty table for two and they faced each other.

"Do you want anything?" she asked.

"Naw, I'm good." He picked up the fork lying to the side and twirled it in one hand. "Man, I can't wait till tomorrow!"

She nodded. "You're not the only one. Richelle's been calling me all week, reminding me to let her know when I get the sign." She shook her head.

"I think we're all on pins and needles, wondering what's going to happen."

"Some enlightenment would be good."

"I'm so ready!"

She decided to change the subject. "So how does it feel to be heading back to university?"

"Totally excited! Not that assignments are that much fun but I missed my friends and the whole university atmosphere. It's addicting."

"How about Janaye? What's happening with the two of you?"

"Well, we've agreed to still see each other, sort of," he said with tilted head. He didn't look sure. "It'll be more of a friendship kind of thing. We'll email each other."

"You're not good with emails."

"She suggested writing letters. Can you believe that?" His eyes got big, filled with incredulity.

"You've never written a letter in your entire life."

"I know!"

"Remember how you promised me you'd keep in touch with email before you went to university?"

"Yeah," he said sheepishly.

"I would have been happy with two – one per semester. But you didn't send me even one!"

He held up his hands in surrender. "I know, I know."

"You actually promised Janaye you'd email her?"

"Hey, don't be so hard on me! I can do email. I can do this, Tessa. Come on, I need some support here."

"Do you think this relationship will last?"

"Hey, what's with all the questions? Janaye and I are friends for now. If I meet someone in university and I fall for her, well that's that. I didn't make Janaye any promises. I told her if she finds a guy here that she wants to date, to go for it. I don't want to cramp her style and make her wait for me. We'll just take it as it comes."

"Is Janaye okay with that?"

"Ah, I think she was a bit hurt when I told her. I don't know what else to do. I like the girl; she's sweet and quiet. I hate girls that talk my ear off. I could handle getting to know her better but there's no time right now."

Tessa nodded. The same old Luke – being tied down was not something he gravitated toward.

"She offered to come see me some weekends."

"What did you tell her?"

"I told her not to. I said it would complicate things for me. Weekends are busy with homework, papers and going to sports games. Having her come would just cramp my style."

"You really don't like commitment, do you?" The words were out before she could stop them. It would only remind him of his father.

His smile vanished instantly. "Just like my dad?"

"I didn't mean it that way, Luke. You're just not ready to settle down yet. When the time is right and the girl is right, you'll be committed."

"Look, I've got to run. Call me when it's time to go back to the mansion, okay?" He stood, leaned over and gave her a peck on the cheek.

She grabbed his hand before he could race off. "I'm sorry, Luke. I didn't mean to upset you."

"I know, sweetheart. See you tomorrow." With that he headed to the door and left.

Tessa walked toward the front doors and watched him get into his "green thing." He started it and it sounded a lot better than it had in a while. Had he actually given it a service job? That was hard to believe. Perhaps he did it for the coming school year. There'd be some long trips back and forth. As she watched his car leave the curb, she prayed he'd be able to let go of the pain of his father abandoning him.

~~~~~

Cody took Tessa to his church on Sunday morning. Tessa had to admit that she was really taking a liking to Church On the Move. The pastor was down to earth, completely understandable and utterly relevant to current events. She was increasingly enjoying the services and she respected the vision they had. Their heart to minister to hurting people impressed her more than she could say. Three months ago, when she'd first come, she'd felt completely out of place. She knew she'd changed during the summer. Her capacity to feel the pain of others had expanded and she had a growing desire to do something about it.

The service was as wonderful and hard-hitting as usual. Charlie sat close to the front, eager to hear Chad's words. Richelle arrived late again and Charlie went to join her at the back when she came.

After the service, Charlie and Richelle left together before Tessa had a chance to talk to them. The young people gathered around Cody. His easygoing nature was evident as he talked and kidded with them. He'd taken them roller-skating the night before and then they'd gone for some pizza. Tessa had joined them and admitted it had been a fun evening. She was actually starting to look forward to youth nights. At first she viewed them as an interference in their relationship but now she knew many of the kids by name and considered them friends.

People dispersed and Cody took Tessa for lunch at a family restaurant close to the church. After dropping her off at home, he left to help his sister move. Choey was moving to Chelsey this weekend and Cody was thrilled. Tessa had offered to help but he had declined, admitting it wouldn't take him long. Chondra had come from a furnished apartment in Detroit Lakes so all she had to bring were personal items, packed in boxes.

Tessa waited impatiently for the afternoon to crawl by. She knew this was the day they had to go back for the dinner at the mansion and she didn't know how the sign would come. Sitting and waiting was so boring, especially with the week-long anticipation of the time travel.

After two hours of filling her time with random things, watching T.V. and leafing through a magazine, the doorbell rang. Leaping from her bed, she headed to the front door and pulled it open.

Cody, standing on the front landing, smiled big and said, "Hi there, beautiful. What are you up to?"

"Hi! I'm so glad you're here. I was bored stiff and felt so impatient I hardly knew what to do with myself."

He chuckled and said, "Well, then it's about time I rescued you."

"Yes, you're my knight in shining armor!"

"That's me. Your hero to the rescue!" He grinned and said, "I'd like to take you to an art exhibit downtown. The art gallery just got some new paintings and sculptures and they're having a special display."

"Sure. I'll just grab my things." Tessa went to get her purse and a light sweater.

As they walked around the new display, Cody looked in his element, his attention fixed on the various pieces of art on exhibit. Tessa couldn't quite see the value of some of the paintings but being with Cody was worth it. It helped keep her mind occupied and that was a good thing.

"I want to show you one that I've always really liked. I would love to have a print of it for my apartment but I haven't seen it in any art stores."

They walked over to one that was set off by itself and highlighted with an assortment of small, directed lights that made it shine and seem somewhat alive. The picture depicted a war scene set in the 1800s with men on horses and some on foot, their faces edged with lust for blood, their weapons raised and ready to strike. Two armies converged on a field, racing toward each other, at the brink of inflicting harm on the other. In the sky above them another battle raged, this one between the angels of heaven in fiery chariots, their swords of fire extended, and the demons of darkness in black, leathery skin, blackish wings, talons outstretched, intent on defeating the host of heaven. It was an epic battle between good and evil.

Tessa loved it immediately. It was visually stimulating to see the supernatural forces at play while the physical conflict raged below.

"Have you seen this painting before, Tessa?"

"It looks vaguely familiar. Maybe I've seen it in a magazine somewhere or the local paper. I'm not sure."

"There was a write-up on it in the paper when the gallery first received it. Since the first time I saw it, I loved it."

"Does the artist have a web site where you could request a print?"

"I've checked but can't get a hold of him."

Tessa studied the intricate work. "Would you be able to reproduce it?"

Cody made a low sound deep in his throat. "I don't think so. It's pretty detailed. I'm not that good."

"You could try."

He looked at her. "You have a lot of confidence in me."

"You're a good artist."

"Thanks, but no. There's no way I could replicate this complex painting." He pointed to the battle in the skies. "Just look at the detail of the angels' wings, their intense faces and their intricate swords. The demons look absolutely hideous. The painting has this believable quality about it and the battle scene is so detailed. The way the artist depicts the human anatomy is amazing."

"It is very impressive."

"I love the angel scene in the sky and the way the demons are bent on revenge and yet cringe in terror when accosted by an angel. It's totally gripping and vivid." His eyes were glued to the painting.

"It's an interesting word," smiled Tessa slyly.

Cody turned and gave her a curious stare. "What word?"

She smiled and gave him a sideways look. "Angel."

His eyes lit up. "You heard the bells?"

She nodded.

They did a quick tour of the rest of the art gallery then left. They were both hungry so made a quick stop for a bite to eat at fast food restaurant. Using her cell, Tessa called her friends from the restaurant and they agreed to meet at the mansion in half an hour.

CHAPTER 26

There was a chill in the air. The sun hung low in the sky, spreading a rosy glow across the clear expanse, ready to kiss the horizon. The evenings were growing increasingly cooler, a sign that fall was on its way. Tessa pulled her sweater a little tighter to fend off the cool breeze as she exited Cody's car, stepped up to the curb and onto the sidewalk. He joined her and shivered.

"It's cooling off quickly," he said, as he took her hand in his.

"I know. Our warm summer evenings are drifting away."

"And to think it's only the end of August."

"Our summers are way too short! Tabitha has the right idea. She's planning to move south. Maybe I should join her."

He stared at her. "Tabitha from work?"

"Yeah."

"You better not join her!"

She chuckled. "Why not?"

He shook his head. "Do you even have to ask?"

Turning her face up to meet his, she placed a light kiss on his cheek. "Don't worry. I'm not going anywhere."

Squeezing her hand, he gave her a wink and led her through the gate.

The disappointment she felt over the cool temperature evaporated at the pleasure of Cody's warm hand cupped around hers.

They sauntered over to the big oak and stopped before switching time zones to survey the house. Tessa mused how this forsaken, debilitated thing had changed her summer and future forever.

Cody said, "It's hard to believe this was once a glamorous place."

"Yeah. Very hard to believe. To think I was afraid of this house for so many years is surprising now. It held so much mystery and there were so many stories about it. Lots of people thought it was haunted. It gave me goose bumps even to walk past it."

His eyes studied her face. "And now?"

"I'm no longer afraid. I have concern, compassion maybe, and a heart for these people, your relatives. I wish people didn't have to go through such difficult circumstances."

"My family sure had their share of issues. But they're not the only ones. There are many people who go through terrible situations and yet somehow manage to survive and go on. I know lots of people in our church that have endured horrible backgrounds and yet have found peace and healing through their relationship with their Heavenly Father. It's an awesome thing to witness, people moving from a place of hopelessness to an overwhelming joy." His eyes left her face and focused on the ruined house. "I believe the healing process for my family is just around the corner and that gives me great hope."

She turned to look at the house too. "It sure does look awful."

"But it won't stay that way for long."

"I can't wait to see it totally restored. It will be so remarkable to see this house bring healing to people for a change."

The gate squeaked behind them and they turned to see Charlie and Richelle enter the yard. At the same time Luke called out from down the sidewalk. All heads turned to look. He was holding Janaye's hand as they hurried toward the gate.

"Hey, don't go without us!" he yelled. They were both out of breath as they stopped at the gate.

"We're waiting, Luke," Tessa assured him.

The newly-arrived visitors joined them by the tree and they all proceeded into the yard as everything transitioned to the year 1946. The sky grew a shade darker, shadowing them beneath the boughs of the tree. The snow was gone and the water had mostly disappeared from the pathway. Tessa noticed that the air felt warmer than the other times they'd visited. Winter had given way to spring here even though it still felt cooler here than in their time.

They all entered through the center main entrance and moved to the side of the foyer to wait for the evening to begin. Tessa could feel the suspense in the air and knew instinctively something decisive was about to happen. The others' expectancy was tangible as well.

She scanned the foyer to see if the angel had graced them with his presence but there was no sign of him anywhere. Sounds echoed down from the top floor and gradually grew louder. They all craned their heads in the general direction.

Mary came into view first and descended the stairway, her mother right behind her. Mary wore a beautiful satin teal-green gown that glittered in areas as the light from the chandelier above shone on it. Her brunette hair was pinned up by a sparkling diamond clip and a few tendrils were left out to cascade past her delicate neck and framed her pale face. She looked sophisticated and elegant as she moved gracefully down the stairway. All eyes were peeled on the beauty descending.

An elaborate diamond necklace ornamented Mary's neck and, as she approached, the precious stones glittered copiously. Matching diamond earrings dangled from her ears, the combination almost rivaling the gleam of the chandelier.

Tessa released a deep, pent up sigh. If only there weren't such a contrast between the girl's appearance to what was buried deep in her heart and soul. Her breathtaking beauty spoke of tremendous wealth, sophistication and grace and yet there was such deep sorrow, disappointment and broken dreams within this young girl's heart. Tessa bit her cheek hard to keep from crying at the empathy she felt. How easy it was to judge only from outward appearances, without truly knowing or caring what lay within.

Mrs. Hardington wore a similar gown but in a deep maroon shade. She also wore diamond necklace and earrings, though smaller in size. Her hair was a mixture of brunette and gray, piled high in a style that was quite flattering. She always exuded sophistication, coming from years of wealth and comfort.

When they reached the foyer, Elizabeth turned toward Mary, smiled in admiration and took hold of her hands. "You look wonderful! How do you feel tonight, dear?"

"I'm a little nervous. This is all happening so quickly. I'm not sure I'm prepared for marriage."

"You'll be fine, Mary. Richard seems like a fine young man and even though he's not your first choice, I'm hoping he'll be a good husband to you. I truly believe he'll treat you well."

"I hope so, Mother. Did you love Daddy when you married

him?"

"I admired him a great deal. Love came later for us. I'm sure it will for you too."

"I do hope so." Her eyes scanned the floor and then looked up to meet her mother's eyes. "I have a hard time even admiring Richard."

Concern clouded Elizabeth's eyes.

Mary smiled tightly. "Don't worry, Mother, I'll try my best to be a good wife to him."

Elizabeth smiled reassuringly, released one of Mary's hands and patted the other with her free hand. A female servant appeared from the right side hallway, walked up to the two but held back, hands crossed in front, not wanting to interrupt.

Turning to face the servant, Elizabeth nodded in acknowledgement.

The servant said, "Sorry to interrupt, Mrs. Hardington. The meal is ready any time. Let us know when your guests arrive and we'll begin to serve it."

"Thank you, Gertrude. I'll inform you when we're ready. We're still waiting on our guests."

Gertrude nodded and left the foyer in the direction that she'd come. Mrs. Hardington led Mary toward the dining room and they disappeared through the large, double doors.

The six friends stayed in their positions in the foyer and talked to pass the time. The conversation focused mostly on Luke and his move to Minneapolis. He animatedly talked of his roommate, their apartment and the courses he was taking. Soon they were all chuckling at his stories and he basked in the attention. He was dramatic to the core and his tales never failed to entertain. The more they snickered the more vivacious he became.

For Tessa, even with Luke's narrative, she felt impatient for the evening to progress. After what seemed like an eternity, there was finally a knock at the door.

All talk stopped and every eye turned to the front door.

James, the butler, appeared and opened it. Richard stepped inside first, followed by a distinguished-looking older couple. They shed their coats and handed them to James. With his arms laden down, he first showed them to the dining room and then proceeded down the hallway to find a place for his load. He soon reappeared and walked toward the office door, knocked and opened it.

"Sir, your guests have arrived and have been escorted to the dining room."

"Thank you, James. I'll be right out."

After a few moments William exited his office, dressed in a black tuxedo, white shirt and dark tie. He whistled cheerfully as he headed to the dining room and disappeared inside.

The six friends followed a short distance behind him. He left the door standing half open and they entered slowly and stood at a discreet distance. No one was seated yet. Elizabeth and Mary stood by one of the bay windows with their guests, holding wine glasses, the smooth liquid sparkling in their cups. William shook hands with the Ridgefields, welcoming them.

The Ridgefields were also dressed handsomely. Mr. Ridgefield wore a dark suit, a white, crisp shirt and a dark tie. Mrs. Ridgefield's gown was a bright shade of red with a short, matching jacket over it, framed with a white, fur collar. It looked quite festive. Maybe it was a Christmas leftover. Even though it looked somewhat gaudy, she wore it well. It fit her perfectly and her shape was still stunning despite her years. Her hair was nearly black, shoulder length, curly, with gray strands throughout.

As the parents talked, Richard led Mary by the hand to the far end of the table, farthest from the doorway. He turned and gazed at her, obviously pleased.

Richard was decked out in a black tuxedo, white shirt, and black tie. He looked downright stunning with his natural good looks, dark hair and height. His attire made him appear the perfect gentleman and the two presented a striking couple. If one didn't know what lay behind the masks, their appearance would declare them an ideal match.

"You look beautiful tonight, Mary." He leaned in and whispered, "I wish our wedding was today and tonight our wedding night."

Mary's cheeks blushed a bright red and she looked away.

Looking at her intently, he asked, "I didn't embarrass you, did I?"

Fidgeting with a fold in her skirt, her nervousness plainly visible, she refused to meet his eyes.

"I believe I did embarrass you." He chuckled in amusement.

"You have nothing to worry about, dear. I'll take good care of you. Within a week's time we'll be Mr. and Mrs. Richard Ridgefield. It sounds wonderful to the ear, does it not?"

She finally looked up at him with a tortured expression. "You will be patient with me, won't you?"

Confusion clouded his good looks. "I don't understand."

"I feel anxious about marriage and the wedding night." She shifted her gaze to study her hands, as if embarrassed to speak of these things while looking into his eyes.

Richard took her hands in his. "I'll be patient as long as you don't disappoint me in our marriage bed." He smiled but she didn't return it. "Let's join our parents, shall we?" He led her toward the others and they gradually joined in on the conversation.

A servant appeared in the doorway and waited. Upon seeing her, Elizabeth acknowledged and said, "The meal is ready. Let's sit down." She directed everyone to their positions around the grand table.

The table was set at the far end and the place settings didn't even take up a third of the table length. Richard and Mary were seated side by side at the end of the table. Their parents sat on either side of them. William poured more wine and they continued talking.

A servant girl brought the first course, which consisted of a cream of potato and broccoli soup with an assortment of breads and biscuits. The girl was unfamiliar; either she was recently hired or just hired to help for this evening.

No prayer was uttered before they started on the first course. Tessa focused on Elizabeth, whose discomfort was noticeable. Almost indiscernibly, she lowered her head for a brief moment before reaching for her spoon. Mary's eyes were glued to her mother and she followed her lead.

The servant girl stayed in the room and stood quietly to the side, waiting as the group finished the first course. The bowls were collected as soon as they were completed and then she left the room. The next course arrived in a few minutes and lavish appetizers were placed before those at the table. Twenty minutes later, salads were brought in.

The meal progressed slowly and the six friends couldn't help but drool over the aromas floating through the room. How it was possible to smell the food was still a mystery but it tempted them and caused their stomachs to growl.

The main dish arrived an hour into the meal. It consisted of roast duck, mashed potatoes with gravy, served with a vegetable medley. The wonderful scent filled the room, teasing and enticing the six onlookers. Tessa took a peek at Luke who was always hungry. His eyes held a pained look.

"Are you going to make it, Luke?" she whispered.

"I don't think so. I'm about to go into hunger shock!" Luke placed one hand on his middle and buckled his knees to enact a fainting spell.

"Oh, don't be such a wimp," Richelle mocked beside him, giving him a poke in the ribs.

"Hey, give me a break. They've been eating for over an hour. I've never watched anyone eat that long and not had a bite myself. This is plain torture!"

"You'll survive, big boy!"

"Oh yeah, that's easy for Miss Undernourished Barbie to say. You can survive on a few carrot sticks a day."

Charlie and Cody chuckled.

Richelle gave Luke an icy stare.

He ignored her and turned his attention back to the table.

Mary picked at her plate of food absently, half of it remaining untouched.

"She doesn't look very hungry," Tessa said to no one in particular.

"I'd finish it for her," said Luke.

"I bet you would if you could," said Richelle.

Richard finished his plateful in record time and then reached over and started picking at Mary's unfinished dinner. She looked at him in startled surprise.

Noticing her shocked expression, he asked, "Do you mind?"

"It seems a trite ill-mannered."

"It seems a waste to leave it and I'm still hungry." With his fork poised in midair, his eyes gazed tenderly into hers, pleading for permission.

Mary's expression softened with his boyish petition and desire to please. "Put that way, help yourself." She pushed her plate toward him and he dove right in.

As the plates emptied, the servant girl gathered them up. Esther, whom Tessa recognized from previous visits, entered the room carrying a tray of dessert. She set it down on the sideboard, waiting for the first girl to finish with the plates. As soon as she left the room, Esther started serving the chocolate mousse cake, beginning with Richard's parents. There were a few "oohs" and "aahs" as the china clinked down on the table.

Luke whimpered pathetically.

Giggles followed.

Suddenly Ruth entered, carrying a tray of coffee and tea with cream and sugar. She glanced around nervously before setting the tray on the sideboard. The six at the table waited for the dessert until the coffee and tea had been served. Ruth asked each one what they'd like and then proceeded to prepare their drinks. Ruth handed the elder Ridgefield a steaming cup of coffee stirred with cream.

As she set it before him, he said, "Excuse me. You look very familiar. Do I know your parents, Miss?"

She looked taken back by the question and her eyes darted to Mr. Hardington.

He answered for her. "This girl's name is Ruth Kendal. Her parents own the bakery shop on Chestnut Street. Ruth's been with us now for over a year and has proved a great asset to the household."

Mr. Ridgefield's eyes lit up. "Ah yes, now I know. I know the Kendals at the bakery shop. I went to high school with your mother, Ruth. You look so much like her; that's why you looked so familiar to me. Your mother was always a great beauty."

Looking completely uncomfortable with the praise in this setting, Ruth averted her eyes and said, "Thank you, sir."

Elizabeth's eyes grew concerned. "Ruth, are you feeling okay? You look so pale today."

"I'm fine, Mrs. Hardington." Keeping her eyes diverted, she ignored the attention being drawn to her and quickly finished pouring the coffee and tea.

Once done, she headed quickly for the door. There she glanced back and, in that moment, her eyes locked with Richard's. She motioned for him to come and left the room.

Tessa saw it and her stomach churned. She saw more than that.

Richard's eyes had followed Ruth the entire time she was in the room. But his empathy had turned to anger the moment Ruth motioned for him to follow.

A few moments after Ruth left the room, Esther returned with the coffee and tea tray. She set it down on the sideboard and stood ready to serve seconds.

Richard stood and faced the Hardingtons. "Excuse me, but I do believe I need to use the men's room. Could you please direct me to the one that would be most suitable?"

Elizabeth gave him directions and he apologetically left the room.

As soon as he left, Tessa followed. Cody, Richelle and Charlie were close behind. Luke and Janaye chose to stay in the dining room.

Richard headed down a hallway and the four of them followed.

Anticipation was tangible and growing. Tessa was sure something would be more fully revealed.

Richard stopped at the door of the washroom but didn't enter. He looked down the hall toward the back sunroom. Continuing on, he opened the double doors leading into it. The four held back as he scanned the room.

He entered the room, turned and closed the doors behind him.

The four friends waited a moment and then Tessa opened the door and entered. Charlie was the last in and closed the door behind him.

Ruth was seated on one of the love seats and Richard sat on the edge of the seat beside her but faced her, looking angry.

"Why did you motion for me to come? I don't appreciate that kind of thing, Ruth. I don't want Mary suspecting anything. You'll be fired quickly if you ever try that again. Do I make myself clear?" There was something else in his eyes. Fear flowed from him, maybe of being found out, cutting off his opportunity here.

Ruth looked devastated as tears formed quickly and streamed down her cheeks. Her complexion turned a pasty shade; she did not look well.

"I'm sorry if I've upset you, Ruth, but that's just the way it will be. I will be the master of this home and you are the servant. I don't want you to forget your role." Richard reached for a hanky from his suit pocket and handed it to her. "Now, what was so important that it had to interrupt my dinner?" He still looked angry but his harsh tone had abated.

Ruth dried her tears frantically and tried to contain her emotions. She sniffled a few times and then turned her bright blue eyes to look at him.

"I'm pregnant."

His eyes grew large with shock and his mouth hung open. Drawing himself together, he asked, "Who's the father of the child?"

She stared at him and said, "You are, Richard. You're the only one I've been with."

"How could you know so quickly? It's only been a few weeks since we…you know?"

"Yes, I know, but I'm definitely pregnant and it's your child, Richard."

"Is that why you look so pale?"

"Yes, I'm feeling quite nauseous. But no one can know about this! The Hardingtons would fire me on the spot. What are we going to do, Richard?"

He stood and paced the room, worry lines creasing his forehead. After a few minutes of pacing, he took a seat beside her again.

"All right, this is how we'll handle it. You're going to tell people that you were attacked and raped while shopping downtown. You have no idea who he is and don't know his name."

She watched him, her eyes filled with worry. "But…how will I describe something that didn't happen."

"You'll say he dragged you into an alley. You shouted but no one heard. He misused you but you were too embarrassed to say anything. When you found out you were pregnant, you knew you'd have to tell someone. That should be sufficiently believable and an easy enough story to propagate."

She wrung her hands nervously. "I don't know."

"You'll do this!" he said firmly. "You'll give birth to this child and the child will have your name. I'll make sure that you'll keep your job here. Financially, you'll have no concerns. I'll provide for you and the baby. You will never mention the true identity of the child, either to Mary or to anyone else. If you ever tell its true identity, I'll completely deny my involvement. I will have you thrown out and you will be responsible for this problem on your own. Are we agreed?"

Misery covered her face but she appeared more calm than before. "What if it's a son? He could carry on your name. Will you disown your own son?"

"Son, daughter, it doesn't matter. I'm getting married within a week and I don't want any complications, not now or ever. Am I understood?"

She looked spent and disappointed but answered weakly, "Yes."

Frustrated, he growled, "I can't believe you've done this to me, Ruth! You've become a thorn in my side."

"I don't remember you objecting a few weeks ago," she said softly, her eyes accusing.

Richard stared at her. "I need to get back to the dining room. Look, if it's worth anything right now, I'm sorry for putting you through this. I should have known better than to get involved with a servant girl, no matter how pretty." With that he left the room and closed the door.

The four friends were about to follow him when they heard Ruth speak.

"I'm a person with feelings. I'm not just a servant girl." She then broke down in gut-wrenching sobs.

Quietly, they stepped out of the sunroom and headed back to the dining room. They slipped in silently beside Luke and Janaye, still in their positions in the dining room, and saw Richard taking his seat beside Mary.

Mrs. Ridgefield said, "Are you okay, Richard? You were gone for quite a while. Did you catch whatever Ruth has? You're looking a little pale yourself."

His face did look rather drained.

Everyone's eyes focused on him and chuckles drifted around the room at the amusing comment.

His face displayed sheer irritation. "I'm fine, Mother."

Elizabeth said, "Well, we're done with the meal. Why don't we move on to the sitting room and we'll get one of the servants to bring us some more coffee and tea there." She stood to signal everyone to join her lead then sauntered toward the door.

Esther, standing at the sideboard, picked up the tray of coffee and tea and prepared to leave the room after the guests.

The whole group left the room, the six unseen visitors the last to follow. Richard took hold of Mary's hand as they walked through the foyer and followed their parents into the sitting room.

"What a two-timer!" Richelle said with disgust in her voice. "I wish I could give him a swift kick where it counts!"

Luke asked, "What happened when Richard left the room, guys? It sounds like Janaye and I missed something."

"Why don't we go into William's den and talk about this?" Cody looked around at the others to see their response.

"We might miss something if we go off by ourselves now."

"Richelle, I think it's time we talk things over. I mean for all of us to talk things over." Charlie gazed at Richelle with an intensity that Tessa hadn't seen before.

Richelle looked confused. "Why, Charlie?"

"We might miss something in there," Luke pointed to the sitting room.

Cody said, "I think Charlie's right. It's time we discuss some things."

Curiosity filled Luke's voice. "What's going on? Is this about what happened when Richard left the room? If it is, you can spit it out right here and then we can get back in there." He pointed toward the sitting room again.

Cody responded, "What we need to talk about involves much more than what happened between Richard and Ruth. I need to share some things with the rest of you. I believe you'll find it very interesting." He waited for a moment, then took Tessa by the hand and started for the den down the hall.

Reluctantly, they all followed, except for Charlie who seemed eager. Once there, they situated themselves on the couches. Luke, Richelle and Janaye looked unsure but curious.

Luke was the first to speak. "Okay, what happened with Richard when he left? What did Ruth want with him?"

Tessa retold the event that took place in the sunroom. Luke and Janaye were stunned. Luke looked repulsed and cursed in disgust. Then he turned to Janaye and apologized for his language.

Janaye nodded and said, "I can't believe this Richard guy. He's just a scoundrel."

That was putting it mildly. Tessa felt repugnance over the

whole mess.

Luke shook his head. "Yeah, I know. He doesn't have a shred of integrity in him. I don't know what Mary sees in him. Actually she sees right through him, doesn't she?"

Cody cleared his throat. "I have something I need to unload."

All eyes turned to him.

"I've already told Tessa but I believe the rest of you need to hear this too." He then revealed his relationship to the Hardingtons. "So, that means Richard and Mary are my grandparents."

Tessa watched astonishment and disbelief fill their eyes and noticed the strange expression on Charlie's face. As Cody finished sharing his information, Charlie released a deep breath and said, "You're not the only one related here."

Everyone turned to stare at him in surprise.

"My last name is Kendal. Ruth Kendal is my grandmother. The child she's carrying is my father." He turned to look at Cody. "I guess that makes us cousins. We share the same grandfather."

Now it was Cody's turn to look shocked. "Are you serious?"

"I'm very serious. I suspected it all along. From the first time we saw Ruth I had my suspicions. She looked so much like the pictures of my grandmother and my father looks a lot like her. His hair has always been light and he has the same bright blue eyes."

"Wow! I never knew I had another cousin."

Richelle looked angry as she turned on him. "Why didn't you tell me about your suspicions, Charlie?"

"I don't know why. I guess I didn't want to say anything until I knew for sure. After watching Ruth carefully tonight and knowing that Richard was the one who got her pregnant, all the pieces started to fit together. I never met my grandfather. When my dad talked about him, he'd never mention his name but I always assumed his last name was Kendal. The way my dad talked about him, I can assure you, it was never with any feelings of pride or affection!"

His answer seemed to settle Richelle's offended feelings and she turned to Cody. "So where did the name Fields come from? That's your last name right, Cody?"

"Well my grandparents, Richard and Mary Ridgefield, had two daughters. Their names were Laura, who is my aunt, and Beth, who is my mother. The name Ridgefield died out but I suppose it wouldn't have had to if Richard would have allowed Ruth's child to have his name. That would make Charlie a Ridgefield." Cody glanced at Charlie.

He shook his head and made a face as though the name were an insult.

Cody continued his discourse. "My mother married a man by the name of Philip Fields and that's how I came to carry the name Fields."

"What happened with Richard and Mary's marriage? Did it survive? Did she ever find out about Richard's affair with Ruth? Did Ruth stay at the mansion and have her child?"

"Whoa, one question at a time, Richelle." Cody smiled and continued. "I don't know a lot about what happened after this night. I only know what my mother has shared with me. She told me about growing up here. Her sister was two years older and my mother was the baby. She remembers a boy living with them; he was four years older than her sister and they both played with him like a brother. During her childhood, she grew up believing that this boy was the child of one of the servants and I don't think she ever questioned it. About my grandparents' marriage, I can't really comment. My mother did mention that it was an unhappy home. There wasn't much love lost between her parents and she remembers it being a sad place. Mary was on meds all the years that Beth, my mother, was in her parents' home. Mary took nerve pills and was often too dazed to be much of a mother. I don't know if Mary ever discovered the affair between Richard and Ruth. I never knew about it until this time travel experience."

"So what ever happened to this mansion? Why was it deserted and left to rot?" Janaye asked.

"Richard and Mary lived here for about ten years, from what I can remember my mother telling me. Richard eventually purchased it from the Hardingtons and they were doing well for a while but the banking business didn't go as planned. Richard did eventually take over the bank here but never handled it as well as his father-in-law. I did some internet research. The bank made some bad investments and had too many unpaid loans, ending with the institution declaring bankruptcy."

"A bank declaring bankruptcy! Can they do that?" Luke looked surprised.

"I suppose they can. When that happened, with the bank here, the problems seeped into the one in Chicago. Clients heard of the problems with the bank here in Chelsey and made a rush on the Chicago bank to withdraw their funds. It was apparently quite a scene. It just couldn't function with so much money being withdrawn and closed its doors within a few months."

"What did William and Elizabeth do?" asked Richelle. "Did they stay in Chicago?"

"They did and he went to work for a brokerage firm there. He managed all right financially even though he never did gain the same status he had here."

"How about Richard and Mary? How did they fare?"

"They really struggled financially after the Chelsey bank closed. He went to work for his father but his father couldn't pay him what the bank had. Richard's salary wasn't enough to be able to maintain the house or the style of living they were accustomed to. The house was paid for so they just abandoned it. Why they never sold it I'll never know. Maybe they hoped they'd move back one day. They moved into a small house and lived there until their old age."

Tessa said, "Maybe they eventually stopped paying the taxes or looking after it and it fell into disrepair. I'm surprised the city didn't do anything with this house sooner. It's been sitting here and falling apart for a long, long time."

"Whatever happened to Ruth when they moved out of the mansion?" asked Richelle.

"My mother mentioned that the boy and his mother moved out before they ever left the house. Perhaps Charlie knows more about that part of the story."

"I don't know what happened. My father never spoke about it. All he's ever said is that his father wasn't worth the time of day. I never knew I had any connection here until I saw Ruth. This is all very new to me."

Richelle's eyes glittered with keen interest. "What about your grandmother, Cody? Is Mary still alive?"

"No she's not. She passed away last year."

A disappointed murmur rippled through the group.

Richelle said, "It would have been interesting to hear her side of the story." She looked contemplative for a moment before piping up again. "What about the old lady, Eunice Hardington; whatever happened to her?"

"William and Elizabeth put her into a home that could take care of her before they moved on to Chicago. My mother has mentioned Eunice to me and she remembers going to visit her at a retirement complex as a young child. Eunice would have been my mother's great grandmother. She passed away when my mom was five years old."

The six of them fell into a hush for a while and Tessa noticed a strange glazed look in Luke's eyes.

She decided to ask, "Is something on your mind, Luke?"

He stared at her uncertainly and then glanced at Cody. Sighing heavily, he said, "Cody, you mentioned that your father's name is Philip Fields. Is that right?"

"Yes."

"I guess I have a bomb to drop as well." With a cautious look playing in his eyes, unsure whether to disclose his secret, he took a deep breath and said, "That's the name of my father as well."

His confession left a stunned hush and every eye stared dumbstruck at him.

After a few silent moments Cody asked, "How can that be?"

"My father had an affair with my mother while he was still married to someone else. I believe your mother is the one he was married to."

Cody's confused expression slowly dissipated as the realization hit him fully. "That would make us half brothers." He looked astounded.

"That's right, bro," said Luke. "I kind of suspected that might be the case when I heard your last name. I've never told anyone about my father. I've always gone by my mother's last name. Today when you mentioned your father's full name I knew for sure that we were brothers. I never knew my dad and I don't ever remember seeing him. He left when I was a baby. I've never had a desire to find him, know him or see him. He's never been a father to me and I've survived fine without him. With a jerk of a dad like I have, I don't need one."

Cody said, "Well, I knew him as a father for the first nine years of my life and since that time I've never seen him again. Life was a struggle without him. I was bitter and angry and I ended up almost destroying my life because of it. I can relate to your hatred of Philip Fields because I despised him for years. Accepting Christ as my Savior opened up a relationship with my Heavenly Father that has brought tremendous healing to my life. God promises never to leave us or forsake us, unlike my earthly father, and his love for his children is a perfect love. God has been a perfect Father to me and his love gave me the courage to finally forgive Philip. God will be a perfect Father to you too if you give him a chance, Luke."

"I don't know." He looked unhappy and vulnerable. "I need some time to think about it."

Tessa could easily see that Cody's concern for him was genuine and with the look on Luke's face, he knew it too.

Tessa remembered something. She asked, "Cody, do you remember the diary entry where we read about Mary's choice of names for her children?"

"Yes. One of them was Luke." He turned to Luke. "Do you know why your parents chose that name for you?"

"It was my father's choice."

Cody said, "I remember my mother telling me how she wanted to name me Luke. Her mother, Mary, spoke of wanting to name her son that. Well, Mary never had a son and never had the opportunity to bestow that name. So my mother was determined to give that name to her son. When I came along, my father adamantly refused it. My mother was upset but she gave in to my father's wishes and he named me Cody. I suppose he felt guilty about that and named you Luke when you came along."

With bitterness in his voice, Luke said, "He had a lot to feel guilty about and still does. I wonder how many other half brothers or half sisters we have out there?"

Cody said, "It won't help to dwell on that. God has forgiven me and it's given me the strength to forgive Philip's bad choices."

"I'll never forgive him! He doesn't deserve it!"

"We don't deserve God's forgiveness either but if we accept it, he'll readily forgive us and accept us. Why don't you receive that free gift?"

Warning flashed from Luke's eyes. "Don't pressure me, Cody. Just because we're brothers doesn't give you the right to push your religion down my throat."

"I don't want to push it down anyone's throat but I sure want to offer it because I know it's the only way you'll ever have any peace in your life." Cody removed his intense gaze from Luke and focused on the whole group gathered in the den. "Anyway, I guess I've just gained two new relatives today, a cousin and a brother. This is quite the day!"

Tessa felt a bit shaken at all the secrets exposed within just a few short minutes. "Does anyone else have anything to add to the information data? Janaye, are you related too? Richelle, how about you?"

Richelle said, "Nothing except what I've already told all of you – you know, about my grandmother marrying Henry."

Janaye shook her head. "I'm not related at all."

Tessa tried to take it all in. God's ways were certainly remarkable. Only he could tie all the loose ends together and bring the hidden out into the open. She only hoped she'd be able to decipher what it all meant for her. Although much had been revealed, the purpose in her life still seemed vague.

After some discussion, they decided the puzzle pieces had all been placed. As far as they could tell, they'd discovered what they needed to know. They headed back to the foyer. Voices still drifted from the sitting room. The six stopped for a moment, all realizing that this would likely be the last time they'd go back in time. For Tessa, it brought on a torrent of feelings – sorrow to see the time travel experiences go, relief finally to get back to normal life and anxiety in knowing that now she'd be accountable to take what she'd received and handle it right. The weight of that responsibility lay heavily on her and she prayed silently for clear direction.

Tessa gazed at her circle of friends and felt so much gratitude. "Are you all ready to say goodbye to this time travel?"

There was regret on every face. She could relate to how they felt. It was sad to leave, to say adieu, knowing they'd never be back again.

Cody said, "I don't think we have any choice, dear. I believe it's done."

The others nodded in resigned agreement.

They slowly made their way outside. It was dark, stars twinkling sporadically between a mostly cloud-filled sky, the moon hidden behind their cover.

They gradually made their way across the yard until they came to the big oak tree. All of them turned and looked at the beautiful mansion once more, reluctant to leave its former grandeur, with the lights blazing from nearly every window. Slowly they turned, one at a time, and continued on past the big oak and switched back to the present.

The sky snapped to attention, brightening above them, the sun just setting on the horizon with an array of colors splashed across the heavenly canvass. The air grew instantly warmer and they knew it was done.

Luke was heading off to university in the morning, so they all said their goodbyes. Tessa knew that his life would be forever changed by what he had learned here. Giving her a prolonged hug, Luke gave her a pained smile before he got into his car and drove off with Janaye. How Tessa wished he had made a decision for Christ this evening and prayed he wouldn't wait too long.

Charlie and Richelle were the next to leave. Tessa and Cody watched them walk hand-in-hand to his vehicle. After holding the door for her, Charlie closed it, scooted to his side of the car, waved at them and got behind the steering wheel. It roared to life and they pulled away, the car's tail lights disappearing around the bend.

Cody turned on the sidewalk and gazed at the deserted mansion. Tessa joined him, sorrow in her heart at leaving the Hardingtons behind. But then again, she wasn't leaving them behind. They were all around her; Cody and Charlie were connected. Luke was Cody's brother. She was still in incredulity over that. Even Richelle had a connection.

"It absolutely amazes me," said Cody thoughtfully.

Tessa slipped her hand in his and gazed up at him.

"Who would have thought I had a brother? I never knew," he said.

"And a cousin," she said with a smile.

"I've grown richer within a few short minutes." He shook his head in wonder.

It was then that she noticed "him" standing on the front landing of the neglected house.

She pointed toward to the crumbling porch and asked, "Cody, do you see him standing there?"

"Who?"

"Is that the angel?"

"Tessa, I don't see anyone."

She looked into his eyes and realized he was serious. She was the only one seeing the man in the trench coat. "Do you mind waiting for me? I'll be right back."

"I'll wait here."

Tessa opened the noisy gate and walked back across the yard toward the house. She expected to switch time zones when she passed the big oak tree but nothing happened this time. Grass and weeds poked through the deep cracks in the walkway and tall grass covered the derelict yard. The man stayed in position as she approached. Walking up the rickety steps to the front landing, she made her way across the rough wooden boards, broken pieces of glass crunching beneath her feet. The angel watched her every move until she stopped in front of him. Gazing up at him, she waited for him to speak. He held a seriousness and import, the intensity of his gaze making her nervous.

Finally he said, "It's done, Tessa. The message is complete."

"I still don't know what it all means for me. What's expected of me now?"

"There are so many who are hurting and need the love and healing touch of God."

"I'm only one person. What can one person do? I can't change the whole world."

"No, you can't change the whole world but you can change the whole world for one person, one person at a time."

It sank in deep. This was the message. She still didn't know which avenue this revelation would take her but she finally understood that she was called to do more than keep inventory of numbers in a book. God wanted her to make a difference in people's lives, one person at a time. When and how this would all play out, she didn't know. A confidence was arising deep within that God would reveal the timing and the plan. All that was needed was her willingness and obedience. She nodded to acknowledge the angel's words.

He smiled at her for the first time and dropped his chin in reply.

Tessa gazed at the heavenly messenger in amazement, knowing that she would probably never see him again, at least not visibly. But then again, who knew?

"Thank you for coming and bringing me this message. I know it's changed me forever."

"You need to thank God for it. I'm only a servant."

She nodded, then turned and slowly descended the steps and walked back across the yard to join Cody. Gazing back, she saw the angel had already vanished and only a deserted, shell of a house looked back at her.

The angel's words and what she had been shown would live forever in her heart. This message was sure to motivate her life as long as she lived. This summer had forever changed her and, for the first time in many months, she was grateful for God's re-direction. Each person involved, everyone who experienced the time travel, had been dramatically affected and she smiled at the awesome hand of God working in all of her friend's lives.

kissed her gently and then led the way to his car. As he pulled away from the curb and drove away from the mansion, she realized that meeting Cody and falling in love with him was an integral part of God's plan for her life. Turning to him, she couldn't help the smile tweaking her lips.

Taking her hand in his, he squeezed and asked, "So what did the angel say?"

After telling him, a sudden revelation hit her. Perhaps God's plan for Cody's life was also his plan for hers. His desire to help hurting people was the very thing that God had implanted into her through the time travel experiences. Curiosity tugged at her and she pondered what God would lead her into. A sudden, overpowering anticipation filled her for the future.

###

THANK YOU

Thank you for reading my book. If you enjoyed it, won't you please take a moment to leave me a review at your favorite retailer?

Also, if you'd like to know more of Tessa's story, check out the second book of the trilogy - Time and Healing. The second book follows Tessa's journey of discovery, introduces you to a new character and unravels some hidden secrets.

OTHER NOVELS BY AUTHOR

HEAVEN ON EARTH SERIES:

Assignment Code 110
Assignment Code 123
Assignment Code 321

TIME TRILOGY:

Time and Healing – Book 2 of Trilogy
Time and Restoration – Book 3 of Trilogy

SHORT STORIES:

The author's short stories are on her blog, located on her website - colleenreimer.ca or colleenreimer.com.

For more information about these books or short stories go to www.colleenreimer.ca or www.colleenreimer.com. To sign up to receive her short story notifications, go to her web site and enter your email information.

ABOUT THE AUTHOR

Colleen Reimer lives near Calgary, Canada with her husband and four children, although only the youngest two still live at home. She has lived in multiple places over the years, in many different Canadian cities and also spent seven years in North Carolina.

Besides writing, Colleen also enjoys gardening, travelling, chatting with friends, a hot cup of Chai tea and chocolate.